Howard Williams

Lucian's Dialogues

Namely, the dialogues of the gods, of the sea-gods, and of the dead; Zeus the tragedian, the ferry-boat, etc. Translated with notes and a preliminary memoir by Howard Williams

Howard Williams

Lucian's Dialogues
Namely, the dialogues of the gods, of the sea-gods, and of the dead; Zeus the tragedian, the ferry-boat, etc. Translated with notes and a preliminary memoir by Howard Williams

ISBN/EAN: 9783337413217

Printed in Europe, USA, Canada, Australia, Japan

Cover: Foto ©Andreas Hilbeck / pixelio.de

More available books at **www.hansebooks.com**

LUCIAN'S DIALOGUES

NAMELY

THE DIALOGUES OF THE GODS, OF THE SEA-GODS, AND OF THE DEAD; ZEUS THE TRAGEDIAN, THE FERRY-BOAT

ETC.

TRANSLATED WITH NOTES AND A PRELIMINARY MEMOIR

BY

HOWARD WILLIAMS, M.A.

LATE SCHOLAR OF ST. JOHN'S COLLEGE, CAMBRIDGE

LONDON: GEORGE BELL AND SONS, YORK STREET
COVENT GARDEN
1888

CONTENTS.

DIALOGUES OF THE DEAD.

PREFACE.

For the few ascertained facts in the life of the greatest prose satirist and most brilliant wit of Greek and Latin antiquity, we are indebted, almost wholly, to scattered and incidental allusions in his own various writings.

Like his immediate predecessor, Menippus the satirist; the illustrious Neo-Platonist, Porphyry, in the third; and the orator, Libanius, in the fourth century, Lucian was Syrian by birth. He was born at Samosata—its heap of ruins still retains the old name almost unchanged—on the Euphrates, not far distant from Edessa, and the chief city of the district of Kommagene, in the extreme north-east of Syria, about the year 120 A.D. Tradition protracts the term of his existence to the age of ninety, or even of one hundred years. He thus lived through the reigns of Hadrian, the two Antonines, and Commodus, and (at all events) the earlier part of the reign of Severus—altogether the happiest period of the Roman Empire, and one of the most interesting ages in the world's history. Of his earlier life, the brief record supplied in his incomplete autobiographical sketch, the *Dream*, so often has been repeated, that it is not necessary to do more than to refer to it here. It is enough briefly to repeat that the deliberations of a family council determined his parents, who were in poor circumstances, to apprentice him, at the age of fifteen, to his maternal uncle, a statuary, for whose art he had shown some boyish inclination; that, by a fortunate accident—fortunate, at least, for the world of literary, if not of plastic, Art—the breaking of a piece of marble, he was induced to run away from his master, in resentment at a severe flogging, and to transfer his allegiance to Literature (*Paideia*[1]) ; or, rather, to prepare himself, in the first instance, by a severe course of training, for the profession of a rhetor (in modern phrase, a public speaker), which eventually led him to embrace the career of philosophy and letters.

At this very early stage his memoir, unhappily, comes to an end, and we are left to incidental remarks in his more considerable productions. His experiences for some years lay in the hard school of poverty and neglect (πένης καὶ ἀφανής). In search of employment, or, rather, to master the rudiments of his profession, the young Lucian wandered through the cities of the south-western region of the Lesser Asia, the celebrated and highly-cultured Ionia, gradually getting rid of his provincial manner and dialect, but still conspicuous by his Syrian (or, as he calls it, Assyrian) and un-Greek style of dress (*The Twice-Accused*, 27). In his twentieth year he arrived in Greece, and made his first acquaintance with the Platonic philosopher Nigrinus, who gives the title to one of his *Dialogues*. He next settled in the Syrian capital, Antioch, where he practised at the bar, and acquired considerable reputation as a pleader ; but the chicanery and frauds of the interpreters of the laws soon caused him to abandon that pursuit (*The Fisherman*, 29). The skill thus gained he turned to lucrative account as travelling disputant (*sophistes*, as it was termed)—a popular and profitable calling, which was as common in the philosophic Hellenic and Roman world in the second century, A.D., as it was in Scholastic Europe of the Middle Ages. In that capacity he traversed Syria and Egypt. Soon afterwards he visited Rome (in the year 150), among other reasons, to consult an oculist; and in his *Nigrinus*, the literary result of his visit, he stigmatizes the prevailing corruptions and laborious trifling of the literary as well as fashionable society of the capital. After a stay of two years in Italy, he proceeded to southern Gaul, at that time, and long previously, celebrated for its schools of

---

[1] The fine allegory of the rivalry of *Paideia* and *Techne* ("Trade") may have been suggested to him, in part, by the charming *idyll* of Moschus (in which Europe and Asia appear in a dream to the daughter of Kadmus, and contend for her possession), as well as by the *Choice of Herakles* of Prodikus and Xenophon.

rhetoric. In Gaul he continued his profession of public lecturer for some ten years, his residence in that country being interrupted only by a visit to Olympia. During this period, probably, he composed many of his published rhetorical pieces.

Having now secured an independent income, at the age of forty, Lucian set out again on his travels, and made a journey through Macedonia and Thessaly, on his way to his Syrian home. His stay at Samosata was only temporary; and, inducing his surviving family to remove to Athens, in the next year he himself followed them to the literary metropolis, which to him, as to every Greek or phil-Hellenist, doubtless was an object of supreme intellectual curiosity. It was on his journey to Athens that he had the interview with the Paphlagonian prophet, Alexander, which gave birth to his satire of that name. The contempt openly exhibited by him for that eminent miracle-worker had almost, as he assures us (*Alex.* 56, 57), cost him his life: for the exasperated Alexander had secretly instructed the crew of the vessel, which he had insidiously placed at his visitor's disposal, to make away with their charge—a conspiracy frustrated only by the interposition of the relenting captain. Thus saved from a premature and inglorious end, he proceeded on his journey to Athens, accompanied by that extraordinary adventurer, Peregrinus, or Peregrinus Proteus, whose fiery immolation of himself (like that of another Hercules Furens), before the assembled multitude at Olympia, witnessed by Lucian, in the year 165, forms the principal subject of the *Peregrinus*.

At Athens Lucian seems—for there is no positive evidence—to have taken up his fixed abode for the greater part of his remaining life, occupying himself, as may safely be conjectured, in the highest philosophical and literary studies, and in the enjoyment of the friendship of such exceptional philosophers as Celsus, the famous Platonist-critic of nascent Christianity (in his *True Account*, known to us only through the Reply of Origen, published fifty years later), of the Stoic Sostratus, and the Eclectic Demonax. His sketch of the career of the last, a meritorious ethical teacher, forms one of the not rare proofs of his esteem for real goodness.[1] During this period appeared his masterpieces—his principal theological, philosophical, and ethical *Dialogues*—when that consummate skill in the management of the marvellous Attic dialect had been attained which rivals the style of the best masters, and which, as the acquisition of a foreigner, excites the admiration of all his editors and critics. Perhaps the only other equally remarkable instance of such kind of excellence is that of the African Terence.

When about the age of seventy, impelled, it would seem, by imminent poverty—for authors, then, even of the highest reputation fell very far short of obtaining from the Sosii of the day the immense pecuniary profits now often secured by ephemeral writers—Lucian once more resumed his old occupation of *rhetor* or *sophist*, and produced some of those declamatory essays which appear among his published works. At a fortunate moment, he found relief from his pecuniary difficulties in an official income derived from his appointment to the registrarship or clerkship of the law-courts of the Egyptian capital, the presentation to which office has variously been assigned to Marcus Aurelius, Commodus, and Severus. Chronology seems, on the whole, to support the claims of the last prince, who became emperor in 193, to the honour of saving from destitution the greatest literary ornament of the century. To clear himself from the charge of teaching one thing (in his satire, *On Hired Dependants*) and practising another, by way of supplement to that essay he published his *Apology*. From it, incidentally, we learn that he derived a large salary ($\pi o\lambda v\tau \acute{a}\lambda a\nu\tau o\varsigma$) from his legal post. He alleges the forcible argument that, as the Imperial master of the Roman legions himself—not to mention numerous less exalted personages —by no means refused the richest emoluments of office,

---

[1] The most interesting, and most meritorious, fact recorded in the life of this highly interesting philosopher, who inclined in opinion chiefly to the School of Plato, in practice to that of Antisthenes, is his fine remonstrance addressed to the people of Athens, who were contemplating the introduction of the cruel "sports" of the Roman amphitheatres. "Refrain, Athenians," he protested, "from voting this, until you have first pulled down your altar erected to Pity" (*Dem.* 51). See, too, his very rational remark on sacrifices (*Dem.* 6).

he, the starving critic, could scarcely be blamed for following—in a very humble fashion, and at a very long interval—that elevated example For the most part, his official
duties at Alexandria he devolved upon a deputy, so that
his learned leisure was little disturbed at Athens, where,
as already stated, he died at an advanced age, but at what
date is quite uncertain.

Such are the somewhat meagre facts collected from his
writings. To these his earlier biographers or critics, led
by the lexicographer Suidas, have been pleased to make
some sensational and apocryphal additions. Suidas, of
whom nothing is known except that he belongs to a
very late date in Byzantine literary history, having, probably, in mind the story of the tragic end of the infidel
Euripides, assures his readers that the " blasphemer "
found a well-merited end in having been torn to pieces by
wild dogs ; and, not content with so unique a termination
to his earthly career, adds, as to his posthumous existence,
" in the future, with Satan, he will have his portion in
eternal fire." Another equally discreet authority, of the
sixteenth century, Raffaelle Maffei (or Volaterranus, as he
is called from his birthplace), avers that he was a mali-
cious apostate from Christianity, attributing to him the
bon mot, that he had gained nothing from his old creed but
change of name—Lucianus in place of Lucius (or Lykinus).
To these and similar mendacious assertions Erasmus replies, " they attached to him the name of *blasphemer*, that
is, 'evil-speaker ; ' but they who did so, one may be sure,
were those whose festering sores he had probed." To his
bitter and persistent satirical assaults upon the established
religion, and upon the contending sects of (so-called) " philosophy," we may be sure, not a few (ephemeral) replies
appeared : but no notices of them have come down to
us. While, however, the last echoes of pagan sacerdotal
or sectarian animosity, excited by his exposures, died away
at the establishment of Christianity, orthodox zeal, on the
other side, even still sometimes regards him as the declared
enemy of the Christian faith. The hostility of the earlier
Christian authorities had been aroused, in particular, by
two very famous *Dialogues*—the *Peregrinus* and the *Philopatris* ("The Patriot"). As for the latter, it has been proved,

beyond reasonable doubt, to have been the production of a much later writer, bearing the same name as the reputed author; while, as for the former, the chief offence originated in a mistaken reading or interpretation of the text, where allusion is made to the Founder of Christianity.[1] In fact, the brief allusions of the Greek satirist to the new faith seem to discover less hostility than is displayed in his ridicule of the rival Oriental creeds, of the established religion itself, or of the popular systems of philosophy and ethics.

If Lucian has been thus vilified by the ignorance or malice of critics of early days, on the other hand, from the first moment of his resurrection, at the restoration of learning—from the first appearance of the *editio princeps*, in 1496—he received an enthusiastic recognition of his rare merits from the best scholars of the time. Among them towers conspicuously the illustrious Erasmus, one of the earliest translators (1514), in conjunction with Sir Thomas More, of the great master of Ridicule, whom he himself so admirably imitates in his *Encomium Moriæ*

---

[1] According to the text of Hemsterhuis and Lehmann, the especially significant and highly interesting passage in question—by many critics believed to have been purposely mutilated—reads as follows :—" At which time, he [Peregrinus] made himself thoroughly master of the wonderful philosophy of the Christians, associating, in Palestine, with their priests and scribes. And—for what need of details ?—in a short time he brought them to be all mere children in his hands, aspiring to the character of prophet, to be president of their public services, and convener of their Assemblies ($\theta\iota\alpha\sigma\acute{\alpha}\rho\chi\eta\varsigma$ $\kappa\alpha\grave{\iota}$ $\xi\upsilon\nu\alpha\gamma\omega\gamma\epsilon\grave{\upsilon}\varsigma$), and he was, in fact, all in all to them. Of their books some he interpreted and expounded, many of them even he himself wrote ; and they regarded him in the light of some divine being, set him up as their legislator, and chose and publicly acknowledged him as their special patron [here occurs the suspected *hiatus*]. They, in fact, worship that great man who was crucified in Palestine, because of his introducing into the world this new religious mystery ($\tau\epsilon\lambda\epsilon\tau\eta\nu$)."— *On the Death of Peregrinus*, 11. For $\mu\acute{\epsilon}\gamma\alpha\nu$ his earlier Christian critics seem to have read $\mu\acute{\alpha}\gamma o\nu$ ("magician"), a reading which is approved by Gesner ; while the epithet "wonderful" has been assigned an ironical meaning. Of Peregrinus a more favourable account is given by Gellius (no very high authority), and Ammianus Marcellinus (a late writer), as well as by the Christian writers Athenagoras and Tertullian. The *Philopatris* (in which satirical allusion is made to the visions of St. Paul) is assigned to the year 363, the date of the Emperor Julian's Persian expedition. Cf. *Philopseudes*, 16.

("Praise of Folly"), and, not altogether so happily, in his
Colloquies. Citing the well-known verse of the Latin satirist-
poet,

Omne tulit punctum qui miscuit utile dulci,

he protests :—" no one, if not Lucian, has succeeded in illustrating this truth. He has imitated the raillery, without
copying the wantonness, of the Old Comedy. Gracious
heaven ! [*deum immortalem* is his strong expletive of admira-
tion], with what sly humour, with what grace and elegance,
he touches everything ! With what power of sarcasm he
holds up every folly to ridicule, how he seasons everything
with his wonderful wit—touching no absurdity that he does
not cover with some irony or satire ! Such grace," continues Erasmus, echoing the *dictum* of Archbishop Photius,
" dominates in his style, there is so much felicity of invention, so much elegance in his wit, such pungency in his more
serious assaults ; he so tickles with his allusions, so mingles
the grave with the gay, in such a way does he enunciate
truth with a smile, so admirably does he picture the
manners, the characters, the pursuits of men, as it were,
with a painter's pencil ; in such a manner does he display
things which we can not only read but actually see, that
whether one regards entertainment, or utility and instruction, there is no comedy, no satire, that has a right to be
put in competition with his Dialogues." At the beginning
of the sixteenth century, at least, this high eulogy was
scarcely an exaggeration.

Among the *Dialogues* translated (into Latin) by Erasmus,
it is interesting to note, are the *Timon* and the *Alexander ;*
by More (who, as an ecclesiastical zealot, and as Lord Chan-
cellor, so soon forgot the spirit of his author, and the
principles of his own *Utopia*), the *Menippus*, the *Philopseudes* ("The Lover of Lies"), and the *Tyrannicide*. Even
Melancthon, the associate of Luther in the Reformation
struggle in Germany, assisted in the work of annotating the
great sceptic (1527). Rabelais, although there is no evidence that he took part in illustrating so congenial a mind,
must have been greatly indebted to him. Early in the next
century (1615) his most considerable French editor, Bour-
delot, enthusiastically maintains that, " in proportion as the

influence of Lucian's writings was diffused, the love of knowledge and virtue increased, which still resides in the hearts of a few ; " and goes so far as to affirm that by such influence the culture, and even civilization, of the philosopher's native country perceptibly benefited in the succeeding age. A Dutch critic, Hoogstraaten, believes him to have been "not only the greatest genius of his own age, but even of all antiquity." These high eulogiums, for the most part, have been repeated by later critics to the days of Hemsterhuis and Reitz (whose judicious settlement of the text, and criticism and summary of the labours of preceding editors and annotators, respectively, first made to the world a worthy presentation of his genuine and attributed productions), and by competent judges of our own time. The English historian of Greek Literature, J. W. Donaldson, holds that "his merits can scarcely be over-estimated," and "considering him with reference to his own age, and to the Literature of Greece," justly adds the learned historian, "a position of the utmost importance must be assigned to him, both in regard to the systems of religion and of philosophy to which he gave the death-blow, and in respect to the cultivation of a purer Greek style, which he vainly taught and exemplified." During the sixteenth century sixty-five editions (in Greek or Latin), in the seventeenth twenty-two, in the eighteenth forty-four (besides translations), bore ample witness to the estimation in which he was held by the learned world. In England the first edition of him (and that only in part) did not appear till 1677. The first version (in part) in 1634. No English translation of any pretension appeared till that of Carr (1775-1798), a spirited, but extremely free, presentation of him, which was followed by that of Franklin, Professor of Greek at Cambridge (1780), and of Tooke (1820)—Franklin's, although not very faithful or accurate, being altogether the most valuable of the three chief English presentations of Lucian. Of French translations, Talbot's (1857) has the greatest repute. Of German versions, that of Wieland, the well-known poet and romancist (1788), is easily first ; and, indeed, it is generally held to be entitled to the foremost place among all attempts at a modern representation of the Greek wit.

Lucian is almost encyclopædic in the extent and rarity of his productions — critic, moralist, philosopher, politician, poet, romancist, littérateur. Of the eighty-four separate writings attributed to him, and published in the editions of his works, not a few find an undeserved place there. Some pieces of inferior merit are the production of his earlier rhetorical period, and show sufficiently evident traces of the stilted style characteristic of the fashionable declamatory essay, as well in matter as in manner. Of his undoubted productions, the shorter pieces—*Dialogues of the Gods, of the Sea-Gods,* and *of the Dead*—by reason of their popular subject-matter and peculiar graces of style, have always been most generally read. His more considerable masterpieces are *Zeus the Tragedian,* the *Sale of Lives,* the *Timon,* the *Ferry Boat,* the *Twice Accused,* the *Fisherman,* the *Fugitives,* the *Banquet,* the *Convicted Zeus,* the *Convention of the Gods,* the *Charon,* the *Icaro-Menippus,* the *True History,* the *Prometheus,* the *Philopseudes, How History Ought to be Written* (the first attempt at a philosophy of history, but not of sustained merit throughout), the *Peregrinus, On Sacrifices, On Mourning,* and the *Alexander.* In the *Greek Anthology* twenty Epigrams are ascribed to a writer bearing the name of Lucian. Whether the composition of *the* Lucian or not, they are by no means unworthy of his genius,[1] and they are among the best in the whole extensive Collection.

It is his theological *Dialogues* that have most contributed

---

[1] Especially admirable are those numbered IX., XIII., XCVI. (*Westminster Selection*); XXXVIII., LX., LXII., LXIII. (*Eton Selection*); XXXII., XL., CCLXIII. (*Edwards's Selection*), Bohn's English edition, 1854. *E. g.* :—"The wealth of the soul is the only true wealth " (xx., *Ed. S.*). "Let a seal on words not to be spoken lie on the tongue. A careful watch over words is better than one over wealth" (xL., *Ed. S.*). "Address to the Gout:"—"O Goddess! who hatest the Poor, and art the sole subduer of wealth, who knowest how to live ' well' at all times, thou delightest to be supported on strange feet, and knowest how to wear shoes of felt, and ointments are a care to thee. Thee, too, garlands delight, and the liquor of the Ausonian Bacchus. But these things never exist, at any time, for the Poor. And, therefore, thou fliest from the threshold of Poverty, that has no gold, and art delighted, on the other hand, in coming to the feet of Wealth " (xxxII., *Ed. S.*). This rich subject for satire inspired the burlesque drama of Lucian, entitled *Tragopodagra* (" Gout in Tragedy ").

to his fame. The inimitable Hellenic arts of architecture and of sculpture which adorned, disguised, and, in some measure, served to redeem the character of the religion of Zeus, or Jupiter, had long shown symptoms of decay, the outward and visible sign of a corresponding coolness in the " religious " feeling of the upper classes ; but the religion of Homer and Hesiod still kept fast hold of the affections of the body of the peoples (as it continued to do, in fact, throughout the country districts, long after the State recognition of Christianity), while the great majority of the educated or influential sections of society regarded it as a useful means of retaining the masses in subjection.[1] To undermine this imposing structure of mingled fraud and imposture, the absurdities, the follies, and the hypocrisies of its various adherents, Lucian especially devoted his almost unrivalled powers of wit and sarcasm ; and, if ridicule could inflict a mortal wound, he might have been well satisfied with his brilliant efforts. But reflection on the history of the Past must sometimes have inspired him with some misgiving, or even despair. For he was far from having been the first to expose the character of the orthodox Theology. In the drama, the most popular form of literature in Hellas—in Tragedy, Euripides (of the school of Sokrates) had, in the latter half of the fourth century, given expression to the more rational belief of the best-educated minds of the time; in Comedy, the conservative Aristophanes, in his inimitable dramas, whether purposely or not, had held up to the most open and undisguised contempt the most sacred objects of the national and popular worship. In the two next centuries Scepticism was rampant. In the lighter forms of literature, the *Mimes* (" parodies ") of Sophron of Syrakuse, and the bitter satires (*silloi*, as they were termed) of Timon of Phlius, a disciple of Pyrrho, whose name has given a synonym for the extremest scepticism, held up to derision the occupants of the national Pantheon. Such rationalistic writers, too, as Euhemerus, author of the *Sacred Inscriptions ;* Palæphatus, author of the *Incredible Legends ;* and, in particular, Menippus, were direct predecessors of the satirist of

---

[1] For instances of this doctrine of Expediency, see the remarkably candid admissions of Polybius and of Strabo.

Samosata. But these more popular writers were not the only assailants of the Pagan Pantheon : and it is enough merely to mention the names of Anaxagoras, Xenophanes, Demokritus, Zeno (the founder of the Stoic School), Antisthenes (the founder of the most practical satirists, the Cynics), and, above all, Epikurus, to recall their wide divergences from, and sometimes direct assaults on, the Olympian theology. To Lucian, however, as to Voltaire, in the last century, was reserved, in very special degree, the work of popularizing and bringing within the reach of the most ordinary intelligence the various labours of his predecessors. Of his models in the Dialogue form of writing, Plato and Xenophon are most commonly quoted : but the eloquent founder of the Academy, and the author of the *Œconomicus*, rather improved than originated it. Sophron of Syracuse, and Zeno of Elea in Italy, had already brought it into use. In the following century, Antisthenes also employed it.

As for the ethical character of Lucian, if we may trust to his own representation of himself, it deserves high praise. In the *Dream*, among the superior advantages offered by *Paideia*, he gives prominent place to the virtues of justice, mildness, and reasonableness. In his *Revived Philosophers*, he declares himself to be a hater of falsehood, of imposture, of arrogance, of pride, a lover of truth, of beauty, of sincerity, and all things lovely (ὅσα τῷ φιλεῖσθαι συγγενῆ). He abandoned the profession of the Law from disgust for its iniquity, or for the fraudulent methods of its practisers. He engages, as he declares, in the war against Falsehood quite conscious that he is fighting a desperate battle—that the vast majority are against him (*Fisherman*, 20). In his biography of his friend, Demonax, his appreciation of that superior Cynic exhibits him as a sympathetic admirer of true worth. In one department of Morals—on the assumption of his having been the author of the scandalous *Erotes* ("Loves")—he has been made the subject of undeserved censure ; for its tedious dulness and its frigid and sophisticated tone, alike foreign to Lucian's manner, prove it to be spurious.

It has been sometimes objected to Lucian's philosophical claims, that he made no attempt to build anew upon the ruins of the religious system overthrown by him. But, in the first place, systems of "faith," or "morals," already abounded *ad nauseam*, and to have erected another system of " philosophy " would have been only to add to the existing confusion. The work immediately and urgently needed was that of complete destruction, and the clearing of the ground for the future dissemination of higher and nobler ideas. This he did—at all events, as far as religionism and metaphysical shams were concerned—with the persistent zeal of a sincere reformer. In the second place, if the charge be a substantial one, he shares the blame with almost every destructive critic of after ages, whose opportunities for establishing better faiths have been superior to his. The charge to which he is more justly open—and it is the only grave fault, perhaps, in his writings—is *indiscrimination* in his assaults on the philosophies of the day. His, apparently, contemptuous treatment, in particular, of Pythagoreanism, the parent of Platonism, and the philosophical school which was most productive of examples of the higher virtues as well as of intellectual ability, deserves censure. In his *Sale of Lives*, in the *Revived Philosophers*, and in one of the *Dialogues of the Dead* in particular, he seems to have yielded to the temptation—a sort of temptation to which great wits have always been liable—of utilizing matter so promising as the ridiculous fables which the enemies of Pythagoreanism abundantly supplied.[1] That among the (self-styled) followers of Pythagoras were to be found some pretenders, and not a few extravagant expositors of his teaching—as such are found in all societies or sects— is sufficiently probable; but to hold up indiscriminately to ridicule what was, in the main, a meritorious system of (ethical) philosophy—that, certainly, did not become the character of a just critic. He lived, indeed, before the appearance of the School of New or Newer Platonism,

---

[1] In the *Sale* or *Auction of Lives*, Pythagoras, who responds to the inquiries of the bidder, as to his qualifications, that he does " not eat the flesh of animals, but everything else except beans," is sold at the price of forty pounds. Epikurus (to whose school, if to any, Lucian himself belonged), or rather an Epikurean, is sold for only eight pounds. Yet, in his *Alexander* he speaks of the founder of " The Garden " almost with the profound reverence and esteem of Lucretius.

whose founders, Plotinus, Ammonius, and Porphyry (the most erudite of all the later Greek scholars), belong to the following century. Extravagant as may have been some of their speculations, the New-Platonists, by their noble, if hopelessly futile, attempts to reform and spiritualize the established religion, and by their noble protests against the gross practical Materialism of life, have deserved (equally with the early Christians), among the various contending sects of religion or philosophy, very high esteem. Had he witnessed their self-denying lives, and been acquainted with their exalted ideas and aspirations, we may with some confidence believe that he would have done justice to their real merits, as distinguished from the errors of judgment which lay on the surface, and which were the inevitable outcome of the scientific defects of the age.

The present volume includes what may be termed the principal *theological* Dialogues. In the spelling of Greek names, in the transitional and unsettled state of Greek orthography in this country, any attempt to adopt a more natural method must, necessarily, be a compromise : hence the present version is open to the charge of some orthographical inconsistency. As for the translation itself, the method adopted has been to adhere as closely to the original as essential differences of idiom allow : to represent Lucian's peculiar graces of style no translator can reasonably aspire. The versions, entire or partial, which have appeared up to this time, however *spirited* they may be— and the German Wieland surpasses all his rivals in this respect, in whose hands, as Lehmann expresses it, "all Lucian lives and breathes "—for the most part are not distinguished by any very strict fidelity to their original. The text followed is that of the great work of Hemsterhuis and Reitz (in Lehmann's edition), which has been compared with the alternative readings adopted by Jacobitz.

DIALOGUES OF THE GODS.

I.

PROMETHEUS OBTAINS HIS RELEASE FROM ZEUS BY A PROPHECY.

Prometheus and Zeus.[1]

Prometheus. Set me free, O Zeus, for I have already endured dreadful sufferings.

Zeus. Set you free, say you? you who ought to have heavier fetters, and all Caucasus heaped on your head; and not only your liver gnawed[2] by sixteen vultures, but also your eyes scooped out, in return for your fashioning such animals as men, and for stealing my fire, and fabricating women. As for the tricks you put upon me in your distribution of the flesh meats, in offering me bones wrapped up in fat, and reserving the better portion of the pieces for yourself, why need I speak?

Prometheus. Have I then not paid enough penalty, nailed for such a long period of time to Caucasus,[3] supporting that most cursed of winged creatures, the vulture,[4] with my liver?

---

[1] Cf. Hesiod, Θεογ. 510-560, Ἐρ. καὶ Ἡμ. 48-58; Æschylus, Προμ. Δεσμ.; and the Προμήθευς ἤ Καύκασος of Lucian.

[2] Κείρεσθαι. Lit. "shorn" or "cropped" (*tonderi*), like hair which grows again. The vital parts of Prometheus were each day renewed.

[3] According to Æschylus, Prometheus was destined to suffer for some thousands of years before the advent of his saviour, Heraklês, would deliver him from his agonies. Hyginus, the Fabulist, reduces the time to the comparatively trifling period of thirty years. But, as Wieland not unjustly observes, who would look for chronological accuracy in myth and miracle?

[4] 'Αετόν. Strictly, an "eagle." 'Αετός and γύψ are indiscriminately used by the mythologists for the torturers of Prometheus.

Zeus. Not an infinitesimal part that of what you ought to suffer.

Prometheus. Yet you shall not release me without recompense. But I will impart something to you, Zeus, exceedingly important.

Zeus. You are for outwitting me, Prometheus.

Prometheus. And what advantage should I gain? For you will not be ignorant hereafter of the whereabouts of Kaucasus; neither will you be in want of chains, should I be caught playing you any trick.

Zeus. Say, first, what sort of equivalent you will pay, of so much importance to us.

Prometheus. If I tell you for what purpose you are now on your travels, shall I have credit with you, when I prophesy about the rest?

Zeus. Of course.

Prometheus. You are off to Thetis, to an intrigue with her.

Zeus. That indeed you have correct knowledge of. But what then, after that? For you seem to have some inkling of the truth.

Prometheus. Don't have anything to do with the Nereid, Zeus: for, if she should be pregnant by you, her progeny will treat you exactly as you, too, treated[1]——

Zeus. This do you assert—that I shall be expelled from my kingdom?

Prometheus. Heaven forbid, Zeus! Intercourse with her, however, threatens something of the kind.

Zeus. Good-bye to Thetis, then. And as for you, for these *timely warnings* Hephæstus shall set you free.

---

[1] But for the very hasty interruption of Zeus, Prometheus would have added—"Cronos and Rhea," the parents of the present usurping King of Gods and Men, dethroned by their unnatural son. See Ov. *Metam.* xi. 221-228, where it is Proteus who gives the warning prediction to Thetis.

II.

ZEUS THREATENS TO PUT EROS IN FETTERS.

Eros and Zeus.

Eros. Well, if I have really done wrong at all, Zeus, pardon me : for I am but an infant, and still without sense.

Zeus. You an infant—you the Eros, who are far older than Iapetus?[1] Because you have not grown a beard, and don't show gray hairs, do you really claim on that account to be considered an infant, when, in fact, you are an old scamp?

Eros. But what great injury have I—the old scamp, as you call me—done you, that you intend putting me in irons?

Zeus. Consider, accursed rascal, whether they are trifling injuries you have done me, you, who make such sport of me, that there is nothing which you have not turned me into—satyr, bull, gold, swan, eagle[2]—but not any one of them have you made to be in love with *me* at all; nor have I perceived that, for anything that depends upon you, I have been agreeable to any woman; but I am obliged to have recourse to juggling tricks against them, and to conceal my proper self, while they are really in love with the bull or swan, and, if they have but a glimpse of me, they die of fear.[3]

Eros. Naturally enough, Zeus, for, being mortal women, they can't endure the sight of your person.

[1] One of the Titans, progenitor of the human race, son of Uranus and Ge, and father of Prometheus. " As old as Iapetus " was a proverb with the Greeks, equivalent to our "as old as Adam." Cf. Hesiod Θεογ. 120; Plato Συμπ. ad init., Θ. Δ. vii. 1. and Aristoph. Νεφ. 985.

[2] An epigram in the *Greek Anthologia* thus sums up some of the principal *liaisons*, and the mistresses, of the King of Gods and Men :—

"Ζεὺς κύκνος, ταῦρος, σάτυρος, χρυσὸς δι' ἔρωτα
Λήδης, Εὐρώπης, 'Αντιόπης, Δανάης."

But the catalogue is incomplete. Besides these heroines, have been commemorated Io, Alkmena, Semele, Kallisto, Klytoria, Asteria, Ægina, Mnemosyne.

[3] Like Semele, the Theban princess, mother of Bacchus.

Zeus. How is it, then, that Branchus[1] and Hyacinthus love Apollo?

Eros. But even from him the beauty, Daphne, fled away, for all his flowing locks and beardless chin. If you wish to be loved, don't shake your ægis, and don't take your thunderbolt with you; but make yourself as agreeable as you can, letting down your locks on both sides of your face, and tying them up again under your coronet; wear a fine purple dress, put on golden sandals, step along keeping time to the sounds of the pipe and cymbals, and you will see that more women will follow you than all the Mænads of Bacchus.

Zeus. Get away with you. I would not take the offer of being loved, on condition of becoming such a figure.

Eros. Then, Zeus, don't wish to love, either: that, at all events, is an easy matter.

Zeus. Not so; but I do wish to love, and to enjoy their society in a less vexatious fashion. Upon this, and this condition alone, I let you go.

III.

ZEUS ORDERS HERMES TO SLAY ARGUS, AND TO CONDUCT IO TO EGYPT.

Zeus and Hermes.

Zeus. Hermes, you know the daughter of Inachus, the famous beauty?

Hermes. Yes, you mean the far-famed Io.

Zeus. She is no longer a girl, but a heifer.

Hermes. Prodigious that! But how was she transformed?

Zeus. Hera, in a fit of jealousy, metamorphosed her,[2] and

---

[1] Son of Apollo by a lady of Miletus, from whom the Branchidæ, the guardians of the Oracle of Apollo at Miletus, who surrendered the treasures of their temple to Darius, derived their descent. For Hyacinthus see Θ. Δ. x. 11 ; and Ovid, *Metam.* x. 162-219.

[2] According to Ovid (*Metam.* i. 13-17), it was Jupiter himself who effected the metamorphosis, to save the Argive princess from the rage of Juno. Cf. Eναλ. Διαλ. vii.

not only that, but she has also contrived another sort of new mischief against the unfortunate girl. She has appointed a certain cowkeeper with eyes all over him, who tends the heifer with sleepless care.

Hermes. What must I do, then?

Zeus. Fly down to Nemea—it's somewhere there that Argus tends his charge—and kill him off. But as for Io, bring her away by sea to Egypt, and transform her into Isis.[1] And, for the future, let her be a divinity to the people of the country, and let her raise the Nile, and send favourable winds, and be the patron-saint of sailors.[2]

IV.

ZEUS INSTRUCTS GANYMEDES AS TO THE NATURE OF HIS DUTIES IN HEAVEN.

Zeus and Ganymedes.

Zeus. Come, Ganymede—for we have arrived at the proper place—kiss me now, that you may know that I have no longer crooked beak, nor sharp talons, nor wings such as I appeared to you, under the semblance of a bird.[3]

---

[1] For this, one of the most famous of the metamorphoses of the Greek Theology, see Ovid, *Metam.* i. 13-17. Io appears as one of the *dramatis personæ* of the Προμήθευς Δεσμώτης of Æschylus, where she is represented as brought in her wanderings to the Caucasian Valley, in which Prometheus was impaled, and bewails the διαφθοράν μορφῆς, as she terms it. Cf. the Ἰκέτιδες of the same dramatist. Strabo, Diodorus, Apollodorus, and Pausanias add particulars to the Ovidian story. Evidently the Greeks derived the myth, in the first instance, from the Egyptian priests.

[2] Votive tablets and pictures, suspended in the temples of Isis, recorded the gratitude of rescued passengers and sailors to their protectress. *Pictores quis nescit ab Iside pasci?* demands Juvenal (xii. 28). The Egyptian goddess was in especial favour with the Roman ladies, and her temples were little else than convenient places of assignation.—Juv. *Sat.* vi. 489. Pausanias (Ἑλλάδος Περιήγησις, x. 32) describes the ritual of one of the temples, or shrines, of Isis in Phocis—"the holiest" of all her Greek sanctuaries—and records the punishment of certain rash and inquisitive intruders. "So," adds Pausanias, "Homer's word seems true that the Gods are not seen by mortals with impunity."—See Bohn's Series.

[3] Some authorities represent Zeus as himself, in the shape of his

Ganymedes. Were you not an eagle but just now, fellow, and did you not pounce down and carry me off from the midst of my flock? How then have those feathers fallen off from you entirely, and you have now come out in quite a different character?

Zeus. But, my dear boy, you see neither a man nor an eagle : but it is I here, the king of all the gods, who have metamorphosed myself at the right moment.

Ganymedes. How? what, are *you* the great Pan? Then how haven't you a syrinx, or horns, and hairy legs?[1]

Zeus. Why, do you take him to be the only divinity?

Ganymedes. Yes, and we sacrifice to him an uncastrated he-goat, bringing him to the grotto where the god stands. But as for you, you seem to me to be some kidnapping slave-dealer[2] or other.

Zeus. Tell me, have you never heard the name of Zeus, nor seen on Gargarus an altar to the Rain-Sender, and Thunderer, and Lightener?

Ganymedes. Do you say, fine Sir,[3] that you are the same who but lately poured down on us that quantity of hail, who are said to live up above, who make such a din, to whom my father sacrificed a ram? Then, how have I wronged you that you have carried me off, O king of the Gods? Already, I doubt, will the wolves be falling upon my unprotected sheep and tearing them to pieces.

Zeus. What! Have you, who have been made immortal,

---

favourite eagle, carrying off his future cup-bearer; while others are content with the agency of the "royal bird." Ovid (*Metam.* x. 4) is among the former. Hesiod knows, or says, nothing of the story of the *rapti Ganymedis honores.* According to the *Iliad,* the rape of the handsome son of the Phrygian king is effected by all the gods in a body. (xx. 232-5). The scene, usually, is laid on Mt. Ida. Cicero (*Tusc. Quæst.* i. 26) will not listen to Homer on this matter.

[1] The proper appendages, in the popular belief, of the rural divinity, as displayed in Theocritus and Virgil.

[2] Ἀνδραποδιστής. How flourishing a profession was that of the *kidnapper* in Greek society, may be seen in the *Comedies* of Plautus and Terence, who borrowed their plots from the Greeks. He makes a conspicuous figure, also, in the Greek Romances—in particular, in the Theagenes and Charikleia of Heliodorus. (See Bohn's Series.)

[3] Ὦ Βελτίστε. Translated *feine Herr* by Wieland, who remarks that the Greek expression has a certain comic force hardly to be conveyed in our language.

and who are to live with us here, still a regard for your sheep?

Ganymedes. How do you say? Then will you not this very day take me down home to Ida?

Zeus. By no means. In that case, I should have changed from a God into an eagle to no purpose.

Ganymedes. My father, then, will certainly be looking for me, and be angry at not finding me, and I shall be whipped by and bye for having left my flock.

Zeus. Why, where will he see you?

Ganymedes. Don't *keep me, please,* for I am already longing to see him. And, if you will take me back, I promise you another ram shall be sacrificed by him as my ransom. We have the three-year-old one—that fine one, who leads the flock to pasture.

Zeus (aside). How simple and innocent is the child—a child yet all over, truly! But, my dear Ganymede, bid farewell to all those things and forget them, your flock, and Ida; and you from this place—for you are now enrolled among the celestials—will do many services both to your father and to your country; and, instead of cheese and milk, you will eat ambrosia and drink nectar: this latter, indeed, you shall yourself pour out, and offer to the rest of us. But, what is more than all, you will no longer be mortal, but shall become immortal, and I will make your star shine very bright,[1] and, in a word, you shall be happy.

Ganymedes. And if I want to play, who will play with me? On Ida there were many of us, playmates of the same age.

Zeus. Here, too, you have a playmate—Eros there, and any number of knuckle-bones.[2] Only cheer up, and be bright, and don't hanker after any of the things down below there.

Ganymedes. In what way, please, can I be of use to you? Must I look after flocks and herds here, too?

---

[1] Under the name of Ὑδρηχόος (Aquarius). Hemsterhuis observes that " Hadrian [the Emperor] very fairly imitated Jupiter, and claimed so much of the stars as his own by right as to insert his Ganymede, the dead Antinous, among them: indeed, he wished it to appear that he had discovered his new star." Cf. Suidas.

[2] Ἀστράγαλους. (Lat. *talos.*) A favourite game, from very early times, with the Greek women and children. See Becker's *Charicles.*

Zeus. No, but you shall pour wine into the goblet, and you shall be placed in charge of the nectar, and shall have the care of the Banqueting-Hall.

Ganymedes. That's no hard matter, for I know how to pour in milk, and to pass about the milk-bowl.

Zeus (aside). There again he is thinking of his milk, and fancies that he will have to wait upon mortals.—But this is heaven here, and we drink, as I told you, the celestial nectar.

Ganymedes. Is it sweeter than milk, Zeus ?

Zeus. You shall know for yourself shortly ; and, when you have once tasted it, you will not again have any longing for your milk.

Ganymedes. But where shall I sleep at night ? with my playfellow, Eros ?

Zeus. No. I carried you off on this account—that we might sleep together.

Ganymedes. Why, could you not sleep alone; but is it pleasanter to you to sleep with me ?

Zeus. Yes, with such an one as you, Ganymede, so handsome as you are.

Ganymedes. Why, how will handsome looks give you pleasure, in respect to sleep ?

Zeus They have a certain sweet charm, and bring it on more softly.

Ganymedes. Yet my father used to be annoyed with me, when I slept in the same bed with him, and used to tell me in the morning how I had taken away his sleep by my restlessness and kicking, and talking in my sleep : for which reason he would generally send me to bed with my mother. If it was on that account, as you say, that you carried me off, it is high time for you to put me down on the Earth again ; or you will be annoyed by being kept awake, for I shall disturb you by my continual tossing about.

Zeus. In doing that very thing you will most please me —since I shall keep awake with you in frequent kisses and embraces.

Ganymedes. You would have to see to that yourself. As for me, while you are kissing me, I shall lull myself to sleep.

Zeus. We shall know what is to be done then.—But now take him away, Hermes; and when he has quaffed immortality,[1] bring him to us to be our cup-bearer, having, first of all, instructed him how he is to hand his cup.

V.

HERA UPBRAIDS ZEUS WITH HIS LOVE FOR GANYMEDES.

Hera and Zeus.

Hera. Ever since, Zeus, you carried off that Phrygian youth from Ida, and brought him up here, you pay me less attention.

Zeus. What, are you really jealous, Hera, already, about so simple and very innocent an affair as that ? I thought you were hard only upon the women, who might happen to be intimate with me.

Hera. Your conduct not even in those matters is proper, or becoming to yourself—you, the liege lord of all the gods, to desert me, your lawful, wedded wife, and go down to Earth to intrigue in the shape of gold, or of a satyr, or of a bull.   But, at least, those females of yours remain on Earth, while this youth from Ida you snatched up and flew off with, O most respectable of gods,[2] actually lives with us, put over my head; a cup-bearer, to be sure—in name. Were you so desperately at a loss for butlers, and have Hebe and Hephæstus really become worn out in the service ? And you—you will not take the cup from him otherwise than first kissing him in the sight of us all; and the kiss is sweeter to you than nectar, and, on that account,

---

[1] Cf. IX. i. 595-600. Apuleius, the contemporary of Lucian, concludes the story of Psyche with a similar scene, when the persecuted bride of Eros is admitted to the privilege of immortality and the society of the Celestials by drinking nectar. With the Pythagoreans, ambrosia and nectar were favourite metaphors for the highest spiritual and intellectual enjoyments. "If," says Iamblichus, "partaking of this divine food (of Knowledge) cannot make men immortal, at least it will make them acquainted with matters of eternal import."

[2] Some MSS. have ἀετῶν, "most respectable of eagles."

you are constantly asking to drink, without even being thirsty. When, too, after just tasting it, you hand back the cup to him, and after he has drunk, you receive it from him again, you quaff off the remainder from the place where the boy has drunk from, and where he has applied his lips, that you may drink and kiss at one and the same moment. Nay, but just now you, the King and father of the universe, laid aside ægis and thunderbolt, and sat down to a game of knuckle-bones with him, with all that big beard you have grown.[1] All these fine doings I see, so don't suppose you are unobserved.

Zeus. And what dreadful crime is it, Hera, to kiss so fair a youth between cups, and to derive pleasure from both—the kiss and the nectar ? If, believe me, I were to allow him to kiss you once even, you would never again blame me for thinking the kiss preferable to the nectar.

Hera. This is the talk of a pæderast ! But, for my part, may I never be so mad as to offer my lips to this soft Phrygian boy, so completely effeminated as he is.

Zeus. Do not upbraid me, most admirable of goddesses, with loves of this sort :[2] for this youth, effeminate, a foreigner, soft and girlish as he is, is more agreeable to me and more desirable than—but I have no wish to say it, not to further provoke you.

Hera. Would that you would even marry him, for my own sake ! Don't forget, however, how offensively you

---

[1] Here, as elsewhere, in his references to the personal appearance of the members of the Greek Pantheon, Lucian is describing the well-known characteristics of the famous representations of them in Art. In the present instance, the Zeus of Pheidias at Olympia was, doubtless, especially in Lucian's mind, the most famous of the representations of the " Thunderer ; " as the " Athena Parthenos " and " Athena Promachos " of the same eminent sculptor, on the Acropolis at Athens, and the Cnidian Aphrodite of Praxiteles were of Athena and Aphrodite.

[2] Τοῖς παιδίκοις. Supply ἔρωσι. Lucian satirizes an unnatural vice especially prevalent in his time, and, probably, had in mind, in particular, the shameful attachment of the late Roman Emperor, Hadrian, for the famous Bithynian youth, Antinous, in whose honour, as is well known, temples and statues were erected throughout the Empire. Pausanias, the Greek traveller and antiquary of the second century, a contemporary of Antinous, informs us that Mantinea, in Arcadia, was especially rich in statues and paintings of the handsome favourite, whose death is involved in circumstances of so much mystery (viii. 9).

insult me, in your cups, on account of this male Hebe of yours.

Zeus. Not so : but that son of yours, Hephæstus, must needs act as butler, with his limping gait, coming straight from his forge, still covered all over with sparks, his fire-tongs only just laid aside : and from those fingers of his I had to receive the goblet, and drawing him to me to greet him with a salute between while, whom not even you, his mother, would kiss with any pleasure, with his face completely blackened with soot.[1]   The present arrangement is much more agreeable : for *will you say that it is* not so ? That cup-bearer of yours certainly excellently becomes the table of the gods; while Ganymede must be sent down back to Ida—for he is clean, and rosy-fingered, and hands the goblet deftly; and, what most vexes you, gives kisses more sweet than nectar.

Hera. Yes.   Hephæstus is lame now, and his fingers are not fit to touch your cup, and he is covered with soot, and the sight of him turns you sick—ever since Ida produced that handsome youth with the flowing locks.   Yet, formerly, you did not observe these things; neither the sparks nor the forge turned your stomach so as to prevent your drinking from his hand.

Zeus. You plague yourself to no purpose, Hera, while you intensify my love for him by your jealousy.   Well, if you are annoyed at receiving the goblet from a beautiful boy, let your son pour out your wine, and as for you, Ganymede, hand the cup only to myself, and at each time kiss me twice : when you offer it full, and again whenever you take it back from me.—What's this ?   In tears ?   Don't be afraid; if any one has any intention of annoying you he will have cause to lament.

---

[1] Cf. Il. i. 600; xviii. 410-415; Juv. *Sat.* xiii. 43-45.

VI.

IXION MAKES LOVE TO HERA.

Hera and Zeus.

Hera. This Ixion,[1] Zeus, what sort of character do you take him to be?

Zeus. A good kind of man, and a boon companion: for he would not associate with us, had he been unworthy of our table.

Hera. But he *is* unworthy of it, for he is an insolent fellow: so let him not live with us any longer.

Zeus. Of what insolence or injury has he been guilty, pray? For *I* ought to know too, I think.

Hera. Insolence? and what else—I blush, however, to mention it, such was his daring impertinence.

Zeus. Yet that is the more reason you should tell me, in proportion to the baseness of his attempt. Surely he has not attempted any one's virtue, has he? For I understand the disgraceful conduct to be something of a kind which you would shrink from telling me.

Hera. On mine, and no one else's *has he made his assaults,* now for a long time past. At first I was ignorant of the reason why he kept staring fixedly at me, while he would sigh and secretly drop a tear; and whenever, after drinking, I handed the beaker to Ganymede, he would ask to drink from the very same place, and would take and kiss it between while, and put it to his eyes, and again stare at me. These actions I now began to perceive to be amorous signs. For a long time I felt ashamed to speak to you, and thought that the fellow would cease from his mad folly. But when he dared to make his advances to me in words, I left him still in tears, and prostrate at my feet; and stopping my ears, not to hear even his insolent en-

---

[1] The "perfidious" king of the Lapithæ (father of Peirithous), who had been pardoned by Zeus after a foul murder, and received into heaven, where it was permitted him to sit at the Olympian table. He does not appear among the eminent criminals whom Odysseus meets in Hades, nor is he mentioned by Hesiod. Pindar (Πυθ. II.) exhibits him as a terrible warning.

treaties, I came away to tell you. Now do you yourself look to it, in what manner you shall punish the man.

Zeus. Is this the fine return the cursed villain makes to myself—even so far as to aspire to the favours of Hera? Has he become so drunk on our nectar? But we ourselves are the cause of these outrages, and are out of all measure philanthropic, in making men our boon-companions. They have some excuse, therefore, if, while drinking on equal terms with us, and beholding celestial beauties, and of a sort they never have seen on earth, overpowered by love, they eagerly long to enjoy them. Well, Love is an intractable sort of creature, and governs not only men, but even ourselves sometimes.

Hera. Of you he certainly is very much the master, and drives and leads you captive, "dragging you," as they say, "by the nose;" and you follow him wherever he may lead you, and he easily transforms you into whatever he wishes; and, in fine, you are the mere possession and plaything of Love. And now I know well *why* you extend your pardon to Ixion—inasmuch as you yourself had an intrigue with his wife, who presented you with that Peirithous of yours.[1]

Zeus. What! Must you be for ever bringing up to mind those *little trifles*—whatever sport I have gone down to Earth and enjoyed? But do you know what I have in my mind about Ixion? By no means to punish him, nor to expel him from our table; for that would be an uncourteous act. And since he is in love, and as you say, falls to tears, and feels unendurable——

Hera. What *are you going to utter*, Zeus? For I am

---

[1] Peirithous, reputed son of Ixion, it seems, was the son of Zeus by Dia, Ixion's wife. Seneca represents Juno as bitterly complaining of the infidelities of her lord :—

> " Soror tonantis—hoc enim *solum* mihi
> Nomen relictum est . . . .
> Locumque, cœlo pulsa, pellicibus dedi.
> Tellus colenda est : pellices cœlum tenent."
> *Hercules Furens.*

See *Il.* i. 535-570; iv. 5-67; xv. 15-35, for other memorable grounds for complaint on the part of the queen of heaven. Pausanias (ix. 3), relates a *pleasant* story of the ingenuity of Zeus, on one occasion, in appeasing her jealousy.

afraid you, too, are on the point of saying something impertinent.

Zeus. Not at all. But let us form a phantom out of a cloud like your very self, and when the dinner party is broken up, and he, as is highly probable, is keeping his vigils, under the influence of his passion, let us carry it and lay it down by his side. In this way he would cease to be plagued; supposing he had had what he wanted.

Hera. Get away with you. Plague take him for indulging hopes beyond his station.[1]

Zeus. Put up with it, however, my dear Hera, for what terrible harm could you get from the counterfeit figure, if Ixion shall have to do with a mere cloud?

Hera. Yes, but *I* shall be supposed to be the cloud, and he will perpetrate upon me his foul purpose, through the resemblance.

Zeus. Your objection is nothing to the purpose. For neither will the cloud ever be Hera, nor will you be a cloud, while Ixion will only be deceived.

Hera. But all men are so vulgar-minded and without good taste, when he goes down he will, probably, talk big and recount to everybody that he has enjoyed the favours of Hera, and shared the bed of Zeus; and, maybe, he will even assert that I am in love with him; and, not knowing it was a cloud he was with, they will believe him.

Zeus. Then, if he should say anything of the kind, the wretch shall be thrown into hell, be bound to a wheel, and carried round with it for ever and ever, and shall suffer everlasting torture, paying the penalty not of his love—for that, surely, is not so dreadful a crime—but of his loud boasting.[2]

---

[1] Μὴ ὥραισιν ἵκοιτο τῶν ὑπέρ αὐτὸν ἐπιθυμῶν. Cf. Lucian, Περὶ Ὀρχήσεως, v. Aristoph. Λύσιστράτη 1037. An old Attic form of imprecation, as to the exact meaning of which the commentators are at variance. Another reading is ὥρας.

[2] "It must be understood that Jupiter, with all his *joviality*, was a great master in the invention of horrible tortures and punishments; and he speaks in the true tone of a dilettante in such matters."—Wieland.

VII.

HEPHÆSTUS RECOUNTS TO APOLLO THE ACTIONS OF THE INFANT PRODIGY, HERMES.

Apollo and Hephæstus.

Hephæstus. Apollo, have you seen Maia's baby, which is just born ? What a pretty thing it is, and how it smiles on every one, and already plainly shows he is going to turn out some great treasure !

Apollo. That a baby, or a great treasure, who is older than Iapetus himself, as far as depends on rascality !

Hephæstus. And what possible mischief could an infant just born be able to do ?

Apollo. Ask Poseidon, whose trident he stole, or Ares; for even from the latter he abstracted his sword from the sheath without being found out, not to speak of myself, whom he disarmed of my bow and arrows.

Hephæstus. The new-born brat did this, who hardly keeps on his feet, who is still in his long clothes ?

Apollo. You will know well enough, Hephæstus, if only he come near you.

Hephæstus. Indeed, he already has been near me.

Apollo. Well, have you all your tools, and is none of them missing ?

Hephæstus. All of them *are safe*, my dear Apollo.

Apollo. All the same, examine carefully.

Hephæstus. By heaven ! I don't see my fire-tongs.

Apollo. No, but you will probably see them among the infant's swaddling clothes.

Hephæstus. Is he so light-fingered, for all the world as though he had mastered the purloining art in his mother's womb ?

Apollo. *No wonder you ask*, for you have not heard his glib and voluble prattling. He is, besides, quite ready to wait upon us. And yesterday he challenged Eros, and wrestled with him and threw him, somehow tripping up his feet. Then, while he was getting praised for it, he stole Aphrodite's *cestus*, as she was folding him to her breast on account of his victory; and, while he was laughing, the sceptre of Zeus, also. And, if the thunder-bolt were not a little too heavy, and had a good deal of fire in it, he would have filched that too.

Hephœstus. The child you describe is a regular Gorgon.

Apollo. Not only so, but already he is a musical genius, also.

Hephœstus. From what can you draw your inference as to that ?

Apollo. Somewhere or other he found a dead tortoise, and from it formed a musical instrument : for, having fitted in the horns (or side-pieces) and joined them by a bar, he next fixed pegs, and inserted a bridge beneath them ; and, after stretching seven strings upon it, he set about playing a very pretty and harmonious tune, so that even I, practised as I have long been in playing the cithara,[1] envied him. And Maia assured us that not even his nights would he pass in heaven, but from mere busybodyness he would descend as far as Hades, to steal something from thence, I suppose. He is furnished with wings, and has made for himself a sort of staff[2] of wonderful virtue, with which he chaperones the souls of dead men, and conducts them down *to the infernal regions.*

Hephœstus. I gave him that for a plaything.

Apollo. Then he has paid you back : your fire-tongs——

Hephœstus. Well remembered. So I will march off to recover it, if, as you say, it is anywhere to be found among his cradle-clothes.

---

[1] Κιθαρίζειν. The *cithara* differed somewhat from the *lyra* and resembled rather the modern guitar. Originally, the lyre had three or four strings only : but (650 B.C.) it received the full complement of seven strings. From the tortoiseshell material it received its Latin name, *testudo.* See Smith's *Dict. of Ant.* art. *Lyra.*

[2] The *Caduceus* (as the ῥάβδος was called by the Latins). By a slight change formed, apparently, from καρυκείον, " a herald's wand "— whence the epithet of *caducifer.* See Ἰλ. xxiv. 343 ; Ὀδ. v. 47 ; Virg. *Æn.* iv. 247-253.

VIII.

HEPHÆSTUS [1] ASSISTS AT THE PARTURITION OF ZEUS AND THE BIRTH OF ATHENA.

Hephæstus and Zeus.

Hephæstus. What have I to do, Zeus ? For I am come, as you ordered me, with my sharpest axe, *sharp enough,* even though it were wanted to cut through a stone at one stroke (*displaying his tool*).

Zeus. Well done, my dear Hephæstus. *But don't waste time,* but bring it down with a will, and split my head in two.

Hephæstus. You are trying me, if I am in my right senses ? Order, pray, something else, whatever it is you really want done to you.

Zeus. *I desire* my skull to be split open—that and nothing else. If you will not obey me, it is not the first time you will tempt my anger.[2] Well, now you must come down with all your soul and strength, and that without delay ; for I am simply dying under the pangs of labour, which rack my poor brain terribly.

Hephæstus. Look out, Zeus, that we don't do you some injury ; for the axe is sharp, and not unattended with blood, nor will it act the midwife for you after the fashion of Eileithuia.[3]

Zeus. Bring it down boldly, without more ado, sir. I know what's best.

Hephæstus. 'Tis sorely against my will, but I will down with it, however : for what's one to do, when you order a thing ? (*Starting back in alarm.*) What's this ? A girl

---

[1] The part here assumed by the blacksmith god by other authorities is attributed to Prometheus or Hermes. Lucian follows Pindar, Oλ. vii. 35 (Jacob.). For an etymological disquisition on the name of Athena see Plato, Κρατύλος.

[2] Hephæstus had been expelled, in an ignominious fashion, from heaven on the memorable occasion recorded in Iλ. i. *ad fin.*

[3] The goddess *who comes* with help to women in childbirth. See Iλ. xi. 270, where the poet speaks of more than one Eileithuia, and represents the sisters as daughters of Hera :—

" μογοστόκοι Εἰλείθυιαι
"Ηρης θυγάτερες, πικρὰς ὠδῖνας ἔχουσαι."

Cf. Iλ. xix. 119. Hesiod knows only one, Θεογ. 886-900, 922.

in armour! A mighty pain you had in your head, Zeus. With good reason, I admit, you were so short-tempered, maintaining alive in the *pia mater* of your brain a virgin of such proportions, and that too, in a suit of armour! It was a camp, surely, not a head you have had *all this while* without its being known. Why! she leaps and dances the Pyrrhic dance,[1] and clashes her shield, and brandishes her spear, and is all on fire with martial excitement; and, what is more, in this short time, she has become a very beautiful woman, and is in her full bloom already. She has a fierceness in her bluish-gray eyes[2] to be sure, but her helmet sets off that, too, to advantage. So, Zeus, pay me my midwife-fee, by betrothing her to me now at once.

Zeus. You ask impossibilities, Hephæstus, for she chooses to remain ever a virgin: but I, however, as far as I am concerned, offer no opposition.

Hephæstus. That's all I wanted. The rest shall be my care, and I will carry her off even now.

Zeus. If you find it an easy affair, do so: but I know that you are indulging a hopeless passion.[3]

IX.

HERMES REFUSES POSEIDON ADMISSION TO ZEUS, AND ASSIGNS AS THE REASON THE LYING-IN OF THE KING OF GODS AND MEN WITH BACCHUS.

Poseidon and Hermes.

Poseidon. May one have an interview with Zeus just now, Hermes?

[1] Πυρριχίζει. The Pyrrhic dance (ἡ πυρρίχη) was the famous military dance performed in full armour to the sound of the flute or rather pipe. At Athens it formed part of the Panathenaic festival. The birth of Athena occupied a conspicuous place on the sculptures of the Parthenon. See Pausanias, i. 24.

[2] Γλαυκῶπις. The well-known Homeric epithet of the goddess of War and Wisdom. The exact colour implied in γλαύκος is disputed. As applied to Athena, it included a certain flashing or fierceness of the eyes. Plutarch, Βίοι Παραλ., in his description of Sulla, records of his eyes:—" τὴν τῶν ὀμμάτων γλαυκότητα, δεινῶς καὶ πικρὰν καὶ ἄκρατον οὖσαν, ἡ χρόα τοῦ προσώπου φοβερωτέραν ἐποίει προσιδεῖν." Cf. Ov. *Amores*, ii. 659; Statius, *Theb.* ii. 715.

[3] For a description of a famous Greek painting of this subject see

Hermes. By no means, my dear Poseidon.

Poseidon. At all events announce me to him (*making a forward movement*).

Hermes. (*Interposing himself.*) Don't be a nuisance, I say: for it is quite an unseasonable moment, so you could not possibly see him at present.

Poseidon. He is not engaged with Hera, is he?

Hermes. No, but it is quite another sort of affair.

Poseidon. I understand. Ganymedes is closeted with him.

Hermes. Not that, either. The fact is, he is rather poorly.

Poseidon. From what cause, my dear Hermes? For this is strange news you report.

Hermes. I blush to tell it, such is its nature.

Poseidon. But you need not blush to tell me, your uncle.

Hermes. He has but just now been brought to bed, Poseidon.

Poseidon. Get away with you. He brought to bed? By whom? Is he an hermaphrodite,[1] without our knowing it *all this time?* Yet his person did not discover any symptoms of it.

Hermes. You are right, for the *usual* part did not hold the embryo.

Poseidon. Ah! I know. He has given birth again through his head-piece, as he did to Athena—it's his head he keeps for a breeding-place.

Hermes. No, it was in his thigh that he was pregnant with Semele's[2] infant.

Philostratus, Εἰκόνες, in the French version, *Philostrate Ancien, Une Galerie Antique,* par A. Bougot, Paris, 1881. The highly interesting pictures, described by Philostratus as having been seen by him in a gallery at Naples, appear to have been not frescoes but painted in the studio.

[1] Ἀνδρόγυνος. Plato's Dialogue, the Συμπόσιον, has given celebrity to the word. Another form of it is γυνάνδρος. Hermaphrodite, which frequently appears in Greek Art, is compounded of Hermes and Aphrodite. See Ov. *Metam.* iv. 5, for the story of the Naiad Salmacis and Hermaphroditus.

[2] The story of Semele is to be found in Ovid, *Metam.* iii. 4, 5. Cf. Apollod. iii. 4. It forms the subject of one of the Εἰκόνες of Philostratus, where Semele is represented mounting to Heaven.

Poseidon. Well done, the excellent *parent!* How productive he is all over, and in every part of his body! But who is this Semele?

Hermes. A lady of Thebes, one of the daughters of Kadmus. He paid her a visit, and made her *enceinte.*

Poseidon. Then, did he take her place in the straw, Hermes?

Hermes. Exactly, however strange and paradoxical it appears to you. For Hera—you know how jealous she is —secretly laid a trap for her, and persuaded her to request from Zeus that he would come to her with thunder and lightning. And when he complied, and came with his thunderbolt, the roof of the house was set all on fire, and burnt up, and poor Semele perished in the flames. And he orders me to cut open the lady's womb, and to bring up to him the still imperfect embryo of seven months. When I had so done, he cuts open his own thigh and inserts it, that it might there receive its completion; and now, exactly in the third month, he has given birth to the child and is feeling poorly after the pangs of parturition.

Poseidon. Where, then, is the baby now?

Hermes. I took it off to Nysa, and delivered it to the Nymphs to bring up, after giving it the name of Dionysus.[1]

Poseidon. And is my brother really both father and mother of this Dionysus?

Hermes. So it seems. But I am now off to fetch water for his wound, and to perform the other services which are customary, just as for a lady after confinement.[2]

---

[1] The Greek alternative name for Bacchus, said to be be derived from Mt. Nysa in Thrace or India, with paternal prefix. One of the most famous statues of Hermes, by Praxiteles, represents the youthful god bearing away the infant, as here described. It was discovered by the German Excavation Commission, in 1877, at Olympia, mutilated, but with the features entire. It is one of the most valued discoveries of Greek sculpture of the present time. See Pausanias, v. 17.

[2] Λεχοῖ. Cf. Aristoph. ʼΕκκλης. 530; Euripides, ῞Ηλεκτρα, 652; and see Ter. *Andria,* iii. 2, in the case of Glycerium.

X.

HERMES CONVEYS TO HELIOS THE ORDER OF ZEUS; THAT HE IS TO REFRAIN FROM DRIVING HIS CHARIOT, UNTIL THE COMPLETION OF THE AMOUR OF THE KING OF GODS AND MEN WITH ALKMENE.

Hermes and Helios.

Hermes. Helios, you are not to drive out to-day, Zeus says, nor to-morrow, nor the day after, but to remain at home; and let that interval of time be one long kind of night. So let the Horæ [1] unharness your horses again, and do you put out your fires, and repose yourself for a good long time.

Helios. New and strange instructions these, Hermes, you come to give me. But am I thought to blunder in any way in my course, and to drive beyond its bounds; and is it on that account he is vexed with me, and determined to make the night three times the length of one day?

Hermes. Nothing of the kind, nor will it be always so: but he wants the night just now to be somewhat longer than usual, on his own account.

Helios. And where is he, or whence have you been despatched with this message for me?

Hermes. From Bœotia, Helios, from Amphitryon's wife, with whom he now is, making love to her. [2]

Helios. Then is one night not enough?

Hermes. By no means, for some mighty and much-

---

[1] The Horæ (" Hours "), in the Homeric theology (Ἰλ. viii. 393), are the doorkeepers of Heaven. According to Hesiod, their names are Eunomia, Dike, and Eirene, the daughters of Zeus and Themis (Θεογ. 901). They united with the Charites, and other divinities, in adorning Pandora :—

$$\dot{\alpha}\mu\phi\grave{\iota} \ \delta\grave{\epsilon} \ \tau\acute{\eta}\nu\gamma\epsilon$$
Ὧραι καλλίκομοι στέφον ἄνθεσιν εἰαρινοῖσι.
Ἔρ. καὶ Ἡμ. 74.

See Lucian, Περὶ Θυσίων. The picture of the *Hours*, as described by Philostratus, formed a charming subject.

[2] Upon this *liaison* of Zeus with Alkmena is founded one of the most entertaining of the *Comedies* of Plautus, the *Amphitryon*. In modern times, it has been imitated by Dryden and by Molière, the latter of whom seems to have had this dialogue of Lucian in mind. For an

victorious divinity is to be born from this intercourse. That he should be turned out complete and perfect in one night is simply impossible.

Helios. Well, may he turn him out to perfection, and good luck to him! This sort of thing, however, was not the fashion in the time of Cronos—for we are all alone by ourselves—nor did *he* ever sleep apart from Rhea, nor would *he* leave heaven and go to bed in Thebes: but day was day, and night, according to its proper measure, was proportionate in the number of its hours. And there was nothing strange or confused and interchanged; and he would never have intrigued with a mortal woman. But now, for the sake of some wretched female, everything must be turned upside down, and my horses must become unmanageable from want of work; and the route, by remaining untrodden for three successive days, almost impassable; while as for men, they must pass their time miserably in darkness. Such are the benefits they will enjoy from the amours of Zeus; and they will have to sit down and wait, until he has accomplished this fine athlete, whom you speak of, under cover of prolonged darkness.

Hermes. Hold your tongue, Helios, for fear you may get some mischief from your words. Now I shall be off to Selene and Hypnus, and announce to them, too, the message of Zeus—that the former travel leisurely on her journey, and that Hypnus let not mortals go, so that they may not know that the night has been so long.

XI.

APHRODITE CHARGES SELENE WITH HER LOVE FOR ENDYMION, AND, AT THE SAME TIME, LAMENTS THE TYRANNY OF HER SON, EROS, OVER HERSELF.

Aphrodite and Selene.

Aphrodite. What is this, Selene, they say you do? That when you are over against Karia, you stop your chariot,

account of the wife of the Theban prince compare Hesiod, Ἀσπις Ἡρακ. i. 56; Ov. *Met.* ix. 3; Seneca, *Her. Furens;* Apollod. iv. 4, 8; Diodorus, iv. 1. She is one of the heroines called up by the necromantic skill of Odysseus (Οδ. xi.).

and fix all your gaze upon your Endymion, who sleeps under the open sky like the hunter he is; and that, at times, you even come down to him from the middle of your journey.[1]

Selene. Ask your son, my dear Aphrodite, who is the cause of this conduct of mine.

Aphrodite. Don't speak of him. He is an insolent rogue. Myself, in fact, his own mother, how has he treated me— one while bringing me down to Ida for the sake of Anchises, the Troian;[2] another time to the Libanus, to meet that Assyrian youth, whom he has made an object of desire even to Phersephatte,[3] and thus has deprived me, for half the time, of my beloved. So that I have often threatened,[4] unless he stop such goings on, to break his bow and quiver, and to clip his wings; and before now I have whipped him with my sandal. But somehow or other, though he is frightened for the moment, and begs pardon, he very soon afterwards forgets all his promises. But, tell me, is Endymion handsome; for, in that case, the evil admits of easy consolation.

Selene. To me he seems to be excessively handsome, my dear Aphrodite, and most especially when he throws his cloak down under him, upon the rock, and goes to sleep, grasping in his left hand his javelins which are just slipping from his fingers, while his right arm, bent double upwards

---

[1] Ovid, *De Arte Amandi*, iii. 83, defends the fair fame of the Goddess, or rather, maintains that she had no reason to be ashamed of her weakness :—

"Latmius Endymion non est tibi, Luna, rubori."

Pausanias informs us that, according to a common belief, she bore to her paramour fifty daughters (v. 1). In the Ἰστορία Ἀληθὴς ("True History") Endymion figures as the sovereign ruler of the Moon.

[2] For Hera's ironical allusion to this escapade on a memorable occasion, see Θ. Δ. xx.

[3] A form of the usual name of Persephone. Cf. Soph. *Antigone*, 894. The Assyrian, or rather Syrian, youth is Adonis. Before his death from the wild boar's avenging tusk, the Goddess of Love had eight months' enjoyment of her human favourite each year; after his death, he was granted to her tears by the soverçigns of the lower world for only half the year. See Ov. *Metam.* x. 9, 10; Theok. Ἀδωνιάζουσαι; and the charming *Idyll* of Bion.

[4] See following *Dialogue*, and the Εἰδύλλιον of Moschus on the Fugitive Eros, and the Anakreontic Odes.

round his head, sets off his face in a circular frame ; while, his limbs relaxed in sleep, he breathes forth that ambrosial and divine breath of his. Then, I confess it, descending noiselessly and advancing on tiptoe, that he may not awake and be alarmed——You know *the rest.* Why should I tell you the sequel? However, I am dying for love of him.

XII.

APHRODITE UPBRAIDS EROS FOR HIS MISCHIEVOUS CONDUCT IN THE PAST, AND CAUTIONS HIM FOR THE FUTURE. EROS DEFENDS HIMSELF.

Aphrodite and Eros.

Aphrodite. Eros, my child, just consider your conduct. I don't mean on Earth, what deeds you induce men to do against themselves or one against the other, but even in Heaven—you who show up mighty Zeus himself in a variety of shapes, converting him into whatever you please, at the moment, and drag Selene down from heaven, and force Helios, forgetting all about his charioteering, sometimes to loiter on his way with his Klymene : while in regard to your wanton conduct to me, you act with entire freedom. Nay, most audacious boy, you have induced even Rhea herself, who long ago was an old woman, and the mother of such a number of Gods, to fall in love with boys,[1] and to indulge a passion for the Phrygian youth. And now she has lost her senses by your work, and harnessed lions and taken to her the Korybantes, who are like mad people themselves ; and they tramp up and down about Ida, she making dismal lamentations for Attes. While as for the Korybantes, one gashes his arm [2] with a knife, another letting down his hair rushes like a madman

---

[1] Παιδεραστεῖν. The Phrygian youth is Attis, Attes, or Atys. The Korybantes were the priests of Rhea or Kybele, in Phrygia, who worshipped with rites of the grossest and most frantic kind. See Catullus, *De Atyde,* for a description of one of her emasculated votaries, and Ov. *Fasti,* iv. 181-246.

[2] Πῆχυν. Lit. "fore-arm." Some of the translators, following Erasmus, have interpreted it as *penem,* by "a ridiculous error." See Hemst. Cf. Seneca, *De Vitâ Beatâ,* xxvii.

through the mountains, one blows on the horn, another beats an accompaniment on the drum, or raises a horrible din on the cymbal, and, in fine, all Ida is in tumult and phrenzy. I fear, therefore, everything: I, who brought you into the world to be such a plague, am dreadfully afraid that Rhea, in one of her mad fits, or, indeed, rather, still in her senses, may order her Korybantes to seize you and tear you in pieces, or cast you to her lions. Such is my dread, when I see you running such risks.

Eros. Never fear, mother, for I have been a long time on the best of terms, even with the lions themselves; and frequently I mount on their backs and laying hold of their manes, I drive them as if they had reins, and they fawn on me, and taking my hand in their mouths, after licking it all over, give it back to me. Why, as for Rhea herself, when could *she* have leisure *to do any harm* to me, wholly taken up as she is with Attes? And, besides, what wrong do I do in pointing out beautiful objects such as they are? And as for you others, do you not yourselves long after beautiful things? Then don't accuse me of these offences. And do you yourself, mother, really wish no longer to love Ares, or him you?

Aphrodite. What a dreadful boy you are, and how you tyrannize over all! Well, you will recall my words some time or other.

XIII.

ASKLEPIUS AND HERAKLES QUARREL ON A QUESTION OF PRECEDENCE IN HEAVEN.

Zeus, Asklepius, and Herakles.

Zeus. Do, Asklepius and Herakles, stop your wrangling, just for all the world as if you were a couple of mortals; for this *sort of behaviour* is unseemly, and quite strange to the banquets of the Gods.

Herakles. But, Zeus, would you have that quack drug-dealer there [1] take his place at table above me? [2]

---

[1] Τουτονί. Lengthened *epideictic* Attic form of Τοῦτον: the final vowel having the force of the French *ci*, as in *celui-ci*. Heraklês points his finger contemptuously at the rival pretender.

[2] Προκατακλίνεσθαι. According to Greek custom, literally, to

Asklepius. By Zeus, yes, for I am certainly the better man.

Herakles. How, you thunderstruck fellow,[1] is it pray, because Zeus knocked you on the head with his bolt for your unlawful actions, and because now, out of mere pity, by way of compensation, you have got a share of immortality?

Asklepius. What! Have you, for your part, Herakles, altogether forgotten your having been burned to ashes on Mt. Œta,[2] that you throw in my teeth this fire *you talk of?*

Herakles. We have not lived at all an equal or similar sort of life—I who am the son of Zeus, and have undergone so many and great labours, purifying human life, contending against and conquering wild beasts, and punishing insolent and injurious men; whereas you are a paltry herb-doctor and mountebank,[3] skilful, possibly, in palming off your miserable drugs upon sick fools, but who have never given proof of any noble, manly disposition.

Asklepius. You say well, seeing I healed your burns when you came up but now half-burned, with your body all marred and destroyed by the double cause *of your death*— the poisoned shirt and, afterwards, the fire. Now I, if *I have done* nothing else, at least, have neither worked like a slave, as you have, nor have I carded wool in Lydia,[4] dressed in a fine purple gown; nor have I been beaten by that Omphale *of yours*, with her golden slipper—no, nor did I, in a mad fit, kill my children and my wife.[5]

"recline higher up" on the κλίνη, dining-couch. For a lively quarrel of this kind, see Lucian, Συμπόσιον ἤ Λάπιθαι, ix.

[1] Ἐμβρόντητε. A favourite and forcible expression of Lucian's (see *e.g. Timon*) implying mental as well as physical injury. The insulting epithet was literally applicable to Asklepius, who, just before his promotion to the skies, had been killed by a thunderbolt from the hand of Zeus, for cheating Pluto of his due number of subjects by means of his very singular medical skill.

[2] See Ov. *Met.* ix. 2 ; Seneca, *Her. Œtæus.*

[3] Ἐπιθήσειν τῶν φαρμάκων. Partitive Genitive, used contemptuously. Ἐπίθεσιν has been proposed as a more usual construction. *Herb-doctor*, in the Greek ῥιζοτόμος, lit. "a root-cutter." *Mountebank*, ἀγύρτης, lit. "one who *collects* crowds" (ἀγείρειν) to sell his quack-medicines. Sophokles wrote a drama with the title of Ῥιζοτόμος, as a satire on the medical world of his day.

[4] See the *Epistola Deïaniræ* of Ovid.

[5] Incited to madness by the jealous Hera, the son of Alkmena had killed his wife Megara, daughter of Kreon, king of Thebes, with her

Herakles. If you don't stop at once your ribald abuse of me, you shall very speedily learn your immortality will not much avail you : for I will take and pitch you head first out of Heaven, so that not even the wonderful Pæon[1] himself shall cure you and your broken skull.

Zeus. Have done, I say, and don't disturb the harmony of the company, or I will pack both of you off from the supper-room ; although, *to speak the truth*, Herakles, it is fair and reasonable Asklepius should have precedence of you at table, inasmuch as he even took precedence of you in death.

XIV.

APOLLO RECOUNTS TO HERMES THE MANNER OF THE DEATH OF HYAKINTHUS, AND HIS GRIEF FOR THE SAME.

Hermes and Apollo.

Hermes. Why so gloomy and dejected, my dear Apollo ?

Apollo. Because, Hermes, I am unhappy in my love affairs.

Hermes. Such misfortune is, indeed, worthy occasion for grief : but in what affair is it you are unfortunate ? Does that business of Daphne[2] still affect you ?

Apollo. Not at all. No, I mourn for my favourite, the Laconian, the son of Œbalus.[3]

Hermes. What ! tell me, is Hyakinthus dead ?

Apollo. Too surely.

Hermes. By whose hands, my dear Apollo ? Could there be any one so unloving as to kill that handsome youth ?

children (whom he threw into the fire), and also two of his nephews. See Seneca, *Her. Furens*, Apollod. ii. 4, 12.

[1] Pæon, or Pæan, physician in ordinary to the Court of Olympus, in later Greek theology was identified with Apollo, the divine Healer. See IΛ. v. 395-402 for his successful treatment of the wounds of Aïdes inflicted by Herakles.

[2] Ov. *Metam.* i. 12. Diodorus (Βιβ. Ἱστ.), Pausanias, and the rest of the authorities vary, as usual, in the relation of the story of the Nymph of the laurel-tree. Pausanias relates that Daphne, in place of being the victim, with her attendant nymphs shot with arrows her too daring lover, who had disguised himself in female dress, and followed her to the bath.

[3] Hyakinthus. Ov. *Metam.* x. 5, Philost. Εἰκονες. Upon the tomb of Hyakinthus, Pausanias informs us, was sculptured the figure of his involuntary slayer.

Apollo. It was my own doing.

Hermes. Were you, then, out of your senses, Apollo ?

Apollo. No, but it was a species of ill-luck—an involuntary deed.

Hermes. How ? For I am anxious to hear the manner of it.

Apollo. He was learning to play with the quoit, and I was playing with him. Well, that most cursed of winds, Zephyrus, himself was in love with him, from a long time past; and being neglected, and not able to endure his superciliousness (while I threw my quoit up into the air, as we are accustomed to do), blowing down from Taÿgetus, bore the disc along and caused it to fall on the head of the youth, so that blood flowed from the wound in large quantity, and the boy died immediately. However, I at once avenged myself on Zephyrus by shooting at him with my arrows, pursuing him in his flight as far as the mountain. And to the boy I had a tomb raised at Amyklæ, where the quoit struck him down; and from his blood I caused the ground to send up a flower, the sweetest, Hermes, and the gayest-coloured of all flowers, having, moreover, letters mourning [1] for the dead imprinted on it. Do I appear to you to have been grieved unreasonably ?

Hermes. Yes, my dear Apollo : for you knew that you had made a mere mortal the object of your particular affection. So, pray, don't vex yourself about his death.

---

[1] 'Επαιάζοντα. Lit. "crying *ai, ai.*" Cf. Bion, Είδ. i. (the *Dirge of Adonis*), Αἰάζω τὸν Ἄδωνιν—κ.τ.λ., Moschus (*Dirge on Bion*, 40), Ov. *Metam.* x. 215. What is this famous flower, which thus immortalizes the fate of Hyakinthus, is matter of dispute with the commentators. See Lehmann's Hemsterhuis, and compare Palæphatus.

XV.

HERMES AND APOLLO ENVY THE DEFORMED HEPHÆSTUS THE POSSESSION OF HIS BEAUTIFUL WIVES.

Hermes and Apollo.

Hermes. But the fact, Apollo, that, though he is both lame, and a mere brazier by trade, he has married the most beautiful wives of us all, Aphrodite and Charis![1]

Apollo. A mere piece of good luck, my dear Hermes. But this I do wonder at—that they tolerate having anything to do with him; most especially when they see him running down with perspiration, as he stoops laboriously over his furnace, and with a quantity of soot upon his face. And yet, though he is such a figure, they embrace him, and kiss him, and sleep with him!

Hermes. This, too, I feel indignant about, and envy Hephæstus—whereas you wear long, flowing, hair, and play on the cithara, and pride yourself greatly on your good looks, and I upon my vigour and good habit of body and my lyre, straightway, when we have to go to bed, we shall sleep all alone.

Apollo. Besides, too, as far as I am concerned, I have no fortune in my *affaires de cœur*,[2] and two, at all events, whom I especially loved, Daphne and Hyakinthus—well, Daphne hated me to such a degree that she chose to become a tree rather than have my embraces; while Hyakinthus I killed with that quoit, and now, in place of them, I have *to be content with* garlands.[3]

Hermes. And as for me, Aphrodite I some time since— but one must not brag.

Apollo. I know, and she is said to have presented you with Hermaphroditus. But tell me this, if you know at

---

[1] See 'Ιλ. xviii. 382. She was one of the Charites or "Graces."

[2] Ἀναφροδιτός ἐς τὰ ἐρωτικά. Lit. "unfavoured by Aphrodite in my love affairs." Lat. *invenustus.* Cf. *Andria,* i. 5 (the lament of Pamphilus) :—" Adeon' hominem'sse invenustum aut infelicem quemquam, ut ego sum ! "

[3] The garlands heaped upon his altars by his votaries.

all, how is it Aphrodite is not jealous of Charis or Charis jealous of her?

Hermes. Because, my dear Apollo, the former lives with him in Lemnos,[1] and Aphrodite in Heaven. And besides, the latter is, for the most part, taken up with Arês, and is in love with him, so that she cares little for this brazier fellow.

Apollo. And do you suppose that Hephæstus knows this?

Hermes. He knows well enough : but what could he do, when he sees a fine youth, and that, too, a soldier ? So he keeps quiet. However, he threatens, at all events, that he will devise some kind of fetters for them, and catch them together by throwing a net over their bed.

Apollo. I don't know, but I would devoutly pray that I myself might be the one to be caught in her company.

XVI.

HERA AND LETO DISPUTE ABOUT THE MERITS OF THEIR
RESPECTIVE CHILDREN.

Hera and Leto.

Hera. Fine creatures, indeed, are the children you have presented to Zeus, Leto![2]

Leto. It's not all of us, Hera, who can produce such progeny as your Hephæstus.

Hera. But this same cripple is, at all events, of some use. He is an excellent workman, and has decorated Heaven for us in a thoroughly artistic fashion,[3] and he married Aphrodite, and is made much of by her;[4] while

---

[1] This island of the N. Ægean sea, was the favourite terrestrial abode of Hephæstus, and some authorities place his forge there.

[2] The abrupt beginning of the *Dialogue* implies antecedent conversation. The jealous Hera may be supposed to have begun with some such ironical observation as " you may well be proud of your good looks," or " you may well be proud of your position among us." The relative is sometimes omitted in familiar conversation in Greek as in conversational English.

[3] See Περὶ Θυσίων (" On Sacrifices "), one of Lucian's finest pieces of satire ; and Ιλ. xviii.

[4] Σπουδάζεται πρὸς αὐτῆς. Scarcely borne out by the facts. Cf. Θ. Δ. xvii.

as for *your* children, one of them is beyond all measure,
masculine, and mountainish, and to crown all, has made off
to Scythia, and everyone knows what her diet is there,
slaying strangers, and imitating the Scythians themselves,
who are cannibals.[1] As for Apollo, he makes pretence to
universal knowledge—to shoot with the bow, to play the
cithara, to be a doctor, and to prophesy—and having set up
his oracle-shops, one at Delphi, another at Klaros and at
Didyma, he juggles and cheats those who consult him,
giving crooked answers,[2] and double meanings, applicable
to either side of the question, so that he runs no risk of
failure, and from such trickery he makes his fortune : for
numerous are the fools, and those who offer themselves
willing victims to be cheated and imposed upon. But by
the wiser part of men it is not unknown that he is, for the
most part, a mere juggler in words. The prophet himself,
at all events, did not know he would kill his favourite
with the quoit, nor did he divine for his own advantage,
that Daphne would flee from him ; and that, too, although
he is so handsome and has such flowing locks. So I don't
see why you thought you had finer children than poor
Niobe.[3]

Leto. These same children, however—the murderer of
strangers and the lying prophet—I am well aware how it

---

[1] See Euripides, Ἰφιγενεία ἐν Ταύροις, Herodot. iv. 103, and Göthe's
Iphigenia. The Scythia of the text is the modern Crimea.

[2] Λοξά, whence his epithet Λόξιας—"the ambiguous speaker or
prophet." For some specimens of his prophetic art, see the Ζεὺς
Τραγῳδός, perhaps Lucian's masterpiece. Cf. Herodotus, *passim* ; Clemens Alex. Προτρεπτ. ; Fontenelle, *Hist. des Oracles.*

[3] See Ov. *Metam.* vi. 2, Pausanias i. 21, ii. 21, viii. 20. For an
eloquent description of the most beautiful conception in all remaining
Greek Sculpture, see Shelley's *Letters from Italy.* As for the miraculous metamorphosis of Niobe, Pausanias, who had seen the pillar of
stone, considers that there need be no difficulty in believing it, for it
happened in the old times of frequent miraculous interposition of
Heaven. He is not prepared, however, to maintain that such miracles
take place in his own day, for man's impiety precludes the possibility.
Accordingly, he does not credit the received story that the petrified
Niobe sheds tears, or the popular tales about *lycanthropy*, or that the
Tritons blow through their shells, as the vulgar believe (viii. 2). Cf.
viii. 8. With this expression of pious faith compare, also, the remarks
of Diodorus (B. I. iv. 1), who holds that miraculous stories must not
be inquired into too closely or critically.

vexes you to see them in the company of the gods; and especially whenever the one is commended for her beauty, and the other performs on his cithara, to the admiration of all in the banqueting-hall.

Hera. I could not help laughing, Leto—he an object of admiration, whom, if the Muses had chosen to give a just decision, Marsyas would have flayed, as himself the conqueror in the musical contest.[1]   But, as it was, the poor man was overreached, and perished by an unjust doom. And, as for your beautiful virgin, she is so beautiful, that, when she found she had been seen by Actæon, from fear the youth might proclaim her ugliness, she set on him his own dogs.[2]   *I don't say all I might*, for I omit to dwell on the fact, that, if she were really a virgin,[3] she could not even assist ladies in the straw.

Leto. You bear yourself superciliously, Hera, because you share the bed and throne of Zeus; and for that reason, you utter your insults without fear.   But, however, I shall soon see you in tears again, when he deserts you and goes down to earth again in the form of a bull or a swan.

---

[1] See Ov. *Metam.* vi. 4.   Herodotus, Strabo, Pausanias, and Aulus Gellius all relate the story with perfect faith.   Cf. Apollod. i. 4, and Hyginus.

[2] See Apollodorus, iii. 4, whose enumeration of the thirty-two hounds seems to have been used by Ovid, *Metam.* iii. 3.   According to the Greek mythologist, the dogs, who had torn their master to pieces (transformed, with some poetic justice, into a stag), on discovering their very excusable error, died of grief and remorse.   Cf. Kallimachus, Περὶ τῆς Παλ. βαλ. (" On Pallas's Bath "), and Apuleius (*Metam.*) on the sculpture of Diana and the Dogs.   Palæphatus remarks on the story of the dogs devouring their master, τοῦτο δ'ἐστι ψευδές—for, as he adds, on the contrary, a dog loves, and is faithful to, his master, however unworthy.

[3] Παρθένος γε αὐτὴ οὖσα.   The office of Eileithuia, or Eleithuia, in later times had been transferred, with some impropriety, to Artemis. Cf. Theok. Εἰδ. xxii. ('Οαριστύς) 28, 29.

XVII.

HERMES NARRATES TO APOLLO THE ADULTERY OF ARES AND APHRODITE, AND THE REVENGE OF HEPHÆSTUS.

Apollo and Hermes.

Apollo. Why do you laugh, Hermes ?

Hermes. Because, my dear Apollo, I have seen the most ridiculous sight possible.

Apollo. Then tell me, that I myself too, when I have heard, may be able to join in the laugh.

Hermes. Aphrodite has been caught with Ares, and Hephæstus has captured and bound them.

Apollo. How ? For I fancy you are going to tell me something pleasant !

Hermes. For a long time I imagine he had been aware of this *amour*, and was hunting them down ; and when he had enveloped their bed with invisible fetters,[1] he went back to his forge and worked away as usual. Then Ares enters unobserved, as he supposed ; but Helios looks down upon them and sees them, and tells Hephæstus. And when they had got upon the bed, and were in each other's arms, and were involved within the meshes, the fetters completely entangle them, and Hephæstus suddenly comes upon them. She, you may be sure, had no means—for in fact she was entirely naked—of veiling her shame ; while Ares at first kept making efforts to escape, and hoped to break the bonds ; but afterwards, perceiving himself to be inextricably caught,[2] he began to act the suppliant.

Apollo. What then ? Did Hephæstus release them ?

Hermes. Not at all. On the contrary, summoning all

---

[1] 'Ηῦτ' 'Αράχνια λέπτα—" As fine as a cobweb," according to the poet of the *Odyssey*. (Οδ. viii. 280.) The δεσμὰ of the text, apparently, was an extremely fine wire-net.

[2]

  " Τὼ δ'ἐς δεμνία βάντε κατέδραθον, ἀμφὶ δὲ δεσμοὶ
  Τεχνήεντες ἔχυντο πολύφρονος 'Ηφαίστοιο.
  Θὐδέ τι κινῆσαι μελέων ἦν, οὐδ' ἀναεῖραι·
  Καὶ τότε δὴ γιγνώσκον, ὃτ' οὐκ ἔτι φυκτὰ πελόνται."

Cf. Ov., *Metam.* iv. 2. *Ars Am.* ii. 573. *Amores,* i. 9.

the Gods,[1] he discovers to them their adultery; while the captives bound together naked, with eyes fixed on the ground, show their confusion by their blushes: and the spectacle appeared to me the pleasantest imaginable—all but as good as the *antecedent* event itself.[2]

Apollo. But that blacksmith—does he not himself, too, feel shame in exposing the disgrace of his marriage-bed ?

Hermes. No, by heaven ! not he, who, in fact, stands over them and laughs at them. For myself, however, if one must speak the truth, I did grudge Ares not only his intrigue with the fairest of the Goddesses, but even his being bound with her.

Apollo. Then would you really endure even to be fettered upon that condition ?

Hermes. And would *you* not, my dear Apollo ? Only come and have a look; for I will commend you, if you would not yourself, too, pray for the like good fortune, if you did but see.[3]

XVIII.

HERA DENOUNCES, AND ZEUS DEFENDS, THE CHARACTER OF BACCHUS.

Hera and Zeus.

Hera. I should be ashamed, Zeus, if I had such an

---

[1] The *Goddesses,* as the poet of the *Odyssey* carefully informs us, did not sanction the stratagem of Hephæstus, and absented themselves :—

    Θηλύτεραι δὲ Θεαὶ μένον αἰδοῖ οἴκοι ἑκάστη.—Ὀδ. viii. 324.

[2] Μονονουχὶ αὐτὸ γιγνόμενον τὸ ἔργον. "Ἔργον et ἐνεργεῖν, in re Venereâ, pervulgati sunt usus."—Hemst. One commentator (Jensius) interprets the words of Hermes, τὸ θέαμα ἥδιστον—ἔργον,' as implying : "Scilicet ferme ita hoc spectaculo delectatus fui, quàm si ipse iisdem fruerer gaudiis." Cf. Plato, Πόλ. III., who condemns this, with other Homeric theology, as immoral and improper.

[3] Lucian has not at all "improved upon" the free confessions of Hermes, as given by the poet of the *Odyssey* :—

    "Αἲ γὰρ τοῦτο γένοιτο, ἄναξ ἑκατηβόλ' Ἄπολλον,
    Δέσμοι μὲν τρὶς τόσσοι ἀπείρονες ἀμφὶς ἔχοιεν,
    Ὑμεῖς δ' εἰσορόωτε Θεοί, πᾶσαι τε Θέαιναι,
    Αὐτὰρ ἐγων εὕδοιμι παρὰ χρυσῆ Ἀφροδίτῃ."

Hermes and Apollo are, appropriately, the interlocutors in this dialogue, since they are specially named in the Homeric epos.

effeminate son, and so debauched a drunkard, with his hair bound with the women's head band, associating chiefly with frantic women, more effeminate than themselves, dancing to the noise of drums, and pipe, and cymbals, and, in short, like anything rather than his father.

Zeus. Yet this effeminate mitre-wearer,[1] who goes more delicately than women, Hera, not only conquered Lydia, and took captive the inhabitants of Tmolus, and brought the Thracians under his yoke, but also made an expedition against the Indians with that army of women, took possession of the elephants, and made himself master of the country, and led away captive the king who dared to offer him a brief resistance; and all this he did while leaping about, and dancing with his chorus,[2] bearing the ivy-wreathed thyrsus, drunk, as you say, and in bacchanalian frenzy. But if anyone attempts to insult him by showing contempt for the initiation into his mystic rites,[3] he certainly avenges himself on him either by binding him with vine-twigs, or by causing him to be torn in pieces by his mother like a fawn.[4] Do you observe how manly these actions are, and not unworthy of his father? And if playful sportiveness and wantonness are combined with them, there is no cause for grudging them to him; and, especially, if one considers what he would be sober, when he performs such actions drunk.

Hera. You appear to me to be going to commend also his discovery—the vine and wine—and that, though you see how drunkards behave, staggering along, and betaking themselves to insolence and violence, and, in a word, mad-

---

[1] See Θ. Δ. ii.; Cf. Euripides, Βάκχαι; Ovid, *Metam.* iii. 8. xi. 1-2; Apollod. iii. 5; Hor. *Car.* ii. 19; Virg. *Æn.* vii. 373.

[2] Ὀρχούμενος ἅμα καὶ χορεύων. Χορεύων differs from the preceding verb in implying the circular dance, and has particular reference to the dithyrambic and dramatic *chorus* round the altar of Dionysus. The *thyrsus* was one of the well-known *insignia* of the God of Wine. It was a pole, or wand, enwreathed with vine and ivy leaves, and crowned with a pine cone.

[3] Τὴν τελετήν. Lit., "the perfecting" or "perfection" (τέλος), used of the sacred mysteries. Cf. Herod. ii. 171. iv. 79; Plato, Φαῖδρος, 240.

[4] As was Pentheus, king of Thebes, for opposing the introduction of the Bacchic worship and ritual into his city. See Βάκχαι; Pausanias, ii. 2; Ov. *Met.* iii., 514.

dened under the influence of the drink. As for Ikarius, at all events, to whom he first gave the vine-shoot, his boon companions themselves destroyed him by striking him with their spades.[1]

Zeus. That is nothing to the purpose; for it's not the wine nor Dionysus that does this, but immoderateness in drinking, and filling oneself with unmixed wine beyond what is becoming.[2] But a man, who should drink within the bounds of moderation, will be of a more jovial and genial disposition. And as to the fate of Ikarius, he [Dionysus] could not have designed any harm to any of his boon companions. But you seem to me to be still jealous, Hera, and to remember Semele, since you calumniate the finest and fairest gifts of Dionysus.[3]

XIX.

EROS EXPLAINS TO HIS MOTHER WHY HE DOES NOT ASSAIL ATHENA, THE MUSÆ, AND ARTEMIS.

Aphrodite and Eros.

Aphrodite. Pray, why in the world, my dear Eros, have you completely subdued to yourself all the rest of the Gods—Zeus, Poseidon, Apollo, Rhea, me, your mother— and kept your hands off Athena alone ; and why, as far as she is concerned, is your torch without a spark, your quiver empty of arrows, and yourself without a bow and without practice ?

Eros. I am afraid of her, mother, for she is terrible, and

---

[1] See Apollod. iii. 14, for the fate of Ikarius, who—by a cause opposite to that of the death of Pentheus—fell a victim to Bacchic fury, and for the adventures of his daughter Erigone and her faithful dog Mæra, who, after death, were translated to the heavens.

[2] The Greeks usually drank their wine diluted with water, and it was a mark of intemperance and barbarism to drink it unmixed. The Spartans, according to Herodotus, believed that their king Kleomenes had become mad in this way (vi. 84); Cf. Plato, Νόμ., i. ; Athenæus, Δειπ. vi. ; Ælian, Ἱστ. Ποικ, ii. 37.

[3] Cf. Plutarch, Περί τῆς Σαρκοφαγίας, i. 2. τί καταψεύδεσθε τῆς γῆς ; κ.τ.λ. Even " half and half " was held to be intoxicating, nor was wine ever drunk during eating.

her eyes burn with a fierce brightness,[1] and she is dreadfully masculine. At all events, whenever I advance towards her with bent bow, she shakes her crest at me, and frightens me out of my wits, and I am all of a tremble, and my arrows slip from my hands.

Aphrodite. Why, was not Ares more alarming? and yet you disarmed him in a moment, and have conquered him.

Eros. Yes, but he readily allows me to approach him, and invites me of his own accord, while Athena is always watching me suspiciously and secretly : and once I flew by her, casually, with my torch, and said she, " If you come near me, by my father, I will run you through in a moment with my pretty spear, or I will seize you by the foot and pitch you into Tartarus, or tear you in pieces with my own hand, and be the death of you." Many such threats has she uttered, and she puts on sour looks, and has on her breast a frightful sort of face, with snakes all over for hair, which is my especial horror, for it frightens me like a very Mormo,[2] and I flee whenever I catch a glimpse of it.

Aphrodite. But you fear Athena, as you say, and the Gorgon, and that, though you are not afraid of the thunderbolt of Zeus ! And the Muses—why are they unwounded and out of reach of your darts ? Do they, too, shake crests, and exhibit Gorgons in front of them ?

Eros. I have an awe of them, mother, for they are grave and respectable, and are always in some profound medita-

---

[1] Χαροπή. Lit., " joyous-eyed " (χάρα—ὤψ). Applied to the Goddess of (scientific) War, it denoted an extraordinary combination of brilliancy and fierceness. Cf. Homeric *Hymn to Hermes* (Shelley's version), Hesiod, Θεογ. 321 ; Lucian, Θ. Δ. vii. ; Νεκρ. Διαλ. i. 3.

[2] Μορμολύττεται (Μορμώ). Mormo, Empusa, the Lamia, and other monsters and goblins of the Greek nursery, apparently, were almost as much used to keep children in order as similar objects of popular superstition are (or lately were), employed in the English nursery. Cf. Aristoph. Εἰρήνη, 466. Ἀχαρν. 557. Βατρ. 285-296 ; Theok. Εἰδ. xv. 40, where Praxinoa tells her baby that Mormo " bites." " We relate to children," says Strabo, " pleasing tales to incite them to [any course of] action, and frightful ones to deter them, such as those of Lamia, Gorgo, Ephialtes, and Mormolyca [Mormo-wolf]," i. 2 (Bohn's Transl.). Lamia was a sort of witch, said to suck children's blood (Hor. *Ars Poet.* 340), Ephialtes an " incubus " or " nightmare."

For a forcible representation of the Medusa-head, see the picture of Lionardo da Vinci.

tion or other, and are occupied in song, and I often stand
by them, beguiled by their melody.

Aphrodite. Well, leave them out of the question, too, as
they are grave and respectable. But Artemis—why don't
you inflict a wound on her ?

Eros. In a word, it is impossible even to come up with her,
as she is always fleeing through the mountains.[1] Then,
too, she has already her own peculiar kind of love.

Aphrodite. For what, child ?

Eros. The hunting of stags and fawns, pursuing them
for the purpose of capturing them or shooting them down,
and she is entirely devoted to that sort of thing. When,
however, her brother, although an archer himself and a
far-shooter [2]——— .

Aphrodite. I know, child, you have shot your arrow at
him often enough.

XX.

THE JUDGMENT OF PARIS.

Zeus, Hermes, Hera, Athena, Aphrodite, Paris or Alexander.

Zeus. Take this apple here, Hermes, and hie to Phrygia,
to the presence of the son of Priam, the cowherd—he is
tending his cows on the Gargarus[3]-summit of Ida—and
say to him : " Paris, Zeus bids you, since you are yourself
a good-looking youth, and clever in love-matters, to decide
for the Goddesses *here* which is the most beautiful. And
let the winner receive the apple as the prize of the contest."
And now, *Goddesses*, it is quite time for yourselves to set off
to the presence of your judge. For, for my part, I decline,
for myself, the office of arbitrator, loving you, as I do, with
equal affection ; and, if it were only possible, I would with
pleasure see you all three winners. Especially *do I decline,*

---

[1]   " Qualis in Eurotæ ripis, aut per juga Cynthi,
        Exercet Diana choros. . . ."—*Æn.* i. 498-9.

[2] 'Εκηβόλον. See 'Ιλ. *passim.* Aphrodite supplies the verb for Eros.

[3] Gargarus, one of the three mountains of which Ida consists. In
Strabo's time they still shewed the scene of the famous Judgment upon
the mountain, which at that time was called Alexandria.—Wieland.
The Idæan range formed the southern boundary of the Troad. Gargara
or Gargarus has a height of some 5,000 ft.

as in giving the prize of beauty to one, I must certainly incur the hatred of the rest. For this reason I am myself no suitable umpire for you—but this Phrygian youth, to whom you are going, is of princely birth, and is a relative of Ganymedes here.[1] In other respects, he is simple and mountain-bred. No one would think him unworthy of such a spectacle.

Aphrodite. As far as I am concerned, Zeus, even though you should appoint Momus[2] himself our judge, I will cheerfully go to the exhibition; for, indeed, what could he have to find fault with in *me?* The man, however, will have to satisfy these goddesses, too.

Hera. Oh! it's not we, Aphrodite, who have to fear—no, not though your own Ares should be entrusted with the arbitration. May we, also, accept this Paris, whoever he may be.

Zeus. And does this content you, daughter, too? What say you? You turn away and blush? It is the privilege of you virgins, indeed, to be shy about such matters; but you nod assent, however. Away with you all, then, and see that you are not hard upon your judge—you who have been vanquished, and don't have any mischief inflicted on the youth. For it's not possible for you to be all equally beauties.

Hermes. Let us start off straight for Phrygia, I leading the way, and do you follow me without loitering, and keep up your spirits. I am personally acquainted with Paris; he is a good-looking youth, and amorous into the bargain, and very competent to judge in all such matters. He would not give a bad judgment.

Aphrodite. That is all fair, and you speak quite after my mind—that he is the right judge for us. [Confidentially] But is he a bachelor, or has he some wife or other living with him?

Hermes. Not absolutely a bachelor, Aphrodite.

Aphrodite. How do you mean? •

---

[1] See Θ. Δ. iv. v.

[2] Momus, who acted as Censor and Critic in ordinary at the Olympian Court, according to Hesiod, derived his obscure parentage from the Goddess Νύξ. He does not appear in the Homeric epics. See Lucian's Ζεός Τραγῳδός ("Zeus the Tragedian"), where Momus takes a prominent part, and uses his privilege very much *à propos.*

Hermes. Some lady of Ida[1] appears to be keeping company with him—well enough in her way, but countrified and dreadfully boorish. However, he does not seem to be excessively attached to her. But, pray, why do you put these questions ?

Aphrodite. I asked quite indifferently.

Athena. Holloa ! you Sir, there, you are exceeding your commission in communicating with her in private.

Hermes. It was nothing extraordinary, Athena, and nothing against you. She only asked me if Paris is a bachelor.

Athena. And pray, why is she so inquisitive about that ?

Hermes. I don't know. But she says it occurred to her quite casually, and she had no purpose in asking.

Athena. Well, *is* he unmarried ?

Hermes. I think not.

Athena. What then ? Has he a desire for the military life, and is he at all ambitious for glory, or is he altogether devoted to his herds ?

Hermes. The exact truth I am unable to say : but one must suppose that a young fellow like him would be eager to acquire fame in these things, and would like to be first in fighting.

Aphrodite (pouting). Do you see ? *I* don't find fault, nor charge you with talking to her on the sly—for such sort of *querulousness* is peculiar to people not over much pleased with themselves : it's not Aphrodite's way.

Hermes. Indeed she asked me almost exactly the same question *as she did you:* so don't be in a pet, and don't imagine you are worse treated, if I answered her somewhat frankly and simply. But while we are talking, we have already advanced far on our road, and taken leave of the stars,[2] and, in fact, are almost opposite Phrygia. And now, in fact, I see Ida and the whole of Gargarus distinctly, and, if I am not deceived, Paris himself, your umpire.

Hera. But where is he ? For he is not visible to my eyes.

Hermes. Look carefully there to the left, Hera—not near

---

[1] Œnone, the Naiad or river-nymph. See Ovid, *Œnone Paridi*, and Tennyson's poem.

[2] Ἀπεσπάσαμεν τῶν ἀστέρων.   Cf. Ἰκάρο-Μενίππος. xi.

the top of the mountain, but along the flank, where the cave is; there, where you see the herd.

Hera. But I *don't* see the herd.

Hermes. How? Do you not see tiny cows in the direction of my finger, so,—advancing from the midst of the rocks, and some one running down from the cliff with a shepherd's crook, and stopping them from scattering a-head?

Hera. Now I see, if it really is he.

Hermes. But it is. And since we are now so near, let us, if you please, settle down on *terra firma*, and walk, that we may not quite disconcert him by flying down all on a sudden from the clouds.

Hera. You are right; so let us do—and now we have made our own descent, it is high time for you, Aphrodite, to advance and show us the way. For you, as is reasonable to expect, are well acquainted with the locality, having frequently, as report goes, come down here to Anchises.[1]

Aphrodite. These sneers of yours, Hera, don't disturb me over much.

Hermes. Well, I will act as your guide and chaperon; for I myself, in fact, passed some time on Ida when Zeus, to be sure, was in love with the Phrygian boy;[2] and often have I come here, when sent down to look after the child. And when, at length, he was mounted on the eagle,[3] I flew by his side with him, and helped to support my handsome *charge:* and, if I recollect aright, from this rock here he snatched him up—for the boy happened to be piping to his flock at the moment—and flying down himself, from behind,[4] Zeus very lightly embraced him in his talons, and, grasping his turban with his beak, bore the lad aloft in a terrible state of alarm, as he was gazing on *his ravisher* with neck bent backwards. Then, picking up his shepherd's pipe, for he had let it fall in his fright, I—but *excuse*

---

[1] The father of Æneas. For divulging his intimacy with the Goddess he was either struck dead, or severely injured by lightning.

[2] Ganymedes. See Θ. Δ. iv.

[3] Le Clerc, followed by Jacobitz, interprets Ἐν τῷ ἀετῷ of Zeus, " in the form of an eagle."

[4] Or (perhaps the preferable reading) ὄπισθεν αὐτοῦ, "behind him."

me, for here is our umpire close at hand : so let us accost him.—Good day to you, herdsman.

Paris. The same to you, young man. But who are you, and what is the purpose of your visit to us ? What ladies are these you are conducting ? For such *town* belles as they are, they are not fitted for roving over rough mountains.

Hermes. But they are not women, Paris ; but it is Hera, and Athena, and Aphrodite you see ; and I, I am the God Hermes Zeus has sent *with them.* But why do you tremble and turn so pale ? Don't be frightened, for there is nothing to be afraid of. He only bids you to be the judge of their beauty : "for since," says he, "you are a handsome youth yourself, and clever in love-matters, I entrust the judgment to you ; and when you have read the *inscription on* the apple, you will know the prize of the contest."

Paris. Come, let me see what it all means—"LET THE BEAUTIFUL ONE TAKE ME," it says. How, pray, Sir Hermes, could I, a mere mortal myself, and a simple peasant, too, be a judge of so preternaturally wonderful a spectacle, and one too great for a poor herdsman to decide upon ? To judge in matters of such importance is rather for delicately-nurtured persons and courtiers : but, for my part, whether one she-goat be more beautiful than another she-goat, or one heifer surpasses another heifer in beauty I could per-haps decide *secundum artem.* But these ladies are all equally beautiful, and I don't know how a man could wrench away his gaze and transfer it from the one to the other ; for it will not easily unfix itself, but where it first rests, to that part it clings, and commends what's imme-diately before it. And even though it pass on to another part, that too it sees to be beautiful, and lingers, and is caught by the adjoining charms ; and, in short, their beauty has circumfused itself about me, and wholly taken possession of me, and I am vexed that I, too, cannot, like Argus, see with all my body. I think I should judge fairly, if I give the apple to all : for, indeed, there is this

---

[1] As in other of his similar descriptions, Lucian probably had in mind some well-known picture, or sculpture, of the scene.

difficulty besides; it happens that this lady is the sister and wife of Zeus,[1] and that these are his daughters. How, I should like to know, is not the decision a hard one from this point of view, too?

Hermes. I don't know about that: but it's not possible to shirk the commands of Zeus, *I know.*

Paris. This one thing, Hermes, persuade them to—that the two defeated ladies be not angry with *me*, but consider the error to attach to my eyes alone.

Hermes. (*confers with the Goddesses, apart.*) They promise to comply with your request. And now it is high time for you to proceed with your judgment.

Paris. I will do my best endeavours, for how can one help it? But this first I wish to know—will it be quite enough to view them as they are, or will it be necessary to make them undress for an accurate examination?

Hermes. That must be your part as judge to decide. Give your orders how and in what way you like.

Paris. How I like, really? I wish to see them undressed.[2]

Hermes. Ho, you ladies there, off with your clothes.[3] (*To Paris.*) For your part make a thorough survey—as for me, I avert my face at once.

Hera. Very well *said*, Paris, and I will be the first to undress, that you may perceive that I have not only " white arms," and that I am not proud of having " cow's-eyes "[4] only, but that I am equally and proportionally beautiful all over.

Paris. Off with your clothes, too, Aphrodite.

[1]
      " Ast ego, quæ divom incedo regina, Iovisque
      Et soror, et conjunx."—*Æn.* i. 46, 47.

[2] Γύμνας, which has not, necessarily, the meaning of our word *naked;* but, like the Latin *nudus,* may mean only " stripped to the shirt." Here it must be taken in the former sense.

[3] 'Απόδυτε, ὦ αὖται. " Zieht euch aus, ihr da," remarks Wieland, "addressed to these Goddesses, sounds startling to modern ears; we have, in Lucian, very often occasion to see, that between Greek urbanity and our politeness of to-day, there prevails no little difference."

[4] The well-known epithets applied, in the *Iliad,* to the Queen of Heaven—λευκώλενος and βόωπις; the latter beautiful simile, and distinguished compliment, English translators usually, with some inadequacy, have given as " ox-eyed."

Athena. Don't let her undress,[1] Paris, before she lays aside her cestus[2]—for she is an enchantress—for fear she may bewitch you by its means. Indeed, she ought not either to have appeared here so meretriciously tricked out, nor painted up with so many dyes[3] and cosmetics for all the world as if she were in fact some lady of the demi-monde,[4] but have exhibited her beauty unadorned.

Paris. (*turning to Aphrodite.*) They are quite right as to that cestus of yours : so you must e'en doff it.

Aphrodite. Why, then, do you not also, Athena, doff that helmet of yours, and display your bare head, instead of shaking that plumed crest and terrifying your judge ? Are you afraid that fiercely-glaring look about your eyes,[5] seen without that frightful object, may be set down to your discredit ?

Athena. There, I have taken off this *objectionable* helmet, for your satisfaction.

Aphrodite. There, too, is the cestus, for yours.

---

[1] 'Αποδύσῃς. "Must not Lucian," asks Wieland, "have written ἀπολύσῃς ? Denn Paris zog sie doch wohl nicht eigenhändig aus." But we are not obliged by the received text to suppose that Paris was to undress the Goddess with his own hands.

[2] See 'Ιλ. xiv. for a description of this supreme *charm* of the Goddess of Beauty :—

$$\text{"} \kappa\acute{\epsilon}\sigma\tau\text{o}\nu \; \grave{\iota}\mu\acute{a}\nu\tau a$$

Ποικίλον · ἔνθα δὲ οἱ θελκτήρια πάντα τέτυκτο.
Ἔνθ' ἔνι μὲν φιλότης, ἐν δ' ἵμερος, ἐν δ' ὀαριστὺς,
Πάρφασις, ἥ τ' ἔκλεψε νόον πύκα περ φρονεόντων,"

as borrowed, on a memorable occasion, by Hera, who seems to have forgotten her obligations. Cf. *Gerusalemme Lib.*, xvi. 24, and *Faerie Queen* iv. 5.

[3] Τοσαῦτα ἐντετριμμένην χρώματα. Cf. Aristophanes, 'Εκκλης., 732 ; Λυσιστράτα, 149 ; Lucian, Δὶς Κατηγ, 31.

[4] 'Εταίραν. Here distinguished from πόρνη, "an unfortunate." The former (in the better meaning of the word) belonged, like the celebrated Aspasia, to a class of women who were sometimes in high esteem in Athens. But the distinction did not universally hold. See Becker's *Charicles.* 'Εταίρα, etymologically, means simply "a lady-friend."

[5] Τὸ γλαυκὸν. Alluding to the well-known Homeric epithet γλαυκῶπις. The shade of colour implied seems to be grayish, or light-blue. The original meaning of the word was "bright-glancing" or "glaring." Latin, *cæsius.* Cf. "Cæsia virgo" Ter. *Heauton.* v. 5 ; Cicero, *De Nat. Deor.* i. 30. In the chryselephantine and other statues of the Goddess, Pheidias and other Greek artists, doubtless, gave a wonderfully life-like vivacity to the eyes by means of precious stones and enamels.

Hera. Well, let us undress.

Paris (expressing, in his features, the utmost admiration). O Zeus, worker of miracles! the glorious vision! the beauty! the delight! How superb is the Virgin-Goddess! And how right royally, and with what dignity does this Goddess [Hera] shine in all her splendour! and how truly right worthy of Zeus! But how sweetly does this Goddess here [Aphrodite] look; and what a kind of pretty, seducing smile she has!—Well, now I have enough of this felicity—but, if it is agreeable, I wish to have a look at each of them separately, in private; as, at present, I am really in doubt, and don't know on what part to fix my gaze, for my eyes are distracted in every direction.

Aphrodite. Let us do as he wishes.

Paris. Withdraw then, you two, and do you, Hera, remain.

Hera. I will do so—And, after you have had a good look at me, it will be time for you to consider other matters besides—whether the gifts *at my disposal,* in return for your vote, *do not appear* fair to you. For if, my dear Paris, you award me the prize of beauty, you shall be lord of all Asia.[1]

Paris. Our decision depends not on bribes. Now withdraw, *please;* for whatever seems proper will have to be done hereafter. And, now, Athena, do you approach.

Athena. Here I am at your service. And, in my turn, Paris, if you award to me the prize of beauty, you shall never come out of battle worsted, but always victorious; for I will make a warrior and a conqueror of you.

Paris. I don't want war and fighting, Athena; for peace, as you see, at present, prevails both in Phrygia and in Lydia, and my father's kingdom is free from war. But never mind, for you shall not be the worse for it, even though we do not give judgment for bribes. Well, now put on your clothes again, and replace the helmet on your head, for I have seen enough. It is now time for Aphrodite to appear.

---

[1] In Greek geography, *Asia* was limited (in the Homeric epics) to the S.W. of what is now called, in modern European geography, Asia Minor. Afterwards, it gradually extended beyond the limits of the "Lesser Asia" eastwards to the Euphrates and Tigris, which first was opened to Greek knowledge by the conquests of Alexander of Macedon.

Aphrodite. Here am I at your elbow, and examine care-fully each part of me, one by one, passing over nothing, but dwelling upon every one of my charms; and, if you will, my handsome youth, listen to this from me. *I have reason to ask you to do so;* for I have long ago observed you to be young and good-looking, of such sort, that I doubt if all Phrygia supports another like you, and I congratulate you on your good looks: but I blame you, that you do not leave these *lonely* cliffs and these rocks, and go and live in the city, instead of wasting your sweetness on the desert air. For what enjoyment can such as you obtain from the mountains? And what satisfaction can your cows derive from your handsome face? You ought by this time to have married—not, however, some hoydenish and rustic girl, such as are the women of Ida, but some girl out of Hellas, from Argos, or from Korinth, or a Spartan lady, such as Helen, young and beautiful, and in no way inferior to myself; and, what is, indeed, most to the point, of an amorous disposition. For, I tell you, if she were but only to see you, she would, I am sure, leave all and give herself up soul and body to you, and would follow your fortunes and live with you. But, surely, even you have heard something of her fame.

Paris. Not a word, Aphrodite, and I should now be glad to hear from you a full account of her.

Aphrodite. She is the daughter of Leda, the famous beauty, to whom Zeus flew down in the shape of a swan.

Paris. What is she like to look at?

Aphrodite. Pale and fair, as the daughter of a swan might be expected to be, and delicate, like one bred in an egg; trained naked, for the most part, *in the gymnasium,* and skilled in the art of wrestling.[1] And she has been, in a manner, so much, indeed, in request that there has even been a war on her account, Theseus having run away with

---

[1] The Spartan girls, as is well known, were trained in the same *Palæstra,* or Gymnasium, with the boys, with whom they contended γύμναι, *i.e.,* probably, in their *chitons.* Cf. Λυσίστρατα, and the accom-plishments of the Spartan lady Lampito (80-85). Wieland objects that " Venus here commits an anachronism, apparently: for this gymnastic practice of the Spartan girls is represented as in force *before* the Lycurgan laws."

her when not yet in her teens :[1] not, indeed, but that, since she arrived at her majority, all the greatest princes of the Achæans met together to woo her, and Menelaus, of the family of the Pelopidæ, was preferred. If you wish it, I say, I will bring about the nuptials for you.

Paris. What, with a girl already married ?

Aphrodite. You are young and countrified. *I* know, however, how affairs of this sort are to be managed.

Paris. How ? For I should like to know, too, myself.

Aphrodite. You will set out on your travels, as if with the purpose of seeing Hellas, and, as soon as ever you arrive at Lacedæmon, Helen shall see you ; and from that moment it would be my business that she shall fall in love, and run away with you.

Paris. That's the very thing that seems to me hard to believe—that she should leave her husband, and be ready to sail off with a foreigner and a stranger.

Aphrodite. As far as that's concerned, have no fear, for I have two handsome boys, Desire and Love :[2] them I will give you to be guides of the way ; and Love, stealthily assailing her with all his might, will compel the lady to fall in love, while Desire, shedding his whole influence over yourself, will render you what he is himself, an object of desire and of love—and I will be present in person to assist them. I will request of the Graces, also, to attend you, so that all of us together may persuade her.

Paris. How it will all turn out, is not clear, Aphrodite. But I am already in love with this Helen, and I fancy, I

---

[1] *Ἄωρον.* Lit. "immature." With the aid of his friend Peirithous, Theseus had carried her off to Athens, from which involuntary escapade and captivity she was brought back by her twin brothers Kastor and Polydeukes. Lucian represents her as maintaining her extraordinarily fascinating charms even in the future life. During his memorable visit to the Isle of the Blessed, she again elopes from her husband Menelaus with a certain handsome youth ; although, we are assured, she was this time quickly recaptured by her uxorious lord. See the *Ἀληθής Ἱστ.* ii. 335.

[2] *Ἵμερος καὶ Ἔρως.* See Hesiod. Θεοy. 201. One of the most famous representations of these attendants of Aphrodite was the sculpture of Skopas at Megara. With them was figured, also, Πόθος (" Passionate Longing"), who is introduced below. See *Ἰλ.* iii. 440-445, Lucian, *Ἁλιεύς,* 36, Paus. *Ἑλ. Περ.* i. Pliny, *Hist. Nat.* xxxvi. 5.

don't know how, I even see her, and am on my voyage straight for Hellas, and am staying at Sparta—yes, and am now returning home with my wife, and I feel vexed I am not already engaged about all this.

Aphrodite. Don't fall in love, Paris, before you have rewarded your match-maker and the bridesmaid[1] with your *favourable* sentence: for it would be proper for me, too, to be with you as the bringer of victory, and at once to celebrate your marriage[2] and to sing your triumphal odes. For it is in your own power to purchase everything—love, beauty, marriage—with this apple here.

Paris. I am afraid that, after the verdict, you may forget me.

Aphrodite. Would you have me, then, give you my oath upon it?

Paris. Not at all.   But just promise me once again.

Aphrodite. I promise you, I say, to give over to you Helen for your wife, and that she shall run away with you and shall come to Ilium to you; I myself will certainly be present, and will assist you in everything.

Paris. And you will bring Love and Desire and the Graces?

Aphrodite. Be sure of it, and I will take with me Passionate Longing and Hymen, besides.

Paris. On these conditions, then, I give the apple to you: on these conditions receive it.[3]

---

[1] Νυμφαγωγὸν.   Lit. "the conductor of the bride."   The special name applied to the friend of the bridegroom, who conducted the bride to her new home, when the former was a widower—in which case it was not proper for the husband to fetch her himself.   See Hesychius.

[2] Γάμους.   The plural form, in later Greek, is very frequent.   The word γάμος, strictly, was the "wedding-feast," which, with the Greeks, formed the only *legal* witness of the marriage.   For νικηφόρον "victory-bringer," it has been proposed to read κανηφόρον, "basket-carrier," the young girl who bore the sacred fruits in the Panathenaic festival at Athens.   But neither the authority of the MSS. nor probability recommends the substitute.

[3] See 'Ιλ. xxiv. 25-28 for the only reference to the "Judicium Paridis, spretæque injuria formæ" in the Homeric epic.   For an eloquent description of a representation of this scene on Mt. Ida, in the amphitheatre at Corinth, where the Goddesses are personated by young and beautiful girls, see Apuleius, *De Aureo Asino.*   Cf. Euripides, in his *Andromache* and *Helene.*   In the Greek *Anthologia* an epigrammatist, in

XXI.

ARES RIDICULES THE THREAT OF ZEUS, AND THE CHAIN LET DOWN FROM HEAVEN.

Ares and Hermes.

Ares. Did you hear, Hermes, what threats Zeus uttered against us, how arrogant and absurd? "If I should have a mind to it," says he, "I will let down a chain from Heaven, and you shall hang on it and use all your force to pull me down, but you will labour in vain; for you will certainly not drag me down. Whereas should I wish to drag it up, not only you but both the Earth and Sea I will fasten together and suspend in mid air."[1] And all the other menaces, which surely you have heard. Now I, for my part, would not deny that he is superior to and stronger than any of us taken separately; but that he surpasses so many of us together, so that we could not wear him out, even though we brought to our aid Earth and Sea—that I could not believe.

Hermes. Fair speech,[2] my dear Ares; for it's not safe to speak in this sort of way, for fear we reap some mischief from your idle talk.

Ares. Why, do you suppose that I should say this to everyone, and not to you alone, who, I knew, can hold

reference to three rival beauties of his day, expresses his feeling on the Judgment thus:—

"Rhodope, Melite, Rhodokleia contended with one another, which of the three had the most beauty, and they chose me as a judge; and they stood, as the Goddesses, gazed at from all sides, wanting nectar alone. But clearly knowing what Paris through his judgment suffered, I straight put crowns on the three immortals together." See *Greek Anthology* (Bohn's Series).

[1] See 'Ιλ. viii. 18-27. Lucian more than once seizes upon this fine opportunity for his ridicule. Cf. Ζεὺς Ἐλεγ. 4; Ζευς Τραγ. 45; Πῶς δεῖ Ἱστ. συγ. 8. Plato (Θεαίτ.) says the σειρὴν χρυσείην is nothing less than the Sun.

[2] Εὐφήμει. Lit. "Speak words of good omen." To what extent *Euphemism* was cultivated by the Greeks is well known. It appears conspicuously in such words as *Eumenides, euonymos* (left hand), *euphrone* (night), *Euxeinos* (the Hospitable Sea).

your tongue ?[1] But what, however, seemed to me especially ridiculous, as I listened while he was threatening, I could not possibly be silent about to *you*. Why, I remember, no very long time before, when Poseidon and Hera and Athena rose up[2] and conspired to seize him and put him in fetters, how he resorted to all sorts of devices in his terror, and that, though they were only three *against him;* and, if Thetis, in fact, out of pity, had not summoned to his aid Briareus of the hundred hands,[3] he would have been bound hand and foot, his thunderbolt and all. As I thought of this, it constrained me to laugh at his fine grandiloquence.

Hermes. Hold your tongue, I say. For it is not safe either for you to talk, or for me to hear, this sort of language.

XXII.

PAN URGES HIS CLAIMS TO BE THE SON OF HERMES, WHO IS UNWILLING TO ADMIT HIS PATERNITY.

Pan and Hermes.

Pan. How do you do, my father Hermes ?[4]

Hermes. And how are you ? But how am I your father ?

Pan. Are you not, perchance, the Kyllenian Hermes ?

Hermes. Certainly. How, then, are you my son ?

Pan. I am the result of an irregular intrigue, your love-child.[5]

[1] 'Εχεμυθεῖν. This word which, in other writers, occurs only in Iamblichus, is found also in the 'Αλεκτρύων, 2—Jacob.

[2] See 'Ιλ. i. 399-406, Ζεὺς Τραγ. 40. Cf. Strabo, i.

[3] See Hesiod. Θεογ. 149-153, 617, 714, 734. Virg. Æn. x. 567, Ζεὺς Τραγ. 40.

[4] Pan, the great rural divinity, was generally believed to be son of Hermes by Kallisto, or Penelope, or some other Nymph. Apollodorus makes him the son of Zeus. According to one account, he was son of Penelope by all the wicked suitors. His most remarkable physical characteristics were horns, a tail, and cloven feet. See Pausanias ("Αρκαδ.). In one respect, he may be considered to be the most interesting figure in the Greek and Latin Pagan theologies, since it is from that divinity Christian Diabolism has borrowed the principal and popular (corporeal) features of our Devil.

[5] An alternative reading is ἐξαιρέτος (adopted by Jacobitz), *extra ordinem tibi natus.* Lehmann prefers ἐξ ἐρώτος, as above.

Hermes. By heaven, rather, probably, of an intrigue of goats : for how could you be mine, with your horns, and such a snub nose, and shaggy beard, and cloven feet, and goatish legs, and tail upon your rump ?

Pan. Whatever sneers you aim at me, it is your own son you render an object of reproach, my dear father, but yourself still more, for begetting and making such offspring. I am innocent of it all.

Hermes. And whom do you call your mother ? Have I perchance had an intrigue with a goat without knowing it ?

Pan. You have not committed adultery with a goat : but recollect yourself, if you have never offered violence to a girl of gentle birth in Arcadia. Why do you bite your thumb to find an answer, and remain in doubt so long ? I allude to Penelope, the daughter of Ikarius.[1]

Hermes. Then under what circumstances did she bring you into the world, resembling a goat instead of myself ?

Pan. I will give you her very own story. Well, when she despatched me to Arcadia, "My child," said she, " I am your mother, Penelope, of Sparta, and know you have a God, Hermes, the son of Maia and Zeus, for your father. And if you wear horns, and have the legs of a goat, let not that circumstance distress you ; for, when your father visited me, he gave himself the form of a he-goat, to avoid notice, and for that reason you have turned out very like that animal.

Hermes. In truth, I remember to have done something of the kind. Shall I, however, who pride myself so greatly on my good looks, and am still without a beard, have the reputation of being your father, and incur ridicule at the hands of all on account of my lovely offspring ?

Pan. Yet I shall not disgrace you, father, for I am a musician, and play the pipe with remarkable sweetness ; and Bacchus can do nothing without me, but has made me his companion and thyrsus-bearer for himself, and I lead the dance for him. And if you could see my flocks too, what a large number I possess in the neighbourhood of Tegea

---

[1] King of Sparta. See Hyginus, ccxxiv. The later authorities, deviating from the Homeric *epos*, represent the wife of Odysseus as by no means the paragon of immaculateness of the earlier tradition. Some allege magic.

and all over Parthenius,[1] you would be greatly delighted. And I rule over all Arcadia; and, but lately, having fought on the side of the Athenians, I distinguished myself so much at Marathon, that even a prize of valour was awarded me, the cave under the Acropolis.[2] In fact, if you go to Athens, you will know how great is the name of Pan there.

Hermes. But tell me, have you already married, Pan?—for that, I believe, is what they call you.

Pan. Certainly not, father; for I am of an amorous turn, and could never be content to live with one wife.

Hermes. Then, no doubt, you make love to your she-goats.

Pan. You are indulging in sarcasm. I keep company with Echo and with Pitys,[3] and with all the Mænads of Bacchus, and am made much of by them.

Hermes. Do you know, however, how you could gratify me, my dear son, who ask a favour of you for the first time?

Pan. Lay your commands upon me, father, and let us know them.

Hermes. Come to me, then, and affectionately embrace me: but see that you don't call me father, at least in the hearing of anybody else.

XXIII.

APOLLO REMARKS TO BACCHUS ON THE HETEROGENEOUSNESS OF APHRODITE'S CHILDREN; WHILE BACCHUS EXPOSES THE CHARACTER OF PRIAPUS.

Apollo and Dionysus.

Apollo. What should we say—that Eros, Hermaphroditus, and Priapus are brothers [4] by the same mother, very unlike

---

[1] Tegea, a town of Arcadia; Parthenius, a border-mountain of Arcadia and Argolis, some 4,000 feet in height. Arcadia was the home and especial haunt of the Shepherd divinity. Herod. vi. 105.

[2] Cf. Pausanias, i. 32.

[3] For the Story of Echo see Ov. *Metam.* iii. 6. Pitys, one of the many Nymphs loved by Pan, had been metamorphosed into a Pine-tree.

[4] Eros claimed as his parents Aphrodite and Ares, or, according to some authorities, Zeus or Hermes; Hermaphroditus, as his name im-

though they are in external form, and in their pursuits?
For the one is altogether handsome, and an archer, and,
invested with no small amount of power, rules over all;
while the second is womanish, and only half a man, and of
ambiguous appearance—you could not plainly distinguish
whether he is a young man[1] or a virgin. As for the third,
he is masculine beyond the bounds of all decency—Priapus,
I mean.

Dionysus. There is nothing to be surprised at, Apollo;
for Aphrodite is not the cause of it, but the different
fathers. Often, in fact, where the children are by the
same father, of the same mother, they are, like yourselves,
the one a male, the other a female.

Apollo. Yes, but we are alike, and follow the same pursuits—for we are archers, both of us.

Dionysus. As far as the bow is concerned, your occupation is the same, Apollo: but those *other* things are not
exactly similar—that Artemis murders strangers among
the Scythians, and you act the prophet, and set up for a
doctor.

Apollo. Why, do you imagine that my sister is happy
with the Scythians, seeing she is quite prepared, if any
Greek should ever happen to touch at the Tauric peninsula,
to sail away with him, loathing her sacrificial butchery?[2]

Dionysus. And she does well to do so. As for Priapus,
however—for I will tell you something highly ridiculous—
being lately at Lampsacus, I was travelling by the city,

ports, Hermes and Aphrodite; Priapus, Aphrodite and Dionysus.
Priapus, the personification of natural fertility, was, as regards his
character and worship, like so many other divinities in the Hellenic
theology, a strange amalgam of Eastern and Western fancy. He was
pre-eminent by his ugliness as well as obscenity. As frequently represented in Art, Hermaphroditus was half male, half female. See
Diodorus, iv. 1.

[1] Ἔφηβος. The *ephebus* was the Athenian youth who had reached
the age of eighteen, when he was enrolled on the public Register as a
citizen: although he did not acquire the full rights of citizenship until
the age of twenty. Before taking his place among the *ephebi*, he underwent strict scrutiny and was initiated by public ceremonies of a martial
character, analogously to the prevalent custom in barbarous countries
at this day.

[2] See the Ἰφιγενεία ἐν Ταυρ. of Euripides and the *Iphigeneia* of Göthe.
Cf. Θ. Δ. xvi.

and he received me hospitably, and gave me lodgings in his house. When we had retired to rest, after having sufficiently moistened ourselves at the dinner, somewhere about midnight my excellent *host* got up—but I blush to tell you.

Apollo. Did he make an attempt on your virtue, Dionysus?

Dionysus. Something of the sort.

Apollo. And you, what did you do thereupon?

Dionysus. Why, what else but laugh?

Apollo. Well done! that was *acting* in no unkind or uncivil manner. He was to be excused, indeed, considering his attempt was directed against so good-looking a personage as yourself.

Dionysus. For that same reason, my dear Apollo, he might direct his attention to you, too; for you are a good-looking youth, and adorned with long flowing tresses, so that Priapus might well attempt your virtue even in his sober moments.

Apollo. He will not do so, however, Dionysus; for, with my flowing hair, I have my bows and arrows, also.

XXIV.

HERMES COMPLAINS TO HIS MOTHER OF THE MULTIPLICITY OF HIS EMPLOYMENTS.

Hermes and Maia.

Hermes. (*crying*). Why, mother, is any God in Heaven more thoroughly wretched than I?

Maia. Pray, don't talk in that way, my dear Hermes.

Hermes. Why should not I talk so, who have such a number of duties to attend to; toiling as I do all alone, and distracted to so many services? For, as soon as I am up at daybreak, I have to sweep out our banqueting-hall, and after carefully arranging the couches,[1] and putting each particular thing in order, I have to take my place at the side of Zeus, and carry about in all directions the messages *I receive* from him, running up and down the

---

[1] Τὴν κλισίαν. The *reclining*-couch, on which the guests took their places at the *triclinium*. Hemsterhuis and the older editors read ἐκκλισίαν, " the Council-Chamber."

whole day like a courier.[1]   And, as soon as I have returned
up here again, while still covered with dust, I must hand
him the ambrosia.   Before, too, this lately-purchased cup-
bearer [2] arrived, it was my business to pour in the nectar,
also.   But, what is most dreadful of all, is, that I alone of
all the Gods, get no sleep even at night: but I must needs,
also, be then conducting souls to Pluto, and acting as
marshal of dead men,[3] and dance attendance in his Court
of Justice.   For my employments by day are not enough—
to take my place in the Palæstra, and even to act as herald
in the representative assemblies, and to train orators—but,
parcelled out as I am already, *for all these services*, I must,
also, take part in the affairs of the dead.   And yet the sons
of Leda [4] take their places, each *in turn*, every other day in
Heaven and in Hades : but *I* must perforce, be about my
duties here and there.   The sons of Alkmena and Semele,[5]
too, born of wretched women, *though they be*, feast without
care ; whereas I, the son of Maia, the daughter of Atlas,
wait upon them.   And now, having but just come from
Sidon, from the daughter of Kadmus,[6] to whom he has sent
me to see what the girl is about ; and, before even I have
had time to get my breath, he packs me off again to Argos
to look after Danae.   "Then go from thence," says he,
"into Bœotia, and have a look at Antiope by the way.[7]

[1] Ἡμεροδρομοῦντα.   The ἡμεροδρομοί ("day-runners") were an important class of State *employés* in the Hellenic cities.   Extraordinary feats
of speed and powers of endurance have been recorded of many of them.
Ingens die uno cursu emetiens spatium, is the observation of Livy (*An.*
xxxi. 24).

[2] Ganymedes.   Said to have been νεώνητον, because Zeus had compounded with Tros, the Phrygian king, for the rape of his son, by a
present of horses.

[3] Ψυχαγωγός and νεκροπομπός.   One of the most important, if least
agreeable, of the multiform offices of the son of Maia.   For the most
memorable occasion on which he filled this arduous post see 'Οδ. xxiv.,
where he conducts to Hades the reluctant souls of the wicked suitors of
Penelope.   Cf. *Æn.* iv. 242.   Hor. *Car.* i. 10.   Hermes figures especially
in this character in the *Dialogue*s.   See, particularly, Χάρων.

[4] Kastor and Polydeukes.   See *Apollod.* iii. 11.

[5] Heraklês and Bacchus.

[6] It has been pointed out that Lucian has here made a slip.   Europa
was the daughter of Agenor, and the *sister* of Kadmus.

[7] One of the numerous mortal paramours of Zeus.   See *Apollod.* iii. 5.

In truth, I am quite done up, and give in. If I could, I vow I would gladly claim my right to be sold like those slaves on the earth who are vilely treated.[1]

Maia. Don't mind these things, child; for you must, perforce, be submissive to your father in everything, since you are but a youth. And now, as you have been despatched, march off to Argos, then to Bœotia, that you may not get a beating for your dilatoriness—for people in love are apt to have short tempers.

XXV.

HELIOS, ACCUSED BY ZEUS OF RASH CONDUCT IN GIVING UP HIS CHARIOT TO HIS SON, OBTAINS A CONDITIONAL PARDON.

Zeus and Helios.[2]

Zeus. What have you done, worst of Titans? you have ruined everything on the Earth by trusting that chariot of yours to a foolish youth who has burned up the one half of the world by being carried too near the Earth, and the other half has caused to be utterly destroyed by cold, by withdrawing heat too far from it; and, in fine, there is nothing whatever that he has not utterly thrown into disturbance and confusion. Indeed, if I had not perceived what had happened, and hurled him down with my thunderbolt, there would have remained not even a remnant of the

---

[1] It was almost the only sort of interposition of Greek Law (at Athens) that, upon proof of extraordinarily cruel treatment of a slave by his owner, the victim of his brutality might claim the privilege to be put up to auction.

[2] Helios, in the earlier Greek Theology, was the son of Hyperion and Theia (Θεογ. 371-4). Later he was identified with Apollo. The horses and chariot of the Sun are of later invention than the times of the Homeric epics and of Hesiod, and first occur in the Homeric *Hymn to Helios.* Some of the poets give him a golden boat, the work of Hephæstos, in which he makes his diurnal voyage. Others represent him as making his nightly journey in a golden bed. See *Dict. of Mythology*, etc. ed. by Wm. Smith. Cf. Ov. *Metam.* ii., where the Latin poet devotes large space to the tremendous catastrophe, which he so eloquently poetises, and the death of Phaethon, for grief for whom his august father hid his face; and, " si modo credimus, unum Isse diem sine sole ferunt."

human species. Such an excellent driver and charioteer have you sent forth, in that fine *son of yours.*

Helios. I committed an error, Zeus; but don't be hard upon me, since I was prevailed upon by my son with his frequent entreaties: for from whence could I have at all expected that so tremendous a mischief could come about?

Zeus. Did you not know what extreme caution the matter needed, and that if one swerved ever so little from the road, everything was ruined? Were you ignorant, too, of the temper of the horses, and how absolutely necessary it is to hold a tight rein? For, if one slackens it at all, they immediately take the bit in their mouths; just as, in fact, they ran away with him, now to the left, and, after a space, to the right, and sometimes in the opposite direction to their course, and upwards and downwards, in fine, where they themselves had a mind to go; while he did not know how to treat them.

Helios. All this, indeed, I knew, and for that reason I for a long time resisted, and would not trust the driving to him: but, when he begged me over and over again with tears, and his mother Klymene with him, after mounting him on the chariot I cautioned him how he must stand firmly, and how far he should allow his horses to go into the higher regions, and be borne aloft; then how far he must direct them downwards again, and how he must have complete control of the reins, and not surrender them to the fieriness of his steeds. And I told him, too, how great was the peril, if he did not keep the straight road. Well, he —mere boy that he was—taking his stand upon such a tremendous fire-chariot, and peering down into the yawning abyss, was seized with sudden terror, as was to be expected; while the horses, when they perceived that it was not I who was mounted upon the vehicle, not heeding the youthful driver, swerved from their proper route, and caused this terrific calamity. Then he, letting go the reins from sheer fright, I suppose, lest he should be thrown out himself, clung to the front rail[1] of the chariot—but he now

---

[1] Ἄντυξ was the *curved* rim of the front part of the Greek chariot, which was always circular, or rather elliptical, in form.

has received the reward *of his rashness*, and for me, Zeus, the consequent grief ought to be enough *punishment*.

Zeus. Enough punishment, do you say, you who have rashly risked all this ! However, I will grant your pardon now, for this time : but, for the future, if you transgress at all in a similar fashion, or despatch any similar substitute for yourself, you shall at once know of how much more fiery virtue is my thunderbolt than your fire. So now let his sisters[1] bury him near the Eridanus, whereabouts he fell, when he was pitched out, weeping amber over him; and let them become poplars out of their grief for him : but do you, for your part, put your chariot to pieces again— both its pole is broken in two, and one of the wheels is completely smashed—and yoking your horses drive on once more. Well, keep in mind all these *injunctions*.

XXVI.

APOLLO ASKS HERMES TO POINT OUT TO HIM, OF THE TWIN DIOSCURI WHICH IS KASTOR AND WHICH POLYDEUKES; AND TAKES THE OPPORTUNITY OF CRITICISING THEIR DIVINE PRETENSIONS.

Apollo and Hermes.

Apollo. Can you tell me, Hermes, which of these is Kastor, or which is Polydeukes ? For *I* could not distinguish between them.

Hermes (pointing them out). That is Kastor, who was with us yesterday, and this is Polydeukes.

Apollo. How do you make your distinction ? For they are as like as two peas.

---

[1] Of the *Heliadæ* or *Heliades*, Phœbe, Phaethusa, and Lampetie, whose tears were converted into amber by divine interposition, Ovid has commemorated, in particular, the two last (*Metam.* ii. 3). The Eridanus was the poetic name assigned to various rivers by the early poets, but was, later, identified with the Padus (Pado). Æschylus, in his lost *Heliades*, applied it to the Rhodanus. As for the chariot of the Sun, S. Chrysostom (who, in common with most of the Christian Fathers, and indeed, with much later authorities, found the origin and counterpart of Greek theological myths in the Jewish Scriptures) is persuaded that it is derived from a distorted version of the fire-chariot of Elias.

Hermes. Thus—because this one, Apollo, has upon his face the traces of the wounds which he received from his antagonists when boxing, and especially the wounds which were inflicted on him by the Bebrycian Amykus,[1] when on the voyage with Jason; while the other shows nothing of the kind, but is untouched and unwounded in his face.

Apollo. You have conferred an obligation upon me by indicating the distinguishing marks, since in regard to other parts, all are exactly alike—the half segment of an egg and star above, on their heads, a javelin in the hand, and each mounted on a white horse,[2]—so that I frequently addressed Polydeukes as Kastor, and the latter by the name of Polydeukes. But tell me this, too, why in the world do they not both live with us, but by halves either of them at one moment is a dead man, and at another a divinity?

Hermes. They act so out of brotherly affection. For, since one of the sons of Leda must have died, and the other have been immortal *alone*, they of their own accord divided for themselves immortality between them in this way.

Apollo. A not altogether wise division, Hermes, since by this arrangement they will not even see each other; what, I suppose, they especially desired. For how *can they*, when one is with the gods, and the other with the dead? But, however, just as I deal in prophecy, and as Asklepius deals in medicine, and you, excellent trainer that you are, give instruction in the art of wrestling, and as Artemis acts the midwife, and each one of the rest of us

[1] For this terrific pugilistic encounter, see Theok. Εἰδ. xx. Διόσ-κουροι. ; Apollonius, Ἀργοναύτ.

[2] In Greek and Latin Art, the Dioscuri ("the sons of Zeus" κατ' ἐξόχην) are represented with egg-shaped hat or helmet, stars standing on the fore part of the head, and holding spears or javelins, and mounted on white horses, and as duplicates one of the other. In the Homeric epic they are of human birth, on both sides, and the brothers of Helene. Later authorities assign them various origins. Kastor, the equestrian, was mortal, Polydeukes, the patron of pugilists, immortal. With the Romans, the "fratres Helenæ—lucida sidera," were always in high honour and esteem, as their saviours and patrons in battle. The twin-divinities especially claimed the devotion of sailors. Cf. Apollod. iii. 11. Pausanias, Livy, Hor. *Car.* i. 12. Ov. *Metam.* viii. 373, Lucian, Νεκρ. Διαλ.

exercises some profession useful either to Gods or to men—
what, then, will these *good people* do for us? Will they,
such strapping youths as they are, enjoy the banquet,
without working?

Hermes. By no means, but they have assigned to them
to act as deputies for Poseidon, and they must ride over
the sea, and, if they anywhere perceive sailors overtaken
by a storm, perch themselves on the ship and protect the
voyagers.

Apollo. A good and salutary profession, Hermes.

DIALOGUES OF THE SEA-GODS.

I.

DORIS RIDICULES THE FIGURE AND MANNERS OF POLYPHEMUS,
THE LOVER OF GALATEIA.

Doris and Galateia.[1]

Doris. A handsome lover, my dear Galateia, that Sicilian shepherd they say is so madly in love with you!

Galateia. Don't sneer, Doris, for he is Poseidon's son, whatever he may be like.

Doris. What then? If he were even the son of Zeus himself, and showed so savage and uncouth a figure; and, most unsightly of all his uglinesses, possessed only one eye, do you imagine his birth would at all avail him, in comparison with his shape?

Galateia. Not even his uncouthness and his savageness (as you call it) is without its charm—for it gives him a manly air; and his eye becomes his forehead, and sees not less than if there were two.

Doris. You seem, Galateia, to consider your Polyphemus not as the courting, but as the courted, one, such are your praises of him.

Galateia. Courted, no, but I cannot endure that excessive proclivity of yours to finding fault, and you *others* seem to me to do it from envy; because, when, some time ago, he was tending his flocks, and had a glimpse of us from his cliff, as we were sporting upon the shore, at the foot of Ætna, where it extends between the mountain and the sea, he did not even look at you others, whereas I appeared to

[1] Cf. Theok. Εἰδ. xi. (where the Cyclops charges the Sea-Nymph with cruelty and vaunts his merits), and vi. ; Kallim. 'Επ. xlix. Ov. *Metam.* xiii. 7. Virgil, *Ec.* vii. 37, ix. 39, and see 'Οδ. ix. One of the Εἰκόνες of Philostratus is founded on this subject.

him as the most beautiful of all *of us*, and so he kept his eye
upon me alone.   It is this that vexes you, for it is a proof
that I am superior, and deserving to be loved; while you
other Nymphs have been neglected.

Doris. If you appear beautiful to the eyes of a keeper of
sheep and to a fellow who wants an eye, do you suppose you
are an object of envy? and, besides, what else had he to
commend in you than your white skin? and that, I suppose,
because he is accustomed to cheese and milk: everything,
therefore, resembling those things he considers beautiful.[1]
For as to other charms, whenever you wish to discover
what you are really like, stoop from some rock, when the
sea is calm, over the water, and behold yourself to be
nothing else than an exceedingly white skin; and that is
not commended unless, too, there is colour to set it off.

Galateia. Yet I, so purely white as I am, nevertheless
have a lover, though it's only he; whereas there is not
one of you whom either shepherd, or sailor, or boatman
praises.   And my Polyphemus, among other merits, is also
musical.

Doris. Hold your tongue, Galateia; we heard his singing,
when but now he came serenading to you.   So may
Aphrodite be[2] my friend, one would have imagined an ass
was braying.   And his very lyre—what a thing it was!
The bare skull of a stag, and the horns served as the
handles,[3] and he bridged them, and fitted in the strings,
without even twisting them round a peg, and then began
to perform some horribly unmusical and unmelodious
melody; himself roaring out one thing, and his lyre accom-
panying him to something else, so that we could not even
restrain our laughter at that fine love ditty.   Why, Echo
would not even return any reply to his bellowing, loquacious

---

[1] Polyphemus, in such preference, is not without high authority.
With the poets, indeed, extreme whiteness has been one of the principal
characteristics of feminine beauty.   Spenser's Una is even " whiter than
snow."   As for Galateia, she has her name from her complexion.   *Ex
re nomen habet.*

[2] A suggested alternative reading is " Amphitrite."   Lehmann defends the received text on the ground that the Nymphs are discoursing
of *love matters.*   But, it will be observed, Doris disclaims the power of
the Goddess of Love.

[3] See Θ. Δ. vii.

as she is; but was ashamed to appear to imitate his uncouth, ridiculous music. And, then, the amiable creature was carrying in his arms, for a plaything, a bear's cub, resembling himself in shagginess. Who, pray, would not envy you, my Galateia, such a lover?

Galateia. Do you then, my dear Doris, show us your own *adorer,* who is, doubtless, handsomer, and more of a musician, and better skilled in performing on the cithara.

Doris. Nay, I have no adorer, nor do I pride myself on being admired. But as for your Cyclops, such as he is, with the rank odour of a he-goat—a cannibal, as they say, and who feeds upon strangers who come to his country—may he be yours *and welcome,* and may you fully return his affection!

II.

POLYPHEMUS COMPLAINS TO POSEIDON, HIS FATHER, OF HIS
TREATMENT AT THE HANDS OF ODYSSEUS.[1]

Cyclops and Poseidon.

Cyclops (blubbering). O father, what have I endured at the hands of the cursed stranger, who made me drunk and put out my eye, assaulting me when I was lulled to sleep.

Poseidon. Who dared to do this, my poor Polyphemus?

Cyclops. In the first instance, he called himself Outis;[2] but, when he had got clear away, and was out of reach of my arrow, he said that his name was Odysseus.

Poseidon. I know whom you speak of—him of Ithaka, and he was on his return-voyage from Ilium. But how did he do it, for he is, by no means, a man of too much courage?

Cyclops. Returning from my accustomed tending of my flocks, I caught a number of fellows in my cave, evidently having designs on my herds: for, when I placed the stone block against the door—the rock is of huge size—and had lighted the fire by igniting the tree which I brought from

---

[1] Cf. 'Οδ. ix.; Ov. *Metam.* xiii. 7; xiv. 4; Euripides, Κύκλωψ; Æn. iii. 613—683.

[2] " Nobody." Some of the Homeric commentators ingeniously have accounted for the name by attributing to the hero of many wiles remarkably large ears (Οὖς-ῶτος).

the mountain, evidently they appeared to be trying to conceal themselves. Well, when I had got hold of some of them, I devoured them for a pack of thieves, as was reasonable. Hereupon that most villainous rascal, whether he was Outis or Odysseus, pours out a sort of drug and gives me to drink—sweet, indeed, and of delicious smell, but most insidious, and which caused great disorder in my head: for immediately upon my drinking everything seemed to me to be in a whirl, and the cave itself was turned upside down, and I was no longer at all in my senses; and, at last, I was dragged down into sleep. Then sharpening the bar, and igniting it besides, he blinded me as I slept, and from that time, I am a blind man, at your service, Poseidon.

Poseidon. How soundly you slept, my son, that you did not jump up while you were being blinded! But as for this Odysseus, then, how did he escape? For he could not —I am well assured that he could not—move away the rock from the door.

Cyclops. Yes, but it was I who removed it, that I might the better catch him as he was going out; and, sitting down close to the door, I groped for him with extended hands, letting only my sheep pass out to pasture, after having given instructions to the ram what he was to do in my place.

Poseidon. I understand, they slipped away under them unnoticed. But you ought to have shouted, and called the rest of the Cyclopes to your aid against him.

Cyclops. I did summon them, father, and they came. But when they asked the sneaking rascal's name, and I said it was Outis, thinking I was in a mad fit, they took themselves off at once. Thus the cursed fellow tricked me with his name; and what especially vexes me is, that actually throwing my misfortune in my teeth, "Not even," says he, " will your father Poseidon cure you." [1]

---

[1] See 'Οδ. ix. 525, and the anguished cry for vengeance of the Cyclops in Ov. *Met.* xiv. 192-197 :—

     " O si quis referat mihi casus Ulyssen,

       *   *   *   *   *   *

     Quàm nullum aut leve sit damnum mihi lucis ademptæ."

Cf. Macrobius, *Sat.* v. 13.

Poseidon. Never mind, my child, for I will revenge myself upon him, that he may learn that, even if it is not possible for me to heal the mutilation of people's eyes, at all events the fate of voyagers is in my hands. And he is still at sea.

III.

POSEIDON QUESTIONS ALPHEIUS, A RIVER-GOD, RESPECTING HIS
AMOUR WITH THE NYMPH ARETHUSA.

Poseidon and Alpheius.[1]

Poseidon. What's this, Alpheius ? Of all *rivers* you are the only one that falls into the sea without mingling with the salt water, as is the custom of other streams, nor do you rest from pouring yourself along ; but, in your passage through the sea, contracting and keeping sweet your waters, still unmixed and pure, you hasten I know not where, diving into the depths, like the sea-gulls and herons ; and yet you seem to be ready to pop up somewhere or other, and again discover yourself.

Alpheius. Something of a love-affair, Poseidon, so don't scold. Even you yourself often have been in love.

Poseidon. Is it a woman or a Nymph, or, indeed, one of the Nereids themselves you are in love with ?

Alpheius. No, but with a Fountain, Poseidon.

Poseidon. And she—where in the world does she flow ?

Alpheius. She is a Sicilian islander. They call her Arethusa.

Poseidon. I am aware, Alpheius, she is no ugly creature— this Arethusa. On the contrary, she is beautifully clear and transparent, and gushes out in a pure stream, and the

---

[1] The Alpheius, the modern Rufia, rising in the mountains of Arcadia, disappears after a short course and, again appearing, unites with the Eurotas. The two rivers, some two miles from their conjunction, sink below the earth, to reappear in Arcadia. The mysterious river empties itself into the Ionian Sea, not far from Olympia, in Elis. According to the myth, the nymph Arethusa, one of the Nereids beloved by the river-god, was pursued by him until she was transformed by Artemis into the Sicilian fountain. Alpheius, however, still vainly pursues her. See Ovid's beautiful description, *Met.* v. 572-641.

water gives beauty to the pebbles, showing all silver above them.

Alpheius. How accurately well you know the Fountain, Poseidon! I am now off to her side.

Poseidon. Well, away then, and good luck to you in your wooing. But tell me this, where did you have a sight of your Arethusa, seeing that you yourself are Arcadian, and she is at Syracuse?

Alpheius. You are detaining me, in haste as I am, with your superfluous questions.

Poseidon. You are right. Away to your beloved, and emerging from the sea, mingle harmoniously with your Fountain, and become one water.

IV.

MENELAUS EXPRESSES TO PROTEUS HIS INCREDULITY IN REGARD TO THE ALLEGED MIRACULOUS TRANSFORMATIONS OF THAT DIVINITY.

Menelaus and Proteus.[1]

Menelaus. Well, that you become water, Proteus, is not incredible, seeing you belong to the sea; and that you become a tree, too, may pass—nay, when you get changed into a lion, yet even that is not beyond my powers of belief. But whether it is possible for you to become fire while living in the sea—that I very much wonder at and doubt.

Proteus. Don't wonder, my dear Sir, for I do become such.

Menelaus. I, indeed, saw it with my own eyes. But you appear to me—for I must confess it to you—to apply some kind of jugglery to the business, and to deceive the eyes of the spectators, while yourself become nothing of the sort.

---

[1] Cf. 'Oδ. iv. 450. Ov. *Metam.* viii. 730-737. Virg. *Georg.* iv. 418-452. Diodorus, Βίβ. 'Ιστ. 1. In the *Odyssey* the meeting of Menelaus and Proteus, and the prophecies of the sea-divinity, are related at length. He figures on two important occasions—as the guardian of Helen, and in the annunciation of the birth of Apollonius of Tyana. The dialogue may be supposed to take place in the island of Pharos.

Proteus. And what deception could there be in a case so clear? Did you not with open eyes see into what I transfigured myself?[1] And if you doubt, and the thing seem to you to be unreal, a sort of phantasmagoria placed before your eyes, when I become fire, give me your hand, my excellent Sir: for you shall know whether I am a mere spectral illusion, or whether, in fact, the property of burning then belongs to me.

Menelaus. The experiment is scarcely a safe one, Sir Proteus.

Proteus. But you seem to me never to have seen the polypus even, or to know what are the peculiarities of that creature of the sea.[2]

Menelaus. Yes, I have seen the polypus; but what are its peculiarities I should be glad to learn from you.

Proteus. Whatever rock it approaches and fastens its suckers on, and hangs clinging to in coils, to that it assimilates itself; and it changes its colour in mimicry of the rock, so that it may escape the notice of the fishermen, being thus not at all different, or conspicuous, but closely resembling the stone.

Menelaus. So they say. But *your* case is far more strange, my friend Proteus.

Proteus. I don't know, Menelaus, whom else you would believe, if you don't believe your own eyes.

Menelaus. Since I saw it, I saw it, it is true; but the thing is miraculous—the same person *to become* both fire and water!

---

[1] The poet of the *Odyssey* represents the "old man of the sea" as assuming, successively, the forms of a "lion," a "dragon" or "serpent," a "leopard," a "boar," "water," and a "tree." Ovid adds "fire."

[2] For the natural history of the polypus, or octopus, in Greek science, and for the large space it occupied in Greek *gastronomy*, the reader is referred to Athenæus, *Deipnosophists* (Bohn's Series), where the Comic poets, as usual, are largely drawn upon. Cf. Aristotle, *Z. I.*, Pliny, *Hist. Nat.* ix. 29. Plutarch (Περὶ τῆς Σαρκοφαγίας) represents Diogenes the Cynic as swallowing one of these creatures uncooked.

V.

PANOPE RELATES TO GALENE THE SCENE OF THE INTRODUCTION
OF THE GOLDEN APPLE BY ERIS INTO THE NUPTIAL FEAST OF
PELEUS AND THETIS, THE DISCORD BETWEEN THE THREE
RIVAL GODDESSES, AND THEIR DISMISSAL TO MOUNT IDA
FOR JUDGMENT.

Panope and Galene.

Panope. Did you see, Galene, yesterday, what Eris did
at the banquet in Thessaly, because she was not, also,
invited to the feast ?

Galene. I was not at the banquet with you, for Poseidon
ordered me, Panope, to keep the sea unagitated meanwhile ; but what, then, did Eris, for not being present *as a
guest ?*

Panope. Thetis and Peleus had already gone off to their
bridal chamber, escorted by Amphitrite and Poseidon.
But Eris, meanwhile, unobserved by any—and she could
easily be so, while some were drinking, others making a
clatter, or giving all their attention to Apollo playing on
the cithara, or to the Muses as they sang—threw into the
midst of the banqueting-hall a certain very beautiful
apple, all of gold,[1] Galene. And it was inscribed : "Let
the beautiful one have me." And rolling along, as though
intentionally, it came where Hera and Aphrodite and
Athena were reclining ; and when Hermes, taking it up,
read out the inscription, we Nereids held our tongues,
for what were we to do, in the presence of those *Goddesses ?*
Then they began to put forward each one her pretensions,
and each claimed the apple to be her own. And had not
Zeus separated them, the affair would have ended even in
blows. But, says he, "I will not myself judge in the
matter [although they earnestly called upon him to do
so] ; but go away with you to Ida to the presence of the
youth Paris, who, as he is a connoisseur in female charms,
knows how to distinguish the superior beauty, and he
would not give wrong judgment."

[1] See Θ. Δ. xx.

Galene. What, pray, did the Goddesses do, Panope?

Panope. This very day, I believe, they are off to Ida, and somebody will come shortly to announce to us the winner.

Galene. As I stand here now, I tell you, no other will be victorious, with Aphrodite for competitor, unless the umpire be altogether dull-eyed.[1]

VI.

THE RAPE OF AMYMONE BY POSEIDON.

Triton, Amymone, and Poseidon.

Triton. Every day, Poseidon, there comes a virgin to Lerna[2] to draw water—a very beautiful sort of creature. I don't know, for my part, that I have seen a more beautiful girl.

Poseidon. Some lady, do you mean, Triton, or is the girl of the pitcher some maid-servant?

Triton. No, indeed—but a daughter of that celebrated Danaus, herself one of the Fifty, Amymone by name : for I inquired what her name is, and her family. Now, Danaus brings up his daughters hardily, and teaches them to work for themselves, and both sends them to draw water[3] and educates them, in other respects, not to be idle.

[1] One of the most interesting of Roman paintings that have come down to us has for subject this *fatal* marriage of Peleus and Thetis— the *Noce Aldobrandine*. It was found at Rome, in the seventeenth century, on the site of the gardens of Mæcenas. It consists of ten figures, that of Thetis carrying away the palm of excellence. See *Recueil des Peintures Antiques Trouvées à Rome.* Par Pietro Bartoli, Paris, 1783. Cf. the *Peleus and Thetis* of Catullus.

[2] A place near Argos, famous as the haunt of the monster killed by Heraklês. Amymone was one of the fifty daughters of Danaus, the issue of his various wives, whose names are recorded, together with those of their doomed husbands, by Apollodorus, ii. 1, 5. Cf. Philost. Εἰκόνες; Pausanias, ii. 37 ; Strabo, viii. ; Pliny, *Hist. Nat.* iv. 5. The Danaides, it may be observed, have received their highest immortalisation from Æschylus in his Ἱκέτιδες. For a description of a Triton, see Apollonius, Ἀρy. iv. 1588-1612.

[3] Le Clerc here observes that, in the most ancient times, it was a common custom for girls of high birth to be sent to draw water, and quotes the authorities of Homer and *Genesis* xxiv. 13-15. "So that," remarks Lehmann, "Le Clerc knows more about antiquity than Lucian himself."

Poseidon. But does she travel all alone so long a journey from Argos to Lerna?

Triton. All alone. Argos is " very thirsty,"[1] as you know : so it is necessary to be always fetching water.

Poseiden. My dear Triton, in no small degree have you agitated me by your account of the girl. So let us start at once for her.

Triton. Let us be off. Just now, in fact, is the time for fetching the water, and she is pretty nearly in the middle of her journey, on her way to Lerna.

Poseidon. Harness the chariot, then : or, *stay,* that involves much loss of time, to harness the horses and to get the equipage ready. Do you bring me rather one of your swiftest dolphins; for I shall mount and ride it in the quickest possible time.

Triton. See, here you have the fleetest of dolphins.

Poseidon. Bravely done! Let us drive away, and do you swim by my side, Triton.—And now we are arrived at Lerna, I will lie in ambush somewhere here, and do you keep a look out. As soon as ever you perceive her approach——

Triton (looking out from his hiding-place). She is close by you.

Poseidon. A lovely and blooming girl, Triton. But we have to capture her (*seizes her*).

Amymone. Fellow, why have you thus forciby seized me, and where are you taking me? You are a kidnapper,[2] and I suppose you have been commissioned by my uncle, Ægyptus :[3] so I will call out to my father for help (*screaming*).

Triton. Hush! this moment, Amymone. It is Poseidon.

Amymone. Why do you talk to me of Poseidon? Why do you offer me this violence, fellow, and drag me down thus

---

[1] Πολυδίψιον, the Homeric epithet for the capital of Diomedes, 'Ιλ. iv. 171. Athenæus and Strabo interpret it as πολυπόθητον, "much thirsted for" (by the absent Greeks).

[2] Ἀνδραποδιστής. For the extent and success of this sort of recognised piracy, or trade, among the Greeks, see the Comedies of Plautus and of Terence, and the romances of Heliodorus and other Greek romancists.

[3] Whose fifty sons came to Argos in search of their reluctant brides.

into the sea? I shall sink and be drowned, miserable-fated being that I am!

Poseidon. Have no fear. You shall suffer nothing terrible. On the contrary, I will strike the rock hard by this sea-beach with my trident, and will cause a fountain to spring up here to be called after your name; and you shall be happy, and be the only one of your sisters who, after death, shall not have to draw water.[1]

VII.

ZEPHYRUS RECOUNTS TO NOTUS THE METAMORPHOSIS AND ADVENTURES OF IO.[2]

Notus and Zephyrus.

Notus. This heifer, Zephyrus, whom Hermes is conducting into Egypt, through the sea, has Zeus, overcome by passion, actually debauched her?

Zephyrus. Yes, Notus. But she was then not a heifer, but a daughter of the River Inachus. Now, however, Hera, out of jealousy, has made her such, because she perceived Zeus to be very much in love.

Notus. Is he, then, now still in love with the cow?

Zephyrus. Very much indeed, and for this reason he sends her to Egypt, and has given us orders not to agitate the sea until she shall have swum across, so that, after having given birth to her child there—and she is already *enceinte*—she may become a divinity, herself and her offspring.

Notus. The heifer a divinity!

---

[1] As is well known, the punishment of the Danaides, for their slaughter of their husbands on one and the same bridal night, at the command of their father, was to pour water incessantly into sieves, or rather, bottomless pitchers. Besides Amymone, however, Hypermnæstra must have escaped this infernal torture, since—*splendide mendax*—in return for his abdication of marital rights, she had spared her husband's life. According to some accounts, these devotees of Artemis were purified from the crime of murder by Athena and Hermes at the command of Zeus.

[2] See Θ. Δ. iii. Cf. Palæphatus, who gives a more prosaic account than the mythologists.

Zephyrus. Undoubtedly, my dear Notus, and she will preside as patroness, as Hermes said, of sailors, and will be our mistress, to send out, or prevent from blowing, whomsoever of us she chooses to.

Notus. Since, then, she is now our mistress, Zephyrus, we must cultivate her good graces.

Zephyrus. Yes, indeed, for so she will be the more benevolently inclined towards us. Well, *let us do so now*, for she has already made her passage, and is now escaped safely to land; and you see how she now no longer walks on four feet, and Hermes has set her erect, and has made a very beautiful woman of her again.

Notus. Strange things these, truly, Zephyrus—horns no longer, nor tail, and cloven feet, but a lovely girl! Hermes, however—what has come to him, that he has metamorphosed himself, and, in place of a young man, has become a dog-faced creature?[1]

Zephyrus. Let us not inquire too curiously, since he knows best what he ought to do.

VIII.

AT POSEIDON'S REQUEST, THE DOLPHINS NARRATE TO HIM THE STORY OF ARION'S ESCAPE.

Poseidon and Delphines.[2]

Poseidon. Well done, dolphins! for you are ever philanthropic. Before now you took under your protection Ino's brat, and carried him off to the Isthmus, when it fell with its mother from the Skironian rocks;[3] and now you

---

[1] Known as Anubis in the Egyptian theology: *Anubis latrator*, is the epithet applied by Virgil (*Æn.* viii. 698). Cf. Juvenal, *Sat.* vi. 534, xv. 8; Diod. i. 18.

[2] See Herod. i. 24; Lucian, 'Αλ. 'Ιστ. ii. 205; Ov. *Fasti*, ii. 83-118; Pliny, *Hist. Nat.* ix. 8; Ælian, *Hist. Nat.* vi. 15; Pliny the Younger, *Ep.* ix. 33; Oppian, 'Αλ.; Pausanias, ix. 30. Pliny the Naturalist narrates the marvellous tales of dolphin-philanthropy with entire faith; his nephew, in his *Letters* (see Bohn's Series), with some scepticism. Philostratus, like Herodotus, some ages before him, alleges the brazen statue of Arion at Tænarum, as conclusive proof of the reality of the miracle.

[3] See Ov. *Metam.* iv. 524-571; *Fasti*, vi. 485-504; Apollod. iii. 4. These rocks are off the E. coast of Megaris (in the Gulf of Ægina).

have taken up *on your back* this harper from Methymna [1]
and swum to Tænarum, with his luggage and harp and all,
nor have you allowed him to meet with a miserable death
at the hands of the sailors.

Dolphins. Don't be surprised, Poseidon, if we do kind-
nesses to human animals, since we ourselves were men
before we were fish. [2]

Poseidon. I certainly blame Bacchus for having metamorphosed you after his defeat of you in that naval
battle, whereas he ought only to have reduced you to subjection, just as he subjected the rest. But how, pray, did
this Arion business come about, my dear Dolphin?

Dolphin. Periander, I believe, was pleased with him, and
would often send for him on account of his skill, and when
he had got rich by the prince's *patronage*, he eagerly
longed to make the voyage home to Methymna, to display
his wealth. Accordingly, having embarked on board a
certain passenger ship, belonging to a set of villains (as he
had showed them the quantity of gold and silver he was
taking with him), when they were in the middle of the
Ægean, the sailors conspire against him. "Then," said he
—for, swimming by the side of the vessel, I heard everything—"since you have determined upon this *crime*, at all
events suffer me of my own accord to throw myself overboard, after having assumed my *proper* dress, and sung a
dirge over myself." The sailors gave him leave, and he
assumed his *musician's* dress, and sang very sweetly, and
fell into the sea, as though he was certainly to die that
moment. But I, intercepting him and placing him on
my back, swam off with him to Tænarum.

Poseidon. I commend you for your love of music; a
worthy remuneration, indeed, for your privilege of hearing
him have you paid him.

---

[1] Arion. Methymna was a principal city of the island of Lesbos.
Tænarum, now C. Matapan.

[2] Ἰχθύς. The Greek term, like the English "fish," unscientifically
includes marine *mammalia*.

IX.

POSEIDON AND AMPHITRITE DISPUTE AS TO THE FITTING PLACE
OF BURIAL FOR HELLE, DROWNED IN THE HELLESPONT.
POSEIDON DIRECTS THE NEREIDS TO TAKE UP HER BODY, AND
BURY IT IN THE TROAD.

Poseidon, Amphitrite, and Nereids.

Poseidon. This strait, where the girl was carried away by
the tide, let it be called Hellespontus[1] after her; and do
you Nereids take up the corpse, and bear it to the Troad,
that it may be buried by the people of the country.

Amphitrite. Not so, Poseidon, but let it be buried here in
the sea to which she has given her name; for we compas-
sionate her for her most pitiable sufferings at the hands of
her stepmother.[2]

Poseidon. That, Amphitrite, is not lawful; nor, besides, is
it becoming that she lie under the sand hereabouts. But, as
I said, she shall forthwith be buried in the Troad, or in the
Chersonese, and this will be no small comfort for her—that
Ino, too, shall shortly suffer the same fate, and, pursued by
Athamas, shall fall into the sea from the promontory of
Kithæron, where it stretches itself into the waves, with her
son, also in her arms.

Amphitrite. But we shall have to gratify Bacchus, and
save her, too; for Ino was his nurse and suckled him.

Poseidon. No, we ought not *to save her*, since she is so
wicked: it is not proper, however, to disoblige Bacchus,
Amphitrite.

Nereids. But she—pray, what possessed her to fall off
the ram, while her brother, Phrixus, rides safely?

Poseidon. It happened as might be expected, for he is a
young man and able to hold on against the rapid motion.
But she, by reason of her inexperience, upon mounting the

---

[1] See Apollod. i. 9; Hyg. *Fab.* 2; Pausanias, i. 44. Cf. Palæphatus.
Helle was the daughter of Athamas and Nephele.

[2] Ino, daughter of Kadmus and Harmoneia. Fleeing from their
stepmother's cruel treatment of them, on the golden-fleeced ram the
brother and sister, Phrixus and Helle, escaped through the air. Helle,
as is well known, in her fright fell into the narrow strait which bears
her name. Her brother arrived in the land of Kolchis, where, as we
are assured, he ungratefully sacrificed his saviour to the Gods.

strange vehicle, and gazing into the yawning depths, was stupefied, and, at the same time, overcome by terror; and, becoming giddy from the excessive rapidity of the flight, lost her hold of the ram's horns, to which, until then, she had clung, and fell into the sea.

Nereids. Pray should not her mother, Nephele, have come to the aid of the falling girl?

Poseidon. She ought to have done so. But Fate is much more powerful than Nephele.

X.

IRIS CONVEYS TO POSEIDON THE COMMANDS OF ZEUS THAT HE SHOULD KEEP THE ISLAND OF DELOS STATIONARY, WHERE LETO WAS TO LIE IN.

Iris and Poseidon.

Iris. That wandering island, Poseidon, detached from Sicily,[1] whose fate it is still to be swimming about submerged, "that same," says Zeus, "you are now immediately to bring to a standstill, and bear it up to daylight, and cause it at once to remain firmly grounded, a conspicuous[2] object in the middle of the Ægean, fixing it quite securely: for there will be some need of it."

Poseidon. It shall be done this moment, Iris. What convenience, however, will it afford him, when it has been brought up to the surface, and no longer sails about?

Iris. Leto is to lie in on it; for at this very moment she is ill with the pangs of labour.

Poseidon. What, then? Is not Heaven a fitting place for her to produce her children in? And if that *locality* is not, at all events, could not the whole Earth give shelter to her offspring?

Iris. No, Poseidon, for Hera bound the Earth with a great oath not to afford a receptacle for Leto in her labour. This island, however, is not pledged, for it was invisible.

---

[1] As Hemsterhuis observes, as far as relative geographical position is concerned, it is as likely that Delos was originally part of Cilicia as of Sicily. See Kallim. Ὑμν. ἐπι Δηλ. v. 30.

[2] Δῆλον. Lucian seems to be making a pun. Some of the old etymologists refer the name of the island to this adjective.

Poseidon. I perceive. Stand still, Island, and rise again from the deep, and no longer be borne along under the waves, but remain firm and motionless, and receive and harbour, O most highly-favoured one! the two children of my brother, the most beautiful of the Gods. And do you, Tritons, convey the lady across to it, and let a universal calm prevail. But as for the dragon, which now terrifies and goads her to madness, the infants, as soon as they are born, shall pursue it immediately and avenge their mother. Now, do you carry word to Zeus that everything is in good order. Delos stands immovable : let Leto come at once and lie in.

XI.

THE RIVER XANTHUS SUPPLICATES THALASSA (THE SEA) TO RECEIVE HIM, AND CURE HIS BURNS INFLICTED UPON HIM BY HEPHÆSTUS ON BEHALF OF ACHILLEUS.

Xanthus and Thalassa.[1]

Xanthus. Receive me, O Thalassa, in my terrible sufferings, and quench my *fiery* wounds.

Thalassa. What's this, Xanthus ? Who burnt you up ?

Xanthus. Hephæstus. Yes, I am all burned to a cinder, ill-fated wretch that I am, and I am at boiling pitch.

Thalassa. Why, pray, did he throw fire upon you ?

Xanthus. On account of the son of Thetis here. For when I approached him as a suppliant as he was murdering the Phrygians, and I could not make him cease from his rage, but he kept blocking up my stream under the weight of the corpses ; out of pity for the poor wretches, I rushed upon him, intending to immerse him, that he might be frightened and abstain from *slaughter of* the men. Hereupon Hephæstus—for he happened to be somewhere near —with all the fire, as I imagine, he had in his forge and all he had in Ætna, and wherever else *he may have any,*

---

[1] See 'Ιλ. xxi. for the Homeric story, which Lucian here holds up to ridicule, with his accustomed mercilessness. Known to the Gods as Xanthus, this once heroic River (now, under the name of Mendere, anything but aggressive or formidable) had the *earthly* name of Skamander. It forms one of the Εἰκόνες of Philostratus.

attacked me, and burned up all my elms and tamarisks, and roasted, too, the unfortunate fish and eels ; and, causing myself to boil over, all but entirely dried me up. You perceive, then, how I am affected by these marks of the conflagration.

Thalassa. You are turbid, and feverish and hot, as might be expected. Blood flows from dead bodies ; heat, as you say, from fire ; and not unreasonably, my friend Xanthus, *did this happen to you*, for making an assault upon my grandson, without respecting the fact of his being a Nereid's son.

Xanthus. Should I not, then, have had pity on the Phrygians, my neighbours ?

Thalassa. And should not Hephæstus have shown pity 'to Achilleus, who is the son of Thetis ?

XII.

THETIS RELATES TO DORIS THE STORY OF THE EXPOSURE OF DANAE AND HER INFANT, PERSEUS.

Doris and Thetis.

Doris. Why do you weep, Thetis ?

Thetis. I saw just now a most beautiful girl[1] cast into a chest—herself and her newly-born babe ; and the father gave orders to the sailors to take away the chest, and, when they had got out some distance from the land, to let it drop into the sea, so that the wretched girl might perish, both she and her baby.

Doris. For what reason, my sister ? Tell me, if you know it at all, the whole story exactly.

Thetis. Her father, Akrisius, incarcerating her in a certain brazen chamber,[2] kept her a virgin, most beautiful though she was. Then—if it be true, I can't say—but they do say that Zeus, transformed into gold, flowed in a

---

[1] Κόρη, like the Latin *puella*, is often applied to married women as well as to virgins.

[2] Cf. Ov. *Metam.* iv. 9 ; Hor. *Car.* iii. 16 ; Pausanias (ii. 23). The Greek traveller informs us that this brazen prison underground was visible down to the historical age, and, indeed, had been seen by himself. "As some sager sing," the golden Zeus was no other than Prœtus, the young lady's uncle.

stream through the roof to her, and that she received the fluid God into her arms, and became pregnant. Her father, a savage and jealous sort of old fellow, learning this, was in a great rage, and, suspecting she had been debauched by some *mortal*, thrust her into the chest as soon as ever she had been delivered.

Doris. And she—what did she do, when she was dropped *into the sea ?*

Thetis. As regarded herself, Doris, she was silent, and was content to endure her sentence ; but, for the babe, she kept entreating that it might not die, weeping, and showing it—most beautiful babe that it was—to its grandfather, while the infant itself, in its ignorance of its misfortunes, actually smiled at the sight of the sea. I feel my eyes fill with tears again in recounting them.

Doris. You made me shed tears, too. But are they now dead ?

Thetis. By no means, for the chest is still floating about Seriphus,[1] preserving them alive.

Doris. Why, then, don't we save it by putting it into the nets of those Seriphian fishermen ? And they, no doubt, will draw it out and save their lives.

Thetis. You say well. So let us do ; for neither must she herself perish, nor must the infant, seeing it is so bonny.

XIII.

ENIPEUS REPROACHES POSEIDON WITH THE FRAUDULENT SEDUCTION OF THE NYMPH TYRO. POSEIDON EXCUSES HIMSELF.

Poseidon and Enipeus.[2]

Enipeus. This is no honourable conduct, Poseidon—for the truth shall be told. Having made yourself like me, you stealthily approached my mistress, and debauched the

---

[1] Modern Serpho, a rocky island of the Greek Archipelago, some hundred miles from the head of the Gulf of Nauplia.

[2] See Hyginus, *Fab.* lx.; 'Oδ. xi. 234-250 ; *Strabo,* viii. " Haud sane multum conqueritur de injuriâ sibi a Neptuno factâ, videturque pudi-

girl, while she supposed she underwent this at my hands, and for that reason she yielded herself up.

Poseidon. Yes, for you were disdainful and dilatory— you who neglected so good-looking a girl (who paid you daily visits, dying for love) and took pleasure in causing her pain ; while she, wandering along your banks, and even entering *your stream*, and sometimes bathing, was dying to have your embrace: but you would give yourself airs towards her.[1]

Enipeus. What then ? Ought you, on that account, to have forestalled my love, passed yourself off as Enipeus instead of Poseidon, and cheated a simple-minded girl like Tyro ?

Poseidon. It is now too late for you to be jealous, Enipeus, supercilious before. But as for Tyro, she has not suffered anything very dreadful, since she thinks that she has lost her virginity to you.

Enipeus. Not so, indeed ; for you declared, at your leaving her, you were Poseidon, a fact which grieves her above everything. And I have been injured in this—that you were then enjoying my privileges ; and, by raising a sort of dark wave all around, which concealed you together, you enjoyed the girl in my place.

Poseidon. Yes, for you, my friend Enipeus, had no desire *to have her.*

bunda virgo non nimis indigne tulisse personæ mutatæ fraudem," re- marks Hemsterhuis, in regard to the interview of Tyro's ghost with the son of Laertes in Hades.

[1] He had some right to be supercilious—

“Ὃς πολὺ κάλλιστος ποταμῶν ἐπὶ γαῖαν ἵησι.”—'Οδ. xi. 238.

XIV.

A TRITON RELATES TO THE NEREIDS THE STORY OF THE RESCUE OF ANDROMEDA BY PERSEUS.

Triton and Nereids.[1]

Triton. That sea-monster[2] of yours, Nereids, which you sent against Andromeda, the daughter of Kepheus, did no harm to the girl, as you imagine, while itself has now perished.[3]

Nereids. At whose hands, Triton? Did Kepheus expose the girl as a bait, and rush upon and slay it, lying in ambush with a large force?

Triton. Not so. But you, Iphianassa, know, I suppose, Perseus, Danae's baby, whom with his mother you saved out of pity, when she was cast into the sea in the chest by his maternal grandfather.

Iphianassa. I know whom you speak of, and likely enough he is now a young man, and very noble and handsome to look at.

Triton. *He* has killed the monster.

Iphianassa. Why, Triton? Surely it did not become him to repay us such reward for saving him.

Triton. I will explain to you the whole matter as it hap-

---

[1] Those who wish to learn the names of the Nereides, the charming divinities of the sea, will find them displayed by Hesiod, Θεογ. 240-261; 'Ἰλ. xviii. 38-50; Apollod. i. 26, and by Spenser, in the *Faerie Queen*, iv. 11. They presided over the Greek Sea, κατ' ἐξόχην, the Mediterranean, at the bottom of which they dwelt in beautiful grottos and caves. Their number was limited to fifty. The most famous of them was the wife of Peleus and mother of Achilleus. Cf. the "orca marina" of the *Orlando Furioso*.

[2] Κῆτος. In the Homeric epics vaguely used of any marine *mammalia*. By Aristotle (Z. I.), and succeeding naturalists, applied to the whale and *cetacea* proper. Here it signifies some huge sea-monster, the prototype, probably, of the monster in Raffaelle's "St. Margaret."

[3] For the story of the deliverance of Andromeda, the prototype of most of the "distressed damsels" of mediæval and later romance, see Ov. *Metam.* iv. 10; Hyginus, *Fab.* lxiv.; *Apollod.* ii. 3. For the celestial immortalization of the "starred Æthiop queen," see Aratus, Φαινομ. v. 10. Cf. Pindar, Πύθ., xii. One of the lost tragedies of Euripides was founded on this exposure of Andromeda.

pened. He set out against the Gorgons to perform some arduous deed of that sort for the king ;[1] and, when he arrived in Libya——

Iphianassa. In what fashion, Triton ? Alone, or did he take some others with him as auxiliaries ? *He took companions, doubtless*, for, otherwise, the road is difficult of passage.

Triton. Through the air : for Athena supplied him with wings. And when, accordingly, he came where they were living, they were asleep, I imagine ; and he cut off the head of Medusa, and took to his wings, and made off.

Iphianassa. How did he get a look at her ? For they are not to be seen : or, whoever does have a look at them will never thereafter look at anything else.

Triton. Athena, by holding before him her shield—for I heard him afterwards telling Andromeda and Kepheus so—Athena, I say, upon her resplendent shield, as upon a mirror, allowed him to have a glimpse of the reflection from Medusa ; then, seizing her by the hair with his left hand, and fixing his eyes upon the reflection, he grasped his scimitar with his right, and cut off her head, and flew off before her sisters awoke. And when he had arrived in the neighbourhood of the sea-coast of Æthiopia here, while now flying near to the earth, he sees Andromeda lying exposed upon a certain projecting rock, fast secured to it—a most beautiful object, ye gods ! with her tresses let down, half naked much below the breasts.[2] In the first place, pitying her fate, he began questioning her as to the cause of her condemnation ; but, insensibly captured by passion—for the girl had to be saved—he resolved to bring aid to her. And, when the sea-monster rushed towards her, exceedingly terrible, as though about to swallow Andromeda whole, the youth sus-

---

[1] Polydektes, the king of Seriphos, the island on which the outcasts had found refuge.

[2] In this very favourite subject of modern art she is invariably represented wholly nude. In Greek art she sometimes appears as here described. In the picture described by Philostratus, following Euripides, the chains which bind Andromeda are being unfastened by Eros. With the κῆτος of this romance compare the tremendous Dragon of the Golden Fleece, described by Apollonius, Ἀργ. iv. 127-160, and the prodigious Serpent of the *Thebais* of Statius, which occupies an acre of ground.

pended above, in the air, his scimitar grasped by the hilt, with one hand aims his blows, and with the other displays the Gorgon's head in front of him, and turned the creature into stone; and it died there and then, and the greater part of it, as much as looked upon Medusa, is petrified.[1] Then, unfastening the virgin's bonds, and giving her his hand, he supported her as she descended on tip-toe from the rock, which was smooth and slippery. And now he is celebrating his nuptials in the palace of Kepheus, and he will carry her off to Argos; so that, instead of death, she has found a bridegroom one does not meet with every day.

Iphianassa. Well, for my part, I am not excessively grieved at the event: for how did the girl wrong *us*, if her mother did boast somewhat loudly on that occasion, and claim to be fairer than we?[2]

Doris. *The girl ought to have perished notwithstanding*, for so the mother would have suffered pain, on account of her daughter, if, at least, she is a *true* mother.

Iphianassa. Let us no longer, Doris, bear these *wrongs* in mind, though a female of barbaric birth talked somewhat in a style beyond her proper rank and situation;[3] for, in having been frightened on account of her child, she has paid to us a sufficient penalty. Let us, therefore, rejoice at her wedding.[4]

[1] The bones of this *bellua* (as it is called by Ovid), as we are assured by the naturalist Pliny, were brought to Rome from the town of Joppa, on the Palestinian coast, the supposed scene of the tremendous combat, and were found to be forty feet in length, while the spine was a foot and a half in thickness. *Hist. Nat.* ix. 5. Pausanias (iv. 35), too, makes Joppa the scene of the memorable exposure and combat. He tells us that a spring close by was, in his time, still red with the blood of the monster. Cf. Solinus, xxxvi. As for the rationalising Palæphatus, he considers it absurd to believe in the exposure of girls to sea-monsters. The real monster he finds in a certain king named Keton.

[2]   " That starred Æthiop queen that strove
        To set her beauty's praise above
        The sea-nymphs, and their Powers offended."

[3] Βάρβαρος, usually translated " barbarian," properly denotes merely a non-Hellen, one not speaking the Hellenic language, " a foreigner." The Greeks called all foreigners *barbaroi;* in particular, the highly-civilized Persians. Iphianassa, as a Greek divinity, naturally speaks as a Greek woman.

[4] Γάμος. This term was especially applied to the *wedding supper* (for the feast always took place at night) which, with the Greeks, was the sole witness of the legal solemnization of the rite.

XV.

ZEPHYRUS RELATES TO NOTUS THE MANNER OF THE RAPE OF
EUROPA, AND THE MARINE POMP WITH WHICH SHE WAS
CONDUCTED TO HER NUPTIALS WITH ZEUS.

Zephyrus and Notus.

Zephyrus. Never did I see a more magnificent Procession on the sea, since I was born, and began to blow. But you—did you not see it, Notus ?

Notus. What is this Procession you talk of, Zephyrus, or who were the Processionists ?

Zephyrus. You have missed a most delicious spectacle, the like of which you may never see again.

Notus. Yes, for I was employed in the neighbourhood of the Red Sea, and, indeed, I blow over part of India, as much of the country as stretches along the sea-coast. I know, therefore, nothing of what you speak of.

Zephyrus. But you know Agenor of Sidon ?

Notus. Yes, the father of Europa.[1] What then ?

Zephyrus. It is about herself I will relate to you a story.

Notus. It is not, is it, that Zeus has been for a long time the girl's lover ? For that I knew quite a long while ago.

Zephyrus. You are, then, aware of the amour. But listen now to the sequel. Europa had gone down to the shore in sportive mood, taking with her companions of her own

---

[1] See Ov. *Metam.* ii. 14, iii. 1, and the charming *Idyll* of Moschus, entitled Εὐρώπη. Herodotus, at the beginning of his *Histories*, among the numerous rapes of European and Asiatic women perpetrated by the two races, one upon the other, which he assigns as the original cause of the enmity between them, recounts that of Europa, whom he alleges to have been carried off by Greek traders : a more probable explanation of a Greek myth than many of the solutions of the old historian—χρονίων ὄζων καὶ βεκκίσεληνος. Palæphatus, in his accustomed rationalising spirit, discredits the miracle. " I believe," he affirms, " that neither a bull nor a horse could swim so great a space of sea ; nor do I believe that a girl would mount a fierce bull ; and Zeus, if he wished to bring Europa to Krete, would have found for her a pleasanter way of travelling." The bull, in fact, he resolves into the less prodigious human ravisher, whose name he supposes to have been Tauros.

age.   And Zeus, making himself like a bull, began to
sport with them, seeming a very handsome creature, for he
was perfectly white, and had beautifully crumpled horns,
and was tame and quiet in look. He began, then, as he was,
to frolic about upon the shore, and to bellow most sweetly;
so that Europa ventured even to mount him. And, as soon
as this was done, Zeus started off with her at a running pace
towards the sea; and, plunging in, began to swim. But
she, very much terrified at the occurrence, with her left
hand kept clinging to his horn, that she might not slip off,
while with the other she held together her long flowing
dress,[1] blown about by the wind.

Notus. That was a charming spectacle, Zephyrus, you
witnessed, and an amorous—Zeus swimming, carrying
his beloved.

Zephyrus. Yet what followed was far more delightful,
Notus.   For the sea from that moment was without a
ripple, and, attracting a perfect calm, showed itself smooth
and unruffled.   We, however, keeping quiet, followed,
being no more than mere spectators of what was hap-
pening : and the Loves, hovering a little above the sea,
so as at times to graze the water with the tips of their
feet, with lighted torches, sang together the hymeneal
song : while the Nereids, emerging from the sea, rode by
their side upon dolphins, clapping their hands, most of them
half-naked.[2]   Then, too, the whole tribe of Tritons, and
whatever else of the sea-dwellers is not terrible to the
sight—all led their dances round the girl.   Poseidon,
indeed, mounting upon his chariot, and with Amphitrite
riding at his side, led the way with hilarity, clearing the
way for his swimming brother. To crown all, two Tritons
were bearing Aphrodite, who reclined upon a shell, and

---

[1] The πέπλος was a full, flowing dress worn by Greek ladies. Cf.
'Ἰλ. v. 734; 'Οδ. xviii. 292; Xen. Κυροπ. v. i. 6; Euripides, Μηδ. 1160
(of the fatal *peplos* given to Glauke by Medea). The *peplos* worn by
Athena, in the Panathenaic procession at Athens, is the most celebrated example of it.

[2]   " Νηρεῖδες δ'ἀνέδυσαν ὑπὲξ ἁλός, αἵ δ'ἄρα πᾶσαι
       Κητείοις νώτοισιν ἐφήμεναι ἐστιχόωντο
   *   *   *   *   τοὶ δ'ἀμφὶ μιν ἠγερέθοντο
       Τρίτωνες, πόντοιο βαρύθροοι αὐλητῆρες," κ.τ.λ.
                        Moschus, Εὐρώπη—114-120.

scattered all sorts of flowers before the bride.[1] This took place all the way from Phenicia as far as Krete. But, when he had set foot on the island, the bull was no longer to be seen. Then Zeus, taking her by the hand, conducted Europa to the cave of Dikte, blushing and with eyes cast down: for now she knew to what she was being led. And we, plunging in, set to work to put the sea in commotion, one in one part, and another in another.

Notus. O fortunate Zephyrus, to have seen such a sight ! But I, for my part, had to satisfy my eyes with elephants, griffins,[2] and black men.

[1] This graphic description of the nuptial procession of Europa and Zeus, a sort of description in which Lucian excels, it is highly probable, was suggested by some particular, celebrated, picture. One of the most famous modern paintings of this subject is that of Paolo Veronese, in the British National Gallery.

[2] For this monster, so well known to the mediæval world, cf. Προμ. Δεσμ. 284, where the οἰωνὸν is so interpreted by the *scholia*, &c.; Herod. iii. 116; Pliny, *Hist. Nat.* viii. 21, x. 49 ; Ælian, Περὶ Ζώων Ἰδιότ., iv. 27 ; Philost. Ἀπολλών. iii. 48. Plaut. *Aul.* v. i.

DIALOGUES OF THE DEAD.

I.

Diogenes and Polydeukes.

Diogenes. Polydeukes, I entrust to you the task, as soon as ever you reach the upper world—for it is your turn,[1] I believe, to return to life again to-morrow—if you any-where catch sight of Menippus,[2] the Dog (and you would

---

[1] See Θ. Δ. xxvi.

[2] Menippus, who figures so conspicuously in these *Dialogues*, was a countryman of Lucian, born at Gadara, in Hollow Syria, in the first century B.C. He belonged to the Cynic sect, and by his satirical writings is one of the most famous of that school: but his cynicism did not prevent him from making an extensive fortune in trade as a banker, which he lost by the bad faith of a trusted friend. He then put an end to his life. His *Satires* are known to us only through the fragments of the *Saturæ Menippeæ* of Varro (his contemporary), the learned Latin antiquarian : one of the best of which is the *Prometheus Liber*. Cicero (*Quæst. Academ.*) alludes to the *Menippean Satires* as displaying profound philosophy as well as wit. Marcus Aurelius (Τὰ εἰς Ἑαυτὸν) especially mentions him as a distinguished mocker of human life (χλευαστής). The predecessors of Menippus, in this line, were Demokritus of Abdera (Τὰ περὶ τῶν ἐν Ἀδοῦ), and one or two other less-known names. One of the most interesting of the Lucianic Dialogues, which is a sort of epitome of the *Dialogues of the Dead*, and which might well have given Dante hints for his *Inferno*, derives its title from

probably find him at Korinth, near the Kraneium, or in the Lyceium,[1] deriding the philosophers as they quarrel one with another), to say to him : "Diogenes bids you, Menippus, if things above ground have been sufficiently ridiculed by you, to come hither, to laugh at many more matters. For there your laughter was yet questionable, and frequent was *the objection*,[2] but who knows altogether what is to come after life ? But here you will not cease laughing on firm grounds, as I do now, and most of all when you see the rich, and viceroys, and princes to be so humble and obscure, and distinguishable by their lamentations alone, and that they are soft-hearted and mean-spirited, recollecting their life above."   This tell him, and, further, to come with his scrip filled with a quantity of lupines ; and, if he anywhere find on the cross-roads a supper for Hekate set out, or a purificatory egg,[3] or anything of the sort, *let him bring it*.

Polydeukes. Well, I will give this message, Diogenes. But describe him, that I may know quite certainly what manner of man he is as to looks.

Diogenes. An old fellow, bald, with a little old cloak,[4] with many a hole in it, exposed to every wind of heaven, and variegated with rags and tatters ;[5] and he is for ever laughing, and, for the most part, jeers at those loud-talking philosophers.

Polydeukes. It will be easy to find him by those tokens, at all events.

the Cynic of Gadara—Μενίππος ἤ Νεκυομαντεία. Κύων, "the Dog," is frequently used by Lucian for the adjective κυνικός. Cf. Δὶς Κατηγυρούμενος, 33. The Homeric picture of Hades ('Οδ. xi.) is an especial object of ridicule throughout these Dialogues.

[1] The places especially frequented by Diogenes of Sinope, the famous Cynic. The Kraneium, where he died, was a cypress grove in the suburbs of Korinth. The Lyceium was the Gymnasium, on the S.E. of Athens, celebrated as the scene of the teaching of Aristotle.

[2] Jacobitz translates καὶ πολὺ τὸ, "es kam dir häufig der Gedanke bei," and cites 'Αλεξάνδρος, 20.

[3] It was a common custom with the rich to propitiate the all-powerful and dreaded divinity of the Night, at the end of each month, with certain dishes from their kitchens, and other offerings, consisting, according to the barbarous *mélange* of the sacrificial ritual, of black lambs, and dogs. These highway sacrifices were in high repute and request with the starving poor, who seldom failed to act as the priests of the triune Goddess. Cf. Aristoph. Πλοῦτος, 595-7 ; Mart. *Ep.* vii. 53 ; Petron. *Satyr;* Plut. Συμπ. vii. 6 ; Lucian, N. Δ. xxii. ; Καταπλ. 7.

Diogenes. Are you willing that I give you some commission with respect to those philosophers themselves?

Polydeukes. Speak: for that will not be any trouble either.

Diogenes. In a word, then, exhort them to cease their trifling nonsense, and quarrelling about the nature of the universe, and generating "horns" for each other, and making "crocodiles,"[1] and teaching the young to engage in such futile rubbish.

Polydeukes. But they will say that I am an ignorant and uneducated fellow to denounce their philosophy.

Diogenes. Do you, however, bid them from me to go and howl with a plague to them.

Polydeukes. This message, too, I will give them, Diogenes.

Diogenes. And to the rich, my dearest pet of a Polydeukes, convey this message from me: "Why, O fools, do you guard your gold *so religiously;* and why do you punish yourselves, calculating the interest of your money, and heaping talents upon talents, who must shortly come hither with only a single obolus?"[2]

For the purificatory egg with which the goddess Isis, or her priests, was propitiated, see Juv. *Sat.* vi. 518; and for the Larvæ and Lemures, see Persius *Sat.* v. 185; Ov. *De Arte Am.* ii. 330. See, also, Ov. *Fast.* v. 1. etc., and Suidas.

[4] The τριβώνιον was a specially distinctive mark of the followers of Antisthenes and Diogenes, and frequently figures in Lucian's ridicule of their extravagances.

[5] Ταῖς ἐπιπτυχαῖς κ. τ. λ. is translated by Jacobitz, "mit Lappen von allen möglichem Farben geflickt." See Heliodorus, Αἰθιοπ. vi.

[1] Κέρατα—κροκοδείλους. Technical names in the absurd *Syllogisms* of the school of Zeno and Chrysippus. The syllogism of the "horns" was thus framed: "What you have not lost, you have: You have not lost horns: Therefore you have horns." From this has been supposed (but, probably, without reason) to be derived the proverb of reproach— "to wear the horns." As for the syllogism of the "crocodile," it derived its name from the following illustration:—A crocodile seizes a child on the banks of a river, and promises to restore it to the father if he can tell truly whether the child will be given back or no. How completely the father was placed on the horns of a dilemma needs no demonstration. The illustration is given by Lucian, in his ridicule of the Stoic logic in the *Sale of Lives.* Cf. Quintilian, *Inst.* i. 10, on the *ceratinas et crocodilinas ambiguitates,* Diog. Laert. Lucian, Ἑρμοτ. 81.

[2] The *obolus,* a coin, which in most of the Greek States had the value of twopence in English money, was always most religiously placed in

Polydeukes. This, too, shall be told to them.

Diogenes. Yes, and say to the handsome and the strong, to Megillus of Corinth and Damoxenus the Wrestler,[1] that with us there is neither auburn hair, nor bright nor black eyes, nor a blush upon the cheek any longer, nor well-strung nerves, nor strong shoulders: but all is for us, as they say, "one and the same dust"[2]—skulls bare of all beauty.

Polydeukes. It will be no trouble either to say this to the handsome and strong.

Diogenes. And to the poor, Mr. Laconian[3]—and they are numerous enough, grieving at their lot, and bewailing their destitution—say that they are not to weep or lament; explain to them the perfect equality here; and that they will see those who are rich there (in the upper world) in no way better off than themselves. And your Lacedemonians reprove from me for this, if you like—telling them that they have become remiss and degenerate.

Polydeukes. Not a word, Diogenes, about the Lacedemonians, for I certainly will not tolerate it. But as to what you were saying in regard to the rest, I will deliver your messages.

Diogenes. Let us leave them alone, since such is your pleasure : do you, however, convey from me my words to those whom I before mentioned.

the mouth of the dead, as a *viaticum*, in payment to the ferryman of the Styx and the other infernal rivers. See especially Lucian's Χάρων. The τάλαντον, of Attica, was worth, nearly, £244. Cf. Juv. *Sat.* iii. 267.

[1] The handsome Megillus figures in Charon's boat. Καταπλ. 22; Damoxenus in Pausanias as a famous Syracusan athlete, vii.

[2] One reading has μία Μύκονος "one Myconos," an island of the Cyclades, famous for the number of its bald-headed inhabitants. See Plut. Συμπ. i.; Clemens Alexand. Στρωμ. i. Terent. *Hecyra.* iii. 4; Plin. *Hist. Nat.* x. 37; Strabo, Γεωγ. x.; Erasmus, *Adagia.* Lucian had in mind especially the ἀμενήνα καρήνα, with the sight of which Odysseus was so abundantly favoured on his visit to Hades, 'Οδ. xi.

[3] Polydeukes was one of the twin-children of Leda, wife of Tyndarus, King of Sparta. See Θ. Δ. xxvi.

II.

KRŒSUS, MIDAS, AND SARDANAPALUS COMPLAIN TO PLUTO OF
MENIPPUS THAT HE DERIDES THEM FOR THEIR LAMENTATIONS
OVER THE LOSS OF THE POWER, WEALTH, AND LUXURY WHICH
BELONGED TO THEM ON EARTH.—MENIPPUS, IN SPITE OF
PLUTO'S REMONSTRANCES, PERSISTS IN HIS RIDICULE.

Krœsus, Pluto, Midas, Sardanapalus, and Menippus.

Krœsus (pointing at Menippus). We can't endure, Pluto,
this dog here, Menippus, dwelling near us. So either
establish him somewhere *else*, or we shall change our
habitation to another spot.

Pluto. But what harm does he do you, seeing he is your
fellow-ghost?

Krœsus. Whenever we groan and lament, remembering
our possessions above—Midas here, his gold coin, and
Sardanapalus his abundant luxury, and I, Krœsus, my
treasures—he laughs at and upbraids us, calling us names
—"slaves" and "castaways";[1] and sometimes he disturbs
our lamentations by singing, too; and, in a word, he is a
nuisance to us.

Pluto. What is this they say, Menippus?

Menippus. Quite true, Pluto: for I hate them for
vile and pestiferous fellows, for whom it was not enough
to live badly, but who, even when dead, still remember and
cling to their earthly possessions. I find pleasure, therefore, in vexing them.

Pluto. But it is not right; for they are no small things
they mourn the loss of.

Menippus. Are you, too, for playing the fool, Pluto, and
casting in your vote with these whining fellows?

---

[1] Καθάρματα, in the first instance, "offscouring," "the refuse of a
sacrifice." Used at Athens, in special sense, for certain real or pretended
criminals, who on the occasion of some national calamity were, like the
scape-goats of the Jews, employed as propitiatory sacrifices, and thrown
into the sea. Cf. Aristoph. Πλ. 454. S. Paul, 1 *Cor.* iv. 13.

[2] For ὀλεθρίους, the common reading, Jacobitz has ὀλέθρους. Cf. :
" Destroyers rightlier called, and plagues of men," *Par. Lost,* xi.

Pluto. Not at all : but I would not have you up in arms.

[exit.

Menippus (*shaking his fist*). None the less, basest of Lydians, Phrygians, and Assyrians, be well assured of this —that 1 will never leave off : for, wherever you may go, I will follow. annoying you, and singing to the tune of your wailing, and ridiculing you.

Krœsus. Is this not insolence ?

Menippus. No, but that was insolence of which *you* wero guilty—in requiring worship, and in mocking at and insulting freemen, without having any thought of *the leveller* death at all.   Therefore, bitterly shall you bewail the loss of all these things.

Krœsus. Yes, O heavens, of many and great possessions !

Midas. Of how much gold I !

Sardanapalus. Of how much luxury I !

Menippus. Well done !   So do. - You, for your part, lament and weep, and I will accompany you, and occasionally join in with the refrain, " Know thyself " : [1] for it would be quite a suitable accompaniment to such howling.

---

[1] The famous apophthegm, $\gamma\nu\tilde{\omega}\theta\iota$ $\sigma\epsilon\alpha\upsilon\tau\grave{o}\nu$, has been attributed to various Greek celebrities—Thales, Pythagoras, Sokrates, and others : but it is generally conceded to Chilon, of Sparta, one of the " seven sages," who lived in the seventh and sixth centuries B.C.   See Diog. Laert. $\Pi\epsilon\rho\grave{\iota}$ $B\acute{\iota}\omega\nu$, &c. i. ; the Platonic Dialogue, $'A\lambda\kappa\iota\beta\iota\acute{\alpha}\delta\eta\varsigma$, i. (from which it appears that the words were inscribed on the entrance to the temple at Delphi); Juv. *Sat.* xi. 27.   Menander, the first of the New Comedy dramatists, parodies this well-worn adage, and holds that " Know others " might be more useful—$\chi\rho\eta\sigma\iota\mu\acute{\omega}\tau\epsilon\rho\rho\nu$ $\gamma\grave{\alpha}\rho$ $\tilde{\eta}\nu$ $\tau\grave{o}$ $\Gamma\nu\tilde{\omega}\theta\iota$ $\tau\sigma\grave{\upsilon}\varsigma$ $\check{\alpha}\lambda\lambda\sigma\upsilon\varsigma$.   For Krœsus, see Herod. i.   For some instances of the luxury of Sardanapalus, consult Athenæus, xii. 38, 39.

III.

MENIPPUS RIDICULES THE ORACLES OF TROPHONIUS AND AMPHILOCHUS.

Menippus, Amphilochus, and Trophonius.[1]

Menippus. So then, you two, Trophonius and Amphilochus, dead men though you are, for some reason or other have been thought worthy of temples, and have the reputation of prophets; and the foolish triflers of men have supposed you to be divine.

Amphilochus. Why, pray, are we to blame, if they, in their folly, will have such opinions about dead people?

Menippus. But they would not be holding such opinions, unless, while you were living, you had indulged in such juggling tricks, as though you foreknew the future, and were able to foretell it to those who inquired of you.

Trophonius. Menippus, Amphilochus himself must know what answer he is to give respecting himself: but I, for my part, am a hero, and deliver prophecies, whenever any one comes down to visit me. But you appear never to

---

[1] Amphilochus, with his equally prophetic father, enjoyed great reputation for oracular power. While on earth, they had taken part in the celebrated War of the Epigoni (or "Descendants" of the Seven against Thebes) upon the city of Œdipus. Amphilochus, the murderer of his mother, had shrines at Athens, at Oropus on the confines of Attica and Bœotia, and at Mallus in Cilicia. The Oracle of Amphiaraus was situated near Thebes, at the spot where he had been swallowed up with his chariot, in his flight from the battle before that city. For the still more renowned Oracle and Cavern of Trophonius (who while in the flesh had enjoyed the reputation of an expert thief) at Lebadeia in Bœotia, see Aristoph. Νεφ. 507 ; Diod. *B. I.* xv. ; Philost. *A. T.* viii. 19 ; Maximus Tyrius (Διαλ. xxvi.) ; Origen in Celsus (Λόγος Ἀληθὴς) ; Lucian, Ἀλέξανδρος, 29. The Comic poets (Kratinus and Alexis) had not neglected so promising a subject. Pausanias, ix. 39. Pausanias gives a rather particular account of the Cavern and its preternatural terrors, of which he had himself been witness. Plutarch is said to have left a treatise on the subject, which, very unhappily, has not survived.

have stayed at Lebadeia at all ; for *otherwise* you would not refuse credence to these things.

Menippus. What do you say ? Unless I had gone to Lebadeia, and dressed myself ridiculously in those fine linen robes, and carried a barley-cake in my hands, and had crawled through the mouth, which is low enough *in the roof*, into the Cavern, I could not know that you are a dead man, as we are, superior only by your juggling faculty ? But, in the name of the prophetic art, *what*, pray, is a " hero " ? for I don't know.

Trophonius. A sort of compound of man and God.

Menippus. Which (as you say) is neither man nor god, but both together ? Where, then, has that half of you, the divine part, now gone off to ?

Trophonius. It is delivering oracles in Bœotia, Menippus.

Menippus. I don't know, my friend Trophonius, what you are talking about, indeed. That, however, you are wholly a dead man, I see distinctly enough.

IV.

HERMES DEMANDS FROM CHARON ARREARS OF PAYMENT DUE TO HIM FOR HIS SERVICES ON THE STYX. CHARON EXCUSES HIMSELF ON THE PLEA OF BAD TIMES; NO GREAT WAR OR FAMINE, AS IT HAPPENED, RAVAGING THE EARTH AT THAT MOMENT. HERMES MORALISES ON THE CAUSES OF DEATH, DIFFERENT FROM THOSE OF OLD, WHICH DESPATCH MEN IN CROWDS TO HADES.

Hermes and Charon.

Hermes. Let us reckon up, Mr. Ferryman, if you please, how much you now owe me, so that we may not hereafter quarrel at all about it.

Charon. Let us do so, Hermes ; for it is better to come to a definite understanding about it between ourselves, and less likely to cause trouble ! [1]

---

[1] Or, as Wieland translates, " wir haben gleich eine Sorge weniger."

Hermes. I procured to your order an anchor at five drachmæ.[1]

Charon. A high price!

Hermes. By Pluto, I purchased them at the full sum of the five pieces, and a leathern thong for the oar for two oboli.

Charon. Set down five drachmæ and two oboli.

Hermes. And a darning-needle for *mending* the sail. Five oboli I paid down *for that.*

Charon. Set down those, too.

Hermes. And bees'-wax to fill up the chinks in our little craft, and nails, too, and a small rope, of which you made the brace—two drachmæ in all.

Charon. And you made a good bargain there.

Hermes. That is the *whole sum,* unless something else has altogether escaped me in the reckoning. And when, then, do you say that you will repay me this?

Charon. Just now, my dear Hermes, it is quite impossible. But if some pestilence or war should send us down some shoals *of men,* it will then be in my power to make profits by cooking the accounts of the fares.[2]

Hermes. Am I, then, now to take my seat, praying for the worst to happen, with the mere chance that I may get something from it?

Charon. There is nothing for you, otherwise, Hermes. Just now, as you see, few come to us: for peace prevails.[3]

Hermes. Better so, even though *payment of* your debt due to me must be postponed by you. But, however, the men of former times, Charon—you know in what sort they used to come to us, nearly all of them, covered all over with blood, and riddled with wounds, the majority of them. But, nowadays, it is either some one who has died by poison at the hands of his son or of his wife; or who is swollen out in his stomach and legs by gluttony—pallid and paltry—not at all like their predecessors. The most

---

[1] The *drachma,* the principal silver coin with the Greeks, was, at Athens, nearly equal to the French *franc*—9¾*d.*

[2] For Æakus, the infernal judge, to whom Charon was bound to present his accounts. Cf. Aristoph. Βατρ. 465, κ. τ. λ.; Juv. *Sat.* i. 10.

[3] It will be remembered that these *Dialogues* were composed during the (comparatively) peaceful reigns of the Antonines.

of them come here, by plotting one against the other for the sake of money, to judge by their appearance.

Charon. Yes, for that is an article exceedingly much loved.

Hermes. Then, surely, neither could I be thought to be wrong in so keenly demanding payment of your debt.

V.

PLUTO DIRECTS HERMES TO BRING HIM THE FORTUNE AND LEGACY-HUNTERS AND FLATTERERS OF A CERTAIN RICH MAN, AND TO SUFFER THE LATTER TO OUTLIVE HIS FAWNING SATELLITES.[1]

Pluto and Hermes.

Pluto. You know that old man, I mean the very aged and infirm fellow, the rich Eukrates, who has no children, but fifty thousand legacy-hunters?

Hermes. Yes, you speak of the Sikyonian. What then?

Pluto. Well, let him live on, Hermes; to the ninety years he has already reached dealing out so many again, and, if, at least, it were possible, even yet more. But as for those fawning flatterers of his, the young Charinus, and Damon, and the rest, drag them all down here, one after the other, the whole lot of them.

Hermes. Such a proceeding would appear strange.

Pluto. Not at all, but exceedingly just. For what wrong have they suffered that they pray for his death, or, although no way related, why do they lay claim to his money? But what of all things is most abominable is, that though they entertain such wishes, they yet court and fawn upon him

---

[1] In this and the two Dialogues following, Lucian satirizes a highly-successful and lucrative profession in the Roman world of his time, as well as in the earlier age of Juvenal and Martial. Not unknown among the Greeks (in the New Comedy it occupies a conspicuous place), it flourished to a much greater extent with their (political) masters, the still more corrupt and luxurious Romans. Cf. Plaut. *Miles Glor.* iii. 709-715; Hor. *Sat.* ii. 5 ; Juv. *Sat.* i. and xii.; Mart. *Epigrammata ;* Lucian, *passim.*

in public; and, when he is ill, their designs are very evident to all; but, all the same, they engage to offer a sacrifice if he should get better; and, altogether, the fawning of these gentlemen is of a somewhat subtle and complicated character. So let the one remain untouched by death, and let the others go off before him, while vainly gaping *in affected admiration.*

Hermes. They will suffer a ridiculous fate, rascals that they are. But he, indeed, charmingly cheats and buoys them up with vain hopes exceedingly; and, in a word, while always appearing like a corpse, he has far more strength than the young men. They, however, already have divided out the legacy among themselves, and are living upon it, promising to themselves a happy time of it.

Pluto. Therefore, let him put off his old age and renew his youth like Iolaus;[1] but as for them, in the midst of their hopes, leaving behind them tho wealth they have been dreaming of, let them come *here* this moment, miserable wretches dying miserably.

Hermes. Have no anxiety, Pluto; for I will go after them for you at once, one by one in their order. There are seven of them, I believe.

Pluto. Drag them down. The old fellow shall follow each of them to the tomb, while he himself, from being aged, shall again be in the prime of youth.

---

[1] The nephew and squire of Herakles, whose youth was renewed by Hebe. See Ov. *Metam.* ix. 394—401. Herakles sent him into Sardinia, and Iolaus, introducing civilisation to the inhabitants, was afterwards worshipped by them as a principal divinity.

VI.

TERPSION, A LEGACY-HUNTER, ACCUSES PLUTO AND THE FATES IN THAT, ALTHOUGH ONLY THIRTY YEARS OF AGE, THEY HAD CAUSED HIM TO PREDECEASE THE OBJECT OF HIS TENDER REGARDS, THE MILLIONAIRE NONAGENARIAN, THUKRITUS. PLUTO CONVINCES TERPSION OF THE INJUSTICE OF HIS ACCUSATION; AND THE LEGACY-HUNTER CONSOLES HIMSELF IN THE PROSPECT OF BEING SOON JOINED IN HADES BY HIS LATE RIVALS ON EARTH.

Terpsion and Pluto.

Terpsion. Is this just, Pluto, that I have died at the age of thirty years, while the old Thukritus, above his full tale of ninety, lives on ?

Pluto. Very just, certainly, Terpsion, since he does not pass his life praying for the death of any of his friends, while you the whole time were plotting against him, and expecting his legacy.

Terpsion. Why, was it not fitting, old as he was, and no longer capable of using his wealth, he had departed from life and made way for the young ?

Pluto. You lay down new and strange laws, Terpsion—that a man, who is no longer able to enjoy his money, should die ! But Fate and Nature have ordered it differently.[1]

Terpsion. Then I blame them for that arrangement of theirs ; for the business should have proceeded in some sort of order—the older *should go* first, and after him the next in age—and by no means have been reversed; nor should the man laden with years, with only three teeth still left in his head, seeing with difficulty, crouching and leaning upon the shoulders of four domestics, his nose stuffed with phlegm and his eyes with rheum, with no further perception of anything pleasing, a sort of living tomb, derided by the

---

[1] Compare the scene in the opening of the *Alkestis* of Euripides, where an animated altercation is represented between Apollo and Thanatos, the latter claiming the young as his especial prey and privilege.

H

young, remain alive, while the handsomest and most robust youths die off: for that is a case of the "streams flowing backward " ;[1] or, in the last resort, people ought to know when each particular old gentleman will certainly be on the point of going off, so that they would not fawn upon any of them to no purpose. Now, however, is the proverb verified, " the wagon *drags* the ox."[2]

Pluto. These things, Terpsion, are much more reasonable than they seem to you to be. And you—what possesses you that you gape with open mouth after other people's possessions, and thrust and force yourselves upon childless old fellows? Thus it is you incur ridicule, when you are laid under ground before them ; and the matter affords the greatest delight to most people, for, in proportion as you pray for their deaths is it a pleasure to all that you predecease them. Why, this is some new and strange art you have devised—to make love to old men and old women, most especially if they have no children ; while those who are blessed with progeny have no lovers, as far as you are concerned. However, already many of the objects of your affection, understanding the rascality of your attachment, if they have children, pretend to hate them, so that they too may possess lovers ; accordingly, they who long danced attendance, like a number of satellites, are excluded in the wills ; while the child and Nature, as is just, possess everything, and these gentlemen grind their teeth at having been finely cheated.

Terpsion. True. Yet how many things of mine Thukritus devoured, while always seeming to be just at the last gasp, and (whenever I came into his house) groaning

---

[1] Ἄνω γὰρ ποταμῶν. A Greek proverb, παγαί being understood. The full expression is found in the *Medeia* of Euripides :—

$$\text{Ἄνω ποταμῶν ἱερῶν χωροῦσι παγαί.}$$

" The springs of the rivers flow *up* " (*i.e.*, in the contrary direction to their natural course). Cf. Lucian, Περὶ τῶν ἐπὶ Μισθῷ Συνόντων ; Ov. *Tristia,* ii. 8.

[2] Ἡ ἅμαξα τὸν βοῦν. Sup. ἐκφέρει or ἕλκει. Erasmus, *Adagia,* explains this Greek *Sprichtwort* of the wagon dragging the ox backwards down a steep hill ; but, as Hemsterhuis remarks, that great glory of his country is not always successful *in adagiis explicandis.*

and croaking, in a manner, in the very depths *of his chest*, for all the world like some unformed chicken from an egg; so that I, imagining him to be almost at the next moment ready to embark upon his bier, would send him a number of things, that my rivals in affection might not surpass me in the magnitude of their gifts. And often, kept awake by my anxious cares, I lay counting and settling each particular item. This, in fact, has been the cause of my death—sleeplessness and anxieties; while he, after having swallowed so large an amount of my bait, stood by as I was being buried the day before yesterday, laughing over me.

Pluto. Well done, Thukritus; may you live to the longest possible period, at once rich and having the laugh against such gentlemen; and may you not die before, at least, you have dispatched all your fawning flatterers before you.

Terpsion. This, Pluto, to me, too, would be exceedingly delightful now—if Charœades, in fact, shall be going to his grave this instant before Thukritus.

Pluto. Keep up your spirits, Terpsion, for both Pheidon and Melanthus,[1] and, in fine, all of them, will precede him, *brought here* by the same cares.

Terpsion. That has my full approbation. Long life to you, Thukritus!

VII.

ZENOPHANTES AND KALLIDEMIDES, TWO PARASITES, BEWAIL ONE TO THE OTHER THEIR FATES, IN HAVING BEEN IN THE MIDST OF THEIR SCHEMING UNEXPECTEDLY DISMISSED TO HADES. KALLIDEMIDES, IN PARTICULAR, RECOUNTS THE PLEASANT MANNER IN WHICH HE BROUGHT ABOUT HIS OWN DEATH.

Zenophantes and Kallidemides.

Zenophantes. And you, Kallidemides, how did you come

---

[1] If these are not the names of contemporaries of Lucian, they may be derived from the characters of the New Comedy.

by your death ? For my part, you know that I, who was Deinias's parasite, was choked by gorging inordinately : for you were present at my death.

Kallidemides. I was so, Zenophantes. But my fate was a strange and unusual sort of one. You knew surely something of Ptœodorus, the old gentleman ?

Zenophantes. The childless millionaire, with whom I knew you as chiefly familiar ?

Kallidemides. That's the very man I was always courting, who promised that he would speedily depart this life for my special benefit. When, however, the business was being protracted to an unconscionable length, and the old fellow was extending his life beyond the age of Tithonus [1] himself, I devised an expeditious sort of road to the inheritance. Purchasing a poison, I induced his butler, as soon as ever Ptœodorus asked to drink—and he drinks pretty hard—to put it in his cup and have it ready to give to him ; and, if he would do so, I pledged myself by oath to give him his freedom.

Zenophantes. What happened then ? For you seem to be going to tell some very strange story.

Kallidemides. Well, when we had come from the bath, the lad with the two cups all ready, the one having the poison for Ptœodorus, and the other for me—by some blunder gave me the poison, and Ptœodorus the unpoisoned goblet. Accordingly he drank his *harmlessly*, while in a moment I lay an outstretched corpse, substituted in his place.—Why do you laugh at this, Zenophantes ? Surely it does not beseem you to mock at a gentleman and a friend.

Zenophantes (laughing immoderately). Why, my friend Kallidemides, you experienced a comical sort of fate. But the old gentleman, what did he at this?

Kallidemides. At first he was somewhat disturbed at the

---

[1] A Greek proverb analogous to our "as old as Methuselah," with the added notion of extreme decrepitude—a sort of Struldbrug. Titho-nus (a Trojan prince, the brother of Priam), beloved by Eos, by her intercession was privileged to be immortal ; but the Goddess of the Morning had omitted to demand from Zeus for her lover perpetual youth. At his earnest prayer, he was metamorphosed into a grasshopper. See Hor. *Car.* ii. 16, and Erasmus, *Adagia.* Athenæus (xii. 72) recounts a much less poetical history of the beloved of Aurora, the termination of which, unhappily, is lost.

sudden event; afterwards, understanding, I suppose, what had happened, he began to laugh himself, too, how the butler had served me.

Zenophantes. But, however, you should never have had recourse to the short cut, for it would have come to you more safely by the high-road, even if a little more slowly.

VIII.

KNEMON, A LEGACY-HUNTER, LAMENTS TO HIS NEIGHBOUR DAMNIPPUS, THAT, WHEREAS HE HAD PUBLICLY, IN HIS WILL, BEQUEATHED ALL HIS WEALTH TO THE MILLIONAIRE HERMOLAUS, IN THE EXPECTATION THAT THE LATTER WOULD RECIPROCATE THE BENEFIT, HE, THE SPECULATING TESTATOR, BY HIS SUDDEN DEATH, HAD BEEN FRUSTRATED OF ALL HIS HOPES, AND, BESIDES, HAD LEFT HIS FAMILY DESTITUTE.

Knemon and Damnippus.

Knemon. Here is that saying of the proverb *come true*— "the fawn *slays* the lion." [1]

Damnippus. What are you so angry and indignant about, Knemon?

Knemon. Do you ask what I am indignant about? Miserably tricked, I have left an heir behind me, against my intention, and have passed over those whom most of all I should have wished to have my property.

Damnippus. How did that happen?

Knemon. I was in the habit of courting and flattering Hermolaus, the millionaire, who was childless, in the expectation of his dying *before me;* and he admitted my courtship with no unpleasurable feeling. It appeared to me, in fact, to be a clever device, that of registering my

---

[1] 'Ο νεβρὸς τὸν λέοντα (sup. αἱρεῖ). A Greek adage implying the occurrence of the unexpected—like the French proverb, " C'est l'impossible qui toujours arrive." Hemsterhuis traces it, through Plato, to Kritias. Cf. for other Greek proverbs, Ἀλιεύς. 9 ; Περὶ τῶν ἐπὶ Μισθῷ Συνόντων.

will in public, in which I have left him all my wealth, so that he might emulate my example and do the same.

Damnippus. What then, pray, did he?

Knemon. What he wrote in his own will I know not. I, however, died suddenly, by the fall of the roof of my house upon me; and now Hermolaus holds my property like some sea-wolf,[1] and has snatched away, too, the hook with the bait.

Damnippus. Not only so, but also yourself, the fisherman. So that you have devised your trick against yourself.

Knemon. I seem like it. On this account it is I am groaning and wailing.

IX.

POLYSTRATUS, A CENTENARIAN PLUTOCRAT, UPON ARRIVING IN HADES, NARRATES TO HIS FRIEND SIMYLUS HOW, BY REASON OF HIS GREAT WEALTH, HE HAD ENJOYED THE ADULATION OF THE WORLD AND AN ABUNDANCE OF GIFTS FROM SPECULATING FLATTERERS, AND HOW HE HAD DISAPPOINTED THEM ALL BY HIS WILL.

Simylus and Polystratus.

Simylus. Are you come to us at length, friend Polystratus, even you, after a life, I believe, not far short of the full century?

Polystratus. Ninety and eight years, Simylus.

Simylus. In what manner, pray, did you live the thirty years after me? For I died about the seventieth year of your existence.

Polystratus. Exceedingly pleasantly, however strange and paradoxical that shall seem to you.

Simylus. Paradoxical and strange indeed, that you, aged

---

[1] Λάβραξ (glutton). A species of fish-cormorant, but what exactly it represents in modern ichthyology is not clear. It was a common synonym with the Greek comic poets for a parasite and a glutton. See Athenæus, *passim.* The French equivalent is *loup de mer.*

and feeble, and childless into the bargain, were able to
find pleasure in life.

Polystratus. In the first place, I enjoyed universal power;
besides, I had many and handsome slave-boys, and very
elegant women, and unguents, and fragrant wine, and a more
than Sicilian table.[1]

Simylus. Strange news to me this, for I used to think
you exceedingly parcimonious.

Polystratus. Yes, but, my good friend, the good things
literally used to flow in upon me from the hands of others;
and from early morning they would come straight to my
doors in shoals, and afterwards all sorts of presents were
brought to me from every corner of the earth, the most
beautiful conceivable.

Simylus. Did you become an autocrat after my death,
Polystratus?

Polystratus. No, but I had ten thousand lovers.

Simylus (*holding his sides*). I couldn't help laughing.
You lovers, at your age, with four teeth in your head!

Polystratus. Yes, by heavens! the noblest in the State.
Even old as I was, and without a hair on my head, as you
see, and blear-eyed into the bargain, and my nose stuffed
with phlegm, they were beyond measure delighted to fawn
upon me; and happy was he among them, whomsoever I
merely looked at even.

Simylus. You did not, too, did you, like the Phaon[2] of
the story, carry some Aphrodite over in your boat from
Chios; and then she did not grant to your prayers to bo
young and handsome over again, and a suitable object of
love?

Polystratus. No; but I was the object of their eager desire,
just such as I am.

Simylus. You speak in riddles.

Polystratus. And yet this affection I speak of, with its

---

[1] Proverbial expression for "sumptuous gluttonies" (in Milton's
phrase). Cf. Plato, Πολιτ. iii.; Hor. iii. 1; Macrobius, *Saturnalia*, vii. 5.

[2] Phaon, an old and ugly boatman of Mytilene, in the island of
Lesbos, was metamorphosed into a young and handsome youth by
Aphrodite for having rowed her on one occasion over the sea, without
exacting his fare. His best title to immortality, however, is the love
of Sappho. See Athenæus (xiii. 70), who alleges another Sappho;
Ælian, I. Π. xii. 18.; Ov. *Sappho Phaoni.*

extravagant display in regard to childless and wealthy old gentlemen, is, surely, plain enough *in its origin.*

Simylus. Now I understand all about your charming face, admirable Sir ! that it was from the *golden* Aphrodite.[1]

Polystratus. However, my dear Simylus, I obtained not a few enjoyments from my lovers, and was all but worshipped by them, and I often behaved insolently to them, and closed my doors against some of them at times ; but they would contend with eager emulation, and surpass one the other in their lavish expense and delicate attentions to me.

Simylus. And, at last, pray, how did you devise in regard to your possessions ?

Polystratus. In public I was accustomed to declare that I had left each one of them my heir; and he believed it and equipped himself with more wheedling flattery than ever ; but, *all the time*, I held in my possession the other my real will, and left it behind me, with an injunction to one and all of them to go to the devil.

Simylus. And whom did your last *will* contain as your heir ?   Some one of your own family, I presume ?

Polystratus. By heaven, no, but a certain recently-purchased handsome boy, a Phrygian.

Simylus. About how old, friend Polystratus ?

Polystratus. Somewhere about the age of twenty.

Simylus. Now I understand what favours *he* conferred upon you.

Polystratus. But, however, he was much more worthy to be my heir than they, even though he was a foreigner and a plague ; whom even the great people themselves are already courting.   He, then, was my heir, and now he is received among the nobles of the land (shaved though his chin was,[2] and though he did not know a word of Greek), and is proclaimed to be more nobly born than Kodrus, handsomer than Nireus, and more prudent than Odysseus.[3]

---

[1] Χρυσῆς ’Αφροδίτης. An allusion to the well-known Homeric ascription—’Ιλ. iii. 64 ; ’Οδ. viii. 337. Cf. *Æn.* x. 16—" Venus Aurea."

[2] In the original, ὑπεξυρημένος, lit. " partly shaved." Slaves usually were made to wear the hair of the head closely cropped. Favourite slaves, *ministerio infami,* were shaved on their cheeks and chin. Cf. Τίμων, 22.

[3] Kodrus, according to legendary Greek History, was the last king

Simylus. I don't care about that. Let him even be Generalissimo of Hellas, if they please ; but only don't let *them* get his legacy.

X.

AN ALARMING NUMBER OF GHOSTS CROWD TO THE STYX. CHARON, FEARING FOR HIS BOAT, DIRECTS HERMES TO SEE THAT THEY WERE ENTIRELY STRIPPED OF THEIR VARIOUS INSIGNIA OF POWER, RANK, WEALTH, AND THE WEIGHTY LOAD OF VICES, BEFORE THEY ARE ADMITTED ON BOARD. MENIPPUS, WHO IS ONE OF THE PASSENGERS, AVAILS HIMSELF OF THE OPPORTUNITY FOR RIDICULING AND RAILING AT THE BEWAILING GHOSTS.

Charon, Hermes, and a number of Dead Men.

Charon. Just hear a moment how matters stand with us. Our little craft, as you observe, is a small one, and it is somewhat rotten, and leaks in most parts ; and, were it to incline to either side, it would completely overturn and go to the bottom ; and yet you come crowding together at the same time, each of you carrying a lot of luggage. If, then, you were to embark with all this, I am afraid that you may have reason to repent later, and especially as many of you as don't know how to swim.

Dead Men. What shall we do, then, to secure a safe passage ?

Charon. I will tell you. You must embark stripped of everything, and leave all these superfluous things upon the shore : for scarcely even so will the ferry-boat receive you.—But it will be your care, Hermes, from this moment, to receive none of them who should not come in light marching order, and throw away, as I said, his furniture and movable property. Now, take your stand near the

of Athens (cir. 1070 B.C.). In obedience to an oracle, he had saved his country by getting himself killed by the enemy; and his grateful subjects abolished monarchy in his honour. Cf. Cicero, *Quæst. Tusc.* i. 48, 116. Hor. *Car.* iii. 19. Nireus is celebrated in the *Iliad* as the "handsomest man," next to Achilleus, who marched against Ilium (ii. 671-674). Cf. Ov. *Ep. Ex Ponto,* iv. 13, 15. Propert, *Eleg.* iii. 16, 27. Hor. *Epod.* xv. 22. Nireus is often used by Lucian as the typical fop.

gangway, and narrowly examine them, and help them up, compelling them to embark stripped of everything.

Hermes. You say well, and so let us do.—Who is this first man here ?

Menippus. It is I, Menippus. There, see, Hermes, let my wallet-bag and my staff be both tossed away for good into your lake ; and as for my tattered cloak, I have obligingly not even brought it.

Hermes. Come on board, friend Menippus, best of men, and take the place of precedence, by the side of the helmsman, on deck, that you may supervise the whole of them. But this handsome fellow, who is he ?

Charmolaus. Charmolaus, of Megara, he who was so much run after, whose kiss was worth two talents.[1]

Hermes. So, then, pray, off with your good looks and your lips with their kisses and all, and that long, flowing hair,[2] and the blush on your cheeks, and your entire hide. 'Tis well; you are now succinctly equipped : come on board now. —And you there, the gentleman with the purple robe and the diadem, you with the grim countenance—who may you be?

Lampichus. Lampichus, autocrat of the Gelensians.[3]

Hermes. Why, pray, Lampichus, are you here with so many *valuables?*

Lampichus. What, then ? Ought a prince to come stripped of everything ?

Hermes. A prince, of course not—a dead man, certainly. So divest yourself of these things at once.

Lampichus. There, my wealth has been cast aside, at your pleasure.

---

[1] £480 of Attic coinage. Whether Charmolaus here is a real or a fictitious character is unknown.

[2] Cf. Θ. Δ. *passim.* Long hair was esteemed, in later times, at Athens, an especial mark of effeminacy. With the Comic poets it formed a frequent subject of ridicule. Aristophanes designates the dandy of the period as σφραγιδονυχαργοκομήτης, "a lazy, long-haired exquisite with rings up to his nails." In the Homeric age, long hair was the rule.

[3] Citizens of Gela, a wealthy city on the S. coast of Sicily, founded in the seventh century by Krete and Rhodes together. It was the *metropolis* ("mother city") of the more famous Agrigentum. Gela itself is most celebrated as having held the tomb of Æschylus. Of Lampichus no more is known than of Charmolaus, or Kraton ; but, if (as is probable) they are either historical or poetical characters, Lucian might have obtained his knowledge of them from a lost history or poem.

Hermes. Cast off at once, too, your bloated pride, Lampichus, and your superciliousness; for, if they be shipped with you, they will weigh the boat down.

Lampichus. Permit me, at all events, pray, to keep my diadem and my royal mantle.

Hermes. By no means—but leave them behind too.

Lampichus. Well, what more? for I have abandoned everything, as you see.

Hermes. Your cruelty and your folly, and your insolence and your rage, these you must abandon as well.

Lampichus. See, I am bare of everything, at your service.

Hermes. Come on board now.—Well, you fat, gross fellow, you with the loads of flesh, who may you be?

Damasias. Damasias, the athlete.[1]

Hermes. Yes, so it seems; for I know you from having frequently had a look at you in the Gymnasia.

Damasias. Yes, Hermes; but take me in, now that I am stripped and bare.

Hermes. Not stripped and bare, my fine Sir, so long as you are clothed in such lumps of flesh. So put them off, since you will sink our craft if you put but one foot on board. Yes, toss away at once, also, those crowns, and the records of your publicly-proclaimed victories.

Damasias. See, I am truly and actually stripped, at your service, as you see, and of equal weight with the rest of the dead men.

Hermes. It is better to be thus unweighted. So come on board.—And as for you, Kraton, strip yourself at once of your riches, and your effeminacy besides, and your luxury, and bring neither your funeral-robes[2] nor your

---

[1] He may be the Damasias of Amphipolis, recorded as crowned a victor at Olympia in the Olympiad cxv. Cf. Lucian, Λεξιφ. ii. In the earlier times of the great Panhellenic " Games," the athletes trained, we are assured, on the purest and simplest food. Pausanias ('Oλ. v.) records the name of the first *kreophagist* trainer. They became, at last, synonyms for gluttons and gross feeders. Ælian ('Ιστ. Ποικ. xiv. 7.) records that, on one occasion, the Spartan Ephors publicly threatened a very corpulent citizen (ὑπερσαρκοῦντα καὶ ὑπέρπαχυν) with severe punishment if he did not alter his diet, and cease to bring shame on Sparta and its laws.

[2] 'Εντάφια. They were, in the case of the rich, usually of the most costly kind. See Περὶ Πένθους, 11.

ancestral dignities, but leave behind both your pride of birth and vain-glory, and if ever the State by public proclamation has allowed you inscriptions on your statues, *leave them behind too;* nor bring us any story of their having piled a huge tomb over you. For even the very mention of these things makes a difference in the weight.

Kraton. It's against my will; however, I will cast them off; for what can I do?

Hermes (*seeing a General in full accoutrements*). Bless me! And you gentleman armed *cap-à-pied*, what do you want? or why are you carrying this trophy?

General. Because I gained a battle, and won the prize of valour,[1] and the State did me that honour.

Hermes. Leave your trophy upon Earth; for in Hades reigns peace, and there will be no need of weapons.—But this gentleman, so majestic in his dress, and who gives himself such airs in it, who elevates his eyebrows, who is wrapped in meditation, who is he—he, I mean, who wears the long, thick beard?[2]

Menippus. A species of philosopher (so-called), Hermes; but rather (in fact) a juggler and a fellow stuffed full of preternatural pretensions. So strip him too; for you will see many and truly ridiculous things stowed away under his cloak.

Hermes. Off you, in the first place, with your clothes; next, with all those things there. O Zeus! what arrogance he bears about him, and what ignorance, and disputation, and vain-glory, and useless questions, and thorny argumentations, and intricate conceits! Yes, and a vast

---

[1] The Athenians were accustomed publicly to decorate the soldier who had most distinguished himself in battle. The prize was a complete suit of armour (πανοπλία). So Plutarch, in his Life of Alkibiades, relates that Sokrates, who had saved the life and honour of his young and handsome comrade at Potidæa, and had thus deserved the ἀριστεῖον, relinquished it to his afterwards distinguished pupil.

[2] An amplitude of beard, ragged and untrimmed, was a characteristic of those who most aspired to the " philosophic " reputation—especially among the Cynics and Stoics—familiar to all readers of Lucian, and it figures largely in the Greek poets of the New Comedy. One of the wittiest of the productions of later Greek Satire is the Μισοπώγων of the Emperor Julian, directed against the witty but licentious people of Christian Antioch.

amount of vain labour, and trifling not a little, and non-sense, and frivolous talk, by heaven! (*producing the treasures concealed under the sophist's cloak*) and gold coin here, and hedonism, and shamelessness, and passion, and luxury, and effeminacy.[1] For they don't escape my observation, however well you conceal them about your person. Now, off this instant with your lying, and your swollen pride, and the notion that you are better than the rest of the world; since, if you were to come on board with all this, what ordinary ship of war[2] would ever take you?

Philosopher. I divest myself of them, then, since you so order.

Menippus. Nay, but let him put off, too, that beard, Hermes, heavy and shaggy, as you observe. There are, at the least, five pounds of hair.

Hermes. You are right. Off with that also.

Philosopher. And who will be the barber?

Hermes. Menippus here will take the ship-carpenter's axe and will chop it off, making use of the gangway as a block.

Menippus. No, Hermes; but hand me up a saw—for that will be more entertaining.

Hermes. The axe will do.—Well done! Now that you have divested yourself of your he-goatish odours, you turn out more like a man.

Menippus. Do you want me to remove a little from his eyebrows?

[1] Lucian, it will be observed, is even more severe upon *sham* philosophy than upon the positive crimes and vices of the powerful and wealthy—probably because, having come into nearer acquaintance with the philosophic pretenders, he had frequently experienced their revenge for his scornful treatment of them.

[2] Πεντήκοντορος. A fighting ship of fifty rowers, of the class *Moncris* —or "man of war," of a single bank of oars. The largest vessels, built by the Greeks, of which record is left, are those of Hiero, tyrant, or prince, of Syracuse, and of the Ptolemies. One belonging to Ptolemy Philopator had forty "banks," with dimensions of 420 ft. × 60 ft., and carried 7,000 sailors and marines, besides a large number of attendants, &c. The description of this and of another ship built by this prince and, still more, that of Hiero's, given in Athenæus from contemporary accounts—their extraordinary and extravagant equipment and decoration—almost surpasses the bounds of belief. To launch the latter the services of Archimedes were in requisition. See *Deipn.* v. 36-44.

XI.

KRATES AND DIOGENES, MEETING IN HADES, INDULGE THEIR
SATIRE ON THE SUBJECT OF THE FATES OF TWO MILLIONAIRE
MERCHANTS (COUSINS) WHO HAD BEEN CONSTANTLY PLOTTING,
IN THE USUAL MANNER, EACH FOR THE OTHER'S LEGACY, AND
WHO HAD BOTH PERISHED ON THE SAME DAY BY SHIPWRECK.
THE TWO EMINENT CYNICS CONGRATULATE THEMSELVES ON
THE RECOLLECTION OF THE VERY DIFFERENT CHARACTER OF
THEIR OWN OBJECTS IN LIFE.

Krates[1] *and Diogenes.*

Krates. You used, Diogenes, to know Mœrichus, the
rich fellow, the millionaire—him of Korinth, who owned
those numerous merchant-ships; whose cousin was Aristeas, himself, too, a plutocrat, who used to quote that
verse of Homer :—

"Let one or other lift his man." [2]

Diogenes. Why, Krates ?

Krates. They used to court and wheedle one the other
for the sake of the *expected* legacy (being of the same age),
and publicly registered their wills ; Mœrichus, if he should
die first, leaving Aristeas master of all his property, and
Aristeas Mœrichus, should he predecease the other.   Such

---

[1] A distinguished follower of Diogenes of Sinope. He had abandoned
a large fortune in order to attach himself to the doctrines and practice of
the School of Antisthenes.   Like his master, he lived upon the most
strictly frugal fare : in which abstinent living he was not surpassed by
Epikurus himself, or, perhaps, by any Christian ascetic of later ages.
His marriage was somewhat romantic.   His wife, Hipparchia, who
belonged to an aristocratic family, had united her fate with his, in spite
of great opposition from her friends ; and even declared her resolve to kill
herself, if they refused consent.   Krates, who left behind him some
writings, now lost, lived in the fourth century.   See Diog. Laert.

[2] 'Η μ'ἀνάειρ' ἢ ἐγὼ σέ. Lit. "Either do you lift me up, or I *will* you."
The speech of Telamonian Aias to Odysseus, in the wrestling encounter
between the two heroes.   See 'Ιλ. xxiii. 724.   The version above is
quoted from Prof. Newman's *Iliad of Homer*.   The application of the
Homeric verse by Aristeas is obvious.

were the terms of the wills ; while they were accustomed to surpass one the other in their mutual wheedling and flattery. The prophets, both those who divine the future from the stars, and those who divine from dreams, like the disciples of the Chaldæans—nay, even the Pythian himself —offered the victory now to Aristeas, now to Mœrichus ; and the scales were for inclining at one time in favour of the latter, and now again for the former.

Diogenes. What, pray, was the end of it, Krates ? For it is worth hearing.

Krates. Both have died on one and the same day, and the properties devolved unexpectedly upon Eunomius and Thrasykles—both relatives—who never even dreamed that this would happen. For, sailing across from Sikyon to Kirrha,[1] about the middle of the passage, they were over-taken by the west-north-west wind across their bows, and they were wrecked and lost.   •

Diogenes. It was very kind of them. Well, as for us, when we were in life, *we* entertained no such designs in regard to one another ; neither did *I* ever pray for the death of Antisthenes, that I might inherit his staff—and he used to have a pretty strong one, which he made for himself of wild olive ;[2] nor, I imagine, did *you*, Krates, eagerly desire to inherit my possessions at my death—my tub and my wallet, which held two quarts of lupines.

Krates. No, for I had no need of them ; neither had you, Diogenes : for what we needed, you inherited from Antisthenes, and I from you, possessions far better and more respectable than all the power of the Persians.

Diogenes. What are these possessions you speak of ?

Krates. Wisdom, self-sufficiency, truth, plain-speaking, freedom.

Diogenes. By my faith, yes. I remember also, that, having received this wealth in succession from Antisthenes, I left behind to you, in fact, still more.

---

[1] Sikyon, near Korinth ; Kirrha, a port of Phokis ; both in the Korinthian Gulf. For the wind called *Iapyx*, see Hor. *Car.* i. 3, iii. 27 ; Virg. *Æn.* viii. 710.

[2] Diogenes had reason to remember this fact. Upon his first approaching the founder of Cynicism, Antisthenes, we are informed, drove him away with blows from this same stick.

Krates. However, the rest of the world used to despise such kind of possessions, and no one of them courted *us*, looking to obtain our legacies ; but they all directed their looks to the gold coin.

Diogenes. With good reason ; for they had not where they could receive from us and *stow away* such possessions, gradually leaking and wasting away, as they were, under the influence of luxury, like rotten pouches. So that, if even one were to put into them either wisdom, or plainness of speech, or truth, it would immediately escape and run through, the bottom *of the vessel* not being able to hold it in ; something like what the daughters of Danaus, those famous maidens, experience when they draw water in their perforated pitcher : while as for the gold, they used to guard it with tooth and nail, and every possible contrivance.

Krates. Accordingly, *we* shall possess *our* wealth even here, while *they* will arrive carrying an obolus with them, and even that as far only as their ferryman.

XII.

ALEXANDER OF MACEDON AND HANNIBAL, QUARRELLING FOR PRECEDENCE, SUBMIT THE ARBITRAMENT OF THEIR CAUSE TO MINOS. EACH RECOUNTS HIS EXPLOITS. SCIPIO, THE CONQUEROR OF CARTHAGE, INTERVENES, AND PRONOUNCES IN FAVOUR OF ALEXANDER, CLAIMING THE SECOND PLACE FOR HIMSELF, AND ASSIGNING THE THIRD PLACE TO HANNIBAL.

Alexander, Hannibal, Minos, and Scipio.

Alexander. I ought to be preferred to you, you Libyan, for I am superior to you.

Hannibal. No, indeed ; rather, I ought *to have the precedence.*

Alexander. Let Minos decide then (*appealing to that judge*).

Minos. But *who* are you ?

Alexander. This is Hannibal of Carthage, and I am Alexander, the son of Philip.

Minos. Upon my word, illustrious, both of you! But what is your quarrel about?

Alexander. About precedence; for this fellow affirms that he was a better general than I; whereas I affirm that I surpass not only him, as every one knows, but almost all who have lived before me, in the arts of war.

Minos. Then let each speak in his turn.[1] And do you of Libya, be the first to speak.

Hannibal. In respect to this one circumstance, Minos, I derive much satisfaction—that while here I have thoroughly mastered the Greek language;[2] so that not even in that particular can he have any advantage over me. Now, I affirm that those men are most deserving of eulogy, who, though nothing at starting, none the less arrived at great eminence, by their own efforts investing themselves with power, and being deemed worthy of governing. Well, though I set out with few soldiers for Spain, at first being subordinate to my brother, I was judged to be the most skilful in war, and was deemed fit for the highest *employments;* and I subdued the Keltiberians, and conquered the Gauls of the West; and, crossing the vast mountains,[3] I overran all the plains of the Padus, and laid in ruins so many cities, and subjected to my power the whole plain of Italy, and advanced as far as the suburbs of its Capital city, and slew such numbers on one day that I measured off their rings by bushels,[4] and bridged their rivers with the dead. And all this I accomplished without either getting myself called the son of Ammon, or

[1] Cf. the Καίσαρες of the Emperor Julian.

[2] According to the testimony of the Latin historian, Cornelius Nepos, or Probus (as the case may be), Hannibal was so well versed in the Greek language as to have composed several works in it (*Vitæ Excel. Imper.*); so that Lucian, if the collocation of the words in the text is his own, as Hemsterhuis observes, does not do justice to the great commander's learning. Gesner proposed a slight transposition of the text, more in accord with the facts.

[3] See Livy, *Hist. Rom.* xxi. 35-37; Plutarch, Βίοι Παρ. The satire of Juvenal (x. 166) on this memorable exploit is well known :—

> "I, demens, et sævas curre per Alpes
> Ut placeas pueris et declamatio fias!"

[4] According to some historians, the number of the gold rings of the Roman officers killed at Cannæ amounted to several bushels. Livy

making claim to divinity, or recounting my mother's dreams;[1] but acknowledging myself to be human; and putting myself in competition with the most skilful generals, and engaging with the most warlike soldiers in the world—not contending against Medes and Armenians, who seek refuge in flight before any one pursues, and yield the victory at once to the bold aggressor. Alexander, on the other hand, enlarged a dominion which he had received from his father, and extended it considerably by availing himself of the start given him by Fortune. But, when he had gained the victory over and vanquished at Issus and Arbela[2] that wretched pest Dareius, revolting from the customs of his ancestors, he began to put forth claims to divine worship, and changed his way of life to the Median mode; and polluted his hands in the blood of his friends at his banquets, and seized them for the purpose of putting them to death.[3] Whereas I ruled my country upon terms of equality *with my fellow-citizens*, and when it summoned me to its aid, on the sailing of the enemy to Libya with a great armament, I obeyed with

inclines to one bushel only (xxiii. 12). To compare great things with small, Cannæ was the " Battle of the Spurs " of modern times, as far as similarity of spoil is concerned.

[1] The young King of Macedon was first saluted by the Egyptian priests as the son of Zeus Ammon (Amun), one of the divinities of the Egyptian theology, upon his visit to the oracular temple in the oasis of the African desert. See Arrian, Ἀνάβασις Ἀλεξ., and Plutarch. For the dream of Olympias, see Plutarch, Ἀλεξ. ii.

[2] The battle of Issus (B.C. 333) was fought near the city of that name in the extreme south-east of Cilicia, on the confines of Syria and the Lesser Asia. The Macedonians owed the victory as much to the unwieldy and heterogeneous masses of the enemy as to their own prowess. One of the finest of mosaics of ancient Greek art describes this subject. It was found in a mutilated state at Pompeii; and is supposed to be a copy of a painting of Apelles. The second great overthrow took place at Gaugamela.

[3] The friends and attendants of Alexander who fell victims to his intemperate fits of passion, or to his suspicions well or ill-founded, were Parmenion, to whose skill he owed, in great measure, his chief victories, and his son Philotus; Kleitus, his intimate friend and companion, who had saved his life at the battle of the Granikus, whom he murdered in a fit of intoxication at Baktra; his page, Hermolaus, who, with other alienated or disgusted Macedonians, had conspired against his master, in revenge for a public indignity; and Kleisthenes, a pupil of Aristotle. See Plutarch, Ἀλεξ. 49-55.

speed,[1] and offered myself as a private citizen ; and after condemnation, I bore the matter with good will. These achievements I performed, non-Greek as I was, and un-instructed by a Greek education; neither reciting and de-claiming Homer,[2] as he did, nor educated under Aristotle, that famous sophist; but availing myself of my natural good qualities alone. These are the points as to which I maintain that I am superior to Alexander. And, if this fellow has a handsomer appearance, because he was accus-tomed to encircle his brows with the diadem—with Mace-donians, doubtless, those things are objects of veneration —he surely should not on that account be thought superior to a man of genuine nobility and of true military capacity, who owed more to his judgment than to fortune.

Minos. He has delivered no ignoble plea, and one not such as it was likely a Libyan would, on his own behalf. Now, you, Alexander, what do you say to these arguments ?

Alexander. I ought, Minos, to make no reply at all to so impudent a man ; for Fame is quite enough to instruct you what a king I was, and what a *mere* brigand[3] he was. However, just consider if it is by a small difference I surpass him—I who while yet a mere youth entered upon public business, and became master of a kingdom all in a state of confusion, and pursued and punished my father's

---

[1] When the Romans, under the elder Scipio, carried the war into Africa, which resulted in their decisive victory at Zama, 202 B.C., Hannibal was driven from his country by a hostile faction, with Roman co-operation.

[2] Cf. Plutarch. Dion Chrysostom says that Alexander knew by heart the whole of the *Iliad*, and many parts of the *Odyssey* (Λόγοι iv.). His great exemplar and admiration was the hero of the *Iliad*, Achilleus, whose ideal form and features were infused into his portraits by his laureate-painter, Apelles. As for the character of Hannibal, Valerius Maximus allows to the great enemy of Rome some virtues, for " humani-tatis dulcedo etiam in efferata barbarorum ingenia penetrat " (*De Factis*, &c., v. 1).

[3] There were not wanting, as Hemsterhuis reminds us, some who attached this title to the father of the conqueror of the Persian Empire him-self. Demosthenes publicly stigmatized him as the λῃστῆς τῶν Ἑλλήνων (Φιλ. iv.), just as, in later times, there were some who characterized the Roman generals and armies as " latrones, communisque omnium liber-tatis raptores." Seneca assigns the same character to Alexander—*latro gentiumque vastator, &c. De Beneficiis*, i. 13. Cf. *De Benef.* v. 6.

assassins; and then, by the total destruction of Thebes having terrorized all Hellas, and having been elected by them to the command-in-chief, I did not think fit to confine my cares to my Macedonian dominions, and to be content to rule over what my father had left behind him; but, extending my thoughts to the whole Earth, and thinking it intolerable if I should not become master of the world, with a few soldiers I invaded Asia; and at the Granikus I gained a great battle; and seizing upon Lydia, Ionia, and Phrygia, and, in fine, conquering in succession everything in my way, I advanced to Issus, where Dareius awaited me with an army of many myriads. From that time, Minos, you know how many dead I sent below to you on one day; at all events, the Ferryman says that his boat did not suffice, at that time, for them, but that the majority of them constructed rafts for themselves, and so made the passage. And this I accomplished by being foremost in danger myself, and deeming it glorious to get myself wounded. Not to recount to you my exploits at Tyre, or at Arbela, *not only all that*, but I advanced as far as the Indians, and made for myself the Ocean the boundary of my empire; and I captured their elephants, and worsted Porus. And as for the Scythians, not a people to be despised with impunity, I crossed the Don and conquered them in a great cavalry battle. And I conferred benefits on my friends, and avenged myself on my enemies; and, if I appeared to men to be indeed divine, they are to be excused, in consideration of the greatness of my actions, for believing something of the kind about me. Finally, I died while yet a king, whereas this fellow *died* in exile at the court of Prusias of Bithynia, as it was right a man of the greatest villainy and cruelty should. For *how* he conquered the Italians I omit to say—that he did not do it by force, but by corruption, and not keeping faith,[1] and by stratagems; nothing according to the usages of war or above-board. And, as for his reproaching me with luxury, I think he has forgotten entirely what he was accustomed to do in Capua, living with ladies of the *demi-monde*, and, admirable General, wasting in pleasures the opportunities of war. I, on the

---

[1] "Punica fides" became proverbial with the Romans, but *Romana fides*, perhaps, would have been equally forcible.

other hand, if I had not esteemed the affairs of the West a small matter, and made my first attacks, rather, on the side of the East, what great achievement could I have done—seizing, without shedding a drop of blood, upon Italy, and subjecting to my power Libya and the continent as far as Gades? No; those parts of the world seemed to me not worth fighting for, being already cowed and acknowledging a master. I have said. Now do you, Minos, judge; for, out of many facts, these are quite enough *to decide by.*

Scipio. Not before you have heard me, too.

Minos. Why, who are you, my fine Sir? or as what countryman will you speak?

Scipio. An Italian;[1] Scipio, the general who razed Carthage, and conquered the Libyans in great battles.

Minos. What, pray, would you say?

Scipio. That I am inferior, indeed, to Alexander, but superior to Hannibal—I who vanquished and pursued him, and forced him to a disgraceful flight. How, then, is this fellow not ashamed to contend in rivalry with Alexander, with whom not even I, Scipio, his conqueror, claim to put myself in comparison?

Minos. By my faith, you speak the words of reason, Scipio; so let Alexander be judged to be first, next to him come you; then, by your leave, follows Hannibal third; for neither is he to be despised with impunity.[2]

---

[1] 'Ιταλιώτης. Properly a Greek resident in Italy; but sometimes, as here, used for 'Ιτάλος—an Italian.

[2] In the 'Αληθὴς 'Ιστορία, one of the wittiest and most entertaining of the works of Lucian, and the original of so many other satirical romances, Alexander and Hannibal are again introduced to us contending for precedence, in their posthumous existence, in the Island of the Blessed. On this occasion Rhadamanthys, who is the judge, assigns the first place, also, to the conqueror of Dareius, on a throne by the side of the founder of the Persian monarchy. Scipio does not figure in this scene; and it is a curious fact that no Roman is admitted into Lucian's Elysium. By Livy (xxxv. 14) Hannibal is represented as much more modest than he appears in this *Dialogue;* for, in reply to a question of Scipio, he pronounces Alexander to be the first of military commanders, Pyrrhus, King of Epeirus, second, and himself third; although, if he had been so fortunate as to conquer his questioner, as he had the other Roman generals, he would not have hesitated to give the precedence to himself. Cf. Appian, 'Ιστ. Ρωμ. xi. In

XIII.

DIOGENES JEERS AT ALEXANDER OF MACEDON FOR HIS LATE
PRETENSIONS TO DIVINITY, AT THE SAME TIME SATIRIZING
THE SERVILE ATTITUDE OF THE CONQUERED GREEK STATES
TOWARDS HIM. HE PROCEEDS TO REMIND THE ARROGANT
CONQUEROR OF ALL HIS VAIN POWER AND GLORY, AND
CASTS LARGE PART OF THE BLAME ON ALEXANDER'S PRE-
CEPTOR ARISTOTLE, FOR FLATTERING AND FOSTERING THE
PRIDE AND AMBITION OF HIS PUPIL. DIOGENES, FINALLY,
RECOMMENDS THE DEAD POTENTATE TO DRINK THE WATERS
OF THE RIVER LETHE.

Diogenes and Alexander.

Diogenes. What's this, Alexander? Have you, too, died,
like the rest of us ?

Alexander. You see for yourself *it is so*, Diogenes; but
it is nothing strange if, man as I was, I am dead.

Diogenes. Then Ammon lied in saying that you were his
son, while, in fact, you were Philip's ? [1]

Alexander. Philip's undoubtedly; for had I been
Ammon's, I should not have died.

Diogenes. Yet similar [2] stories used to be told of Olympias
—that a serpent visited her, and was seen in her bed; that

the Καίσαρες of Julian, Alexander is put in comparison with the
"Divine Julius." It is worth notice that the great Roman satirist, who
makes frequent use of the name of the arch-enemy of Rome, selects him
as an example, κάτ' ἐξόχην, of the nothingness of human glory :

> "Expende Hannibalem: quot libras in duce summo
>   Invenies ? "

Fontenelle, the most famous modern imitator of Lucian's *Dialogues of
the Dead*, has imitated this *Dialogue* in his *Jules César et Charles XII.*
(*Dialogues des Morts*).

[1] According to Plutarch, it was the ignorance of Greek on the part
of the priests of Ammon which assigned to him a divine father. Intending to greet him with the words Ὦ παιδίον, they addressed him as
Ὦ παῖ Διός (son of Zeus) a slight verbal error, which Alexander was
not anxious to correct.

[2] Hemsterhuis would substitute for ὅμοια of the received text ὁποῖα
(*qualia*). As for the prodigy of the Serpent, Scipio Africanus aspired
to the same semi-reptile origin. Livy, xxvi. 19. Cf. Ælian, Περὶ
Ζώων. xii. 30.

then you were born from such intercourse, and that Philip was altogether deceived in supposing you were of his begetting.

Alexander. I, too, like you, used to hear these tales; but now I see that neither my mother nor the Ammonian prophets spoke at all rationally.

Diogenes. But their lie was not unserviceable to you, Alexander, in regard to your exploits; for many were cowed, under the impression that you were a God. But, tell me, to whom have you. left behind this so great empire of yours?

Alexander. I don't know, Diogenes; for I had not made any arrangements about it beforehand, or only this much —that on my death-bed I gave over my ring to Perdikkas.[1] But, however, why do you laugh, Diogenes?

Diogenes. Why, at what else than the recollection of the doings of Hellas, that servilely flattered you, who had but just succeeded to the throne, and elected you to the hegemony and command-in-chief against the foreigners. And some even added you to the twelve *principal* deities,[2] both building to you temples and sacrificing to you as to a Serpent's son! But, tell me, where did the Macedonians bury you?

Alexander. I am still lying in Babylon, after three days, *unburied;* but Ptolemæus, of my foot-guards, promises, if ever he has leisure from the troubles immediately before him, to carry me away to Egypt and bury me there, so that I may become one of the Egyptian divinities.

---

[1] One of the principal generals of Alexander. Appointed to the regency, and trusting to this mark of confidence on the part of his dying master, he laid claim to the supremacy. He was defeated, and slain by his own troops, in Egypt, while making war on Ptolemæus Soter, 321 B.C.

[2] The *Dii Majores*, as they were called in the Latin theology, who, in the Homeric and Hesiodic theogony, occupy, as the third dynasty, the summits of Mount Olympus. See Plutarch's fine reflection upon the perverse *titular* ambition of the kings and conquerors. Eulogizing the just moderation of Aristeides, he remarks:—Ὅθεν ἀνὴρ πένης καὶ δημοτικὸς ἐκτήσατο τὴν βασιλικωτάτην καὶ θειοτάτην προσηγορίαν—τὸν Δίκαιον. Ὁ τῶν βασιλέων καὶ τυράννων οὐδεὶς ἐζήλωσεν, ἀλλὰ Πολιορκηταὶ καὶ Κέραυνοι καὶ Νικάτορες, ἔνιοι δ' Ἀετοὶ καὶ Ἱέρηκες ἔχαιρον προσηγορεοόμενοι· τὴν ἀπὸ τῆς βίας καὶ τῆς δυνάμεως, ὡς ἔοικε, μᾶλλον ἢ τὴν ἀπὸ τῆς ἀρετης δόξαν ἀγαπῶντες (Βίοι Παρ. Ἀριστ.).

Diogenes. May I not, pray, be excused for laughing, Alexander, at seeing you even in Hades still playing the fool, and expecting to become an Anubis or Osiris? But, however, don't for a moment expect it, most respectable of godships; for it is not allowed to any of those who have once crossed the Lake, and passed within this side of the mouth *of the Cavern,* to go back up *to Earth.* For Æakus is not so careless, nor is Kerberus so easily to be despised. However, I would gladly learn this from you—how you endure, whenever you reflect upon it, *the thought* of how much happiness you have left behind, above ground, to come here — body-guards, your picked corps of shield-bearers,[1] and satraps, and gold in such heaps, and adoring nations, and Babylon and Baktra, and the huge elephants, and honour, and glory, and the riding *in your chariot* with all the insignia of your rank, with your head encircled with a white fillet,[2] arrayed in a brooch-fastened purple robe. Do not these things cause you grief, when they recur to your memory?—Why do you weep, fool? Did not the wise Aristotle instruct you even so much as that—not to suppose the gifts of Fortune to last for ever?

Alexander. He wise, who was the most inveterate of all flatterers?[3] Just let me alone for having some know-

---

[1] Ὑπασπιστάς. The name given to the select body-guard of foot soldiers formed by Alexander. They numbered 3,000 men, and acted a considerable part in the achievements of the Macedonian army. Their splendid *shields* gave them their distinguishing name. Besides these were a body-guard called *Argyraspids,* " with the silver shields." But the most magnificent " household-troops " were the " horse-guards," 1,200 in number, in imitation of the Persian " Immortals."

[2] Ταινία. The original form of the *diadem.* A narrow band of white wool, worn by the Persian monarchs round the *tiara.* Cf. Xenophon, Κυροπαιδεία, viii. 3 ; Arrian, Ἀνάβασις, vii. 22. In Greek dress, it was the narrow band worn by women under the bosom, beneath the *chiton.* See Becker, *Charicles.*

[3] Plutarch quotes letters from Alexander to Antipater and Kassander, in which the pupil of the Stageirite charges his former preceptor with the same courtier-like behaviour. As for the charge of extorting large sums of money, the great natural philosopher expended at least a great part of the gift in making his great Zoological Collection, the outcome of which is preserved to us in his Ζώων Ἱστορία. Cf. the Πράσις Βίων. For the Τἀγαθόν, (*summum bonum*), see Plato Πολ. vi ; and cf. Cicero, *De Fin.* v. 6., &c.

ledge of the character of Aristotle—how many things he begged of me, what sort of letters he sent me, and how he abused my zeal for learning, cajoling and eulogizing me now for my beauty (as though that, too, were a part of "the *summum bonum*"), and now for my actions and riches; for, indeed, he was used to consider that, also, " a good," so that he did not blush, even himself, to take it— a juggling fellow, Diogenes, and a crafty trickster. But, however, this benefit I have gained from his philosophy —to be grieved at the loss of those things as the greatest "goods," which you but just now enumerated.[1]

Diogenes. Well, know you what you should do? I will suggest to you a remedy for your grief. Since hellebore[2] does not grow hereabouts, do you, at least, even gulp down and drink with wide-opened mouth forthwith the waters of Lethe, and drink again and often; for thus will you cease to be troubled at " the goods " of Aristotle. —Why, really, I see the Kleitus *you know about*, and Kallisthenes, and many others rushing towards you, as though they would tear you in pieces, and wreak their vengeance upon you for what you did to them. So step off you by this other path, and [*shouting after him*] drink often, as I told you.

[1] Plutarch quotes a letter from Alexander to Aristotle, in which he finds fault with him for publishing to the world his *esoteric* teaching (τοὺς ἀκροαματικοὺς τῶν λόγων), and so depriving him of the *sole* possession of such lucubrations.

[2] A plant which grew, in particular, in two places—Anticyra, a small island off Phokis, and Anticyra in Thessaly—hence often used as synonyms for hellebore itself—having reputation in Greece and Italy as a specific for madness, and recommended by the authority of Hippokrates. Cf. Aristoph. Σφῆκες, 1489; the poets of the New Comedy, *passim;* Strabo, ix. ; Pliny, *Hist. Nat.* xxv. 5; Plautus, *Pseudolus*, iv. 7; Persius, *Sat.* iii. 63, iv. 16, v. 100; Juv. *Sat.* xiii. 96, 97; Hor. *Sat.* ii. 3, *Epist.* ii. 2; Lucian, *passim.*

XIV.

PHILIP, KING OF MACEDON, RIDICULES HIS SON ALEXANDER'S ABSURD ARROGANCE IN CLAIMING TO BE THE SON OF AMMON, AND CALLS IN QUESTION THE GREATNESS OF HIS MILITARY ACHIEVEMENTS.   ALEXANDER DEFENDS HIMSELF.

Philip and Alexander.

Philip. Now then, Alexander, you will not be for denying that you are my son; for, had you been Ammon's, you had not died.

Alexander. Nor was I myself ignorant, father, that I am the son of Philip and grandson of Amyntas; but I accepted the oracle as supposing it to be of service to the success of my undertakings.

Philip. What do you say? Did it appear to you to be of advantage—the giving yourself up to be deceived out-and-out by the prophets?

Alexander. Not that; but the non-Greeks were struck with consternation, and not one of them any longer resisted, thinking that they were fighting with a divine being; so that I kept gaining victories over them with the greater ease.

Philip. And what people worth fighting with did *you* gain victories over, you who always came into conflict with cowards, defending themselves with miserable bows and paltry light shields, and Persian bucklers of osier-twigs? [1] To conquer Hellenes—Bœotians, Phokians, and Athenians —was an achievement, and to utterly defeat the heavy-armed troops of Arkadia, and the Thessalian cavalry, and the javelin-armed soldiers of Elis, and the Mantineian

---

[1] Πελτάρια καὶ γέρρα οἰσύϊνα.   The Πέλται were a light kind of shield covered with leather, adopted from the Thracians by Iphikrates, the famous Athenian military commander, about 390 B.C.   With his *peltasts* Iphikrates gained some decided victories over the heavily-armed Spartans.   The γέρρον, also, was a light, wicker-made shield, oblong in shape, and covered with ox-hide, used chiefly by the Persian troops. See Herod. vii. 75; Xen. Κυροπ. vii. 1, 33.

peltasts, or Thracians, or Illyrians, or Pœonians—those *were* great deeds.[1] But as for Medes, and Persians, and Babylonians, and gold-equipped and effeminate soldiers, do you not know that ten thousand men, who marched up with Klearchus, vanquished them before your time; while they did not endure even *so much as* to come to close conflict, but fled before an arrow reached them?

Alexander. But the Scythians, father, and the elephants of the Hindus was not a kind of work to be lightly despised. And yet, without stirring up dissensions among them, or purchasing my victories with treasons, I got the mastery over them; nor did I ever perjure myself, or falsify my promise, or commit any breach of faith for the sake of conquest. And, as regards the Hellenes, while some I received under my dominion without bloodshed, as for the Thebans, you probably know by report how I punished *them.*

Philip. I know all this; for Kleitus brought me word, whom you murdered with your own hand while at dinner by running him through with a hunting-spear, because he dared to eulogize me by comparison with your deeds. Well, you threw aside the Macedonian short cloak and exchanged it, as they say, for the Persian flowing robe,[2] and put on your head the towering tiara, and claimed divine honours from the Macedonians, from free people,—and the most ridiculous circumstance of all,—you were accustomed to imitate the manners of the conquered! I omit to mention all your other *bad* actions,—your shutting up men of culture with lions,[3] and contracting marriages of such a kind

---

[1] Philip refers to his own military exploits. He owed, however, as much to gold as to steel. See the Λόγοι of Demosthenes. Cf. Hor. *Car.* iii. 16.

[2] The χλάμυς was worn originally, or chiefly, by horsemen. The κάνδυς of the Persians was a thoroughly oriental sort of dress. The *chlamys*, adopted from the Macedonians, was put on by the Athenian when he had attained the age of an *ephebus.* See Plutarch, 'Αλεξ. 45.

[3] A rhetorical exaggeration, if not altogether a myth. Several writers have recorded the story of the imprisonment of Lysimachus (one of the most distinguished of the Macedonian generals, who afterwards possessed himself of the dominions of Alexander) in a lion's den. They assert that, like his anti-type Richard "Cœur de Lion," he killed the wild beast by his natural arms alone, and in consequence

as you did,[1] and entertaining an excessive affection for Hephæstion.[2] One circumstance only that I have heard I commend—your keeping your hands off the wife of Dareius, who was a beautiful woman, and your taking care of his mother and his daughters : for that was conduct becoming a prince.

Alexander. But my eagerness to incur dangers, father, do you not praise, and the fact that at Oxydrakæ I was the first to leap down within the fortifications, and received so many wounds ?[3]

Philip. I don't commend this conduct, Alexander, not because I don't think it to be honourable for the king sometimes to get wounded, and to incur danger on behalf of his army, but because such conduct least of all suited *your* character. For if, with the reputation of being divine, you had ever received a wound, and they had seen you carried out of the battle in a litter, flowing with blood, groaning by reason of the pain from the wound, that had been subject for ridicule to the spectators, how even

of this display of courage was pardoned by his king. Curtius (*De Rebus Gestis Alex.* viii.) assigns the origin of the legend to an encounter of Lysimachus with a lion of heroic size in Syria. Justin (*Hist. Philip,* xv. 3), a later writer, credits the more sensational account.

[1] With Roxana, the Baktrian princess, captured in the Fort of Sogdiana (327 B.C.). His second wife, Stateira, a daughter of the Persian king Dareius, was afterwards treacherously murdered at Babylon by her rival Roxana, who herself, with her son, was murdered by Kassander in 311 B.C.

[2] A native of Pella in Macedonia, one of the two especial " favourites " of Alexander, with whom he had been brought up as a foster-brother. He died at Ekbatana, in 325. The extravagance of the grief and mourning of Alexander is well known. Horses were shorn, the walls of cities pulled down, and the physician whose accidental neglect had caused or hastened the favourite's death was crucified. Upon his tomb 10,000 talents (about two millions and a half) were expended. The other chief favourite, Kraterus, between whom and Hephæstion frequent quarrels arose, as related by Plutarch ('Αλέξανδρος) served as a principal *medium* between his royal patron and the Macedonian officers, as Hephæstion for the Orientals.

[3] Oxydrakæ, a people of Hindustan inhabiting what is now called the Punjaub. Arrian (vi. 11) rejects the story. Diodorus and Plutarch join together the Malli and Oxydrakæ on the occasion. Plutarch tells us that the breaking of the scaling-ladder forced Alexander to leap down into the midst of the enemy, who were so much alarmed by the flashing of his armour that they took to flight.

Ammon had been convicted of being a mere juggler and false prophet, and the prophets of being mere flatterers. Or who would not have laughed at seeing the son of Zeus swooning, begging the aid of his physicians? For now, when you are dead in fact, do you not suppose there are many who make cutting sarcasms upon that pretension of yours, when they see the corpse of the god lying stretched out, already clammy with decay and swollen out, according to the law of all bodies? Besides, even that, which you were saying was of service to you, Alexander, the fact of your easily conquering by this means—it deprived you of much of the glory of your actual successes; for, thought to be achieved by a divine being, anything would appear to fall short *of what it ought to have been.*

Alexander. These are not the thoughts men have about me—on the contrary, they put me in rivalry with Herakles and Dionysus;[1] indeed, I was the only one to conquer that famous Aornos,[2] neither of them having got possession of it.

Philip. Do you observe that you are talking of these exploits as though you were son of Ammon, in comparing yourself with Herakles and Dionysus? And do you not blush, Alexander, and will you not unlearn even that puffed-up pride of yours, and know and perceive yourself to be now a mere dead man?[3]

---

[1] Because those divinities had preceded him in the invasion of India. From the Nysa in the Punjaub, Dionysus, according to some authorities, derived his name.

[2] A hill-fort on the Indus, ἡ ἄορνος πέτρα, "the rock inaccessible to birds." See Curtius, *De Gestis Alex.* viii. 11.

[3] Among the modern imitators of Lucian, Fontenelle and Lord Lyttelton have treated this subject not unworthily of their master. In the dialogue, *Alexandre et Phrine* (Phryne), the celebrated original of the *Aphrodite Anadyomene*, after a comparison of her conquests to those of her quondam admirer, concludes: "Quand on ne veut que faire du bruit, ce ne sont pas les caractères les plus raisonables qui y sont les plus propres." She also makes the, perhaps, too philosophic reflection : " Si je retranchois de votre gloire ce qui ne vous en appartient pas, si je donnois à vos soldats, à vos capitaines, au hazard même, la part qui leur en est dûe, croyez-vous que vous n'y perdissiez guère ?"—*Dialogues des Morts.* Cf. Lyttelton's *Alexander the Great and Charles XII.*

XV.

ANTILOCHUS, THE SON OF NESTOR (ONE OF THE GREEK HEROES
WHO FELL DURING THE SIEGE OF ILIUM), REMONSTRATES WITH
HIS FRIEND ACHILLEUS FOR HAVING GIVEN UTTERANCE TO
THE WORDS .PUT INTO HIS MOUTH BY THE POET OF THE
ODYSSEY—THAT HE WOULD RATHER BE A SLAVE ON EARTH
THAN KING IN HADES—SHOWS HIM THE USELESSNESS OF
REGRETS IN THE UNDER-WORLD, AND, AT THE SAME TIME,
ATTEMPTS TO CONSOLE HIM WITH THE REFLECTION THAT HE
IS FAR FROM BEING ALONE IN HIS FATE. ACHILLEUS TAKES
THE ADMONITION OF HIS FRIEND IN GOOD PART, BUT REFUSES
TO BE COMFORTED.

Antilochus and Achilleus.

Antilochus. What sort of language was that, Achilleus,
you addressed to Odysseus the day before yesterday about
death; how ignoble and unworthy of both your teachers,
Cheiron and Phœnix![1]   For I overheard you, when you
were saying that you would wish to be a servant, bound to
the soil, in the house of any poor man "whose means of
support were small,"[2] rather than to be king over all
the dead. These sentiments, indeed, some abject Phrygian,
cowardly, and dishonourably clinging to life, might, perhaps,
be allowed to utter, but for the son of Peleus, the most
rashly daring of all heroes, to entertain so ignoble thoughts
about himself, is a considerable disgrace, and a contradic-
tion to your actions in life; you who, though you might

---

[1] Cheiron, the most renowned of the Kentaurs, had instructed the
father of Achilleus also—in the art of obtaining an immortal wife,
Thetis. He was slain accidentally by Herakles with his poisoned arrows.
Phœnix, the Dolopian prince, who had been forced to flee from his
country on account of having seduced his father's mistress, and had
found refuge at the court of Peleus, was appointed by him his son's
tutor.

[2] An allusion to the confession of Achilleus to Odysseus in Hades :—

Βουλοίμην κ' ἐπάρουρος ἐὼν θητευέμεν ἄλλῳ
Ἀνδρὶ παρ' ἀκλήρῳ, ᾧ μὴ βίοτος πολὺς εἴη,
Ἡ πᾶσιν νεκύεσσι καταφθιμένοισιν ἀνάσσειν.

Od. xi. 488-490; Cf. *Æn.* vi. ; Plato, Πολ. iii. (*ad init.*), deprecates the
sentiment.

have reigned ingloriously a length of time in Pthiotis, of your own accord preferred death with fair fame.[1]

Achilleus. But, O son of Nestor, at that time I was still unacquainted with the state of things here, and was ignorant which of those two conditions was the better, and used to prefer that wretched paltry glory to existence ; but now I already perceive how profitless it is, even though the people above ground shall parrot-like sing its praises to the utmost of their power. With the dead there is perfect sameness of dignity ;[2] and neither those good looks of mine, Antilochus, nor my powers of strength are here : but we lie all alike under the same murky gloom, and in no way superior one to the other; and neither the dead of the Trojans have fear of me, nor do those of the Achæans pay me any court : but there is complete and entire equality in address, and a dead man is the same *all the world over*— " both the coward and the brave."[3] These thoughts cause me anguish, and I am grieved that I am not alive and serving as a hireling.

Antilochus. Yet what can one do, Achilleus ? For such is the will of Nature—that all certainly die : so one must abide by her ordinance, and not be grieved at the constituted order of things. Besides, you observe how many of us, your friends, are about you here. And, after a short space of time, Odysseus, too, will certainly arrive ; and community in misfortune, and the fact that one is not alone in suffering, brings comfort. You see Herakles and Meleager ;[4]

---

[1] Yet the *invulnerable* hero of the *Iliad* frequently bewails his apportioned brief career—μινυνθάδιον περ ἐόντα.

[2] Elsewhere termed by Lucian ἰσοτιμία. Cf. *Ecclesiastes, passim.* Seneca, *De Irâ*, iii. 43. " Venit ecce Mors, quæ nos pares faciat. Ridere solemus," he proceeds, " inter matutina arenæ spectacula, tauri et ursi pugnam inter se colligatorum : quos cum alter alterum vexârit, suus confector expectet. Idem facimus : aliquem nobiscum alligatum lacessimus, &c."

[3] Ἐν δὲ ἰῇ τιμῇ ἠμὲν κακος ἠδὲ καὶ ἐσθλός, the words of Achilleus to Odysseus ('Ιλ. ix. 319).

[4] The principal hero in the famous Calydonian hunt of the wild boar, whose conquest needed all the chivalry of Hellas ; who in fleetness, if not in prowess, were surpassed by the virgin Atalanta, with whom at first they had refused to associate in that arduous enterprise. The Calydonian prince had, also, been one of the Argonautic heroes. See Apollonius, 'Αργ. i. and cf. 'Ιλ. ix. 525-600.

and other admired heroes, who, I imagine, would not accept *the offer of* a return to the upper regions, if one were to send them back to be hired servants to starvelings and beggars.

Achilleus. Your exhortation is friendly and well meant : but, I know not how, the remembrance of things in life troubles me, and I imagine it does each one of you, too. However, if you do not confess it openly, you are in that respect worse off, in that you endure it in silence.

Antilochus. No, rather better off, Achilleus, for *we* see the uselessness of speaking *about it.* And we have come to the resolution to keep silence, and to bear, and put up with it, not to incur ridicule, as you do, by indulging such wishes.

XVI.

DIOGENES, THE CYNIC, EXPRESSES HIS ASTONISHMENT TO HERAKLES AT SEEING THE SON OF ZEUS IN HADES, LIKE THE REST.   THAT HERO PRETENDS THAT HIS ACTUAL SELF IS IN HEAVEN, WHILE IT IS HIS *eidolon,* OR PHANTOM, WHICH IS AMONG THE DEAD.

Diogenes and Herakles.

Diogenes. Is not this Herakles ? It is, indeed, no other, by Herakles !—the bow, the club, the lion's skin, the bulk —it is Herakles all over.   Then, with all his being son of Zeus, has he died for good and all ? Tell me, " O glorious victor," [1] *are you* a dead man ? for I used to offer sacrifice to you above ground, as if you were divine.

Herakles. And you did perfectly right; for the true

---

[1] Καλλίνικε. So called from a hymn to him by Archilochus, sung at the Olympic Games, beginning with Καλλίνικ' ἄναξ Ἡράκλεις.— Bourdin.

Herakles himself is in the company of the Gods in heaven, and

> " Enjoys Hebe of the beautiful ancles," [1]

while I, his ghost, am here.

Diogenes. What—a ghost of a God ?   And is it possible for one to be a God in one half *of one's person,* and to have died in the other half ?

Herakles. Yes : for *he* has not died, but I, his simulacrum.

Diogenes. I understand.   He handed you over as a substitute, in place of himself, to Pluto ; and you, therefore, are a dead man in the stead of that hero.

Herakles. Something of the sort.

Diogenes. How, pray, did Æakus, who is so particular, not distinguish you were not he, but accepted a supposititious Herakles,[2] as soon as ever he appeared ?

Herakles. Because I resembled him so exactly.

Diogenes. You speak the truth : for so exactly *do you resemble him* that you are he.   Consider a moment, however, whether the contrary is not the case—you, in fact, are *the* Herakles, while it's your ghost that has married Hebe in heaven.

Herakles. You are an insolent and prating fellow ; and, if you don't stop your jeering at me, you shall presently know of what sort of God I am ghost.

Diogenes. Your bow, indeed, is out of its case,[3] and ready to hand : but I,—why should I, once dead, any longer be

---

[1]   Καὶ ἔχει καλλίσφυρον Ἥβην.
The whole Dialogue is a parody of the account in the *Odyssey* of the interview of the hero (among other ἀμενήνα καρήνα of celebrities in Hades) with that of the son of Alkmene :—

ἐσενόησα βίην Ἡρακληείην
Εἴδωλον· αὐτὸς δὲ μετ' ἀθανάτοισι Θεοῖσι
Τέρπεται ἐν θαλίῃς καὶ ἔχει καλλίσφυρον Ἥβην
Παῖδα Διὸς μεγάλοιο καὶ Ἥρης χρυσοπεδίλου.
            Ὀδ. xi. 600-604.

The visit of Odysseus to the infernal regions, or, at least, his method of conjuration, it must be admitted, is barbarous enough to excuse severer satire than even that of Lucian.

[2] Ἀντανδρὸν. A word peculiar to Lucian. Cf. Κατάπλους ἢ Τύραννος, the offer of the tyrant Megapenthes to Klotho :—εἰ βούλεσθε δὲ, καὶ ἀντανδρὸν ὑμῖν ἀντ' ἐμαυτοῦ παραδώσω τὸν ἀγαπητόν.

[3] Parody of Ὀδ. xi. 606.

afraid of you ?   But tell me, in the name of your own
Herakles—when he was alive, did you associate with him
at that time as his ghost; or, were you one and the same
during your life, and, when you died, did you separate and
did he fly off to heaven, and you, the ghost, as was natural,
come to Hades ?

Herakles. I ought not even to have replied to a man who
talks thus lightly.   However, pray, just hear this, too.   As
much as there was of Amphitryon in Herakles,[1] that has
died, and I am all that; but what there was of Zeus is
living with the Gods in heaven.

Diogenes. Now I clearly understand.   For Alkmene gave
birth, you imply, to two Herakleses at the same time—the
one by Amphitryon, and the other from Zeus; so that, without its being known, you were twins, born of the same
mother.

Herakles. No, vain trifler: why, we both were one and
the same person.

Diogenes. It's not so easy to understand this—that there
were two Herakleses compounded into one—excepting, perhaps, in the manner, as it were, of some hippocentaur, you
had grown together, man and god.

Herakles. What ! don't you suppose all men to be so composed of two parts—soul and body ?   So what is to hinder
the soul from being in heaven, which was from Zeus, and
the mortal part—myself—from being with the dead ?

Diogenes. Nay, most excellent son of Amphitryon, you
would have fairly advanced that argument if you were a
body ; but now you are a bodiless ghost.   So you are
perilously near making Herakles just now into a trinity.

Herakles. How a trinity ?

Diogenes. In this way about.   If the one, whoever it is,
is in heaven, and the one who is with us are you the ghost,
while your body has already been dissolved and become
dust on Æta,[2] these surely are three.   And consider, therefore, whom you will devise for the third parent for your
body.[3]

Herakles. You are an impudent and sophistical fellow.
And who, pray, may you happen to be, too ?

---

[1] See Θ. Δ. x.   [2] See Θ. Δ. xiii. and Ἑρμοτίμος, vii.

[3] Hemsterhuis quotes a Latin epitaph which divides the human

Diogenes. The ghost of Diogenes, the Sinopian. But, on my faith, *he* is not "with the Gods immortal"[1]: nay, rather, I associate with the best of the Dead, and laugh heartily at Homer and such like frigid nonsense.

XVII.

MENIPPUS DERIDES THE FABLE AND FATE OF TANTALUS.[2]

Menippus and Tantalus.

Menippus. Why weep you, Tantalus, or why stand you by the lake and bemoan yourself ?

Tantalus. Because, Menippus, I am dying of thirst.

Menippus. Are you so lazy as not to stoop and drink, or, by all that's sacred, even to draw up *water* in the hollow of your hand ?

Tantalus. No good, if I were to stoop down, for the water flees away whenever it feels me approaching it. And if even, too, I drew any up and put it to my mouth, I have not wetted the tip of my lips, before somehow or other it

animal into four distinct elements, destined for as many separate habitations:—

> "*Bis duo sunt homines—manes, caro, spiritus, umbra;*
> *Quattuor has partes tot loca suscipiunt.*
> *Terra tegit carnem, tumulum circumvolat umbra,*
> *Orcus habet manes, spiritus astra petit.*"

[1] The well-known hemistich from the *Iliad.*

[2] Another satire on the poet of the *Odyssey*, and on the received theology :—

> Τάνταλον εἰσεῖδον, χαλέπ' ἄλγε' ἔχοντα
> "Εσταοτ' ἐν λίμνῃ—

Cf. Ov. *Met.* iv. 458 ; Hor. *Sat.* i. 68 ; *Epod.* xvii. 66, &c. ; Lucian, Περὶ Πένθους, Νεκρομαντεία. Euripides ("Ορεστ. 5) repeats another account of his torture, by which he floats in the 'Tartarean air, and is in constant terror from a rock suspended over his head : a version of the fable which Lucretius follows :—

> " Nec miser impendens magnum timet aere saxum
> Tantalus, ut famast, cassà formidine torpens.
> Sed magis in vitâ," &c.   *De Rer. Nat.* iii. 900.

flows through my fingers, and leaves my hand again as dry as ever.

Menippus. Your experience is somewhat of the miraculous, Tantalus. But tell me why, pray, have you even any need to drink? For you have no body; but that which could suffer hunger and thirst, lies buried somewhere in Lydia: and as for you, the spirit, how can you any longer be thirsty, or drink?

Tantalus. That's the very *nature* of the punishment—that my spirit should thirst as though it were body.

Menippus. Well, I will believe it to be so, since you declare you are being punished by the feeling of thirst. But what, pray, will there be terrible to you in that? Is it that you fear *dying* from want of something to drink? *But that can't be,* for I do not observe another Hades after this one, or another death *to go to,* from here to another place?

Tantalus. You are right, and this, in fact, is part of my sentence—the longing to drink, without having any need to do so.

Menippus. You talk nonsense, Tantalus; and you seem truly enough to be in need of a draught—unmixed hellebore, by heaven!—who have experienced a fate the opposite to that of those who have been bitten by mad dogs,[1] since you are afraid, not of water, but of thirst.

Tantalus. Not even hellebore, Menippus, do I refuse to drink; let me only have it.

Menippus. Keep up your spirits, Tantalus, since neither you nor anyone else of the Dead will drink: for it's an impossibility. However, not all, like you, by the terms of their sentence, thirst for water that will not stay for them.

---

[1] "Mad" dogs, evidently, were not unknown in ancient cities, maddened, doubtless, by much the same causes as in modern days— terror, ill-treatment, bad, and insufficient food. Horace numbers them among the terrors of the streets of Rome. For a panic excited by a supposed mad donkey, see Apuleius, *De Aureo Asino.* Cf. Goldsmith, *Citizen of the World,* lxix.

XVIII.

MENIPPUS DESIRES HERMES TO POINT OUT TO HIM THE BEAU-
TIFUL WOMEN AND HANDSOME MEN CELEBRATED BY THE
POETS. HERMES SHOWS HIM THE GHOSTS OF THE MOST
FAMOUS OF THEM, AND, IN PARTICULAR, THAT OF HELENE.
MENIPPUS CYNICALLY EXPRESSES HIS ASTONISHMENT THAT
A BARE SKULL SHOULD HAVE CAUSED A GREAT WAR, AND
THE DEATHS OF SO MANY THOUSANDS.

Menippus and Hermes.

Menippus. And where are the *belles* and the *beaux*,
Hermes? Be my *cicerone*, for I am a new arrival.

Hermes. I have no leisure, Menippus: look carefully,
however, at that spot, to the right, where are Hyakinthus,
and Narkissus, and Nireus, and Achilleus, and Tyro, and
Helene, and Leda,[1] and in fine all the beauties of old?

Menippus. I see only bones and skulls, bare of flesh,[2] for
the most part all alike.

Hermes. Yet these are the bones that all the poets rave
about, which you appear to contemn.

---

[1] Propertius (*Eleg.* ii. 21), in praying for the safety of his mistress,
recounts some of the famous beauties of Greek antiquity, who, he thinks,
ought to be enough to satisfy Pluto :—

> " Sunt apud infernos tot millia Formosarum :
> Pulchra sit in superis, si licet una locis.
> Vobiscum est Iole, vobiscum candida Tyro,
> Vobiscum Europe, nec proba Pasiphae.
> Et quot Iona tulit, vetus et quot Achaia Formas,
> Et Thebæ, et Priami diruta regna senis."

Cf. Θ. Δ. ii. Tyro and Leda were among the many *belles* who appeared
to Odysseus in Hades. 'Οδ. xi. 234-296.

[2] According to the poet of the *Odyssey*, ghosts are divested of the
" muddy vesture " of flesh and bones :—

> Οὐ γὰρ ἔτι σάρκας τε καὶ ὀστέα ἶνες ἔχουσιν.
> Ἀλλὰ τὰ μέν τε πυρὸς κρατερὸν μένος αἰθομένοιο
> Δαμνᾷ, ἐπεί κε πρῶτα λίπῃ λεύκ' ὀστέα θυμός
> Ψυχὴ δ'ἠΰτ' ὄνειρος, ἀποπταμένη πεπότηται.
> 'Οδ. xi. 2.

Menippus. However, point me out Helene : for I could not distinguish *her*.

Hermes. That skull is Helene.

Menippus. Then, on account of this, those thousand ships were equipped from the whole of Hellas, and so many Hellenes and foreigners fell, and so many cities have become ruins !

Hermes. But you never saw the lady alive, Menippus ; for even you would have acknowledged it was not a matter to excite indignation that they :—

" For such a woman many a year choose bitter woe to suffer." [1]

For, in fact, if one looks at withered flowers, when they have lost their brilliant colour, it is plain that they will seem to him to have lost all their beauty. While, however, they are in bloom and retain their colour, they are very beautiful.

Menippus. 'Tis this, however, I wonder at, Hermes,— that the Achæans did not know they were suffering for a thing so shortlived and quickly fading.

Hermes. I have no leisure, Menippus, to engage in a philosophical chat with you. So do you choose out for yourself a spot, wherever you like, and throw yourself down and there lie ; while I shall straightway go and look after the rest of the dead men.

---

[1] Τοιῇδ' ἀμφὶ γυναικὶ πολὺν χρόνον ἄλγεα πάσχειν.   A quotation of 'Ιλ. iii. 157, where unwilling admiration is excited in the aged Priam and Trojan chiefs (as they watch the *causa teterrima belli* from the walls of the city), who exclaim :—

Οὐ νέμεσις Τρῶας καὶ εὐκνημῖδας 'Αχαιοὺς
Τοιῇδ' ἀμφὶ γυναικὶ πόλὺν χρόνον ἄλγεα πάσχειν
'Αινῶς ἀθανάτῃσι Θεῇς εἰς ὦπα ἔοικεν.

See the remarks of Quintilian, *De Inst. Orat.* viii. 4 : " *Quænam* igitur illa forma credenda est ? Non enim hoc dicit Paris, qui rapuit, non aliquis juvenis, non unus e vulgo ; sed senes et prudentissimi et Priamo assidentes," &c. For an enumeration of the lovers of Helen, see Apollodorus, iii. 10. The sum-total amounts to no less than twenty-eight.

XIX.

PROTESILAUS, ONE OF THE VICTIMS OF THE TROJAN WAR, SEEKS
TO AVENGE HIMSELF BY AN ASSAULT ON HELENE——ÆAKUS,
GATEKEEPER AND ONE OF THE HIGH COURT OF JUSTICE IN
HADES, REMINDS HIM THAT IT IS MENELAUS, THE COMMANDER-
IN-CHIEF OF THE ACHÆAN ARMY AGAINST ILIUM, WHO IS THE
PROPER OBJECT OF HIS VENGEANCE. MENELAUS SHIFTS THE
RESPONSIBILITY TO THE SHOULDERS OF PARIS. PARIS LAYS
THE BLAME UPON EROS. ÆAKUS DECIDES THAT PROTESILAUS
HAS ONLY HIMSELF TO BLAME FOR PREFERRING MILITARY
GLORY TO A YOUNG AND BEAUTIFUL WIFE; BUT CONCEDES
TO PROTESILAUS THAT THE BLAME, IN THE LAST RESORT,
LIES WITH THE FATES.

Æakus, Protesilaus,[1] *Menelaus, and Paris.*

Æakus. Why are you falling upon Helen, and throttling
her, Protesilaus ?

Protesilaus. Why ? Because it was through her I met
with my death, Æakus, leaving behind me my house half-
finished, and my newly-married wife a widow.

Æakus. Blame Menelaus, then, who led you to Troy,
for the sake of such a woman.

Protesilaus. You are right. It's he I have to call to
account.

Menelaus. No, not me, my fine sir, but Paris more likely,
who, contrary to every principle of justice, ran off with the
wife of his host—myself. Why, this fellow deserves to be
throttled not by you only but by all Hellenes and foreigners,
seeing he has been the cause of death to such numbers.

Protesilaus. Better so. Never, therefore, I assure you,

[1] A prince of Thessaly who led a number of confederated Thessalian
tribes to Ilium. First to leap out of his ship on to the enemy's coast, he
was the first slain of the Achæans. The story of the devotion of his
wife, Laodameia, is well known. Cf. 'Ιλ. ii. 698-703 ; Ov. *Laodameia
Protesilao ;* Catullus, *Ad Manlium,* 70-108 :—

> " Quo tibi tum casu, pulcherrima Laodameia,
>   Ereptum est vitâ dulcius atque animâ
> Conjugium : tanto se absorbens vortice amoris
>   Æstus in abruptum detulerat barathrum."

will I let you out of my hands, "ill-fated Paris,"[1] (taking him by the throat).

Paris. Then you do an injustice, Protesilaus, and that, too, to your fellow-craftsman. For I myself, also, am a devotee of Eros, and am held fast prisoner by the same divinity. And you know how involuntary a sort of thing is *love*, and how a certain divinity drives us wherever he wishes, and it is impossible to resist him.

Protesilaus. You are right. Would therefore it were possible for me to get hold of Eros here!

Æakus. I will maintain the cause even of Eros against you. Why, he would himself acknowledge that, likely enough, he was the cause, as regards Paris, of his falling in love; but that of your death, Protesilaus, no one else was the cause but yourself, who, entirely forgetful of your newly-married wife, when you brought your ships up at the Troad, so rashly and foolhardily leapt out before the rest, enamoured of glory; on account of which you were the first, in the disembarkation, to die.

Protesilaus. Then, I shall, in defence of myself, make a still juster reply to you, Æakus. *You will confess it*, for it is not *I* am responsible for all this, but Destiny, and the fact that my thread of life was so spun[2] from the first.

Æakus. Rightly, too. Why, then, do you blame them?

---

[1] A parody of 'Ιλ. iii. 39, where Hektor taunts his brother with his cowardice :—

  Δύσπαρι, εἶδος ἄριστε, γυναιμανὲς, ἠπεροπευτὰ, κ. τ. λ.

imitated by Ovid (according to the revision of Heinsius)

  " Dyspari Priamide, damno formose tuorum."
            Laod. Prot. 43.

Euripides uses a similar amalgam in Δυσελέναν (" ill-fated Helene"). 'Ορέστης, 1391.

[2] 'Επικεκλῶσθαι. Namely, by Klotho, the one of the three sisters whose province it is to *spin* out the fated life of man. See Hesiod. Θεογ. 905-910, and Lucian, Κατάπλους ἤ Τύραννος.

XX.

ÆAKUS, AT THE ESPECIAL REQUEST OF MENIPPUS, INTRODUCES
HIM TO THE GHOSTS OF THE MOST CELEBRATED POTENTATES
OF ANTIQUITY, WHEN THE CYNIC AVAILS HIMSELF OF HIS
OPPORTUNITY FOR RIDICULE AND DERISION. MENIPPUS IS
NEXT INTRODUCED TO THE MOST FAMOUS PHILOSOPHERS,
WHOM HE TREATS WITH NOT MUCH GREATER CONSIDERA-
TION. THE DIALOGUE CONCLUDES WITH THE INTERVIEW
WITH SOKRATES, WHOSE FOIBLES, REAL OR PRETENDED, ARE
MADE THE SUBJECT OF SATIRE.

Menippus and Æakus.[1]

Menippus. In the name of Pluto, Æakus, be my chaperon,
and conduct me round all the sights of Hades.

Æakus. No easy thing, Menippus, *to do* everything.
As regards, however, the principal sights, learn *as follows :—*
that this creature here is Kerberus you are aware ; and
this ferryman, who conveyed you across, and the lake,
and Pyriphlegethon,[2] you have seen but now at your
entering——

Menippus. I know all that, and you, that you are the
gate-keeper, and I saw the king, and the Erinyes :[3] but point

---

[1] Jacobs (ap. Porson, *Adversaria*) thinks this Dialogue to be not
worthy of the genius of Lucian. But, as Lehmann justly remarks,
although it has some parts not so highly finished as is usual with Lucian,
" omnino tamen ubivis spirat aura Luciani."

[2] The "flaming" river, or lake, surrounding Hades. The other
infernal streams are the Acheron (the *joyless* river), the Kokytus (the
river of *wailing*), and the Styx (*the hateful* river). See that eloquent re-
pertory of fantastic superstition or imagination, the *Phædon*—to which
the Christian *Inferno* and, in particular, that of Dante is indebted.
According to Plato, Acheron and the Acherusian lake, the pagan
Purgatorio, await those "too black for heaven, and yet too white for
hell," who, after expiating their offences, receive the reward of their
good deeds. Into "Tartarus horriferos eructans faucibus æstus," the
worst criminals are thrown headlong, to endure everlasting fire and
tortures. Cf. Æn. vi., *Georgica*, ii. 490-492 ; Lucretius, *De Rer. Nat.* iii.

[3] The *avenging* divinities, the Latin *Furiæ*, in Hellenic euphemism
usually known as the *Eumenides* (the "kindly disposed"). The *triad*
is found first in Euripides. The individual names Alekto, Megæra,

out to me the men of old times, and especially those of them who are famous.

Æakus. This is Agamemnon, and this Achilleus, and this Idomeneus close by, and this Odysseus; next are Aias and Diomedes, and the most valiant of the Hellenes.

Menippus. Bah! Homer, what creatures are the principal ornaments of your rhapsodies, that are tossed about on the ground, shapeless, mere dust all of them, and empty trumpery, in very truth "fleeting forms!"[1] And this fellow, Æakus, who is he?

Æakus. It is Cyrus, and this Krœsus, and the one above him Sardanapalus, and the one above them Midas; and he here is Xerxes.

Menippus (*to Xerxes*). Then, vile refuse, it was at *your* bridging the Hellespont that Hellas shuddered, and at your ambition to sail through the mountains?[2] And what a

and Tisiphone appear first in the Hellenic theological writers of late times. In the Εὐμενίδες of Æschylus, their number is unlimited.

[1] Cf. Aristoph. 'Ορνίθες, in the magnificent choral parabasis :—

> Φύσιν ἄνδρες ἀμαυρόβιοι, φύλλων γενεᾷ προσόμοιοι,
> 'Ολιγοδρανέες, πλάσματα πηλοῦ σκιοειδέα φῦλ' ἀμενηνά,
> 'Απτῆνες ἐφημέριοι, ταλαοὶ βροτοὶ, ἀνέρες εἰκελόνειροι.

Moschus :—

> Εὔδομες εὖ μάλα μάκρον ἄτερμονα νήγρετον ὕπνον.

Juvenal, *Sat.* x. 172 :—

> "Mors sola fatetur
> Quantula sint hominum corpuscula," &c.

[2] Menippus alludes to the canal across the Macedonian peninsula of Chalkidike (of which Mount Athos is the Southern extremity) formed by order of Xerxes, to avoid the dangerous passage round that cape. The canal, of which traces are visible, had a length of one and a-half miles. Juvenal, who, in common with many ancient and modern writers, was incredulous, thus refers to it :—

> "Creditur olim
> Velificatus Athos, et quidquid Græcia mendax
> Audet in historiâ; constructum classibus îsdem
> Suppositumque rotis solidum mare."
> *Sat.* x. 174-177.

Some one hundred and fifty years later a yet more ambitious, and much less praiseworthy, work was proposed by an architect in Alexander of Macedon's train—the transformation of Mount Athos into a gigantic statue of that conqueror, holding in one hand a city of 10,000 inhabitants, and in the other a river. See Plutarch, Βίοι Παρ. 'Αλεξ.

figure, too, is the famous Krœsus ! And as for Sardanapalus, Æakus, just permit me to give him a cuff on the ear.

Æakus. By no means, for you would shiver his skull in pieces, it is so like a woman's.

Menippus. Well, then, I will, at least, certainly spit upon him for a woman-man.

Æakus. Would you like me to show you the philosophers, too?

Menippus. In heaven's name, yes.

Æakus. First of all, this is your celebrated Pythagoras.

Menippus. Good-day to you, Euphorbus, or Apollo,[1] or whatever you like *to be.*

Pythagoras. The same to you, with all my heart, Menippus.

Menippus. Have you no longer a golden thigh ?

Pythagoras. Why, no; but come, let me see if your wallet contains anything eatable.

Menippus. Beans, my dear sir—so that's not in your way of eating.

Pythagoras. Only give them to me.   Other opinions hold among the dead ; for I have learned that beans and one's parents' heads are not all on an equality here.

Æakus. This is Solon, the son of Exekestides, and that

---

[1] Euphorbus, a Trojan hero, slain by Menelaus, who hung up his enemy's shield, as a trophy, in a temple at Mykenæ. Pythagoras, who, according to the fable, asserted himself to have been, in one of the various stages of the metempsychosis, Euphorbus, proved his identity by selecting his shield by the faculty of *reminiscence,*   Compare Lucian's Πρᾶσις Βίων, and Ὄνειρος ἤ Ἀλεκτρυών, 16; Diog. Laert. Περὶ Βίων κ. τ. λ. (Πυθαγ.); Ov. *Metam.* xv., which book contains, as Dryden justly observes, the finest passage in that charming poem—the Pythagorean precepts in regard to humane living. As for the absurd legend of the " golden thigh," repeated unquestioningly by so many writers, old and modern, see Ὄνειρος, Ἀλεξ. 40 ; Diog. Laert. viii. &c. For the more historical prohibition of beans (to the highest class of his initiated followers) see Porphyry's Βίος Πυθαγ. ; Plut. Συμπ.; Diog. Laert.; and the commentaries of Hemsterhuis and Lehmann. In a well-known passage, Horace refers to the prohibited bean :—

" O quando faba Pythagoræ cognata, simulque
Uncta satis pingui ponentur oluscula lardo ?
O noctes cænæque deûm ! "—*Sat.* ii. 6.
Cf. Juv. *Sat.* xv. 170-174.

Thales, and by their side Pittakos and the rest;[1] and there are seven in all, as you observe.

Menippus. These, Æakus, are the only ones of all of them without grief and cheerful. But the one covered with cinders, for all the world like a loaf baked in the ashes, who blossoms all over with blisters, who is he ?

Æakus. Empedokles, Menippus, come from Ætna, half-boiled.

Menippus. Fine Sir of the brazen foot, what possessed you that you threw yourself into the craters *of Ætna ?*[2]

Empedokles. A sort of melancholy madness, Menippus.

Menippus. Not so, by heaven! but vain-glory and puffed-up pride, and much drivelling—these things burned you to

---

[1] The four other " Sages," to whom allusion is here made, are Bias, Periander, Cheilon, and Kleobulus. By far the most distinguished of these " seven wise men," as they were called κατ' ἐξόχην, are Thales, the celebrated *savant* of Miletus, the originator of the theory of the Aqueous origin of the Universe, and Solon, the Attic legislator. Of the remaining five, their titles to supreme wisdom are not altogether unquestionable. Periander, tyrant of Korinth, in the sixth century B.C. (if justice or humanity enter into the idea of " wisdom "), had the least indefeasible claim of all. In fact, by some authorities he was excluded from the magic number.

[2] As in the case of Pythagoras, Lucian chooses to adopt the absurd popular legend, or hostile calumny, which represents this distinguished philosopher as throwing himself into the crater of Ætna, that his miraculous disappearance might acquire for him the honours of divinity. Cf. Ἱστ. Ἀληθ. ii. 289 ; Περὶ τῆς Περεγρίνου Τελεύτης, i. ; Diog. Laert. ; Strabo, vi. ; Ælian, Ποικ. Ἱστ. xii. 32 ; Horace, *Ars Poet.* 464. Diogenes informs us that the Pythagorean philosophers were in the habit of wearing sandals or slippers of brass; but Lucian's epithet, χαλκόπου, as Wieland points out, may be derived from Ἰλ. xiii. 23, and from the Ἤλεκτρα of Sophokles, 492. In spite of alleged eccentricities, Empedokles has deserved to be regarded as one of the most distinguished *savants* and geniuses of old Hellas. The greatest of Latin poets speaks of him in terms of the highest and most enthusiastic praise. Celebrating the glories of Sicily, Lucretius adds :—

> " Nil tamen hoc habuisse viro præclarius in se
> Nec sanctum magis et mirum carumque videtur.
> Carmina quin etiam divini pectoris eius
> Vociferantur et exponunt præclara reperta,
> Ut vix humanâ videatur stirpe creatus."
> *De Rer. Nat.* i. 729.

Of his principal poem, Περὶ Φύσεως, considerable fragments remain.

ashes, slippers and all, not unworthy *of your fate.* But the clever trick did you no good; for you clearly were proved to have died.—— Sokrates, however, wherever in the world is he, pray?

Æakus. He is generally talking nonsense, with Nestor and Palamedes.

Menippus. None the less I would wish to have a look at him, if he is anywhere here.

Æakus. Do you see the bald-headed man?

Menippus. All of them are bald-headed together. So that would be the distinguishing mark of all.

Æakus. I mean the snub-nosed one.

Menippus. That, too, is all one;[1] for they are the whole lot of them all snub-nosed.

Sokrates. Is it me you are inquiring for, Menippus?

Menippus. Yes, indeed, Sokrates.

Sokrates. How go things in Athens?

Menippus. Many of the young men say they are engaged in philosophy. And if one were to regard their ways of dressing and walking alone, they are tip-top philosophers.

Sokrates. I have seen very many of them.

Menippus. But you have observed, I suppose, in what style Aristippus[2] came to you, and Plato himself; the one reeking of perfume, and the other after having thoroughly learned the art of courting Sicilian despots.[3]

Sokrates. But about me what opinions do they entertain?

Menippus. You are a lucky fellow, Sokrates, as to that sort of thing, at all events. All, in fact, consider you to have been an admirable man, and to have known every-

---

[1] 'Ομοΐον, the French *tout égal,* of the use of which idiom a highly entertaining illustration may be seen in *Tristram Shandy,* vii. 34.

[2] A disciple of Sokrates, and founder of the *Cyrenaic* School, as it is called. For his selfish and sensual principles of life, see Diog. Laert.; and compare the Βιῶν Πρᾶσις, Athenæus, xiii. Horace expresses his admiration for him in well-known verses, *Ep.* i. 1, 17, 23, 24, and *Ep.* i. 1, 18.

[3] The two Dionysii, uncle and nephew, the celebrated tyrants of Sicily. According to some of the biographers or historians, Plato suffered for his plain-speaking to the despots. See, in particular, Plutarch. *Dion.*

thing; and that, too—for one must, I suppose, tell the truth—when you knew nothing.[1]

Sokrates. And I myself kept telling them that, but they would imagine the thing was pretended ignorance *on my part.*[2]

Menippus. And who are these about you ?

Socrates. Charmides, and Phœdrus, and the son of Kleinias.[3]

Menippus. Well done, Sokrates ; for even here you pursue your peculiar profession, and don't altogether despise the handsome fellows.[4]

Sokrates. Why, what else could I engage in more pleasantly ?　However, do you, please, recline close by us.

Menippus. No, faith, for I shall go off to join Krœsus and Sardanapalus, to take up my abode in their neighbourhood.　I think, in fact, that I shall laugh not a little in listening to their doleful lamentations.

Æakus.　I, too, will now be off, for fear that some one or other of the dead may get clear away without my perceiving him.　As for the remaining *sights* you shall see them at another time, Menippus.

Menippus. Take yourself off at once ; indeed, these sights here are quite sufficient, Æakus.

---

[1] The Delphic Oracle had pronounced the philosopher " the wisest man," we are assured, because for himself he constantly professed that he knew nothing.　How far this exaggeration of a truth was carried by his disciples in the " New Academy " is well known.　Of the scepticism of Pyrrho, who probably was considerably influenced by Sokratism as well as by Demokritus, an entertaining parody is given in the Πρᾶσις Βίων.

[2] Εἰρωνείαν, the special character of the Sokratic Dialogue, whence the English *irony.*　See 'Αλ. 'Ιστ. ii. 232.

[3] Charmides, the uncle of Plato, and Phœdrus have given their names to two of the *Dialogues* of Plato.　The son of Kleinias was Alkibiades, who occupies a conspicuous place in the Συμπόσιον, and gives his name to two Platonic *Dialogues.*

[4] See 'Αληθὴς 'Ιστορία (ii. 225), which gives an highly entertaining account of the manner of life of some of the celebrities met by the enterprising travellers in the Island of the Blessed.

XXI.

MENIPPUS INQUIRES OF KERBERUS, THE CANINE GUARDIAN OF THE ENTRANCE TO HADES, AS TO THE DEMEANOUR OF SOKRATES UPON HIS FIRST ARRIVAL THERE.

Menippus. My friend Kerberus—for I am your kinsman, being myself a dog, too,[1]—tell me, in the name of the Styx, what was Sokrates like when he was coming down to us: it is to be expected that you, as you are divine, not only bark but also utter human sounds whenever you have a mind to do so.

Kerberus. At a distance, Menippus, he appeared, in every way, to be approaching with undisturbed countenance, seeming to fear death in no great degree, and desirous to make this evident to those who stood outside the entrance. But when he stooped down and peered within the yawning cavern, and saw the darkness, and when I gave him a bite as he was long dallying with the hemlock,[2] and dragged him down by the foot, he began to squall like an infant, and to bewail his little children, and to take all possible forms *in his terror.*[3]

Menippus. Was then the fellow a mere sophist? and did he not, in fact, have contempt for the event *of death?*

Kerberus. No, he had not; but when, in fact, he saw

[1] See N. Δ. i. ; Περὶ Πένθούς, 4 ; Μενίππος ἢ Νεκυομ. 10; Aristoph. Βατρ. Kerberus, like most of the *monsters* of Hellenic fancy or Mediæval superstition, was, chimæra-like, a compound of dog and serpent—the reptile part of the monster adorning its back and forming its tail. See Apollod. ii. 5, 12. The Dog, it has been observed, has been deified (in the two principal religions of the ancient western world), in Heaven, on Earth, and in Hades, as Seirius, Anubis, and Kerberus.

[2] Διαμέλλοντα αὐτὸν δακὼν τῷ κωνείῳ, κ. τ. λ. There is some ambiguity in the connection of τῷ κωνείῳ. Fritzsche connects them with δακὼν. The order of the text is that adopted by Jacobitz. Cf. Aristoph. Βατρ. 124.

[3] Παντοῖος ἐγένετο. Nahm alle möglichen Gestalten an, d. i. war ganz ausser sich, wuste nicht, was er machen sollte. Cf. Νιγρίνος, 4, Θ. Δ. xxi. 2.—Jacobitz. This account of Kerberus differs altogether from that given by Plato in his Φαίδων:—" οὐδὲν τρέσας, οὐδὲ διαφθείρας οὔτε τοῦ χρώματος οὔτε τοῦ προσώπου, ἀλλ᾽ ὥσπερ εἰώθει, ταυρηδὸν ὑποβλέψας." Cf. Xenophon, οὐδὲ πρὸς τὸν θάνατον ἐμαλακίσατο, ἀλλ᾽ ἱλαρῶς, κ. τ. λ. ('Απολογία) Ælian. Π. Ι. ix. 7 ; Cicero, *Tusc. Disp.* iii. 31.

that it was necessary and unavoidable, he began to show himself courageous, as though, forsooth, ready to suffer not unwillingly what he was bound certainly to undergo, so that the spectators might admire *his conduct.* And, in short, about all such persons I could tell you, up to the entrance they show daring and manliness; but what happens within is a clear proof *of their fear.*

Menippus. And I, what did you think of *my* coming below?

Kerberus. You alone, Menippus, and Diogenes before you,[1] *made the descent* in a manner worthy of your species; because you entered without being compelled, or pushed in, but of your free will, laughing, after having bidden all the world to go to the devil.

XXII.

CHARON DEMANDS FROM MENIPPUS HIS ACCUSTOMED FEE. UPON THE ABSOLUTE REFUSAL OF THE CYNIC TO PAY, A LIVELY ALTERCATION ENSUES.

Charon and Menippus.

Charon. Pay me, damned rascal, my passage-fee.

Menippus. Bellow, if that is more agreeable to you *than* anything *else,* Charon.

Charon. Pay me, I say, for my having ferried you across.

Menippus. You will not get anything from a fellow who has nothing.

Charon. And is there any man in the world who has not a couple of pence?[2]

---

[1] The manner of the death of Diogenes is variously related. See Diog. Laert. Lucian in his Πρᾶσις Βίων makes him kill himself by swallowing an uncooked polypus. Cf. Plutarch, Περὶ τῆς Σαρκοφαγίας. He is, however, usually represented as having died of old age (at ninety) at Korinth, the year of the death of Alexander of Macedon.

[2] Ὀβολὸν. See Περὶ Πένθους, ii. (the principal authority on the subject); Aristoph. Βατρ. 140; Diodorus, ii. 5; Juvenal, *Sat.* iii. 267 :—

     "Infelix, nec habet quem porrigat ore trientem."

Also Staekelberg's *Die Gräber der Hellenen.* Apuleius (*De Aureo Asino*), on the descent of Psyche to the Infernal Regions, refers to this practice :—
"*in ipso ore duas ferre stipes, quarum alteram primam transvectionem, reditum altera mercetur,*" for (as we are told) *et inter mortuos Avaritia vivit.*

Menippus. If there is anyone else *who hasn't got them* I don't know; but *I* have not got them.

Charon. By Pluto, I will certainly throttle you, villain, if you don't pay up (*taking him by the throat*).

Menippus. And I will beat and break your skull to pieces with my staff.

Charon. Then you will have made your so long voyage in vain.[1]

Menippus. Let Hermes, who handed me over to you, pay you for me.

Hermes. Much profit should I get, faith, if I am going to pay for the dead, too!

Charon. I shall not let go of you (*tightening his grasp*).

Menippus. Then haul your craft on shore, and stop *till you get it.*[2] But, however, how can you receive what I have not got?

Charon. But did you not know it is absolutely necessary to provide oneself *with it?*

Menippus. I knew well enough: but I had not got it. What then? Ought I not to be dead on that account?

Charon. Are you then to be the only one to boast of having made the passage *gratis?*

Menippus. Not *gratis*, my fine Sir! For indeed I baled out the bilge-water, and lent a hand at the oar, and was the only one of all the passengers not to weep.

Charon. That's nothing to do with the ferryman. You must pay your twopence. It's not lawful and right for it to be otherwise.

Menippus. Then take me back to life again.

Charon. A pretty idea—to get blows for my pains from Æakus, into the bargain!

Menippus. Don't bother me, then.

Charon. Show us what you have got in your wallet.

Menippus. Lupines—if you want them—and Hekate's supper.[3]

---

[1] " The meaning is: You will in vain have made so long a voyage, for if you do not give me the *obolos*, you will have to return to the upper world."—Jacobitz.

[2] The ναῦλον or "fee."

[3] See N. Δ. i. The Lupine (a species of flowering *pulse*) was the common and staple food of the disciples of Antisthenes. See Diog.

Charon. From where in the world did you bring us this dog, Hermes? And what language he used during the passage—laughing and jeering at all the whole lot of passengers, and, while the rest were groaning and lamenting, the only one to give us a song!

Hermes. Don't you know, Charon, what personage it is you have brought over—a free man and no mistake; he cares for nobody. He is the famous Menippus everyone knows.

Charon. All the same, should I ever catch you (*shaking his fist*)—

Menippus. *Should* you catch me, my fine Sir: but you don't catch me *twice* (*making off*).

XXIII.

PROTESILAUS, AN ACHÆAN HERO, WHO HAD FALLEN BEFORE ILIUM, SUPPLICATES PLUTO TO PERMIT HIM TO RETURN TO LIFE, FOR A DAY, TO VISIT HIS WIFE LAODAMEIA, AND ADDUCES AS PRE-CEDENTS THE EXAMPLES OF ORPHEUS AND ALKESTIS. AT THE INTERCESSION OF PERSEPHONE, PLUTO AT LENGTH GRANTS THE FAVOUR.

Protesilaus,[1] *Pluto, and Persephone.*

Protesilaus. O Lord, and King, and our God *here below,* and you, daughter of Demeter, do not contemn a lover's prayer.

Pluto. And you—what do you want from us, or who may you be?

Protesilaus. I am Protesilaus, the son of Iphiklus, of Phylake, who fought with the Achæans, and was the first of the army against Ilium to die, and my supplication is that I may have leave of absence for a short time, and return to life again.

Pluto. That's a sort of love, Protesilaus, all dead people indulge in: but not one of them will ever succeed in it.

Laert. With the poets of the New Comedy it was a fertile subject for ridicule, as displayed in Athenæus.
 [1] See N. Δ. xix.

Protesilaus. But it's not life, Aïdoneus,[1] I am in love with, but my wife, whom I left behind still a young bride in the bridal chamber, and went off on the voyage: for, ill-fated wretch, I died by the hands of Hektor, at the disembarkation.[2] Love for my wife, accordingly, wears me away immeasurably, my Lord, and I am ready, after having appeared to her, if only for a brief time, to come down again.

Pluto. Did you not drink the water of Lethe, Protesilaus?

Protesilaus. Yes, indeed, my Lord: but the matter was beyond all bounds.

Pluto. Then just wait for her; for she, too, will arrive at some time or other, and there will be no need for you to go up above.

Protesilaus. But I can't endure the delay, Pluto. You've been in love [3] yourself, before now, and you know what a thing love is.

Pluto. Besides, what good will it do you to live again for one day, when you will have to experience the same griefs shortly afterwards?

Protesilaus. I think I shall persuade her, too, to follow me to you, so that, in a little while, in place of one you will receive two dead people.

Pluto. It is not lawful and right that this should be, nor has it ever been so.

Protesilaus. I will refresh your memory, Pluto. Why, on this very same plea you delivered up Eurydike to Orpheus, and you sent off my kinswoman Alkestis to gratify Herakles.

Pluto. But would you wish thus, with your bare and ugly skull, to appear to that beautiful bride of yours? and how, too, will she admit you to her, when she is not able even to distinguish you? Why, she will be frightened, I am well

---

[1] A paragogic form of *Aïdes* or *Hades.*

[2] In the *Iliad* (ii. 695) his slayer is anonymous. Lucian here follows Ovid (*Metam.* xii. 67) or some other authority.

[3] With Persephone, in particular, who :—

> " Gathering flowers,
> Herself a fairer flower, by gloomy Dis
> Was gathered."

assured, and will flee from you, and you will have made
your long journey to the upper world to no purpose.

Persephone. Do you all the same, my husband, set that
right, and direct Hermes, as soon as ever Protesilaus is in
daylight, to touch him with his caduceus,[1] and make him
a handsome youth again, such as he was *when he came out*
from the nuptial chamber.

Pluto (to Hermes). Since it's Persephone's pleasure, conduct this man to the upper regions, and just make him a
bridegroom again.—(*To Protesilaus.*) And do you remember you have got only one day.

XXIV.

IDOGENES DEMANDS OF MAUSOLUS, THE KARIAN SATRAP, THE
REASON OF HIS ARROGANCE AND PRIDE, AND RIDICULES THE
VANITY OF HIS GRANDEUR AND POWER ON EARTH, AND, IN
PARTICULAR, THE USELESSNESS TO HIM OF HIS MAGNIFICENT
TOMB AT HALIKARNASSUS. HE CONCLUDES HIS DIATRIBE
WITH CONTRASTING HIS OWN COMPLETE IGNORANCE AND IN-
DIFFERENCE IN REGARD EVEN TO THE MANNER, OR PLACE,
OF HIS OWN SEPULTURE.

Diogenes and Mausolus.[2]

Diogenes. For what reason are you so high and mighty,
and claim to have precedence of us all in honour, Karian?

Mausolus. Indeed, by reason of my kingdom, O Sinopian—seeing I was king of all Karia, and ruled over some

---

[1] For the magic property of the ῥαβδος, see Θ. Δ. vii.

[2] Mausolus was Satrap of Karia, on the S.W. of the Lesser Asia,
under the Persian monarch Artaxerxes the Second, or Mnemon (as he
was called by the Greeks). With other Satraps he revolted, and established himself as an independent prince—377-353 B.C. At his death,
his sister and wife Artemisia, who succeeded him, built the splendid
monument which has given its name to succeeding edifices of the kind—
none of which in the Western world have any title to rivalry with it.
For a description, see Pliny, *Hist. Nat.* iv. 36. More justly than were
most of the others, it was reckoned among the " seven wonders." In
modern times, however, in the Eastern world the tomb of Mausolus
has been surpassed by that paragon of architectural beauty, the Taj
Mahal at Agra.

of the Lydians, also, and subjugated to my dominion several islands, and advanced as far as Miletus, overrunning the greater part of Ionia. And I was handsome and great, and strenuous in wars. But, what is greatest *reason* of all, is that I possess in Halikarnassus a very great monument lying over me, of dimensions such as no other dead man has; nay, nor one so elaborately beautified—horses and men having been copied with the greatest accuracy in the most beautiful marble—of such sort as one could not easily find even a temple. Seem I not to you justly to be high and mighty on those grounds ?

Diogenes. On account of your kingdom, you say, and your handsome appearance, and the weight of your tomb ?

Mausolus. Assuredly, on those grounds.

Diogenes. But, my handsome Mausolus, neither that power of yours nor your figure any longer pertains to you. If, however, we should choose some judge of good looks, I am unable to say why your skull should be preferred to mine; for both are bald and bare, and we display our teeth with equal prominence, we are both deprived of our eyes, and have been both provided with snub-noses. And as for your tomb, and those costly marbles, they, perhaps, may be *of use* to the good people of Halikarnassus, to show off for their own benefit and to get honour for themselves from strangers and visitors as having, no doubt, a certain big building. But as for you, my fine Sir, I don't see what benefit *you* derive from it, unless [1] you affirm this—that you bear a heavier burden than we, inasmuch as you are weighed down by such huge stones.

Mausolus. Will all those things, then, be of no advantage to me, and will Mausolus and Diogenes have an equality of privilege ?

Diogenes. Not an equality of privilege, most excellent Sir,—certainly not. For Mausolus will groan and lament, in remembering his possessions above ground, in which he used to imagine himself to be happy, while Diogenes will laugh at him. And as for the tomb at Halikarnassus—he

---

[1] Πλὴν εἰ μή. "Lucian himself has animadverted upon this expression in his *Solœcistes;* for correct writers wrote πλὴν εἰ, or εἰ μή. But Lucian has often not attended to his own rule."—Hemst.

will call it his own, though it was constructed by his wife and sister Artemisia; whereas Diogenes does not know whether even he has *any* tomb for his carcass; for he did not even bestow a thought about it;[1] but he has left behind, for the best part of mankind, the memory of himself as of a man, who has lived a life much more sublime than your monument, greatest of Karian slaves, and built on a firmer foundation.

XXV.

NIREUS AND THERSITES, DISPUTING WHICH OF THEM WAS THE MORE DISTINGUISHED BY GOOD LOOKS, APPEAL TO MENIPPUS. MENIPPUS, DISREGARDING THE AUTHORITY OF HOMER, PRONOUNCES THE ἰσοκάλλος AS WELL AS THE ἰσοτίμια, IN HADES, TO BE AS COMPLETE AS IT IS UNALTERABLE.

Nireus, Thersites,[2] and Menippus.

Nireus. See, I say, Menippus here shall judge which of the two is more shapely.—Say, Menippus, don't I seem to you the better-looking?

Menippus. But *who* are you, really? For it is first necessary, I suppose, that I know that.

Nireus. Nireus and Thersites.

Menippus. Which, pray, is Nireus, and which Thersites? For that's not clear as yet.

Thersites. This one point *in my favour* I have already— that I am like you, and that you by no means are so far

---

[1] See N. Δ. i. His master Antisthenes, the founder of the Cynic School, displayed equal indifference to the rites of sepulture.

[2] For Nireus, see N. Δ. xviii. The agreeable picture of this representative demagogue, Thersites, painted by the poet of the *Iliad*, is well known :—

$$\text{αἴσχιστος δὲ ἀνὴρ ὑπὸ Ἴλιον ἦλθε·}$$
$$\text{Φολκὸς ἔην, χωλὸς δ' ἕτερον πόδα · τὼ δὲ ὤμω}$$
$$\text{Κυρτὼ, ἐπὶ στῆθος συνοχωκότε · αὐτὰρ ὕπερθε}$$
$$\text{Φοξὸς ἔην κεφαλὴν, ψέδνη δ' ἐπενήνοθε λάχνη.}$$
ii. 216-219.

See 'Αλ. 'Ιστ., where Thersites brings an action (γραφὴ ὕβρεως) against the poet for calumny, before the Court of Rhadamanthys, and gains his case (ii. 280).

superior as Homer, that blind fellow, commends you *for being*, when he calls you a finer man than the rest of us; whereas I, the peak-headed and almost bald-pated individual, did not appear at all inferior in the eyes of our judge.—But do you see, Menippus, whom you consider really the finer gentleman ?

Nireus. Me, to be sure, the son of Aglaia and Charops,

> " Of all the Danai 'neath Ilion who mustered,
> The man of fairest form." [1]

Menippus. You, by no means, however, came below ground very much like a *beau*, as I imagine; on the contrary, your bones were all much alike, and your skull could be distinguished, I suppose, from that of Thersites in this respect only—that yours is easily smashed; for it is a brittle and no virile one you have.

Nireus. Indeed, ask Homer what I was like when I was campaigning with the Achæans.

Menippus. Mere dreams: I see, however, what beauties you have just now, and as for those former *graces of yours*, the people of those times know all about that.

Nireus. Have I, then, here *no* superiority in good looks, Menippus ?

Menippus. Neither you, nor anyone else, have any pretensions to good looks; for perfect equality *prevails* in Hades, and all are alike.

Thersites. For me, I assure you, that is quite enough.

[1]
$$\text{"Ὅς κάλλιστος ἀνὴρ ὑπὸ Ἴλιον ἦλθον.}$$
Ἰλ. ii. 673.

Cf. *Æneis*, vii. 649, of the Son of Mezentius. Nireus and Thersites became a sort of proverb for masculine beauty and ugliness. Plato, in his representation of the various choices made by human souls, for their second lives, makes Thersites adopt that of an ape.—Πόλ. x. *ad finem.*

XXVI.

CHEIRON IMPARTS TO MENIPPUS HIS REASON FOR PREFERRING HADES TO HEAVEN AND IMMORTALITY.

Menippus and Cheiron.[1]

Menippus. I heard, Cheiron, that though divine, you had a great desire to die.

Cheiron. You heard quite right, Menippus; and I have died, as you see, when I might have been immortal.

Menippus. Pray, what love of death possessed you, a thing undesired by most people?

Cheiron. I will tell you, as you are not altogether without sense. I had no longer any pleasure to get from immortality.

Menippus. It was no pleasure to you to live and see the light of day?[2]

Cheiron. No, Menippus, for I, for my part, hold pleasure to be something which is variable, and not simple. But I was always living and in the enjoyment of the same things —sun, light, food; and there were the same seasons, and everything happened, each in its own order, following, as it were, one after the other—I became, therefore, satiated with them : for my pleasure was dependent not on its permanence, but on the not being constantly participant in it.[3]

[1] The most famous of the Kentaurs, and instructor of Peleus, Achilleus, and other heroes. He met his death by an accident, at the hand of Herakles. As the son of Cronos, he was immortal; but, preferring death, Zeus permitted him to transfer his deathlessness to Prometheus. See Apollod. ii. v. &c.; Hyginus ; Ov. *Met.* ii.

[2] "No longer to behold the light," to the Hellene, and, in particular, to the Athenian, living under pure, translucent skies, and physically and mentally sensitive in a high degree to the enjoyments of life, was the one great cause of regret at the moment of death—as depicted by their tragic dramatists. See, especially, Euripides, Ἰφιγενεία ἐν Αὐλ., 1359-1362.

> Ἰώ, ἰώ, λαμπαδοῦχας ἁμέρα,
> Διὸς τε φέγγος, ἕτερον, ἕτερον,
> Αἰῶνα καὶ μοῖραν οἰκήσομεν!
> Χαῖρε μοι, φίλον φάος.

Cf. the exquisite lines in the *Cenci* of Shelley (v. 4).

[3] Le Clerc supposes Lucian to have derived this philosophy of Pleasure from the Ὑποβολιμαῖος of Menander, who, in his turn, was indebted to Alexis. The fragment has been preserved by Stobæus. For ἐν τῷ μετασχεῖν ὅλως, Lebmann would read, with other MSS., μεταβαλεῖν—"in constant change."

Menippus. You are right, Cheiron; but how do you endure the state of things in Hades, ever since you came here by preference?

Cheiron. Not disagreeably, Menippus, for your equality is very democratic, and the circumstance of being in daylight or in darkness brings no difference with it: besides, one has not to be thirsty nor hungry, as up above, for we are without all those *wants.*

Menippus. Take care, Cheiron, that you are not caught in your own words, and your argument does not come round to the same thing.

Cheiron. How do you mean?

Menippus. That if everlasting sameness and similarity of human life was the cause of your *ennui,* here, too, the sameness of things must be equally matter for satiety for you; and you will be obliged to seek some means of migrating from here, also, to another life, a thing which, I imagine, is impossible.

Cheiron. What should one do, then, Menippus?

Menippus. According to what is commonly said, I suppose that a sensible man is pleased and content with his present circumstances, and thinks none of them intolerable.

XXVII.

THE PHILOSOPHERS DIOGENES, ANTISTHENES, AND KRATES RESOLVE TO MAKE FOR THE ENTRANCE TO ORCUS, TO OBSERVE THE QUALITY AND CONDUCT OF THE NEW ARRIVALS. ON THE WAY THEY ENTERTAIN THEMSELVES WITH RECOUNTING THEIR SEVERAL EXPERIENCES OF THE BEHAVIOUR OF THEIR TRAVELLING COMPANIONS TO HADES. UPON THEIR ARRIVAL AT THEIR DESTINATION, DIOGENES INTERROGATES A POOR MAN AS TO THE CAUSE OF HIS LAMENTATION.

Diogenes, Antisthenes, Krates,[1] *and Poor Man.*

Diogenes. We are at leisure, friends Antisthenes and

[1] See N. Δ. xi.

Krates: so why should we not set off for a walk straight for the place of descent, to observe the new *arrivals* coming down [1] to us, what they are like, and what each of them is about?

Antisthenes. Let us be off, Diogenes, for, indeed, the spectacle would be a pleasant one—to see some of them weeping, and some entreating to be let go, and some making the descent with reluctance, and, though Hermes gives a push to their shoulders, resisting, and struggling on their backs, to no purpose.

Krates. I, also, will relate to you what I saw by the way, when I was coming down.

Diogenes. Give us the story, Krates, for I fancy you have seen some uncommonly laughable *scenes*.

Krates. There were several others who made the descent in my company, and conspicuous among them were Ismenodorus our countryman, the millionaire, and Arsakes the Median Satrap, and Orœtes of Armenia.[2] Well, Ismenodorus —for he was murdered by the robbers of Kithæron, while proceeding on foot to Eleusis, I believe—began groaning and covering his wound with his hands, and kept calling upon the new-born infants whom he had left behind him, and accusing himself of rashness, for crossing Kithæron, and traversing the neighbourhood of Eleutheria[3] (left altogether desolate by the ravages of war), and for taking with him

---

[1] Τοὺς κατιόντας. The term applied to exiles returning home, and there is reference to this in the text. See Herod. i. 62, iii. 45, Æschylus, Ἀγαμέμ., 1283.

[2] It is uncertain whether the two last names represent historical personages, or are merely fictitious. The first is certainly either fictitious, or that of some person of whom nothing more is known than what we are here told, that he was a countryman of Krates, and therefore a Theban. Arsakes is the name of the founder of the Parthian Monarchy, which, like that of Cæsar with the Roman Emperors, was adopted by all his successors. The first of the Arsacidæ is said by Ammianus Marcellinus to have died a natural death; while Suidas follows the account of Lucian. An Orœtes figures in the Χάρων (14); the Satrap who, as Herodotus informs us. crucified Polykrates of Samos (iii. 130). Hemsterhuis thinks that all the three characters may be derived from the New Comedy.

[3] A town or village at the foot of Kithæron, on the confines of Attica and Bœotia. The wars referred to were, probably, those waged by Alex-

only two domestics, and that, though he had with him five
bowls of gold, and four cups. As for Arsakes—now advanced in age and, indeed, not without some dignity about
his appearance, he was annoyed after the fashion of the
foreigner, and was highly indignant at trudging on foot,
and claimed it as his right that a horse should be supplied
to him; and, in fact, his horse had died with him, both
having been run through, at one stroke, by some Thracian
peltast, in the engagement on the Araxes with the
Kappadocian.[1] For Arsakes charged, as he declared to
us, far in advance of the rest; while the Thracian, awaiting
the attack, covers himself with his round shield, and wards
off the spear-shaft of Arsakes, and, couching his own
Macedonian lance, runs him and his horse through *at the
same time.*

Antisthenes. How was it possible for that to be done at
one stroke, Krates?

Krates. Very easily, Antisthenes. For he began charging,
pushing before him a spear-shaft of twenty cubits; while
the Thracian, when with his shield he warded off from
himself the onslaught, and the spear-point passed him,
sank on his knees, and received the attack with his spear,
and wounds the horse under the chest, who ran himself
through by his own ardour and the vehemence of his speed.
And as for Arsakes, he is run right through from the groin
to the buttocks. You see something of what it was like:
the action was rather that of the horse than of the hero.
He was indignant, nevertheless, at being on a level with
the rest in point of dignity, and considered it as his right to
come down in the capacity of a knight. But as for Orœtes,
he was very tender-footed, and was not able even to stand
on the ground, not to say anything of walking—all Medes,
in point of fact, have this experience, on dismounting from
their horses : they walk as though upon thorns, on tiptoe,
and with difficulty get on at all—so that, when he threw

ander of Macedon and his successors.—Jacob. The range of Kithæron
was thickly wooded, and favourable for robbers.

[1] In Armenia. By the Kappadokian, probably, is to be understood
Eumenes, whom Perdikkas (who had usurped the chief command of the
Macedonian army at the death of Alexander) had appointed to the post
of Lieutenant in Kappadocia and Paphlagonia.—Jacob.

himself down, and lay there, and would by no means allow himself to be set on his feet again, the excellent Hermes took him up and carried him as far as the ferry-boat; while I set myself laughing.

Antisthenes. Well, as for myself, when I was making the descent, I did not at all mix myself up with the rest, but, leaving them to lament, I ran forward to the ferry-boat, and took my place beforehand, that I might have a comfortable passage. In fact, during the voyage they were shedding tears, and suffering from sea-sickness, while I was exceedingly entertained by them all.

Diogenes. You, Krates, and you, Antisthenes, chanced to fall in with fellow-travellers of such description. My fellow-travellers down were Blepsias the money-lender, from Pisa, and Lampis of Akarnania, who had been captain of mercenaries, and Damis the millionaire, he of Korinth. Damis died from poison administered by his son ; Lampis cut his own throat for love of Myrtium, the celebrated courtesan ; while Blepsias, the poor wretch, was said to have slowly starved to death ; and he showed it clearly enough, appearing pallid to excess, and attenuated to the most extreme point. I, although aware of the facts, began to question them as to the manner of their deaths. Then, when Damis was accusing his son, " You suffered, however, no unjust fate at his hands," said I, " since, while you at once possessed a quarter of a million, and lived in luxury yourself, nonagenarian as you were, you used to supply a youth of eighteen with just sixpence. And as for you, Mr. Akarnanian (for he, too, was uttering groans, and imprecating curses on Myrtium), why do you blame Eros, when you ought to accuse yourself ? you who, while you never trembled at the enemy *in battle*, but used to fight, regardless of danger, in the front ranks, were caught, admirable man, by the made-up tears and sighs of a common prostitute !¹ As for Blepsias, he anticipated *blame* and accused himself, of his own accord, of excessive folly, in that he hoarded up his money for heirs in no way related to him, thinking, the fool ! to live for ever. However, to me they afforded no common amusement by

¹ Cf. 'Εταιρῶν Διαλ.

their groans then——.   But, now we are at the entrance,
we must watch and observe carefully the arrivals, while yet
at a distance.   Bah! they are numerous and various enough,
and all in tears, except these newly-born children and
infants.   Nay, even the very old fellows are bewailing
themselves.   What's this?   Has the magic potion of life,
forsooth, got them under its influence?   However, I want
to question this superannuated old man.—What are you
weeping about, dying at your time of life?   Why are you
indignant, my fine Sir, and that, when you have arrived at
a good age?   You were, doubtless, some king?

Poor Man. Not at all.

Diogenes. Well, some satrap or other?

Poor Man. Not that, even.

Diogenes. Then you were, doubtless, a rich man, and it
troubles you, I suppose, to have died and left behind you
much luxury?

Poor Man. Nothing of that sort; on the contrary, I had
arrived at about the full age of ninety years, and led a life
of want, sustained by means of my fishing-rod and line,
excessively poor, childless, and lame, into the bargain, and
half blind.

Diogenes. Then, though you were in such a condition, did
you wish to go on living?

Poor Man. Yes, for the light of day was sweet to me,
and to die is a terrible thing and to be avoided.

Diogenes. You are bereft of your senses, old man, and
behave in the face of inevitable Necessity like a child; and
that, though you are a contemporary of the Ferryman *there.*
What, pray, could one in future say as regards the young,
when people of your time of life are so fond of living, who
ought to pursue Death as the one remedy for the evils
essential to old age?—But let us be gone, now, for fear
someone may suspect us of wishing to run away, if he sees
us crowding about the entrance-gate.

XXVIII.

MENIPPUS RIDICULES THE STORY OF THE PROPHET TEIRESIAS AS FOUND IN THE POETS AND THEOLOGISTS, AND, IN PARTICULAR, HIS METAMORPHOSIS INTO A WOMAN.

Menippus and Teiresias.[1]

Menippus. Whether, in fact, you are blind, Teiresias, it is no longer easy to distinguish; for the eyes of all of us alike are empty, and only their sockets remain; and, for the rest, you would no longer be able to tell which was Phineus,[2] or which Lynkeus. That, however, you were a prophet, and that you are the only one who has ever been of both sexes—both a man and a woman—I am aware, having heard so from the poets. In heaven's name, therefore, tell me which life did you find by experience the pleasanter—when you were a man, or was the woman's superior?

Teiresias. The woman's, Menippus, far away, for it was more free from the cares *of life,* and the women lord it

---

[1] The famous prophet of Thebes, who figures conspicuously in the Sophoklean drama. His blindness has been variously accounted for. One narrative attributes it to the indignation of Athena, whom he had chanced to see in the bath, who, however, gave him, by way of compensation, the prophetic faculties. His transformation into one of the opposite sex is attributed to his having killed a female serpent, and his double experience induced Zeus to make him arbiter in his dispute with Hera upon the question, which sex has the greater enjoyment; and, when he pronounced in favour of the weaker, the indignant Hera deprived him of sight. See Apollod. iii. 6 ; Ov. *Met.* iii. 318-338. Cf. 'Οδ. xi. where Odysseus, by means of his barbarous magic rites, evokes the spectres of the dead.

[2] Phineus, the Thracian king and prophet in one, famous as having been the especial object of the persecution of the 'Αρπυῖαι (on account of his cruelty to his sons), and as the instructor of the Argonauts. The cause of his blindness is variously given. See Apollod. i. 9, 21, 22; iii. 14, 7 ; Apollonius, 'Αργ. Milton celebrates the blind prophets and poets of Hellas in the well-known passage in his *Par. Lost* :—

> "Blind Thamyris, and blind Mæonides,
> And Teiresias and Phineus, prophets old."
>
> (iii. 35.)

over the men, and they are not forced to go to fight in war,
or to stand sentinel at the battlements, or to wrangle in
parliament, or to be cross-examined in law courts.

Menippus. Have you not heard, Teiresias, the *Medeia* of
Euripides, how she pities the female sex, in her speech, as
wretched, and having to undergo certain intolerable pangs
—those of childbirth? [1] But tell me—for the *iambics* of
Medeia remind me of it—did you ever have a child, when
you were a woman, or did you continue barren and un-
fruitful in that state of life?

Teiresias. Why do you ask that, Menippus?

Menippus. No offence intended, Teiresias; but answer
me, if it is agreeable to you.

Teiresias. I was not barren, and yet I did not have a
child at all.

Menippus. That's quite enough. If you had a womb, in
fact—I wished to know that.

Teiresias. Of course I had.

Menippus. And was it in course of time that it disap-
peared, and the sexual part was obstructed, and your
breasts were removed, and the manly parts sprang into
existence, and you grew a beard; or did you immediately
from being a woman turn out a man?

Teiresias. I don't see what your question means exactly.

---

[1] The forsaken wife of Iason thus expresses the unhappy condition of
her sex :—

Γυναῖκες ἔσμεν ἀθλιώτατον φυτόν·
Ἃς πρῶτα μὲν δεῖ χρημάτων ὑπερβολῇ
Πόσιν πριάσθαι, δεσπότην τε σώματος
Λαβεῖν· κακοῦ γὰρ τοῦδ' ἔτ' ἄλγιον κακόν,
Κἂν τῷδ' ἀγὼν μέγιστος, ἢ κακὸν λαβεῖν
Ἢ χρήστον. Οὐ γὰρ εὐκλεεῖς ἀπαλλαγαὶ
Γυναιξίν, οὐδ' οἷον τ' ἀνήσασθαι πόσιν.
Εἰς καινὰ δ' ἤθη καὶ νόμους ἀφιγμένην
Δεῖ μάντιν εἶναι, μὴ μαθοῦσαν οἴκοθεν,
Ὅτῳ μάλιστα χρήσεται συνευνέτῃ.

*   *   *   *   *

Λέγουσι δ' ἡμᾶς, ὡς ἀκινδύνον βίον
Ζῶμεν κἀτ' οἴκους, οἱ δὲ μάρνανται δορί
Κακῶς φρονοῦντες · ὡς τρὶς ἂν πὰρ' ἄσπιδα
Στῆναι θέλοιμ' ἂν μᾶλλον ἢ τεκεῖν ἅπαξ.

231-251.

M

But you appear to me, however, to doubt that these things were so.

Menippus. Why, is not one allowed to have any sort of doubt in these cases, Teiresias; but, like some simpleton who doesn't inquire into the truth, must one receive them as gospel, whether they are possible or not'?

Teiresias. Do you not, pray, believe other things to have so happened *as they are related*—when, *for example*, you hear that certain persons have been changed from women into birds, or trees, or quadrupeds ; into Philomela,[1] or Daphne, or the daughter of Lycaon ?

Menippus. If ever I come across them, I shall know—what they say.   But you, my fine Sir, when you were a woman, did you play the prophet then, as afterwards, or did you learn to be man and prophet at the same time ?

Teiresias. Just see.   You are ignorant of everything that concerns me—how I put an end to a certain quarrel among the gods, and how Hera blinded me, *in consequence;* and how Zeus consoled me for my misfortune by the gift of prophecy.[2]

Menippus. Do you still stick to your lies, Teiresias ? However, you do so quite in prophetic style ; for it is the custom of you people to say nothing rational or true.[3]

---

[1] For the tragic and frightful story of Philomela (from which Shakspere, or whoever was the author, derived the idea of the tragedy of *Titus Andronicus*), see Ov. *Met.* vi. 424-676.   For Daphne, *Met.* vi. 205, and Θ. Δ. ii., xv.   For the daughter of Lycaon (the impious king who served up human flesh to Zeus during his wanderings in Arkadia), Callisto, see *Met.* ii. 496.

[2] See Ov. *Met.* iii. 333-338 :—

> gravius Saturnia facto,
> Nec pro materiâ fertur doluisse ; suique
> Judicis æternâ damnavit lumina nocte, etc.

[3] Cf. Aristoph. 'Ορνίθες, 960-991 ; Juv. vi. 512-591 ; Apul. *De Aur. Asino ;* Lucian, 'Αλέξανδρος, Νίγρινος, etc.

XXIX.

AGAMEMNON INQUIRES OF (TELAMONIAN) AIAS THE REASON OF
HIS LATE COOL RECEPTION OF ODYSSEUS, WHEN HE CAME
DOWN TO LEARN THE FUTURE FROM TEIRESIAS. AIAS JUS-
TIFIES HIS HOSTILE FEELING BY ALLEGING THE CONDUCT OF
ODYSSEUS TO HIM, IN THE MATTER OF THE COMPETITION FOR
THE ARMS OF ACHILLEUS.

Aias and Agamemnon.[1]

Agamemnon. If you in a fit of madness, Aias, killed
yourself, and intended also to murder us all, why do you
blame Odysseus; and, the day before yesterday, why did
you not even look at him, when he came to consult the
oracle, or deign to address a word to your old comrade
and companion, but haughtily passed him by with huge
strides ?[2]

Aias. With good reason, Agamemnon; for he was the
actual and sole cause of my madness, seeing that he put
himself in competition with me for the arms.

Agamemnon. And did you consider it your right to be
unopposed, and to lord it over all without the toil of
contest ?

Aias. Yes, indeed, in such respect; for the suit of armour
was my own, as it was my uncle's.[3]   Indeed, you others,
though far superior *to him,* declined the contest for yourselves, and yielded the prize to me; whereas the son of
Laertes, whom I often saved, when in imminent peril of
being cut to pieces by the Phrygians, set himself up to be
my superior, and to be more worthy to receive the arms.

Agamemnon. Blame Thetis, then, my admirable Sir,
who, though she should have delivered over the heritage of

---

[1] Cf. 'Oδ. 542-563 ; Soph. Aἴας, 1355 ; Ov. *Met.* xiii. 1-398, where, at
the close of the lengthy harangues of the rival competitors, Odysseus
prevails,

" fortisque viri tulit arma disertus."

[2] The Homeric phrase—μακρὰ βιβάς.

[3] Peleus: Telamon and he being brothers.

the arms to you as her relative, took and deposited them for general competition.

Aias. No, but Odysseus, who was the only one to put himself forward as claimant.

Agamemnon. It is excusable, if, human as he was, he had great longing after glory, a very pleasant acquisition, for the sake of which every one of us, also, underwent dangers ; seeing, too, he conquered you, and that before Trojan judges.

Aias. I know what Goddess gave sentence against me: but it is not allowed one to say anything *true* regarding the divinities.   But as for your Odysseus, however, I could not by any means cease from hating him, Agamemnon ; not even if Athena herself should enjoin it upon me.[1]

XXX.

SOSTRATUS,[2] FOR HIS CRIMES, ABOUT TO BE CONSIGNED BY MINOS TO THE TORTURES OF TARTARUS, PROTESTS AGAINST THE INJUSTICE OF HIS SENTENCE; SINCE, UPON THE ADMISSIONS OF HIS JUDGE HIMSELF, HE HAD BEEN A MERE INSTRUMENT IN THE HANDS OF FATE. MINOS, MOVED BY THE PLAUSIBILITY OF HIS PLEA, REPRIEVES HIM.

Minos and Sostratus.

Minos. Let this brigand Sostratus be cast into Pyri-phlegethon, and let the sacrilegious rascal be torn piecemeal by our Chimæra ;[3] and, as for this tyrant, let him be ex-

---

[1] Athena had favoured the pretensions of her protégé. Her inter-position at a still more critical juncture, between the two principal Achæan chiefs, quarrelling for the captive girls, Briseis and Chryseis, may be seen in 'Iλ. i. 193-222.

[2] Of this follower of Prokrustes, nothing more is known than his name. Lucian (as remarked by Du Soul), from a passage in his Δημώναξ seems to have written his life, and, in the 'Αλεξάνδρυς, he is numbered among the worst criminals.

[3] This divine monster, who has given to the modern languages a word expressive of the fabulous or impossible, was a composition of lion, goat, and dragon or serpent, as described in 'Iλ. vi. 180-183 :—

posed, Hermes, side by side with Tityos,[1] and have his liver gnawed, too, by the vultures. But as for you good people—depart with all speed to the Elysian field, and inhabit the Islands of the Blessed,[2] in recompense for your just actions in life.

Sostratus. Hear me a moment, Minos, *and judge* whether I appear to you to say what is just.

Minos. Must I listen to you again? Why, have you not been out-and-out convicted, Sostratus, of being a bad man, and of having murdered a number of people?

Sostratus. I have been condemned, it is true; but consider whether I shall be, in fact, justly punished.

Minos. Very certainly you will be; if, at least, it is just to suffer merited punishment.

ἡ δ' ἄρ' ἔην θεῖον γένος, οὐδ' ἀνθρώπων·
Πρόσθε λέων, ὅπιθεν δὲ δράκων, μέσση δὲ χίμαιφα,
Δεινὸν ἀποπνείουσα πυρὸς μένος αἰθομένοιο.

Hesiod makes her still more formidable by giving her, like Kerberus, three heads. Θεογ. 319-325. The fire-breathing monster, we are informed by that poet, was killed by Bellerophon and Pegasus. It was thenceforth settled (according to Virgil, *Æn.* vi. 288) at the entrance to Orcus, the most dreaded of the infernal terrors. So Ov. *Tristia*, iv. 7. Cf. Lucretius, *De Rer. Nat.* v. 904-906.

[1] Tityos, one of the chief criminals in Tartarus, was the gigantic son of Zeus or of Gaia, and had his habitation in the island of Eubœa. It was an attempted outrage on Leto, or her daughter Artemis, which entailed upon him his tremendous penalty in Tartarus, where, like Milton's Satan, he lay " stretched out huge in length " :—

Viscera præbebat Tityos lanianda, novemque
Jugeribus distentus erat. (Ov. *Met.* iv. 456.)

Cf. Lucretius, iii. 984-994; Virg. *Æn.* vi. 595; Statius, *Thebais* i. Apollod. i. 4. 1.

[2] For a description of the Homeric Paradise, see 'Οδ. iv. 565-570 :—

Τῇ περ ῥηίστη βιοτὴ πέλει ἀνθρώποισιν·
Οὐ νιφετὸς οὔτ' ἄρ χειμὼν πολὺς, οὔτε πότ' ὄμβρος, κ. τ. λ.

Cf. Hesiod, 'Ερ. καὶ 'Ημ, 170-174; Pindar, 'Ολ. ii. 109 :—

Ἴσον δὲ νύκτεσσι αἰεὶ,
Ἴσα δ' ἐν ἀμέραις ἅλι—
ον ἔχοντες, ἀπονέστερον
'Εσθλοὶ νέμονται βίο—
τον. . . .

See *Æn.* vi. 743; Ov. *Amor.* ii. 6, 49-58; Plato, Φαίδων; Lucian, Περὶ Θυσίων; 'Αλήθ. 'Ιστ. ii., and a charming description in an epigram in the *Anthologia Græca*, addressed to Πρώτη :—

Οὐκ ἔθανες, Πρώτη, μετέβης δ'ἐς ἀμείνονα χῶρον, κ. τ. λ.

Sostratus. However, answer me, Minos : for I will put briefly a certain question to you.

Minos. Speak, let it only not be long, that we may pass judgment on the rest of them forthwith.

Sostratus. Whatsoever actions I performed in my life, whether did I do them, of my own free will, or had they been spun out for me by the Fate?[1]

Minos. By the Fate, to be sure.

Sostratus. Well, then, did all of us who have the reputation of being good or bad, do those actions *of ours* as subservient to her?

Minos. Certainly to Klotho, who appoints to each one at birth what he is to do.

Sostratus. If, then, a man, forced by another, should murder some one, having no power of resisting his compulsion, such as a public executioner or an officer of the guard—the one obeying the judge, the other the prince—whom would you charge with the murder?

Minos. It is clear *one would have to charge* the judge or prince ; since it is not the sword itself *we must accuse,*[2] for that, as the instrument for his rage, is merely the minister of him who first gave the occasion *for its use.*

Sostratus. Bravo, Minos, for giving more forcible illustration to my instance.—And if a man, when his master sends him, comes in place of his master, with gold or silver, to whom must one attribute the favour, or whom must one register as the benefactor?

Minos. The sender ; for the carrier is an agent *merely.*

Sostratus. Do you see, then, how unjustly you act in

---

[1] Namely Klotho, the Μοῖρα whose particular province it was to *unwind* or *spin out* the thread of human existence, whence her name. See Ἐλεγχομ. She occupies a prominent place in the Κατάπλούς ἤ Τύραννος. Cf. Χάρων. 13, 14 ; Νεκρ. Διαλ. xix. *ad fin.*

[2] " Lucian seems to make sarcastic allusion to a religious ceremony of the Athenians at the festival of the Βουφονία (" Ox-Murder "), when the priest-butcher of the cow or ox fled for his life ; while the axe, by which the murder was effected, was brought to trial and condemned as the guilty accomplice. This subject may be seen described at length in Meursius, and Castellanus on the Hellenic Festivals."—Jens. This very significant survival of early sacrificial ritual took place at the *Dipolia* (" Festival of Zeus "). See Aristoph. Νεφ. 985, 986. Cf. Porphyry, Περὶ τῆς Ἐποχῆς.

punishing us, who are simply ministers and agents, in respect of the orders of Klotho, and in rewarding those who are only ministers of the good deeds of others ? For, surely, no one could maintain this, at all events—that it was possible to resist commands imposed with the whole force of necessity.[1]

Minos. My friend Sostratus, you might see many other things, too, which are not to be squared with Reason exactly, if you inquire with any diligence. But, however, *you* will derive this advantage from your questioning—that you appear to be not only a brigand, but also a sort of sophist.—Let him go, Hermes, and let him receive no further punishment. (*To Sostratus.*) Beware, however, that you don't put the rest of the Dead up to propounding questions of a like kind.

[1] This sort of special pleading has been most wittily used by Lucian in his Ζεὺς Ἐλεγχόμενος. For a memorable instance of this appeal to "Necessity, the tyrant's plea," see, in the *Letters of Phalaris*, the defence of himself by the famous tyrant of Agrigentum (for his treatment of the constructor of the brazen bull, and of his other victims), addressed to the Athenians, in which he adopts the highly convenient doctrines of Predestination and "fixed Fate," advanced by Sostratus.

ZEUS THE TRAGEDIAN.

[ZEUS, gloomy and in tragic distress, is implored by
Hermes and Athena to divulge the cause of his melancholy condition ; while Hera, true to her Homeric character,
confidently attributes it to another earthly amour. The
king of gods and men, thus adjured, announces the true
reason of his anxiety—daring assaults upon the character
of himself and the rest of the Olympian divinities, and, in
fact, denial of their very existence, by the skeptics, represented by an Epikurean philosopher named Damis ; and the
weakness of the arguments of their over-zealous apologists,
the Stoics, represented by a champion named Timokles :
which all-important controversy he had chanced to over-
hear when present, on the day preceding, at a sacrificial
feast given to the Gods at Athens.

He proceeds to request the opinions of the three divinities upon the best course to be pursued, in the emergency.
Hera and Hermes propose a Council of the Gods ; Athena,
a private settlement of the business. The former opinion
prevails, and Zeus directs Hermes to summon the rest of
the Gods to a general Council, which the Olympian herald
proceeds to do in the orthodox Homeric style, after some
reluctance on account of his want of poetic skill, and in
face of the discouraging example of Apollo, whose prophetic utterances (in verse) had become the object of so
much ridicule. Some difficulty arises, at the outset, on
the question of precedence, both because (the representative
statues of the divinities being variously formed of gold,
silver, ivory, and bronze) it was a question whether it
should be decided by the material, or by the excellence of

the workmanship; and, also, by reason of the numerous recent additions to their august body. Zeus rules that gold must have the preference. By this decision the old-established, genuine Hellenic divinities find themselves forced to give way to the *novi homines*, not without much and protracted squabbling. In the end, by the ruling of the president, the members of the celestial Senate have to take their places promiscuously, on the principle of "first come first served."

Silence having been secured, Zeus rises to open the deliberations. An unaccustomed nervousness and hesitation threaten to spoil his *exordium*, and even to ruin everything, by raising suspicion of the soundness of their cause. At length, at the suggestion of Hermes, discarding the well-worn Homeric *exordium*, he opens in the words of a famous oration of Demosthenes. He sets forth the cause of the summoning of the Council, and reports the circumstances which led to his presence at the dispute between the Epikurean and Stoic champions, in the Painted Porch at Athens, and its fortunate interruption at a critical moment by the pressure of the crowd, with its consequent adjournment. The Gods, whom age and standing permit, are then invited to deliver their several opinions upon the course of action to be adopted. Momus, the Censor of the Olympian Court, rises, and, with his usual candour, affirms that the objections and arguments of their avowed enemies are not at all to be wondered at; and, in fact, himself points to the prevalence of injustice and cruelty, the triumph of the bad, and the oppression and sufferings of the good on the Earth. He takes occasion to ridicule the studied ambiguity and obscurity of Apollo and his oracular prophecies, and the mischiefs arising from them; and next criticises the policy which admitted so many strange and outlandish divinities to the rights of Olympian Godship.

Poseidon and Apollo next address the Council; the former voting for violent and summary measures—nothing less, in fact, than the destruction of Damis by a thunderbolt; in which opinion (later) he is vigorously supported by Herakles. The latter calls attention to the inferiority, and confused and illogical method, of their apologist, and advises that an associate-advocate be supplied to him, to whom alone it should be allowed to speak, Timokles acting merely as his prompter.   The opportunity is not lost by Momus for sarcastic allusion to Apollo's own confused prophetical style; and, ridiculing the proposition of an associate-advocate, he calls upon him opportunely to give some *ex tempore* specimens of his oracular faculty.   Thus urged, with much reluctance and diffidence Apollo complies, to the great entertainment of his censor.   At this juncture there arrives in hot haste, fresh from the yesterday's scene of verbal conflict at the Painted Porch, Hermagoras, a statuary, who, like the Ephesian town-clerk, may be supposed to have been a not entirely disinterested well-wisher to the Olympian Establishment.   In iambic verse he announces the approaching renewal of hostilities, in the oracular strain so dear to Apollo, and so well known to readers of Herodotus, of the 'Ορνίθες and 'Ιππεῖς of Aristophanes, and of Lucian.

The Celestials arrange themselves in attitudes of eager expectancy; and the verbal duel below begins with a vituperative onslaught (in which controversial virtue Zeus recognizes their champion's strength to lie) on the part of Timokles, and a dispute on the question upon which of the two rested the *onus probandi*.   This being settled, at length, by the concession of Damis in favour of his opponent, the combatants engage in earnest.   As the fortune of the day seems to incline to this side or that, the celestial spectators express, chorus-like, their hopes or fears—the latter, however, very greatly preponderating; Momus not omitting to exercise his powers of sarcasm.   Timokles, after vainly throwing overboard his sheet-anchor—in the shape of a remarkable syllogism—takes refuge, as his opponent tauntingly expresses it, at the altars.   Damis, claiming the victory, now retires from the scene, pursued by the vituperation and even missiles and blows of his enraged antagonist.   The celestial clients of Timokles disperse, consoled by the reflection of Hermes, that, in spite of all the arguments of the wicked philosophers, at all events the larger part of the world, Greek as well as barbarian, will continue to be on their side, and not cease to supply them with the rich steams of sacrifice.   Zeus, however, cannot refrain from the expression of his feeling, that he would rather have one such able champion as the Epikurean, than a thousand conquests by stratagem or force.

This masterpiece of Lucian opens with parodies (in hexameter and iambic verse) of the Homeric epics, of Euripides, and the tragic poets.]

Zeus, Hera, Athena, Aphrodite, Apollo, Hermes, Poseidon, Herakles, Kolossus, Momus, Hermagoras, Timokles, Damis.

Hermes. O Zeus! why pensive mutter'st inward words,
Re-pacing, lonely, as a student pale?
To counsel call me : cast on me thy care,
Scorn not thy servant's chat nonsensical![1]
 Athena. Yea, thou supreme of governors, our father,
  child of Kronos,
I, owl-eyed goddess, Trito-born, cling to thy knees im-
  ploring.
Speak out, and no concealment make ; thereby we all shall
  know it,
What plotting gnaweth inwardly thy secret heart and vitals,
Or what draws out thy heavy moan, and stains thy cheek
  with pallor?[2]
 Zeus. (*to himself.*) No dire disaster, so to say, exists,
No woe so terrible and tragical,

[1] These iambics parody some unknown tragic dramatist. They are thus translated by Wieland :—

  O Zeus, was ist dir, dass du so allein,
  Gedankenvoll und grüngelb, mit der Farbe
  Von einen Philosophen, auf und nieder gehst,
  Und mit dir selber sprichtst? Entdeck' es mir.
  Lass mich an deinen Sorgen antheil nehmen ;
  Vielleicht kann eines treuen Dieners Rath,
  So schlecht er ist, dir noch zu statten kommen.

The English version of the hexameters has been modelled on the metre of Professor Newman's *Iliad of Homer*.

[2] A parody of 'Οδ. i. 45, and 'Ιλ. iii. 35, and other Homeric passages :—

  Auch ich, O unser Vater Kronion, der Könige höchster,
  Ich, die grauaugige Göttin, aus deinem Haupte gebohren,
  Knie vor dir. O höre mich an! verhehle nicht länger
  Was am Herzen dir nagt! Was ist dir, lass es uns wissen,
  Dass du so schwer erseufzest, und deine Wange so blass ist?

But Gods in heav'n must toil beneath the load.[1]

Athena. Apollo ! what an overture of speech ![2]

Zeus. (*to himself.*) Rascals ! infernal nurselings of the Earth,
And thou, Prometheus ! Oh, how deep thy stab ![3]

Athena. Say, what ? for only we thy friends will hear.[4]

Zeus. (*to himself.*) O whirr of lightning's mighty crash,
      what now wilt thou avail me ?[5]

Hera. Calm your wrath, since we cannot all play comedy,
Zeus, like these *geniuses*, nor have we swallowed Euripides
whole[6] so as to respond to you in tragic guise. Do you suppose
us not to know the cause of your grief, what it really is ?

Zeus. Thou know'st not: else loud clamour would'st
      thou raise.

Hera. I know the real source of your sufferings—a love-
affair. However, from force of habit I no longer make a
clamour, having been often before now insulted by you in
that sort of thing. Likely enough, no doubt, you have
found a Danae, or Semele, or a Europa again, and are tor-
mented by your passion, and so are planning to take the
form of some bull, or satyr,[7] or to become gold and flow in a
stream through the roof into the bosom of your mistress :
for these are the signs—these heavy sighs and tears and
pallor—of nothing else than of love.

Zeus. Silly creature, to suppose our trouble to have anything to do with love and such trifles ![8]

---

[1] Parody of opening verses of the *Orestes* :—

    Es giebt, um alles auf einmal zu sagen,
    Kein Ungemach, kein Leiden, kein Tragödien-Unglück,
    Womit wir Götter uns nicht placken müssten.

[2]   Apoll ! was kündigt uns der Eingang an !

[3]   Kann was verruchters sein als diess
    Pedantenvolk auf Erden ?   O Prometheus !
    Was hast du mir für Uebel zubereitet !

[4]   Was ists denn ?   Rede frei, du sprichst ja nur
    Zum Chor von deinem Hausgenossen—

[5]   O du, des fürchterlich rasselnden Blitzes Gepolter—was hilfst du ?

[6] Borrowed from Aristophanes, Βατρ. etc.

[7] To make love to Antiope, daughter of the River-God Asopus, and
mother by Zeus of Amphion and Zethus. She is named again below.
Cf. Milton :—

    " Some beauty rare, Calisto, Clymene," etc. (*Par. Reg.* ii. 186), etc.
See Aristoph. Ὀρνίθες. 554-560, Νεφ. 1063-4.

[8] This response of Zeus, as has been pointed out, by a very slight

Hera. But what else, if not this, annoys you—considering you are Zeus himself?

Zeus. In peril dire, affairs divine are placed, and here is the proverb verified, Hera, "it now stands upon a razor's edge,"[1] whether we are to have honour any longer paid to us, and to have our *accustomed* honours on Earth, or, in fact, to be altogether neglected, and to have no reputation at all.

Hera. The Earth has not produced any Giants again, has it? Or have the Titans burst their chains, and overpowered their guard, and do they once again take up arms against us?

Zeus. Fear not: no danger threatens from below.[2]

Hera. What else, pray, could there be to alarm? For I don't see, if something of the sort does not distress you, for what reason you leave your proper character, and come out as another Polus or Aristodemus.[3]

Zeus. Timokles the Stoic, and Damis the Epikurean, Hera, yesterday, from some discourse or other begun between them, were disputing on the subject of Providence, in the presence of a very numerous and select audience—a circumstance which especially annoys me; and Damis affirmed that neither have the gods any existence, nor do they exercise any supervision at all over what happens *on Earth*; while Timokles, best of men, endeavoured all he could to maintain our cause. At this juncture, a dense mob surging against them, there was no definite conclusion of the conference; for they separated, after agreeing to consider the remaining arguments at some future time. And now all are in a state of suspense in regard to this discussion, as to which shall have the best of it, and be

alteration of the first word, and the addition of the beginning of Hera's reply, may be resolved into iambics:—

Ὦ μάκαιρ'

Ἥτις ἐν ἔρωτι, καὶ τοιαύταις παιδίαις
Οἴει θ'ἀμέτερα πράγματ' εἶναι ἄλλο τί.

[1] A common Greek proverb. Cf. 'Ιλ. x. 173; Theognis, 557; Herod. vi. 11; Æsch. Χοεφ. 883; Soph. Ἄντ. 996.

[2] A parody, perhaps, of Euripides, Φοιν. 118;—

Θάρσει· τὰ γ' ἔνδον ἀσφαλῶς ἔχει πόλις.

[3] Celebrated tragedians of the age of Demosthenes. See Lucian's Νεκυομαντεία. 16.

judged to have the more truth on his side. You see the danger, how our interests are altogether in a strait, risked upon *the ability* of one man.' And one of two things *must happen*—either we must be despised, and be voted mere names, or we are to be honoured as heretofore, supposing Timokles shall have the best of the argument.

Hera. A terrible state of things, this, of a verity ; and not without reason, Zeus, were you acting the tragedian, under the circumstances.

Zeus. And you imagined that, in such trouble, I had thought of a Danae or Antiope !—What now, Hermes, and Hera, and Aphrodite, should we do? Do you together, according to your several ability, devise something.

Hermes. For my part, I hold you should summon an Assembly, and refer the consideration of the matter to the whole body *of the Gods.*

Hera. I am exactly of the same way of thinking.

Athena. I, however, have the contrary opinion, father—that we don't throw heaven into utter confusion, nor make it plain that you are disturbed by the occurrence, but manage this business privately, in such manner that Timokles shall have the best of it in argument, and Damis leave the conference an object of thorough ridicule.

Hermes. But since the contest of the philosophers will be in public, these things will not be unknown, Zeus, and you will have the repute of being tyrannical, should you not throw open to all *a discussion* about matters of so much importance and general interest.

Zeus. Well, then, make your proclamation at once, and let all of them put in an appearance—for you are right.

Hermes. (*mounting the bema.*) Halloo! I say, come together, you Gods, to a meeting; don't loiter, come all, in a body, come ! we shall discuss business of great importance.

Zeus. Is it in this bare, unornamental, and prosaic style you make your proclamation, Hermes; and that, too, when you are summoning them on matters of highest import ?

Hermes. Well, but how, Zeus, do you require me *to do it ?*

---

[1] Zeus may have condescended to borrow this expression from the famous Funeral Oration of Perikles, as reported by Thucydides :—μὴ ἐν ἑνὶ ἀνδρὶ πολλῶν ἀρετὰς κινδυνεύεσθαι εὖ τε καὶ χεῖρον εἰπόντι πιστευ θῆναι. ii. 35.

Zeus. How do I require you to do it? I say you ought
to impart solemnity to your proclamation by some sort of
verse, and with poetical magniloquence, that they may be
induced to assemble with more alacrity.

Hermes. Yes, but such is the business of versemakers and
professional reciters, while I am not the least of a poet. So
I shall completely spoil my proclamation, by stringing
together verses either with too many or too few feet, and
shall be the object of their ridicule for my want of poetic
skill.   In fact, I observe that even Apollo himself is laughed
at for some of his oracular responses,[1] although his obscurity[2] conceals the greater part *of his blunders*, as his
hearers have not too much leisure for examining his
metrical effusions.

Zeus. Then, Hermes, mix up in your proclamation,
chiefly, verses from Homer, in the manner he was wont to
convene us.   Of course, you call them to mind?

Hermes. Not so very accurately and readily ; but, all the
same, I will try (*much preliminary clearing of the throat*):—

Let none of Gods, whate'er the sex, fail to obey my summons,
Nor any River stay behind, except the stream of Ocean,
Nor any Nymph: but haste ye all to swell the lofty Council
Of Zeus, whoe'er at hecatombs illustrious are feasted,
Modest howe'er your rank—if mean, or even stark ignoble,
Come hither, all, whoever sit beside the steaming altars.[3]

---

[1] The oracles were delivered in verse. Herodotus has preserved for
us some remarkable specimens of these ingeniously ambiguous prophetic
utterances. See, especially, Herod. i. 46-56, vii. 140-144; Thucyd. ii.
54; and cf. the very witty parodies and ridicule of Aristoph. in his masterpiece, the ’Ορνίθες (960-988) ; Lucian, Θεῶν ’Εκκλ., ’Αλεξ. ; Juv. *Sat.* vi.
555, etc.

[2] ’Ασαφείας. Or, reading τῆς μαντικῆς (with Jacobitz), " oracular
skill."

[3] Dass kein weiblicher Gott, dass keiner vom Männergeschlechte,
Noch der Flüsse, der Söhne des alten Oceanus einer,
Noch der Nymfen sich säume! Kommt alle zu Jovis versammlung,
Die ihr an festlichen Tagen die Hekatomben verschmauset,
Alle, so viel' als euer, vom ersten Rang und vom zweyten
Bis zu den Nahmenlosen herab, an bekränzten Altären
Sitzet, und gierig den Rauch vom brennenden opferfett einschlürft!
(Wieland.)

Hermes is indebted, in particular, to ’Ιλ. viii. 7, xx. 7, ix. 228, xiii. 227,
successively, for the *farrago* of his parody.

Zeus. Bravo, Hermes. You have performed your crier's part most admirably; and, indeed, they are already rushing together. So take and seat them, each according to rank, as it belongs to him by reason of material or art—the Golden in the front rank, then next to them the Silver; next in due order all the Ivory ones; after them the Bronze or the Marble; and among these same let those of Pheidias, or Alkamenes, or Myron, or Euphranor,[1] or of similar artists, have the best places. As for these rabble, and inartistic fellows, let them be crammed together somewhere at a distance, and serve only to fill up the House as dummies.

Hermes. So it shall be, and they shall take their seats as is proper. But it's not so easy to know—when any one of them is of gold, indeed, and of many hundredweight,[2] but not perfect in workmanship, but plainly vulgar and plebeian, and badly proportioned, shall he seat himself before the bronze gentlemen of Myron, and of Polykleitus,[3] and of Pheidias, and the marble ones of Alkamenes? Or must we consider Art to have precedence?

Zeus. So it ought to be; but, all the same, preference must be given to Gold.[4]

[1] The first of these most distinguished sculptors and statuaries of Hellas and the world is sufficiently well known. Alkamenes, the most eminent of the pupils of Pheidias, was especially famous for a statue of Aphrodite. Myron, the sculptor of the well-known *Discobolos*, an elder contemporary of Pheidias, was the Landseer of Greek sculptors. His Cow was especially in high repute, and in the Greek *Anthologia* thirty-six epigrams celebrate her praise. It was removed from Athens between the age of Cicero and that of Pausanias. This beautiful statue survived, at least, to the sixth century. Of the works of Euphranor, a native of Korinth, but, like most of the great artists, resident at the "hospitable" Athens, most celebrated was his representation of Paris, of which the statue in the Museo Pio-Clementino is probably a copy. See Pliny, *Hist. Nat.*

[2] Πολυτάλαντος τὴν ὁλκήν. Lit. "many talents in weight." The τάλαντον, both gold and silver, was used as a measure of weight varying at different periods. Here the *gold* talent, probably, is intended.

[3] Polykleitus, of the Argive and Sikyon School of Sculpture, a contemporary of Pheidias, has been ranked second only to the Koryphæus of Greek Art. The Argive was more celebrated for *human*, the Athenian for *divine* figures. The most famous of his works were the *Doryphorus*, or *Kanon* (as it was termed, from being held to be the ideal of the human form), and his *Hera*. See Pliny, *Hist. Nat.*

[4] "An excellent trait," remarks Wieland, "of the *anthropomorphic* character of this Jupiter."

Hermes. I understand you to direct me to seat them according to wealth and property, not according to excellence and real value.—Come, then, to the front seats, you golden gentlemen. (*In a whisper.*) The foreigners, Zeus, appear to be the only ones likely to occupy first places; for you observe of what description the Greeks are—elegant and good-looking enough, and artistically fashioned, but, none the less,[1] all of marble or bronze, or (at all events) the most costly of them are ivory, with just a little gold gilding so as merely to have a surface tint and veneer *of that metal;* but inside they are, in fact, all wooden, sheltering whole troops of rats, that form regular colonies there; while Bendis here, and that Anubis there, and Attis at his side, and Mithras and Meen [2] are all of solid gold, and pretty costly, and no mistake.

Poseidon. Is really this justice, Hermes, that this dog-faced fellow of Egypt should have place before me—actually before Poseidon, God of the Sea, himself!

Hermes. Yes, but, Earth-shaker,[3] Lysippus [4] fashioned you as a poor fellow of bronze—for the Korinthians had then no gold, and that is more precious than all the other metals put together. You must, therefore, submit to be thrust aside, and not be angry, if a fellow with such a huge snout [5] of gold has been preferred to you.

Aphrodite. In that case, Hermes, take me, too, and give me a seat on the front row; for *I* am golden.

Hermes. Not as far as I can see, Aphrodite: but (unless

---

[1] Jacobitz has ὁμοίως, "alike."

[2] Bendis, a Thracian divinity, whom Hesychius identifies with Artemis. See Ἰκαρο-Μένιππος, 24; Strabo, x. Mithras, the Persian solar divinity, represented in sculpture in a Phrygian dress, kneeling on a prostrate bull, whose throat he is cutting. Meen, or Lunus, a Phrygian divinity. Consult Spanheim, *De Usu Numism.* For Attis and Anubis, see Θ. Δ. xii., N. Δ. xiii., Ζεὺς Τραγ., Ἐκκλ. Θεῶν.

[3] Ἐννοσίγαιε—the Homeric epithet for Poseidon.

[4] Lysippus, of Sikyon, the distinguished sculptor-laureate of Alexander of Macedon, whose statues in bronze (in which material only he worked) are said to have been 1,500 in number. With Apelles in painting, he had, in sculpture, the monopoly of Alexander's portraits, of which he executed a large variety, none of which have come down to us.

[5] Anubis. "Plangentis populi currit derisor Anubis."—Juv. *Sat.* vi. 534.

I am altogether purblind) after having been hewn out of white marble from Pentele, I imagine, you then, at the good pleasure of Praxiteles, became Aphrodite, and were handed over to the Knidians.[1]

Aphrodite. Indeed I have a very credible witness I shall quote to you—Homer himself, who up and down his poems calls me the " Golden Aphrodite."

Hermes. Why, indeed, the same Homer says that Apollo, too, is very golden and rich:[2] but now you will see even him seated somewhere in the third class,[3] deprived of his crown by thieves, and completely robbed of the pegs of his cithara. So be satisfied that even your place in the assembly is not, in fact, among the lowest classes.

Kolossus (of Rhodes). With me who would venture to compete, for I am the very Sun himself, and of size so enormous ?[4] If, to be sure, the Rhodians had not thought fit to construct me of so portentous and excessive dimensions, at an equal expense they could have made for themselves sixteen Gods of gold. So that, by the rules of proportion, I should be considered of all the greater value;

---

[1] The Knidian Aphrodite, one of the most celebrated statues of antiquity, and the production of one of the most eminent of Greek sculptors, perished by fire at Constantinople, in the reign of Justinian. It had the reputation of being the most perfectly beautiful of the statues of the Goddess, and was modelled from the famous *hetæra*, Phryne, who, also, was the original of the equally famous picture of Apelles—the *Aphrodite Anadyomene* (" Aphrodite Rising from the Sea "). Cf. Lucian,'Ερῶτες, 11, κ. τ. λ. Pentelicus, an offshoot of the Mt. Parnes range, in Attica, famous for its marble, derived its name from the borough of Pentele.

[2] " He is called ' rich,' but nowhere in Homer πολύχρυσος, which is the usual epithet of Venus in Hesiod."—De Soul.

[3] 'Εν τοῖς Ζευγίταις. Among the *Zeugitæ* (those who could afford to have a *yoke* of oxen), the third class of the citizens in the timocratic constitution of Solon. The income of the *Zeugite* was fixed at from about £8 to £12 *per annum*. The *Thetes*, whose property-qualification fell below £8, formed the fourth and lowest class. The *Pentecosiomedimnoi*, who possessed a *minimum* income of 500 *medimni* or *drachmæ* (about £20), were ranked in the first class.

[4] He was the work of Chares of Lindus, 280 B.C. This gigantic bronze statue of Apollo, one of the " Seven Wonders," had a height of over 100 feet. It was thrown down by an earthquake about fifty years after its creation, and lay where it fell until the year 667 A.D., when the Saracen Arabs broke it up. The extraordinary fable, so often repeated by modern writers, of its striding the Rhodian harbour, originated in the sixteenth century. See Pliny, *Hist. Nat.* xxxv. 10.

and the artistic skill is to be counted into the bargain, and the perfection of the work in a statue of such magnitude.

Hermes (aside to Zeus). What must I do, Zeus? For this for me, at least, is a hard business to determine: for if I should regard solely the material, he is bronze; but if I should reckon at the cost of how many thousands he has been fabricated, he would be far above the first-class *claimants.*

Zeus (aside to Hermes). Why, what must he, too, needs come here for, to reproach the insignificance of the rest, and to be a nuisance to the company? (*To the Kolossus*) Well, but hark you, most excellent Rhodian, even if you are to be preferred to the utmost to your golden *rivals,* how in the world would you ever occupy the front place, unless all have to stand up, that you alone may be accommodated, and occupy the whole Pnyx[1] with one of your buttocks? So you will do better to give your vote standing up, and make your bow to the council.

Hermes. Here, again, is another difficult thing. They are both of them, in point of fact, bronze, and of the same workmanship—each of them the work of Lysippus, and, what is most important, of the same rank as to birth— seeing both are sons of Zeus—Dionysus here and Herakles. Which of them, pray, shall have precedence? For they are wrangling, as you observe.

Zeus. We are wasting time, Hermes; whereas we ought long ago to have been at business. So now let them take their seats higgledy-piggledy, where each has a mind to; and, at some future time, a sitting shall be given to settle that point, and I shall know then what is the rank to assign to them.

Hermes. But, Herakles! what an uproar they make with their clamours for their vulgar and every-day wants— "doles! doles! where is our nektar? The ambrosia runs short. Where are the hecatombs? The sacrificial victims for the public!"[2]

---

[1] A semicircular hill, near the Areiopagus, on which the Athenian 'Εκκλήσια, or Commons' House, held its sittings. For an entertaining scene at one of these sittings, see Aristoph. 'Αχαρ. 1-202.

[2] A double satire on the celestial gourmandism and the selfish policy of the imperial Roman Government in keeping the populace of

Zeus. Silence them at once, Hermes, that they may learn on what account they have been assembled, and drop this nonsense.

Hermes. Not all of them, Zeus, understand Greek, and I am not much of a linguist, so as to make my proclamations intelligible to Tartars, and Persians, and Thracians, and Kelts. It will be better, therefore, I imagine, to make signs, and *in that way* to enjoin silence.

Zeus. So do.

Hermes. Capital: they have become dumber than the philosophers themselves. So it is high time for you to harangue them. You observe they have been long regarding you fixedly, expecting what you will say.

Zeus (aside to Hermes). Yes, but what my feelings are, Hermes, I will not shrink from imparting to you, as you are my son. You are aware how bold and magniloquent I always was in our public Assemblies.

Hermes. I am, and I used to dread hearing your harangues; most especially when you would threaten to drag up from their foundations the earth, and sea, and the Gods and all, by simply letting down that golden chain of yours.[1]

Zeus. However, now, my son, I don't know whether it is from the magnitude of the present pressing dangers, or from the number of the company—for our Parliament is crowded by the Gods to an excess, as you see—but I am utterly confused in mind, and am all of a tremble, and my tongue seems tied. But, what is strangest of all, I have clean forgotten the *exordium* to my speech, which I had prepared for myself, so that it might have as specious a beginning as possible.

Hermes (in a whisper). You have ruined everything, Zeus; they suspect your silence, and expect to hear some very great calamity as the cause of your hesitation.

the capital dependent on periodical supplies for their sustenance. Juvenal, *Sat.* x. 78-81, alludes to this policy :—

" qui dabat olim
Imperium, fasces, legiones, omnia, nunc se
Continet, atque duas tantum res anxius optat—
Panem et Circenses."

Cf. Aristoph. Ὄρνιθες, 1515-1524.

[1] See Θ. Δ. xxi.

Zeus. Would you have me, then, Hermes, begin to recite to them that celebrated prelude of Homer?

Hermes. Which?

Zeus. " Hear my words, all ye Gods and all ye Goddesses, listen ! " [1]

Hermes. Get out with you. Those introductory verses have been enough used up by you in our wine-parties. But, if you like, drop the bother of metre, and do you string together, of the harangues of Demosthenes against Philip, whatever parts you choose, with a few variations. At least, that's what most orators do nowadays.

Zeus. Excellent, a compendious sort of oratory, and a convenient and facile resource for those who are at a loss, that *you suggest.*

Hermes. Lead off, then, at last, pray.

Zeus (mounting the tribune). I think, gentlemen [2]—Gods, I mean—you would choose before a good deal, that it should be clear to you what at length this matter in truth is, with respect to which you have been brought together. This being the case, then, it is proper you should listen to me with all attention. The present crisis, O Gods, indeed, all but declares aloud in words that we must vigorously apply ourselves to the matters before us, while we seem to be very remiss in regard to them. Now I desire—Demosthenes, to confess the truth, fails me here—to explain clearly to you the business about which I am so perturbed, and for which I convoked Parliament. Well, yesterday, as you know, on the occasion of Mnesitheus, the sea-captain, offering a thanksgiving sacrifice for the safety of his ship, which had been all but lost off Kaphereus,[3] we were feasting

---

[1] " Κέκλοτε μου πάντες τε Θεοὶ πᾶσαι τε Θέαιναι."—*Il.* viii. 5.

[2] 'Ω ἄνδρες Θεοί. " The wit of this address can only be imperfectly expressed in a foreign language. The general opening of Demosthenes, and of all, who declaimed before the sovereign people at Athens, was 'Ω ἄνδρες 'Αθηναιοί. Jupiter, who in his embarrassment begins to quote the introduction to the first *Olynthiac* Oration of Demosthenes, in his anxiety forgot to change the words, and is on the point of addressing the Gods in those identical terms. When the ἄνδρες is already out, he bethinks himself all at once, and hence the ἄνδρες Θέοι in the original, which in a Greek audience must have excited loud laughter."—Wieland.

[3] A rocky promontory off S.E. Eubœa, in modern days known by the

at the Peiræus, such of us as Mnesitheus invited to the
sacrifice. Then, after the libations, you turned yourselves to your several occupations, each according to
his fancy; but I, for it was not yet very late, went up to
the city, to have an evening walk in the Kerameikus,[1]
reflecting, at the same time, on the niggardliness of Mnesitheus, who, to entertain sixteen Gods, slaughtered only a
single cock, and that, too, a long since old and wheezy one,
and four grains of exceedingly mouldy incense,[2] so that it
was at once consumed on the coals, and did not afford as
much smoke as could be smelled by even the tip of our
nostrils; and that, though he promised whole hecatombs,
when his ship was just being carried on to the rocks, and
was actually within the breakers. And, when pondering
these things, I find myself near the Stoa,[3] I observe a very
large crowd of people jammed together—some within, in
the Hall itself, but many in the open air; and some
persons shouting and vehemently clamouring, seated on
the benches. Guessing then, what indeed was the fact,
that these were philosophers of those contentious sort, I
had a mind to stand by and listen to what they say; and
(for I had enwrapped myself, as it chanced, in a cloud of
the densest), by disguising myself in their fashion, and by
letting down my beard, I had a pretty close resemblance
to a philosopher. Well, I say, elbowing aside the crowd,
I enter without being known who I was. There I find
the Epicurean Damis, the practised villain, and Timokles,
the Stoic, best of men, disputing with uncommon vehemence. Timokles, in fact, was actually all in a perspiration,
and already becoming hoarse, by his loud shouting; while

Italian name of Capo d'Oro. It was the scene of the shipwreck of the
confederated Achæan fleet on the return from the destruction of Ilium.

[1] There was an inner and outer *Quarter of the Potters*. The former,
embraced within the city, included the *Agora*; the latter was the
principal suburb of Athens. It was the inner Kerameikus that Zeus
chose for his walk.

[2] Alkiphron, the well-known epistolary writer, a younger contemporary of Lucian, has the same words in a passage in Book iii. 35, as
pointed out by Reitz.

[3] Τὴν Ποίκιλην, sub. Στόαν. One of the numerous lounging Halls in
Athens, so called from being *decorated* by frescoes by the painter
Polygnotus, representing scenes in the battle of Marathon.

Damis, making fun of him sardonically, still further provoked his antagonist. Their whole argument, forsooth, was about us. Why, that accursed Damis was affirming that neither do we exercise any providence over men, nor superintend their actions; maintaining nothing else than our entire non-existence, for that plainly was what his argument amounted to. There were some who applauded him. But the other, Timokles, took our part, and fought for us vehemently,[1] and fell into a passion, and struggled for us in every possible way, glorifying our providence, and recounting with what beautiful order and suitable arrangement we plan and dispose each particular part. He, also, had some backers, but, indeed, he had already tired himself out, and was speaking badly, and the majority were beginning to fix their attention entirely on Damis. I, perceiving all that was imperilled, ordered Night to envelop them and break up the meeting. Thereupon they went off, after agreeing to discuss the subject fully on the next day; and I, joining the crowds, listened to their praises of Damis's arguments, while they were on their way to their homes, and already choosing his side in far the larger numbers : there were some, however, who thought it fair not to condemn beforehand the opposite arguments, but to wait *to see* if Timokles shall say anything *to the point* to-morrow.

These are the reasons for which I called you together; no trifling ones, O Gods, if you shall consider how our whole honour, and glory, and revenue consist in men. If they should be persuaded either that we don't exist at all, or that, existing, we yet are altogether regardless of them and all their concerns; as far as regards the Earth, we shall be deprived of victims, dignity, or honour, and we shall sit idly in Heaven,[2] attacked by famine, as we shall be deprived of *the benefits of* those feasts of theirs, and their holy-days, and public-games, and sacrifices, and vigils,[3] and solemn processions. Wherefore, in view of matters of such importance, I say that we ought all to devise some means of safety, in our

---

[1] Ὑπερεμάχει, or "beyond his strength;" or simply "fought for us."

[2] "Magna otia Cœli."—Juv. *Sat.* vi. 394. Cf. Aristoph. Ὀρνιθ. 610-637, κ.τ.λ.

[3] Παννυχίδων (Lat. *pervigilia*), lit. "all-night festival, or watching." See Aristoph. Βατρ.; Eurip. Ἑλένη. 1365; Herod. iv. 76; Plato, Πολ.

present circumstances, and by what means Timokles shall
conquer, and be reputed to have more truth on his side, and
Damis be derided by the audience: for I, for my part, have
not excessive confidence in this Timokles, that he will
conquer by himself, if he do not receive some help from us.
Do, then, your herald's duty, Hermes, and make your proclamation according to the legal forms, that they may all
stand up and record their votes.

Hermes (shouts). Attention! Silence! Order! Which
of the full-grown Gods,[1] who are privileged, wishes to
speak?—How's this! No one get up! Ah! you are
tongue-tied and dumbfounded at the bigness of the
message, are you?

Momus. "May all of you, I pray, be turned straightway
to earth and water."[2]   Now, I, if I be allowed, at least, to
speak with perfect freedom, should have a good deal to say,
Zeus.

Zeus. Speak, Momus, with all boldness; for you are
plainly going to unburden your mind freely for the public
good.[3]

Momus. Hear then, all you Gods, what comes from the
heart, as they say.   Why, I have been quite expecting our
affairs to come to this pitch of perplexity, and that many
sophistical fellows of this sort would sprout up against us,
who would get from ourselves the source of their daring.
And, by Themis, we have right to be angry neither with
Epikurus, nor with his associates and propagators of his
arguments, if they have supposed such kind of things about

---

328. A Latin poem by an unknown poet, which celebrates the vigils
of a lover, has come down to us with the title of *Pervigilium Veneris.*

[1] Τελείων.   "Wer unter den volljährigen Göttern."—Wieland.
With preceding commentators Wieland erroneously supposes the limit
of age in the Athenian ἐκκλησία to have been fixed at thirty years. All
citizens from the age of eighteen or twenty had the right, or rather duty,
of taking part in their truly popular Legislature, nor was any *precedence*
legally given to age, although by the Solonian constitution such priority
had in the earlier period prevailed.   Hermes, in inviting discussion,
employs the regular Athenian formula, τίς βούλεται ἀγορεύειν;

[2] Ἀλλ' ὑμεῖς μὲν πάντες ὕδωρ καὶ γαῖα γένοισθε, the objurgation of
Menelaus, addressed to the assembled Achæan chiefs, who thought
proper to decline the challenge of the " glorious " Hektor ('Ιλ. vii. 99).

[3] Or, according to the common reading, " you are well known to speak
your mind," &c.

us. For what, pray, would anyone expect them to think, when they see such confusion in *human* life—their good men neglected, perishing in poverty, and diseases, and slavery; while thoroughly bad and rascally men are preferred to honours, and abound in wealth, and lord it over their betters; [1] the sacrilegious [2] not punished, but getting off scot-free, the innocent impaled alive, or sometimes beaten to death? Naturally, then, when they see these things, do they determine thus about us, as non-existent at all, especially when they hear the oracles pronounce that a certain man, by crossing the Halys, will destroy a mighty kingdom, [3] but don't explain, however, whether it is his own or that of his enemies *he will destroy;* and, again, "By thee, O Salamis divine, children of women shall die," [4] for, in fact, both Persians and Greeks, I imagine, were children of women. Nay, when again they hear the epic poets and reciters *to the effect* that we fall in love, and get wounded in battle, [5] and serve as slaves, and are put in chains, and engage in civil wars, and have ten thousand troubles of every sort, and that, too, while we claim to be blessed and incorruptible—what else *can they do* than laugh at us, and justly enough, and hold our power in contempt? However, we get into a rage if a few men (not entirely fools) convict us of these things, and reject our providence; whereas we ought to be content, if there are still any who sacrifice to us, after such scandalous behaviour.

[1] Cf. Hor. *Sat.* ii. 1 : "Cur eget indignus te divite ?" &c., and Milton :—

 " If every just man, that now pines with want,
 Had but a moderate and beseeming share
 Of that which lewdly-pampered luxury
 Heaps now upon some few with vast excess,
 Nature's full blessings would be well dispensed," &c.—*Comus.*

[2] Ἱερόσυλους. Lit. "robbers of temples," who, to judge from their frequent juxtaposition with the worst characters, had no better repute in pagan Hellas than in mediæval Europe.

[3] One of the many responses given to Krœsus by the Delphic Oracle, on inquiring as to the event of the impending war with the Persian monarch. The Halys was the boundary river. See *Herod.* i. 53. Cf. Plut. Θεμιστ.

[4]   Ὦ θείη Σαλαμίς, ἀπολεῖς δὲ σὺ τέκνα γυναικῶν,
  Ἢ που σκιδναμένης Δημήτερος, ἢ συνιούσης,
the conclusion of the twelve verses of the second oracle delivered to the inquiring Athenians.

[5] As recounted in Ἰλ. iii., where Aphrodite, among the rest of the celestials, loses the divine *ichor,* "such as spirits bleed."

And here, Zeus—for we are all by ourselves, and no human creature is present in this Assembly, except Herakles, and Dionysus, and Ganymedes, and Asklepius,[1] those illegally enregistered *Gods* there—answer me truly, if you have ever had so much care for human affairs as to trouble your head as to who of them are bad, or who are good. But you cannot say *you have.* If, in fact, Theseus on his way from Trœzene to Athens, as a sort of diversion on the journey, had not exterminated those rascals, as far as depended on you and your providence nothing would have prevented Skeiron, and Pityokamptes, and Kerkyon,[2] and the rest from being now alive and revelling in the murders of travellers. Or, unless Eurystheus, a man of old-fashioned morality and of some forethought, out of pure philanthropy had investigated the condition of every people, and despatched his domestic here [*pointing to Herakles*], an active fellow, and eager for adventures and toils, little you would have cared, Zeus, about the Hydra, and the Stymphalian birds, and the Thracian horses, and the wanton and drunken insolence of the Kentaurs. Nay, if the truth must be told, we sit here looking out only for this—whether there is anyone sacrificing and raising the fat steam of burnt offerings at the altars, while everything else is borne down the stream *of fate,* swept along as the chance of each directs. Accordingly, we now suffer what might have been expected, and we shall suffer still, when men, little by little rising up from their prostrate condition, shall find that they get no profit by their sacrifices to us and religious processions. So, I suppose, in a short time, you will see the Epikuruses, and Metrodoruses,[3] and

---

[1] These new "creations," however, were all only semi-human, being, on one side, of divine parentage. Cf. Cicero, *De Div.* ii. 56, 115.

[2] The two former were robber-chiefs, who infested the Korinthian isthmus and the mountain-borders of Attica and Bœotia. For Sinis or Pityokamptes (so called from his method of killing his captives—by tearing their limbs asunder between the branches of pine trees), see Apollod. iii. 16, whose unfinished Βιβλιοθηκα terminates with a notice of this conquest of Theseus. Kerkyon, a son of Poseidon, or Hephæstus, and tyrant of Eleusis, was also slain by the Athenian hero. Cf. Ov. *Met.* vii. 438-448, and N. Δ. xxx, and see Plutarch, Θήσευς.

[3] The most eminent of the immediate disciples of the great master— Epikurus—and destined to succeed him in the direction of the Garden

Damises ridiculing us, and our advocates vanquished and effectually muzzled by them. So it should be your business to put a stop to and heal such *scandals*, since it was you *Gods* who brought them to this pass. As for Momus, it will be no great matter to him, if he shall be disfranchised; for not even in the good old times was he of the number of glorified ones, while *you* were yet in prosperity, and feasting and revelling on the sacrifices.[1]

Zeus. Let us leave this fellow, Gods, who is always morose and critical, to go on talking his nonsense. For, as said the admirable Demosthenes, to bring charges, to find fault, and to chide is an easy matter, and within the power of anyone who wants to do so; but to take measures how the present state of things shall be improved, that, of a verity, is the part of a wise counsellor;[2] and this, I am well assured, the rest of you will do, even though this fellow hold his tongue.

Poseidon. Now, I, for my part, live mostly, as you know, under water, and do my business[3] at the bottom of the sea, as far as in me lies and, according to the best of my ability, protecting voyagers, and escorting ships, and mitigating the violence of the winds. All the same, however (for I take an interest, too, in your affairs here), I affirm that we ought to put this Damis out of the way, before they come to the contest, either by a thunder-bolt, or by some other contrivance, for fear he get the better in argument—for you say, Zeus, he is a persuasive kind of fellow. For we shall prove to them, at the same time, how we punish those who institute such *critical inquiries* to our damage.

Zeus. Are you joking, Poseidon, or have you entirely for-

---

at Athens, but he died before his master in 277 B.C. Seneca says of his diet that he almost attained to the extreme frugality of his master, and managed to live on something like sixpence of our money a day (*toto asse*).—*Ep. ad Lucilium*, xviii. Cf. Cicero, *De Fin.* ii. 28.

[1] " Momus belonged, indubitably, to the *Saturnine* Court of Heaven. Because, however, he had never been promoted to any department in the administration of earthly affairs, nor, otherwise, had made it worth their while to honour him, he was, in spite of his old and genuine divinity, nowhere honoured by men as his godship deserved."—Wieland.

[2] See Demos. 'Ολ. i. 6.

[3] " Treibe meine Geschäfte" (Wieland), or simply "reside." The notion of πολιτεύεσθαι, originally, is " to be a free citizen."

gotten that nothing of this sort depends upon our power, but the Fates spin out for each one his end—this one to die by a thunder-bolt, another by the sword, a third by fever or consumption ? For, in fact, were the matter in my power, should I have suffered, think you, those sacrilegious wretches the day before yesterday to get away from Pisa,[1] without being knocked on the head with a thunder-bolt, after having shorn me of two of my locks, which weighed each six pounds;[2] or you, would you yourself have permitted with impunity at Geræstus[3] the fisherman from Oreus to filch away your trident ? Besides, too, we shall have the look of being in a rage, and of being downcast about the business, and of being afraid of the arguments of· Damis, and for that reason *we shall be thought* to have made away with the man, and not waited for him to pit himself against Timokles. So what else shall we have the repute of doing but of conquering in this way, by default *of the enemy ?*

Poseidon. Indeed, I thought I had devised a short sort of cut to victory, by that *method,* I did.

Zeus. Get away—a very fishy idea,[4] indeed, Poseidon, and quite too clumsy, to murder one's adversary beforehand, that he may die unvanquished, and leave the controversy a drawn game, and undetermined !

Poseidon (*peevishly*). Then devise something better, you others, since you throw my suggestions in this way to the tunnies.

Apollo. If it had been permitted by law to us, who are still young and unprovided with a beard, to address the House, perhaps I might have contributed something useful to the discussion.

Momus. Our deliberation, Apollo, is about matters of

---

[1] In Elis, in the Peloponnese.

[2] From the famous statue of Pheidias at Olympia, which Pisa here represents. The latter city had been entirely destroyed by the Eleians in the sixth century B.C., and was never rebuilt. The theft, to which Zeus refers, probably had been effected in Lucian's day. The locks, it may be inferred, were golden.

[3] Geræstus was a port in the island of Eubœa, where Poseidon had a temple. Oreus was a town in the same island.

[4] Θυννῶδες τὸ ενθύμημα, which Wieland translates " eine feine Wallfischmässige erfindung." The original is " tunny-fishlike device" or " device worthy of a tunny-fish."

such importance, that leave to speak is not regulated by age, but is thrown open to all : for a pretty thing it would be if, while we were in extremest peril, we should split straws about legal qualification. And, besides, you have this long while been quite legally capable of speaking ; for you have long ago emerged from the state of minorship, and have been inscribed on the register of the Twelve,[1] and are not so far from having been a member of the Council in the time of Kronos himself. So don't affect youthful modesty with us, but speak boldly now your opinions, without bashfulness for having to harangue the House without a beard ; and that, especially, when you have a son, Asklepius, with so thick and fine-grown a one. Besides, it were surely fitting for you most particularly to show off your wisdom on the present occasion, unless you sit on Helikon, philosophizing with the Muses, to no purpose.

Apollo. But it's not for *you*, Momus, to give such permission, but for Zeus ; and should he bid me, I might, perhaps, say something not altogether unworthy of the Muses, but befitting our meditative studies on Helikon.

Zeus. Speak, my child, for I give full permission.

Apollo. This Timokles is, indeed, a good and pious man, and he has thoroughly acquired the methods of argument of the Stoics ; so that he associates, in fact, with many of the youth for the purpose of teaching them philosophy, and he pockets no small pay upon this account ; for he is exceedingly persuasive whenever he disputes in private with his pupils ; but in a crowd he is very timid in speaking, and is vulgar and provincial[2] in language, so as to incur ridicule in his controversies on that account, from not connecting his sentences, but stammering and getting confused; particularly when, though such is his peculiarity, he wishes to show off his graces of oratory. For, in mere intelligence, indeed, he is acute and subtle to an excess, as say those who best know the learning of the Stoics : but, in speaking and expounding, he spoils and confuses it by *this* weakness, as he does not explain his meaning clearly,

---

[1] *Dii Majores*, or *Dii Majorum Gentium*, as they were termed in the Latin Theology. They were Zeus, Hera, Poseidon, Apollo, Aphrodite, Ares, Hermes, Hephæstus, Athena, Demeter, Hestia, Artemis.

[2] Μιξοβάρβαρος—lit. " half-foreign."

but offers arguments very like riddles, and, besides, replies
much too ambiguously to the questions *put to him*, and
people who don't understand him laugh outright at him.
One ought, however, I imagine, to speak with clearness, and
to pay great attention to this point especially—that one's
hearers shall understand one.

Momus. You are perfectly right in this, Apollo, in com-
mending those who speak clearly, even though you do not
yourself altogether practise it in your oracles ; for you are
ambiguous and enigmatical, and safely marshal them, for
the most part, in a neutral position between both camps,[1] so
that the hearers want another Pythian Apollo to interpret
them. But what do you advise next ? what remedy to
apply to the feebleness of Timokles in argument?

Apollo. To supply, Momus, if by any means we can, another
as his mouth-piece,[2] one of those clever fellows, to speak
suitably what the other may think out and suggest.

Momus. The remark, that, of a beardless youth with a vengeance, and who still needs his tutor—that his mouth-piece
should take his stand by his side, in a conference of philosophers, to act as interpreter of the sentiments of Timokles
to the audience ; and that Damis should speak in his own
person, and by his own mouth, while the other have the
aid of a public interpreter to privately whisper in his ear,
and *prompt him to speak* his own sentiments ! And an interpreter is to act the orator, who probably even does not
understand himself what he hears ! How can these things
not be a source of ridicule for the multitude ? Nay, let
us consider this matter in a different fashion. And you,
excellent Sir—for you profess, in fact, to be a prophet, and
have procured no small quantity of profit for such work, so
far even as before now to have received gold bricks[3]—why
did not you seasonably exhibit to us your art, by predicting
which of the philosophers will come off conqueror in the

---

[1] 'Ες τὸ μεταίχμιον, or, " on a neutral frontier." Wieland translates
" zweideutiges zwischen Ja und Nein." Cf. Θεῶν 'Εκκλησία.

[2] Ξυνήγορον—lit. " associate-pleader ;" an " advocate," a recognized
institution in Athens. They were of two kinds—public and private.
See Liddell and Scott, 1883.

[3] For the splendid profits acquired by the patron-God of Prophecy
on one memorable occasion, see Herod. i. 50.

dispute? For you know, I presume, what will be the result, as you are a prophet.

Apollo. How is it possible to do so, Momus, when neither my tripod is at hand, nor altar-incense, nor oracular fountain like Kastalia.

Momus (laughing). There! though you are caught in a corner, you are for escaping conviction.[1]

Zeus. All the same, my child, speak, and don't afford this calumniator here a handle for calumniating and mocking at your *art*, as though it depended upon a tripod, and water, and incense; as though, if you have not these appliances, you would be deprived of *the power of exercising* your art.

Apollo. It were better, father, to perform such functions at Delphi or Kolophon,[2] with all my useful tools at hand, as is my wont. All the same, even though thus destitute of those things, and unequipped, I will do my endeavour to prophesy to which of the two the victory will belong. But will you bear with me, if I should not speak in regular metre?

Momus. Speak, but only clearly, Apollo, and not *verses* that themselves need a mouth-piece or interpreter; for, indeed, there will be no lamb's flesh and tortoise boiling just now in Lydia.[3] But you are aware what our deliberation is about.

Zeus (to Apollo, in whom the signs of the prophetic afflatus are visible). What in the world are you going to say, my child? For the preludes to your oracular deliverances—they are, as it is, already alarming enough. Your complexion has completely changed colour, and your eyes roll in your head,

---

[1] Τὸν ἔλεγχον, or the *reductio ad absurdum.* An allusion to the logic of the Porch. Cf. Πρᾶσις τῶν Βίων; Diog. Laert. ix. 22.

[2] Actually at Klaros, a small town near the Ionian city of Kolophon, on the S.E. coast of the Lesser Asia, whence he was known as the Klarian Apollo. See Δὶς Κατηγ. i. and Ov. *Met.* i. 516.

[3] To test the truth of the oracles, in Hellas and in Libya (before consulting them as to the result of the impending war between himself and the Persian king), Krœsus, king of Lydia, sent messengers simultaneously to demand of each one of them what he was actually doing on the day of inquiry. The ingenious monarch, on the day fixed (the hundredth from the departure of his envoys), cut up a lamb and a tortoise, and boiled them together in a brazen cauldron. The Delphic oracle alone gave the right answer, or, rather, the responses of the rest were not deemed worth preservation. See Herod. i. 46.

and your hair stands on an end, and your movements are Corybantic,[1] and your whole appearance betokens possession, and is horrifying, and mystic in the extreme.

Apollo. Hear the prophetic word divine, of me the seer
        Apollo,
About the chilly strife of tongues, which men sharp-scream-
        ing jabber,
With closely-fitted argument, accoutred as with armour.
By hubbub of alternate cluck, triumphant, hither, thither,
They many a vessel's stern strike down, of oft-repassing
        plough-tail;
But if the vulture's crooked grasp, sharp-talon'd, seize the
        breast,
Then shall the crows, who augur rain, their last forebodings
        utter.
The mules are victors: but the ass shall butt his fleeter
        children.[2]

Zeus. Why do you thus burst out laughing, Momus? Surely the circumstances before us are no laughing matter. Stop, wretch! you will literally be choked by your hilarity.

Momus. And how is it possible, Zeus, *not to be choked* by such a clear and transparent oracle?

Zeus. Then be so kind as at once to interpret its meaning for us.

Momus. Excessively clear and simple *are the verses*, so

[1] The characteristic symptoms of the phrenzied priestess as she delivered the responses of the God, seated on the tripod, over the mephitic and intoxicating fumes which issued from the caverns of Delphi. See Heliod. Αἰθ. iii.

[2] "Höret was Phöbus, der Seher, in hoher Begeisterung weissagt,
    Über den grausen Streit, der zwischen zwei Schreyern entstanden,
    Die mit scharfen Sophismen bewaffnet, gleich kämpfenden Dohlen
    Gegen einander die Schnäbel eröffnend, mit wildem Gekreische
    Hoch aus der Luft die Spitze der dichten pflugsterz erschüttern:
    Aber so bald der krummklauige Geyer die Heuschreck erfasst hat,
    Werden die regenbringenden Krähen zum letztenmal krächzen:
    Wie auch der Esel mit böckischer Stirn die Schnellfüssigen Kinder
    Anfällt, und um sich stösst; der Sieg wird dem Maulthieren bleiben!
                                                        Wieland.

Lucian's satire on the laboured unintelligibility, and laughable absurdity, of the prophetic utterances of the Hellenic oracles, is not in the least hyperbolic, and was probably suggested, especially, by the specimens quoted by the pious Herodotus (see i. and vii.). The ἄκρα κόρυμβα ("towering sterns" of the ships) is derived from 'Ιλ. ix. 241.

that we shall have no need of a Themistokles :[1] for the divine oracle says thus explicitly, that this *prophet* is a quack, and that we are a set of pack-asses, by Zeus, and mules for putting faith in him, and have not even as much sense as a lot of locusts.

Herakles. Well, father, although I am *only* a resident-alien, all the same I, for my part, will not shrink from declaring my opinion. As soon as ever they meet for discussion, then, should Timokles have the better of it, we will allow the controversy to proceed in our favour; but, if something untoward should fall out, at that moment I will myself, if you like, give a tremendous shake to the Stoa itself, and bring it on Damis's head, so that, cursed rascal as he is, he may not go on with his insolent talk against us.

Momus. Herakles, O Herakles, that is a bucolical and terribly Bœotian[2] remark of yours—with one worthless fellow to destroy such a number of people, and the Stoa into the bargain, with Marathon, and Miltiades, and Kynægeirus,[3] and all! And how, if all this perished at one blow, could the orators ever again flourish their oratory, deprived *as they would be*, of the greatest subject for their speechifying? Besides, when you were alive *on the earth*, it was, perhaps, possible for you to effect this; but since you have become a god, you have learned, I presume, that the

---

[1] We are told by Herodotus that, upon the Athenians applying a second time to the Delphic Oracle, on the eve of the Persian invasion, Apollo, through his priestess, returned for answer, after other admonition, that :—

Τεῖχος Τριτογενεῖ ζύλινον διδοῖ εὐρύοπα Ζεῦς.
Μοῦνον ἀπορθήιτον τελέθεῖν, τὸ σε τεκνα τ' ὀνήσει.

*   *   *   *   *

'Ω θείη Σαλαμὶς, ἀπολεῖς δὲ συ τέκνα γυναικῶν,

which the Athenian statesman and admiral skilfully interpreted for the benefit of his country.

[2] Herakles being a Bœotian by birth. To be a native of Bœotia, as well as of the Thracian Abdera, was a standing reproach. Cf. Pindar, 'Ολ. vi. Hor. *Ep.* i. 244 :—

" Vervecum in patriâ, crassoque sub aere nasci."

[3] Kynægeirus, who figured prominently in the frescoes of the " Painted Porch," was a principal hero in the battle of Marathon. He was a brother of Æschylus. Cf. Herod. vi. 114. Pliny, *Hist. Nat.* xxxix. 8.

Fates alone can do such things, and that we have no control over[1] them.

Herakles. Then, even when I killed the lion or the hydra, was it the Fates that performed those actions through me?

Zeus. Most certainly.

Herakles. And now, if anyone be insolent to me, by plundering my temple, or overturning my statue; unless it may have been long ago decreed by the Fates, I am not to knock him on the head?

Zeus. Certainly not.

Herakles. Then just hear me, Zeus, speak my mind freely, for, as the comic poet[2] says, "I am rough and ready, calling a spade a spade."[3] If such is the state of our affairs, I will bid a long farewell to your dignities here in heaven, and your sacrificial steam, and bloody victims; and I will go down to the infernal regions, where even the ghosts of the monsters I killed will be afraid of me with my bow, stripped and naked though I should be.

Zeus. Excellent! the *hostile* witness is found at home, as they say.[4] By your suggestions to Damis you save him, at all events, *trouble.*—But who is this coming towards us in all haste, this blacksmith, this graceful, this well-formed gentleman, he who is so old-fashioned in the style of wearing his hair?[5] Nay, rather, he must be your brother, Hermes, he of the market-place, who stands by the Painted Stoa.[6] At all events, he is besmeared from top to toe with

---

[1] Ἄκυροι (Jacobitz). Ἄμοιροι (another reading) seems to be a play on the preceding Μοῖραι.

[2] Aristophanes, according to the commentators, who quotes the proverb in one of his lost comedies. Cf. Πῶς δεῖ Ἱστ. Συγ. 41.

[3] Τὴν σκάφην, σκάφην. Lit., "a tub a tub."

[4] Οἴκοθεν ὁ μάρτυς. "The witness comes from home." "Save me from my friends." Wieland translates: "da haben wir einen Zeugen unsrer eigenen familie gegen uns!"

[5] Ὁ ἀρχαῖος τὴν ἀνάδεσιν τῆς κόμης. Lit. "Old-fashioned in the manner of *fastening up* his hair." Thucydides informs us that the old Athenian beaux almost up to the time of his writing (circa B.C. 410), bound up their hair in a knot with golden cicadas—χρυσῶν τεττίγων ἐνέρσει κρωβόλον ἀναδούμενοι τῶν ἐν τῇ κεφαλῇ τριχῶν, i. 6. Cf. Aristophanes, Νεφ. 971.

[6] For the bronze Hermes *Agoraios* ("Hermes of the Market") at the *Stoa Pækile* see Pausanias, Περιήγησις Ἀττ. Hermagoras, the newcomer, is this Hermes merely disguised in terrestrial form; whence the paternal salutation of Zeus.

pitch, by having impressions taken off him every day by the statuaries.—Why, my child, have you come here at such a racing speed? Do you, I wonder, bring any news from Earth?

Hermagoras. Exceeding important news, Zeus, and requiring serious attention.

Zeus. Say at once, if some new revolt has broken out without our knowledge.

Hermagoras. Just now my breast and back in pitchy clay
By copper-working men was plaster'd o'er:
Around my body swung right ludicrous
A breastplate, framed by imitative art—
All as mere moulding for a copper-seal.
Then saw I crowds approaching: 'mid them two
Pallid, high-brawling, fisticuffers keen
With quibbling logic. Damis one was called,
The other——[1]

Zeus. Stop, most excellent Hermagoras, your manufacture of iambics—for I am aware whom you mean. But tell me this, whether the clash of battle has long begun between them.

Hermagoras. Not yet: they were still skirmishing, engaging one another with light artillery, and vituperating one another somewhere or other at safe distance.

Zeus. What further, then, remains for us to do, Gods, than to stoop down and listen to them?[2] So let the Hours remove the bars and chains at once,[3] and, dispelling the

---

[1] " So eben hatten unsre Bildergiesser
Mich unter Händen; sie bepichten mich
An Brust und Rücken, und ein lächerlicher Panzer,
Mit nachgeahmter Kunst mir um den Leib
Gegossen, drückte meine ganze Form
Wie ein in Wachs gedrucktes Siegel ab:
Auf einmal seh' ich Volk zusammenlaufen, und
Darunter ein paar blasse kreischende
Sophismenfechter, Damis und "—Wieland.

Lucian, according to his custom, parodies some verses from one of the numberless lost tragedies of Euripides, or of some other Greek dramatist.

[2] See Ἰκαρομένιππος, 25, where the father of Gods and men, preparing to listen to the prayers of mortals, seats himself on a golden throne, or seat, placed at a number of trap-doors (θύριδες) at which he listens.

[3] See Περὶ θυσίων, 8.

clouds, let them throw wide the gates of Heaven. (*Starting back in alarm*) Herakles! What a multitude have met together to hear the philosophic disputation! But this Timokles does not altogether please me—he is all of a tremble and confused; that man will ruin everything to-day. It is plain, at all events, he will never be able to raise himself even to the level of Damis. However, what is most in our power,[1] let us pray for him.

"In silence, to ourselves, indeed, lest Damis chance to hear us."[2]

(*The scene changes from Heaven to the Stoa Pœkile at Athens.*)

Timokles. What do you say, you robber of temples—that the Gods don't exist, nor exercise any providential care over men?

Damis. No, but you, first of all, answer me, by what reasoning were you persuaded that they do exist?

Timokles. Certainly *I shall* not : rather do you, abominable villain, reply *to me.*

Damis. No, indeed; you, rather, *make answer to me.*

Zeus (*looking up from his trap-door*). Our friend so far exhibits his wrath in much better and more euphonious fashion. Bravo, Timokles! pour out upon him *all the vials of* your vituperative powers, for in that lies your sistrength; since, in other respects, he will shut you up, and make you *as dumb as* a fish.

Timokles. No, by Athena! no, I will not answer you first.

Damis. Then, pray, put your questions, Timokles, for you have conquered me by that oath : but without bad language, if you please.[3]

Timokles. You say well. Tell me then, accursed villain, do you not believe the Gods exercise providence?

Damis. By no means.

Timokles. What do you say? Do all these things, pray, go on without providential interference?

---

[1] Jacobitz, without MS. authority, apparently, has δυνατόν in place of δυνατώτατον.

[2] Σιγῇ, εφ᾽ ἡμείων, ἵνα μὴ Δάμις γε πύθηται, a parody of Ἰλ. vii. 195.

[3] Lucian, probably, had in mind, in this altercation, the famous scene in the Νεφέλαι of Aristophanes, between Δικάιος and Ἄδικος Λόγυς (879, 929-934), and in the Ἱππεῖς between Δῆμος and Κλέων and the Sausage-Seller.

Damis. Yes.

Timokles. And is the care of the Universe not placed under the superintendence of any God at all, then ?

Damis. No.

Timokles. And are all things borne along at random, by irrational impulse ?

Damis. Yes.

Timokles (*to the audience*). And so you good people endure to hear this, and you will not stone the impious sinner ?

Damis. Why do you incite the people against me, Timokles ; or, who are you, to be angry on behalf of the Gods, and that when they themselves are not angry ? At all events, they have taken no very severe measure against me, though they have heard me this long time, supposing they do hear.

Timokles. Yes, Damis, they hear, they do hear, and will punish you sooner or later, hereafter.

Damis. And when could they have leisure *to look* after me, seeing they have, as you say, so much business on their hands, in administering the affairs of the universe, infinite in number ? So that they have not even yet punished you for the perjuries you are constantly committing, and the rest of your crimes, *on which I am silent*, that I may not be myself compelled to use vituperative language, contrary to our agreement. Yet I do not see what other greater proof of their providence they could produce than by making a miserable end of a miserable man like you. But they are, evidently, away from home, beyond the Ocean, perhaps, " with the blameless Æthiopians." [1] At least, it *was* their custom constantly to go to them to dinner ; sometimes, too, at their own invitation.

Timokles. What can I say to such shameless ribaldry ?

Damis. That particular thing which I have for some time been longing to hear from you, Timokles—*how* you were persuaded to think that the Gods exercise providential care.

Timokles. Well, the ordinary arrangement of all Nature,

---

[1] Ζεὺς γὰρ ἐπ' 'Ωκεανὸν μετ' ἀμύμονας, Αἰθιοπῆας
Χθιζὸς ἔβη μετὰ δαῖτα·   Θεοὶ δ'ἅμα πάντες ἕποντο,

as his divine mother informs the complaining Achilleus, 'Ιλ. i. 423.

in the first place, persuaded me—the Sun always holding the same course, and the Moon in the same way; and the revolving Seasons, and the growing vegetation, and the birth of animated beings, and these same animals furnished with so beautiful a mechanism, so as to feed themselves, and to be capable of reflection, and of movement, and of walking, and of doing carpentry, and making shoes, and the rest—do not these things appear to you to be the actions of rational provision?

Damis. You are, I take it, begging the very thing in question,[1] for it is not yet proved whether each of these things *is* effected by rational provision. But that the order of Nature is such *as you say* I could readily affirm myself. It is not, however, a necessary *conclusion*, to be persuaded forthwith that it comes about by any intelligent contrivance: for it is possible that, having begun fortuitously, the universe is now kept together similarly and after a like fashion. But you call their orderly arrangement *necessity.* Next, you will get into a rage, I suppose, should one not follow you in your enumeration and eulogy of all things that happen, of whatever sort; and in your belief that they are a proof of the intelligent ordering of each one of them by providential design: so that, according to the comic poet:—

"Too wretched this: another plea produce."[2]

Timokles. I don't believe there is need of any further demonstration upon this matter. All the same, however, I will ask, and answer me then, do you think Homer to be a most excellent poet?

Damis. Of course.

Timokles. I believed him, then, when he declares the providence of the Gods.

Damis. Well, admirable Sir, all persons will concede to you that Homer was a good poet, but not that, of such matters, either he or any other poet is a trustworthy witness. For they care not for truth, I imagine, but for enchanting their hearers, and, therefore, they charm them by their verses and

---

[1] Αὐτο που τὸ ζητούμενον ξυναρπάζεις. "You are running off with the thing in question."

[2] From which one of the vast number of poets of the New Comedy who have perished this verse is taken, or parodied, is unknown.

instruct them by their fables; and, in fine, use every device with a view to delighting. However, I should be truly glad to hear by which of Homer's verses you were especially persuaded. Was it, perhaps, those in which he speaks of Zeus, how his daughter, and brother, and wife formed a conspiracy to put him in fetters; and, unless Thetis, as cognisant of the occurrence,[1] had summoned Briareus, our most excellent Zeus would have been carried off and actually put into prison?[2] In return for which *good offices*, calling to mind his debt of gratitude to Thetis, he deceives Agamemnon by sending him a certain lying dream, so that many of the Achæans perished.[3] Do you observe? It was impossible for him to hurl his thunderbolt and burn up Agamemnon there, on the spot, without acquiring the reputation of an impostor. Or, is it hearing these particulars that have chiefly forced you into belief—how Diomedes wounded Aphrodite, and afterwards Ares himself, at the instigation of Athena; and how, a little after, the Gods themselves engaged in battle, and fought duels, ladies and gentlemen indiscriminately: and how Athena conquers Ares, as he had been, I suppose, beforehand disabled by the wound which he had received from Diomedes,[4]

"Luck-bringer Hermes stout defied the deity of Leto,"[5]

---

[1] Reading (with Jacobitz) ὡς νοήσασα, instead of ἐλεήσασα, "pitying."

[2] See 'Ιλ. i. 397-406.

[3] For this οὖλον ὄνειρον, see 'Ιλ. ii. 1-35, for which, among other things, Plato finds fault with the poet:—Δεῖ περὶ Θεῶν καὶ λέγειν καὶ ποιεῖν, ὡς μήτε αὐτοὺς γοήτας τῷ μεταβάλλειν ἑαυτοὺς, μήτε ἡμᾶς ψεύδεσι παράγειν ἐν λόγῳ ἢ ἔργῳ . . . τοῦτο οὐκ ἐπαινεσόμεθα—τὴν τοῦ ἐνυπνίου πομπὴν ὑπὸ Διὸς τῷ Ἀγαμέμνονι. Πολ. ii. Macrobius (*Somnium Scipionis*, i. 7), and other pagan theologians, have laboured to prove that there was no real deception.

[4] See 'Ιλ. v. 310-909 :—

$$\text{ῥέε δ'ἄμβροτον αἷμα Θεοῖο}$$
$$\text{'Ιχώρ, οἷος περ τε ῥέει μακάρεσσι Θεοῖςι. κ.τ.λ.}$$

"from the gash
A stream of nectarous humour flowed
Sanguine, such as celestial spirits may bleed."
Par. Lost, vi. 331.

For the indiscriminate battle among the Gods, see 'Ιλ. xx.

[5] Λητοῖ δ'ἀντέστη σῶκος, ἐριούνιος Ἑρμῆς.
'Ιλ. xx. 72.

or do those stories about Artemis appear to you particularly
worthy of credit—when she complains and is indignant
because she was not invited by Œneus to a feast, and
accordingly sends a certain wild boar, of huge size and
irresistible strength, against his country.[1] Is it, indeed,
by such narratives that Homer has persuaded you, pray ?

Zeus (*in alarm, to the Gods*). Bless me ! how the mob shout
applause of Damis ! while our man seems like one in
despair.   He is certainly afraid, and is all of a tremble, and
evidently is on the point of throwing away his shield,[2] and
already is casting about how he shall steal away and escape.

Timokles. Does not even Euripides, pray, seem to you to
speak with any reason, whenever he mounts the Gods themselves upon the stage ; and represents them as protecting
the good heroes, and crushing the wicked, and wickedness
such as yours ?

Damis. But, most admirable of philosophers, if the tragic
poets by so doing have persuaded you, one of two things
must follow : either, that you regard Polus and Aristodemus,
and Satyrus,[3] on those occasions, as divine ; or, the very
masks of the Gods, and the tragic boots, and the long-
flowing dresses, and the short mantle, and the flowing
sleeves, and the false paunches, and paddings, and the other
things by which they give the grand air to tragedy : *a
supposition* which I presume to be highly ridiculous.   For,
whenever Euripides, in his own person, is speaking his own
opinions, when the requirement of the dramatic action
does not constrain him, hear him declaring boldly :—

> " See'st thou this vast expanse of air above,
> In whose moist arms our Earth is firmly poised ?
> That, that for Zeus ; that only God accept."

And again :—

> " Whoe'er Zeus be : for nought of him I know
> But by report," [4]

and the like.

---

[1] See 'Ιλ. ix. 530-550; and Swinburne's *Atalanta in Calydon*.

[2] The last and irretrievable disgrace of the Greek soldier.   See
Aristoph. Σφ. 19, 23 ; and cf. Plut. 'Αλκιβ. 10.

[3] Famous actors ; the two former of the tragic, the last of the comic
stage.   Satyrus is said to have given lessons to Demosthenes.

[4]   'Ορᾷς τὸν ὑψοῦ, τὸν δ'ἄπειρον αἰθέρα,

Timokles. Have all mankind, then, and all nations been deceived in believing in gods, and solemnly celebrating them?

Damis. Capital, Timokles, for you bring to my mind the received belief among different nations, from which one may most certainly be assured that their language about Deity has nothing sure or certain about it. For many are their confused contradictions, and some believe and practise one thing, and some another. The Scythians offer sacrifices to a Dagger,[1] the Thracians to Zamolxis,[2] a runaway slave who came to them from Samos; the Phrygians to Meen,[3] the Æthiopians to the Day, the Cyllenians to Phales,[4] the Assyrians to a Dove,[5] the Persians to Fire, the Egyptians to Water. Although this water is a divinity common to all the Egyptians, yet, locally, the ox is the divinity of the people of Memphis, the onion of the people of Pelusium, the ibis of others, or the crocodile, the dog-faced baboon, the cat, or the ape.[6] Nay, more, in the country districts, to some his godship is the right shoulder, while to those living on the opposite side *of the*

Καὶ γῆν πέριξ ἔχονθ' ὑγραῖς ἐν ἀγχάλαις;
Τοῦτον νόμιζε Ζῆνα, τόνδ' ἡγοῦ Θεόν.

Ζεύς, ὅστις ὁ Ζεύς, οὐ γὰρ οἶδα, πλὴν λόγῳ
Κλύων.

Quotations from lost dramas of Euripides. See, too, Ἑκάβη, 460; Ὀρεστ. 401; Τρωάδες, 846–850. Cf. the pantheism of the Latin poet :—

"Jupiter est quodcunque vides, quocumque moveris."

[1] Ἀκινάκῃ. See Lucianic Dialogue, Τόξαρις, 38; Herod. (iv. 62), who relates, in detail, the mode of the horrid sacrifice to this outward and visible symbol of War.

[2] Cf. Ἀληθ. Ἱστ. ii. 220; Herod. iv. 95.

[3] See above, page 177; and cf. Ἐκκλ. Θεῶν.

[4] Who is meant by "Phales" is conjectural. Gesner would read "Phanes," whom Macrobius identifies with the Sun. Lehmann supposes him to be the Ithyphallic Mercurius, to whom, according to Pausanias (vi. 26), the Kyllenians of Elis dedicated a temple.

[5] See the Lucianic treatise, Περὶ τῆς Συρίης Θεοῦ, 33, 54   The dove is said to have been symbolical of, and sacred to, the Assyrian Semiramis. The Assyrians had not too much respect for *their* divinity.

[6] See Herod. ii. 65-76; Diod. Sic. i. 84; Strabo, xvii.; and cf. Juvenal, *Sat.* xv.:—

river he is the left shoulder; to some half of a head, to others a drinking-flagon, or dish of earthenware. How is all this not matter for ridicule, you charming Timokles?

Momus (*triumphantly*). Did not I say, Gods, that all these things would come to light, and would be minutely inquired into?

Zeus. You did say so, Momus, and you rightly chided us; and I, for my part, will do my best to set these matters straight, if we get clear off from this danger before us.

Timokles. But, you enemy of the Gods, the Oracles, and Prophecies of future events—whose work would you affirm them to be, rather than that of the Gods and of their providence?

Damis. Don't say a word, excellent Sir, about the Oracles; since I shall ask you which of them, in particular, you would like to mention. Is it the one which the Pythian returned to the Lydian, which was beautifully two-edged and double-faced, such as are some of our Hermæ,[1] double and alike on both sides; to whichever part of them you turn. For *what did it mean?* That Krœsus, by crossing the river Halys, will destroy his own kingdom, or rather that of Cyrus? Yet that pest of Sardis purchased this ambiguous verse at the cost of not a few thousands.

Momus. The man is discussing and handling pretty nearly the very things, Gods, which I especially had dreaded.— Where, now, is that handsome lute-player of ours? (*To Apollo*) Go down at once, and make your defence in reply to these charges.

Zeus. You kill me entirely, Momus, by your unseasonable sarcasms.

> " Inde furor vulgo, quod numine vicinorum
>   Odit uterque locus, quùm solos credit habendos
>   Esse deos, quos ipse colit."

[1] Heads of Hermes on quadrangular pillars which, at Athens especially, were found everywhere. So great was the demand for these *Hermæ*, that they gave a name to the Art of Sculpture—ἡ ἑρμογλυφική. See Lucian, Ἐνύπνιον, 7. For the oracle, see above, page 185. Cf. Juv. *Sat.* viii. 53 :—

" Nil nisi Cecropides, truncoque simillimus Hermæ."

Timokles. Observe what you are about, you impious sinner; you are within an ace of overturning the very seats of the Gods, and their altars, by your argument.

Damis. Not *all* the altars, as far as *I* am concerned, Timokles; for what great harm indeed arises from them, *so long as* they are full of incense and pleasant odours *only?* But I should be glad to see those of Artemis among the Tauri utterly overturned from their foundations; upon which the Virgin [Goddess] finds pleasure in such horrid feasting.[1]

Zeus (with tragic air). Whence falls upon us this insuperable misfortune?—for not one of the divinities does the man spare, but is as free in language as a carter,[2]

"One after other carping at, innocent or guilty."[3]

Momus. Indeed, Zeus, you would find few innocent among us; and it is just possible the fellow will proceed and attack even some one of those nearest the throne.

Timokles. So, then, do you not heed or hear Zeus, even when he rolls his thunders, you enemy of the Gods?

Damis. And how could I fail to hear thunder, Timokles? But whether it is Zeus who thunders,[4] you might know better than I, as you have come, perchance, from that quarter, direct from the Gods. Yet some, who come from Krete, tell us a different tale—that a certain tomb is shown there; and that a column stands close by informing us that Zeus would never thunder again, as he had been dead ages ago.[5]

---

[1] See 'Ιφιγενεία ἐν Ταύριδι of Euripides, and Θ. Δ., and Lucretius, *De Rer. Nat.* i. 80-100.

[2] 'Εξ ἁμάξης παῤῥήσιαζεται. A proverbial expression, derived from the licence allowed to the frequenters of the Dionysiac Mysteries, who travelled in their country-wagons, or from the reputation of cartwrights for Billingsgate. See Aristoph. Πλοῦτος, 1014; 'Ιππεῖς, 462, where the Chorus demand of Kleon :—

Οἴμοι, σὺ δ'οὐδὲν ἐξ ἀμαξουργοῦ λέγεις;

Cf. Bentley's *Phalaris.*

[3] Μάρψει δ'ἐξείης, ὅστ' αἴτιος, ὅστε καὶ οὐκί. 'Ιλ. xv. 137. The charge of Athena against Zeus himself.

[4] For a highly-humorous scene, in which Sokrates rationalizes this popular prerogative of Zeus, see Aristoph. Νεφελαί, 394-406, and cf. Τίμων, 1-6.

[5] See Τίμων, 6, *ad fin.* Among the Christians, Lactantius, in particular, triumphs in this fact.

Momus. This I long ago knew the man would say. But why, Zeus, pray, have you turned so pale, and why do you let your teeth chatter so with fright? You must keep up your spirits, and never mind such paltry fellows.

Zeus. How do you say, Momus? Never mind them! Don't you see what a number are listening, and how already they have been convinced, one and all, against us, and how Damis has fast fettered them, and how he leads them away by the ears?

Momus. However, Zeus, whenever you care to do so, you may let down your golden chain, and all of them

"Aloft you draw with Earth itself, and Sea, and all within them." [1]

Timokles, Tell me, cursed rascal, have you ever before now been at sea?

Damis. Yes, Timokles, often.

Timokles. Then were you not, on those occasions, carried along either by the wind blowing upon the mainsail, and filling out the stay-sails, or by the rowers? And did a certain single individual stand at the helm, and guide and keep the ship safe?

Damis. Undoubtedly.

Timokles. Then, I suppose, the ship did not proceed on its voyage without being steered. And think you that this Universe is carried along without a helmsman and ruler?

Zeus. Capital! That argument of yours, Timokles, *you drove home* with force by your *simile.*

Damis. But, O Timokles, cherished favourite of heaven, that same helmsman you would see to be always devising for the best, and fully equipping his ship before the time of *sailing*, and giving directions to his sailors; while the vessel had nothing useless or purposeless *about it*, nothing which was not undoubtedly serviceable and necessary to them for the voyage. This helmsman of yours, however, whom you claim to have command of this great ship *of the universe*, and his fellow-sailors, arrange nothing

---

[1] Αὐτῇ κεν γαίῃ ἐρύσαις, αὐτῇ τε θαλάσσῃ. 'Ιλ. viii. 24. The English version is borrowed from the *Iliad of Homer* of Prof. Newman (1871).

reasonably or fittingly: but the mainstays,[1] if chance so
direct, are stretched to the stern, while both the sheet-
ropes *are stretched* towards the prow; the anchors often
are of gold, the figure-head[2] of lead; the parts of the
ship below water are ornamented, the parts above unsightly. And, of the sailors themselves, you may see
the one who is idle, and unskilful, and without heart
for his work, in the position of second or third officer;[3]
and another, who is a skilful swimmer, and agile in
leaping up into the yard-arm, and who is skilled in each
thing pertaining to useful *navigation*, he is just the only
one *you will see* set to bale out the bilge-water. So, too,
among the passengers, *you will see* some worthless fellow
seated by the side of the captain, in the most commanding
place, and being made much of; and another, some unnatural wretch, or parricide, or swindler, honoured above
all the rest, and occupying the highest posts in the vessel;
many persons of good taste or feeling crowded into a corner
of the ship, and trampled upon by those really inferior to
themselves. Consider, in fact, in what manner Sokrates and
Aristeides made their voyage, and Phokion, who had not even
sufficient bread to eat,[4] nor even were able to stretch their legs
upon the bare planks along the hold; while in the midst of
how many good things *lived* a Kallias, a Meidias,[5] and a
Sardanapalus rioting, and insulting those under them.

[1] Πρότονος. In the Greek ship, the two ropes which were fastened to
the top of the mainmast, and descended to the prow: the πόδες were the
ropes which fastened the ends of the square sails to the stern by rings.

[2] Χηνίσκος (χὴν a goose). The ἀκροστόλιον, or figure-head, was so
called from the ordinary device for the ship's prow. It was usually pro-
tected by plates of brass or copper, and in later times of gold, and served,
with the ἔμβολοι (*rostra*, or "beaks"), as a ram against the enemy's
ships. The latter were sometimes above and sometimes below the water.

[3] Διμοιρίτην ἢ τριμοιρίτην. Lit.: "a commander of two or of three
divisions or companies," or "of a second or third part of the ship."

[4] Aristeides suffered exile; and Phokion died (like Sokrates) by the
Athenian mode of capital punishment—drinking hemlock, 317 B.C., at
the age of eighty-five. See Plutarch. Βίοι Παρ.

[5] Meidias was a wealthy Athenian citizen, who owes his fame to his
hostility to Demosthenes. The Kallias here referred to, presumably,
is the stepson of Perikles, and brother-in-law of Alkibiades, and the
host of the guests of Xenophon's Συμπόσιον. Lucian's examples of
iniquity are not always the most superlatively striking.

Such is the state of matters on board your ship, most sapient Timokles; whence those innumerable shipwrecks. Now if any captain were in command, and observed and ordered each particular thing; in the first place, he would not be ignorant who are the good, and who the bad among the ship's company; in the next place, he would suitably distribute to each his proper post—the better place, up above by his side, to the better men, and the lower place to the inferior; and some of the superior men he would admit to his own table, and appoint them to be of his council; and of the sailors, the most zealous would have been appointed to the care of the forepart of the vessel, or to the captaincy of the forecastle,[1] or, certainly, in a place above the rest: while the sluggish and negligent would be corrected a dozen times in the day with the rope's end about his shoulders. So, admirable Sir, this *simile* of yours of the Ship is in some danger of being completely wrecked, from having chanced upon this incompetent captain.

Momus. This *contest* proceeds swimmingly for Damis now, and he is being borne onwards full sail to victory.

Zeus. Rightly do you conjecture, Momus, and as for Timokles, he devises no firm and consistent method of argument: but these commonplace and vulgar proofs he pumps out one after the other, all only to be easily overturned.

Timokles. Then, since my comparison of the ship appears to you to be of no such great weight, listen now to the " sacred anchor,"[2] as the proverb has it, which you will not shatter by any possible means.

Zeus (all attention). Whatever in the world is he going to say, then ?

Timokles. Well, you shall see if I put these arguments into syllogistic sequence, and if you can overturn them anyhow. If there are altars there are also Gods : but there are certainly altars ; there are, therefore, Gods.[3] What do you say to that ?

---

[1] Τοίχου ἄρχων (usually written τοίχαρχος), lit. " the captain of the rowers at the *sides* of the ship." See Suidas, *sub voce*, and cf. Διαλ. Ἑταίρων, 14, 3.

[2] Τὴν ἱεράν ἀγκυράν—A Greek proverb denoting the last resource or hope. Cf. Lucian, Δράπεται, 13.

[3] " This argument," says Wieland, " is for a ' sheet-anchor' (*Noth-anker*) not the strongest : but it is by no means to be supposed that

Damis (choking with laughter). As soon as ever I have laughed my fill I will reply to you.

Timokles. But you don't seem at all likely to stop grinning. Tell me, however, whereabouts my allegation appears to you ridiculous.

Damis. It's because you don't perceive you suspended your anchor, and that, too, " the sacred one," upon a fine thread. For, in connecting the existence of the Gods with the existence of altars, you imagine you have made your anchorage secure thereupon. So, since you say you have nothing else " more sacred " than this to say, let us at once depart.

Timokles. Do you confess, then, you are worsted, as you leave first ?

Damis (calmly). Yes, Timokles ; for you, like those who are getting the worst of it, you have sought refuge at the altars. So, by the " holy anchor," I am ready to make a treaty of peace with you this moment, with a libation upon the altars themselves, so that we may no longer wrangle on these matters.

Timokles (in a violent rage). You say this to me ironically, you plunderer of tombs,[1] you abominable villain, you utterly contemptible wretch, you good-for-nothing slave, you infamous hang-dog—why, don't we know who your father was, and how your mother got her living, and how you throttled your brother, and what a debauched fellow and corrupter of youth you are ; you chief of gluttons and of shameless rascals.—(*As Damis is retiring*)—Don't run off, pray, before you have got some reminders from me to take away with you : indeed, I am ready to slay you this very

---

Lucian would have put it into the mouth of Timokles, if the Stoics were not accustomed to make use of it. It is quite of a similar character and strength to the brilliant syllogism of Balbus in Cicero's *De Nat. Deor.* (iL 4) : — *quorum interpretes sunt, eos ipsos esse certe necesse est : Deorum autem interpretes sunt : Deos igitur esse fateamur."*

[1] Τυμβωρύχε. Lit. " digger into tombs." Cf. Aristoph. Βατρ. 1147. The tombs, as being often the receptacles of valuable treasures, were a common and rich hunting-ground of robbers, if, at least, we may trust the Romances of the fifth and sixth centuries A.D. Hence the imprecations on desecrators of them, inscribed on many of the slabs. Slaves sometimes were set to keep guard. See Νιγρίνος, 30. For a display of the vituperative powers of the Greek vocabulary see Aristoph. Νεφ. 444-450, and elsewhere.

moment with this potsherd here, superlative villain that
you are (*throwing the missile at him*).

Zeus. One of them, O Gods! is running away in fits of
laughter; and the other pursues him with vituperation, as
he cannot endure Damis's making merry over him : indeed,
he seems actually about to strike him over the head with
his potsherd.   And we—what are we going to do hereupon ?

Hermes. The comic poet appears to me to have rightly
said,

> " Don't own defeat, you've suffer'd then no harm." [1]

For, indeed, what mighty evil is it, if a few men go away
convinced of these things ?   For those who hold the contrary opinion are sufficiently numerous—the greater part
of the Greeks (the mass of the people, and the rabble), and
all the non-Greek peoples.

Zeus. However, Hermes, that saying of Dareius, which
he uttered in the case of Zopyrus, is exceedingly good.
So, too, I myself would have wished to have one such as
Damis, as an ally, rather than the possession of ten thousand
Babylons.[2]

---

[1] Οὐδὲν πέπονθας δεινὸν, ἂν μὴ προσποιῇ.   A fragment of Menander.
Προσποιεῖσθαι, " to affect not to notice," is used by Thucyd. iii. 47, and
by Theophrastus in a passage in the Χαρακτῆρες quoted by Arnold.
(*Thucydides*, i. 496.)

[2] Zopyrus, a Persian noble in the army of Dareius besieging Babylon,
having voluntarily mutilated himself in a frightful manner, fled to the
enemy, pretending that he had escaped from the atrocities of the
Persian king.   After the betrayal and slaughter of several thousands of
his countrymen—with the consent of his master—for the purpose of
still further deceiving the Babylonians, he at length found his opportunity for delivering the city to the Persians.   Upon which event, the
despot is reported to have condescended to remark, that he would have
foregone the possession of twenty Babylons rather than that his devoted
slave should have inflicted so much injury upon himself. See Herod. iii.
153-160.   It is evident that Lucian does not think himself bound, in
every case, to repeat with the strictest accuracy the *on dits* of
History.

THE CONVICTED ZEUS.[1]

[Cyniskus, a Cynic philosopher (as his name imports), encouraged by Zeus to ask a favour, protests that his request will be a very modest one and very easy to grant : he is not

[1] Ζεὺς Ἐλεγχόμενος—"Zeus Convicted," "Confuted," or "Cross-Examined." Of this *Dialogue* Wieland remarks :—"Never, probably, had any writing a more appropriate title than this, in which Jupiter, in a *tête-à-tête*, is forced by the straightforward and undaunted Cynic, in a way such as, probably, he had never yet experienced from any son of Earth, to confess the truth. The worst blow, to which dogmas, that are not grounded upon Reason, can be submitted, is when one holds up their mutual contradictions to the light. One spares oneself, by this means, the trouble of refutation, and can calmly see them, like the armed men sown by Kadmus, annihilate themselves. This is the spectacle which Lucian gives us, in this *Dialogue*, in his best manner.

"The inconsistencies of the Pagan doctrines of a Fate, of the Providence of their Gods, and of the system of Rewards and Punishments after death, appears in it in a light, by whose brilliance Jupiter himself is quite dazed and reduced to silence ; or, what is still more humiliating, to so miserable a shift, that Cyniscus himself, at last, out of mere pity, and content with having deprived him, after complete overthrow in open field, of his power, his dignity, and his kingdom, and leading him in triumph mortally wounded, presents him with his life for so long as in the course of Nature it might be expected to last. The questions which he lays before Jupiter had, in fact, been already debated in the *Jupiter in Tragedy*, between Damis and Timokles, not to the advantage of the party of the Gods. But Lucian, as it seems, held it to be necessary to deliver a last decisive assault. Jupiter had to be driven out altogether from his last lurking-holes, and to be convicted of his wicked deeds so completely, that the most shameless sycophant must blush any longer to undertake his defence. This it is, that Lucian, as it seems to me, in this little *Dialogue*, in so masterly a way, and with so much fineness of touch, manages to effect, that I know no more complete example of the transformation of the antipodes of reason (as Homer expresses it) 'into earth and water.'"

P

going to petition for wealth or power, but simply for en-
lightenment on certain perplexing points of theology and
metaphysics. He begins with a request to be informed as
to the truth of the statements of Homer and Hesiod
respecting the Fates, and their absolute control over human
life. Zeus assures him of their omnipotence. The apparent
contradictions of the Hellenic Scriptures are easily ex-
plained by the circumstance that their inspiration had not
been constant : that, when those theologian-poets spoke of
their own free motion, they were, like ordinary mortals,
liable to error ; but everything uttered by them under
direct inspiration of the divinities is entirely to be received.

Cyniskus then inquires whether Zeus himself acknow-
ledges subjection to the Fates, to Chance or Fortune (also
the object of the popular Creed) ; and, upon the assent of
the " King of Gods and men," he proceeds to quote the
well-known passage in the *Iliad* on the " Golden
Chain," and, sarcastically, remarks that the Fates themselves
more justly might boast of suspending *him* in mid-air.
Becoming more and more uneasy at every new question,
Zeus professes himself to be at a loss to divine at what his
interlocutor is driving. Nor is his alarm without some
reason, since the Cynic next inquires the purpose of the
hecatombs of slaughtered victims for the altars, and of all
the costly sacrifices ? Instead of direct reply, Zeus takes
occasion to denounce the philosophers and sophists, and their
well-known impiety. Pressed on the question of utility,
he defends the sacrificial system upon the pretext of its
being an outward and visible sign of respect and honour
on the part of men for what is greater and nobler than
themselves. To which the Cynic retorts that one of these
wicked philosophers might be disposed to ask *in what* consists the superiority of the Gods, seeing that they are subject and subordinate to Fate : for the accident of " immortality," so far from being an advantage, retains them in
everlasting servitude. Nor, if the Hellenic theology was
to be believed, could it be said that all divinities are in
enjoyment of so much happiness—a position which Cyniskus
illustrates by some conspicuous examples. Zeus now resorts
to indirect menaces, and angrily hints at some supernatural
punishment of the audacious sceptic : but the philo-

sopher calmly expresses his confidence that he can suffer nothing which has not been, by the Fates or Destiny, fore-ordained. Besides, he observes that not even the most audacious insulters of the Gods themselves—the many plunderers of their temples—seem to be any the worse off for their sacrilege, while the innocent frequently fall victims to the indiscriminating thunderbolts.

Driven to bay, the champion of the orthodox Olympian theology reprobates the philosopher as one of those who are for destroying all idea of a divine providence ; Cyniskus inquires who or what is *Providence*, and how exercised, and is told that he is becoming grossly impertinent ; but he extracts the reluctant admission that the Gods, after all, are nothing but the agents and ministers of Destiny. Zeus, however, attempts to rescue himself and his colleagues from the consequent position of utter superfluousness and contempt by claiming credit for oracles and prophecies. The Cynic retorts, of what use are warnings against the *inevitable* —to say nothing of the ambiguous and misleading character of these divine oracles. Zeus makes some feeble attempt at an apology, and then, not obscurely, threatens the *dernier ressort* of the most forcible of his arguments—the thunderbolt. Cyniskus tauntingly remarks that what is fated is fated—and he is quite prepared to receive the inevitable. He wishes to know how it happens that such men as Aristeides, Sokrates, Phokion, suffered, while the tyrants of the world, for the most part, have been allowed to flourish. That is easily answered, rejoins the king of Gods, for are not men to receive their deserts in a future life ? His unrelenting tormentor retorts once more that, for his part, he would rather escape certain misery and suffering in this life than have the offer of not altogether certain happiness in another state of existence. But, continues the Cynic, if Fate or Predestination, ordain and control everything, how, in fine, can there be any logical place for a Minos to distribute rewards and punishments ? Zeus disdains to answer so captious a question, and stigmatizing his satirical examiner as impudent and sophistical, abruptly leaves him. As a parting shot, the Cynic bawling after him desires to learn, particularly, where, after all, these Fates are to be found—or how they

manage to transact so enormous an amount of business, with
their extremely limited number, and ventures to think that
they themselves must have been born under a not too
propitious destiny. As for himself, he professes himself
quite satisfied with the information he has extracted from
the highest authority, and contents himself with the reflection, that, as for the points upon which he had failed to
receive information, it was, apparently, not in "the fates"
that he should be enlightened.]

Zeus, Cyniskus.

Cyniskus (with wallet and tattered cloak). I will not
trouble you, Zeus, about such matters—asking for wealth,
gold, and kingdoms, which are objects most fervently
prayed for by the rest of the world, and which are not
altogether easy for you to grant. I observe, indeed, that
you generally turn a deaf ear to their prayers.[1] But there
is one thing, and that a very easy thing to grant, I did
wish to obtain from you.

Zeus. What is that, Cyniskus? For you shall not fail
to get it, especially since, as you say, it is a modest favour
you ask.

Cyniskus. Just give me an answer in regard to a certain
not difficult question.

Zeus. Your petition, of a truth, is a small matter and
soon settled : so ask whatever you have a mind to ask.

Cyniskus. Here it is then, Zeus. You read, doubtless,
you as well as the rest, the poems of Homer and Hesiod.
Tell me, pray, are those things true which these poets have
so magnificently declaimed about Destiny and the Fates—
that whatever *lot* they spin out for each mortal, at his
birth, is not possible to be avoided ?[2]

Zeus. Indeed, all that is quite true : for there is nothing

---

[1] See 'Ικαρο-Μένιππος, 25.

[2] See 'Ιλ. xx. 128 (the words of Hera) ; 'Οδ. i. 17-19, 35-40 (where
the conflict between Fate and Providence involves the *reductio ad absurdum) ;* Hesiod, Θεογ. 905, 906 ; Theognis, Γνωμ. 815.

that the Fates do not ordain; but all things that happen, whatever they are, are turned upon their spindle; and they have, each one of them, their final event, from the very first, strictly determined: nor is it possible or right for it to be otherwise.

Cyniskus. Then, when the same Homer, in another part of his poem, says:

"Lest to the house of Aïdes, despite of Fate, he send thee,"[1]

and that sort of thing, we must say, I suppose, that he is then talking nonsense?

Zeus. Certainly. For nothing could happen so, independently of the law of the Fates—nothing beyond the stretch of their thread. But, as for the poets, whatever they sing under the constraining inspiration of the Muses, that is truth: when, however, the Goddesses desert them, and they poetize of themselves, on such occasions, I say, they are liable indeed to error, and are apt to contradict their former assertions. And they may be pardoned, if, as they are but men, they don't know the truth, after it has left them, which, so long as it was present, poured forth its strains through them.

Cyniskus. Well, we will say so then. But further answer me this, too. Are there not three Fates—Klotho, Lachesis, and Atropos?

Zeus. Of course.

Cyniskus. Destiny,[2] then, and Chance—for they, too, are

---

[1] Μὴ καὶ ὑπὲρ Μοῖραν δόμον Ἄϊδος εἰσαφίκηαι,

'Ιλ. xx. 336.

The warning of Poseidon to Æneas not to engage in battle with Achilleus. If we choose to read μοῖραν, Poseidon might, perhaps, be relieved of the charge of having perpetrated a ridiculous "bull." Gellius (*Noct. Att.* xiii. 1) takes ὑπὲρ μοῖραν to be simply *præter naturam*, "unnaturally," "violently." But the interpretation of Cyniskus is the probable one.

[2] "Lucian means what we call 'Destiny' (*Schicksal*), Εἱμαρμένην. This word seems to have a meaning identical with Πεπρωμένη, and is used by some writers as a synonym for Μοῖρα; by others, however, it is distinguished from her, and even from *Pepromene*, so that the question of Cyniskus, who does not know too well what he was to make out of all these names, is quite natural. Since, however, Jupiter knows no more of the matter than other people, so he gets out of the difficulty with the accustomed answer in such cases—'it is not permitted to us to see clearly in these things.'"—Wieland.

much in everyone's mouth—who ever are *they*, and what power does each of them exercise ? Have they a power equal to that of the Fates,[1] or something even above them ? I hear, however, everyone say that nothing is more powerful than Chance and Destiny.

Zeus. It is not permissible for you to know everything, Cyniskus. And with what purpose, pray, did you ask this question about the Fates ?

Cyniskus. I will tell you, if you will tell me first, Zeus, this too—do they govern you, as well ; and is it, really, a matter of necessity for you to hang suspended by their thread ?

Zeus. It is matter of necessity, Cyniskus. But why did you smile, pray ?[2]

Cyniskus. I called to mind those verses of Homer, in which you have been represented by him as declaiming in the popular Assembly of the Gods, when you threatened

---

[1] Ταῖς Μοίραις—the Latin *Parcæ*. The Latins gave these dread divinities the names of Nona, Decuma (or Decima), and Morta (or Mœra), according to an authority quoted by Gellius, iii. 16. The etymology of both Μοῖραι and *Parcæ* seems to be the same, and to denote the *distributive* or *apportioning* powers.

[2] " Here, too, Jupiter answers conformably to the Homeric and popular Theology, which makes the Gods dependent on Fate (*Schicksal*), or Necessity (*Nothwendigkeit*), and, also, even upon the Parcæ, who execute the laws of Necessity. As, however, nothing was firm or stereotyped in the Greek Theology, the common belief did not hinder many, to whom the consequences of such teaching were a stumbling-block, from thinking otherwise. Pausanias, where he speaks of the statues of Jupiter Olympius at Megara, gives as the reason why the *Horæ* and *Parcæ* are represented hovering above the God's head, that it was pretty generally recognized that *Pepromene* (' Fate '), is subject to Jupiter alone, and that the *Horæ* are ruled by him, and kept in due order. But Lucian's Jupiter, weak as he was, had, at least, so much understanding as to know that a *Necessity*, subject to his absolute will, could be *no Necessity ;* and is, accordingly, resolved not to overstrain his power, either in regard of the *Parcæ* that hover over his head at Megara, or of the statues and altars, which, according to the testimony of Pausanias, he possessed here and there under the name of *Moiragetes* (' Ruler of the Fates ') : but, rather, with a good grace confessed that not only could he not alter the laws of Fate, but that he was, as regards his own person, subject to them. Lucian could with so much the greater justice make his Jupiter confess this, because the Delphic Apollo himself, when Krœsus bitterly reproached him after the unlucky event of his war with Cyrus, excused himself in the same way (Herod. i. 91)."—Wieland.

them to suspend the universe by a certain golden chain—
for you asserted that, of yourself, you would let down the
chain in question from Heaven, and that all the Gods together, if they chose, might hang by it and use all their
force to pull it down, but that they certainly would not
drag the chain down, whereas you yourself, whenever you
wished, easily

"Aloft could draw the Earth itself, and Sea, and all within them."[1]

On those occasions, I confess, you appeared to me to be
admirable in your strength, and I used to shudder with
terror while I listened to those verses; whereas now I see
that all this time you have been yourself suspended
with your chain and all your threats, by a slight thread,
as you admit. Klotho, it seems to me, according to
this, might boast with far more justness, as it is she
who drags up and hangs *you* in mid air by her spindle,
for all the world as fishermen do their little fish from their
rod and line.

Zeus (*indignantly*). I don't know what these same questions of yours mean.

Cyniskus. This, Zeus—and, by the Fates and by Destiny,
do not hear me with harsh or angry feeling, if I speak the
truth with freedom. Why, if this is so, and the Fates
rule all things, and nothing of what has once been decreed
by them can be altered by anyone, with what purpose do we
men offer sacrifices and present whole hecatombs to you,[2] with
prayers for good things from you. For I don't see what
advantage we could get from this piece of attention, if
neither it is possible for us to find, through vows and prayers,
means of averting evils, nor to obtain any heaven-given good.

---

[1] 'Ιλ. viii. 26. See Θ. Δ. xxi.

[2] The Homeric *hecatomb* (lit. "sacrifice of a hundred victims)," hyper-
bole as it might seem, was upon occasion, even vastly exceeded. The
Jewish and Pagan priesthoods and ritual were alike insatiate in their
sanguinary sacrifice, for almost every occurrence of public or private
life: and the thirst for blood rose with the magnitude of the event to
be celebrated. For example, see 1 *Kings*, viii. 63 (22,000 oxen, 120,000
sheep); Suetonius (*Vitæ Duod. Cæsarum, Caligula*, 14), records that
100,000 various victims were sacrificed, at one time, to the *divinity* of
Caligula. See Juv. *Sat.* xii. 101-120; Clement Alex. *Pædag.* ii. 1;
Lucian, Περὶ Θυσίων.; Porphyrius, Περὶ 'Εποχῆς.

Zeus (vehemently). I know where you get those pretty questions from—from those cursed sophists, who assert that we don't even exercise any providential superintendence over men ; and without doubt, they ask such questions out of sheer impiety, diverting the rest of mankind from sacrifice [1] and vow-making, as being quite useless : seeing, *as they affirm,* we neither pay any regard to what is done among you, nor, in fine, have any power at all in respect to earthly affairs. However, they shall have no reason to be pleased by their pursuance of such *inquiries.*

Cyniskus (calmly). No, by the spindle of Klotho, I declare, Zeus, it was not from being influenced by those people that I put these questions to you ; but our line of discussion itself, I don't know how, has gone on till it ended in this—that sacrifices are supererogatory and superfluous. But again, if you please, I will put the question to you briefly, and do not shrink from answering me, and *be so kind* as to give a more candid reply *than is your wont.*

Zeus. Ask away, *if* you have leisure to talk such trifling nonsense.

Cyniskus. You affirm that everything is done by the Fates ?

Zeus. Well, I do.

Cyniskus. But that it is in your power to alter *their* decrees, and to spin them back ?

Zeus. Not at all.

Cyniskus. Would you have me, then, lead up to the necessary consequence, or is it plain enough without my mentioning it ?

Zeus. Oh, quite plain. But those who sacrifice, do so, not on account of any need *for it*—to make a return, and, as it were, to purchase good things from us ; but, in a particular manner, out of honour for what is superior *to themselves.* [2]

---

[1] Zeus, apparently, had quite forgotten the consolatory observation of Hermes at the conclusion of the memorable debate between Damis and Timokles.

[2] Jacobitz, departing from the authority of the *Codices,* reads ἀλλά for ᾔ, by which the meaning of the reply of Zeus is considerably altered. According to the generally received text, we read, " but those who sacrifice do so, not by reason of any need *of ours,* but to make a

Cyniskus (triumphantly). That's sufficient—since even you allow that the sacrifices are of no earthly use, but *are offered simply* by way of friendly feeling on the part of men, who honour the superior power. Yet if any one of those sophists *you speak of* were present, he would ask you *why* you affirm the Gods to be superior, and that, seeing they are fellow-slaves with men, and under subjection to the same mistresses—the Fates. For the plea of immortality will not avail them, so as, on that account, to gain the reputation of superiority: because that accident, in fact, makes it far worse for them, seeing that death would have removed them to a state of freedom; while, *as it is*, your business ends only with infinity, and your slavery, wound up with that long-reaching thread, is everlasting.

Zeus. But, Cyniskus, that eternity and that infinity of ours is a blessed one for us, and *we* live in the enjoyment of all good things.

Cyniskus. Not all of you, Zeus. On the contrary, even among you your concerns have been variously portioned out, and considerable confusion exists in your midst. *You*, indeed, are fortunate, for you are king, and can hoist up Earth and Sea by just letting down a bucket-rope, as it were. But Hephœstus now, he is lame, and a sort of mechanic and blacksmith by trade; as for Prometheus, he was once upon a time crucified[1]—and as for your own father, what shall I say of him, who is still a prisoner in chains in Tartarus? They do say that you *Gods* even play the gallant, and get wounded in battle, and sometimes work with men as slaves, as certainly did your own brother with Laomedon, and Apollo with Admetus. These circumstances don't seem to me to be very happy ones; on the contrary, some individuals among you appear to be fortunate and lucky, and others the opposite. I omit, in fact, to mention that you are apt to fall among thieves,[2] just as we are, get robbed by plunderers of your temples, and

return for favours received, and, as it were, to purchase good things from us, &c." Jacobitz's revision is more consistent with the reply of the Cynic.

[1] See Θ. Δ. 1 ; Æschyl. Προμ. Δεσμ.; and the humorous scene in Aristoph. 'Ορνίθες, 1494-1551.

[2] Even in Heaven itself, among themselves. See Θ. Δ. vii.

from a state of the greatest wealth become paupers, in the twinkling of an eye. And many before now have been melted down, for all their being of gold or silver; to whom, I presume, that fate had been destined.

Zeus (*frowning*). There! These, now, are mere wanton insults of yours, Cyniskus. Indeed, you will repent of them some time or other.

Cyniskus. Spare your threats, Zeus, as you know that I shall suffer nothing, which has not been determined by Fate before you had anything to do with it: since I notice that not even the robbers of your temples themselves are all punished; on the contrary, the majority of them get away from you scot-free. In fact, I suppose it had not been fated for them to be caught.

Zeus. Did I not say that you are, without doubt, one of those fellows who are for doing away with providence by your style of argument?

Cyniskus. You are terribly afraid of them, Zeus, I don't know why. Everything, in fact, I say, whatever it may be, you suspect to be their teaching. But I—from whom else should I learn the truth *rather* than from you?—I should be glad to ask you this, too, who is this " Providence "[1] of yours ; is it some Fate, or a divinity even above her,[2] as it were, ruling over *the Gods* themselves?

Zeus. I told you already before that it is not lawful or proper for you to know everything. And you, although at the beginning you said you would ask a certain single question, don't stop a moment, putting a number of hair-splitting subtleties to me ; and I see it is the chief aim of your discourse, to prove we exercise no providential care over human concerns in anything.

Cyniskus. That is not my affair : but you affirmed, a little before, that they are the Fates that accomplish everything ; unless, perchance, you repent of making those concessions,

---

[1] Πρόνοια. " So the Stoics named 'Providence' (*die Forschung*), which they attributed to the Gods, without detriment to their necessary Fate, and on account of which they were in perpetual feud with the Epicureans."—Wieland. Cf. Herod. iii. 108 ; Plato, Τιμ. 44 ; Cicero, *De Div.* i. 51 ; Seneca, *De Providentiâ ;* Macrob. *Sat.* i. 17.

[2] Jacobitz reads ὑπὲρ ταύτην in place of ὑπὲρ ταύτας, upon what authority does not appear.

and recall again what you have said, and put in a claim for "Providence," and thrust Destiny aside altogether.

Zeus. By no means; on the contrary, it is Fate that brings each thing to pass through our agency.

Cyniskus. I understand. You say you are a kind of agents and ministers of the Fates. But, however, even so, it would be they who exercise providence, while you are, as it were, a sort of tools and instruments of theirs.

Zeus. How?

Cyniskus. How? Why, just as, I suppose, the carpenter's axe and auger work together, in some sort, for *the creation of* the work: but no one would say that they are the workman himself, nor the ship the work of the axe or the auger, but of the shipwright. Analogously, then, Destiny is she who acts as the shipwright in regard to each particular, while you are, I presume, the axes and augers of the Fates: and, as it seems, men ought to offer their sacrifices to Destiny, and demand their good things from her; whereas they approach *you*, honouring *you* with their processions and sacrifices. And yet they would not do it reasonably, even in honour of Destiny. For I don't suppose it to be possible even for the Fates themselves to change or upset anything of what has been originally decreed respecting each several event. At all events, Atropos[1] would not tolerate it, if anyone were to turn back the spindle, and undo the work of Klotho.

Zeus. And do you, Cyniskus, now require that not even the Fates be held in honour by men? Well, you seem to have for your object to throw everything into confusion. We, however, if for nothing else, should be justly honoured, at least, for our giving out oracles and predicting every particular thing which has been determined by the Fates.

Cyniskus. Upon a survey of the whole matter, it is useless, Zeus, for those to whom it is altogether impossible to guard themselves against them, to foreknow events that are to take place; unless you say this—that one who has learned beforehand that he will have to die by an iron spear-head, might be able to escape death by shutting himself up. But that is impossible: for Fate will drag him

---

[1] As her name implies, the *irreversible* one, "with whom is no variableness, neither shadow of turning."

out to set him hunting, and will deliver him up to the spear; and an Adrastus will hurl his javelin against the wild boar, and will miss *him*, but will slay the son of Krœsus; just as though the javelin had been carried against the youth by irresistible command of the Fates. The saying of Laius is, indeed, ridiculous, which says:—

> " Sow not, in heav'n's despite, a field of sons :
> Sure death you'll meet from your own progeny." [1]

For an exhortatory warning against events that will certainly so happen is, I imagine, superfluous. So, in fact, after the oracle, he did "sow," and "the progeny" slew him. Therefore, I don't see upon what pretence you demand pay for your oracular art. Why, I omit to mention that you *Gods* are accustomed to return to the majority *of your clients* oracular responses of double and ambiguous meaning, and don't make it over clear, whether the one who crosses the Halys will destroy his own kingdom, or that of Cyrus:[2] for the oracle might be made to mean both.

Zeus. Apollo, Cyniskus, had some cause for anger against Krœsus, inasmuch as he tempted him by boiling lamb's flesh and a tortoise together.[3]

Cyniskus. As a God, he ought not even to have been angry: but, however, it had been fated, I presume, for the Lydian that he should be deceived by the oracle; and, besides, Destiny spun for him, that he should not understand too clearly what was in store for him. So even your oracular art is her work.

Zeus. And do you leave nothing for us, but are we Gods without any purpose, and do we not import any sort of providence into *human* affairs, and are we, like a lot of axes and augers, in actual fact, unworthy of sacrifices ? Indeed, I think you quite reasonably have a supreme contempt for

---

[1]   Μὴ σπεῖρε τέκνων ἄλοκα δαιμόνων βίᾳ·
        Εἰ γὰρ τεκνώσεις παῖδ ἀποκτενεῖ σ' ὁ φύς.
Eurip. Φοιν. 118, 119.

" Besäe nicht die Kinderfurche, dir verbieten es
Die Götter ! thust du es, so tödtet dich dein Sohn."
Wieland.

[2] See Ζεὺς Τραγῴδος, 29-31 ; Ἐκκλ. Θεῶν.   [3] *Ibid.*

me, because, as you see, I forbear my hand, although ready to hurl my thunderbolt at you, all the time you are making all these *cavillings* against us.

Cyniskus. Shoot away, Zeus, *if* it has been fated for me to be struck by a thunderbolt; and I will not blame *you* at all for the stroke, but Klotho, who wounds me by your agency: for I would not affirm even that the thunderbolt was the cause of the wound. However, I will ask this of you— yourself and Destiny—and do you answer me, also, on her behalf; for you reminded me by your threat: Why ever in the world do you leave alone robbers of your temples and pirates, and such a number of insolent wrong-doers, and men of outrage and violence, and perjurers, and frequently cast your bolt against some poor oak, or rock, or mast of a ship that has done you no harm; and, at times, against some good and just traveller?[1] Why are you silent, Zeus? Or is it not lawful and right for me to know even thus much?

Zeus. Why, no, Cyniskus; and you are a meddlesome sort of fellow, and I don't know where you come from with these jumbled-up *arguments.*

Cyniskus. Then may I not even ask you this—you, I mean, and Providence and Destiny—why ever did Phokion, that good man, die in such poverty and want of the actual necessaries of life,[2] and Aristeides before him; while Kallias and Alkibiades, youths unbridled in their licentiousness, abounded in wealth, and Meidias, the insolent upstart,

---

[1] See Τίμων. 1-5.

[2] This well-known Athenian statesman and military commander, contemporary with the Macedonian Philip and Alexander, fell a victim to the unjust suspicions of his countrymen of traitorous designs. He died by the ordinary Athenian method of public execution—the administration of hemlock—in his eighty-fifth year. Upon what authority Lucian reduces him to actual *poverty*, is not clear. Plutarch, who gives the details of his life, informs us that he was distinguished by his frugality and simplicity of diet, but does not state that he ever suffered from destitution. Lucian ('Αληθ. 'Ιστ. ii. 23) places him in the Elysian paradise. As for Aristeides, his poverty seems to have been his own choice. It is of him that Plutarch makes the admirable remark at the expense of the kings and heroes of History. The Kallias here referred to, the stepson of Perikles, was known for his extravagant dissipation. Xenophon's Συμπόσιον takes place at his house. Cf. Ζεὺς Τραγ. 48; Τίμων. 24.

and Charops of Ægina, a man of infamous debauchery,[1] who killed his mother by starvation. And, again, Sokrates, why was he handed over to the Eleven, while Meletus was not so?[2] and Sardanapalus, why had he kingly power, with his debauched character, and why were such a number of good and honourable Persians impaled or crucified by him, because they were not content with his proceedings? Not to mention to you things of the present time, or further particularize—the wicked and the avaricious happy and fortunate, the good driven and carried off into captivity, oppressed through poverty, by diseases, and ten thousand evils.

Zeus. Why, don't you know, Cyniskus, what punishments the wicked endure after this life, or in how much happiness the good pass their time?

Cyniskus. You talk to me of Hades, and the Tityuses and Tantaluses. But, as far as I am concerned, whether there is anything at all of the sort I shall know clearly enough when I am dead : and, as for the present, I would prefer to pass my life happily during this life, as long as it might be, and, after death, to have my liver gnawed by sixteen vultures—but not, while here, to be as thirsty as Tantalus; and in the Islands of the Blessed to drink, reclining in the Elysian meadows with the heroes.[3]

Zeus. What do you say? Do you disbelieve or doubt that there are certain punishments and rewards, and a judgment-seat, where at length each one's life is inquired into?

---

[1] Meidias, an Athenian plutocrat, is chiefly known as the enemy of Demosthenes the orator, who was deterred from delivering his carefully-prepared speech against the plutocrat by dread of his powerful influence. —See Plutarch, B. II. Of Charops of Ægina nothing seems to be known.

[2] Meletus, or Melitus, a bad tragic poet, was the public accuser put forward by the enemies of Sokrates. Like other similar *sykophants,* he was afterwards made a sort of scape-goat by the fickle Athenian demos. The real *informers* were Anytus and others.—See Xenoph. Ἀπομν. i.; Lucian, Δημῶναξ. 11; Δὶς Κατηγ. 6. The *Eleven*, or Νομοφύλακες, were officers entrusted with the execution of the decrees of the Areiopagus and of the Heliasts, and with the safe keeping of prisoners.

[3] For Lucian's idea of the Elysian Fields, see the charming description of the Isle of the Blessed (in his Ἀληθ. Ἱστ. ii. 5-27) and its vanishing joys, in which some of the Lucianic commentators have discovered a covered satire on the Ἀποκάλυψις of the Christian Scriptures.

Cyniskus. I hear that a certain Minos, a Kretan, acts as judge in such matters; and answer me somewhat about *him*, too : for he is said to be your son.

Zeus. And why do you ask about him, Cyniscus?

Cyniskus. *Whom* does he punish chiefly?

Zeus. The wicked, of course, such as murderers and temple robbers.

Cyniskus. And whom does he despatch to the heroes?

Zeus. The good and holy, who have lived virtuously.

Cyniskus. Why, Zeus?

Zeus. Because some deserve reward, others punishment.

Cyniskus. And, if a man have done some dire action unwittingly, does he deem him deserving, too, of being punished?

Zeus. By no means.

Cyniskus. Nor, I suppose, if a man does some good action against his will, would he think it proper to reward him either?

Zeus. Why, no, to be sure.

Cyniskus. Then it befits him, Zeus, neither to punish nor to reward anybody?

Zeus. How, not anybody?

Cyniskus. Because we men do nothing of our own wills, but are compelled by some inevitable necessity, if, at least, those things are true which have been before admitted— namely, that Fate is the cause of everything. In fact, if a man commit a murder, she is the real murderess; and if he rob a temple, he does what it has been ordered him to do. So, if Minos intend to give just judgment, he will punish Destiny instead of Sisyphus,[1] and Fate instead of Tantalus. For what wrong did they commit, since they obeyed their orders?

Zeus (in a towering rage). It is no longer worth while

---

[1] The well-known king of Korinth, equally famous for his commerce and his craft—ὁ κίρδιστος γένετ' ἀνδρῶν. 'Ιλ. vi. 153. By the poet of the *Odyssey* he is tortured in Tartarus for his misdeeds by the everlastingly rolling rock, or huge stone, which, as soon as pushed up the hill, rolled back again, 'Οδ.' xi. 593-599. Cf. Lucretius, *De Rerum Nat.* iii. 1013; *Æn.* vi. 602; Ov. *Met.* iv. 460; Cicero, *Disp. Tusc.* i. 5, 10; Aristotle ('Ρητορ. iii. 19) represents the poet as employing the fable metaphorically. For Tantalus, see Νεκ. Διαλ. xvii.

even to reply to you and your questions—for you are an impudent fellow, and a sophist into the bargain; and I will leave you and go away this moment.

Cyniskus (*calling after him*). I did want to put to you again this question, too—Where do the Fates spend their days, or how do they manage to reach to the superintendence, even to the smallest particular, of so many matters— and that, though they are *only* three ? For they seem to me to live a laborious and no enviable sort of existence, in having such a quantity of public business; and, as it appears, they were born under a not altogether propitious Destiny, even they. I, at all events, if choice were given to me, would not exchange my own life with them, but would pass through life still poorer than I am rather than sit plying my spindle full of such a quantity of trouble- some business, and looking after each particular item. However, since it is not easy for you to reply to them, Zeus, we shall be even content with those answers which you have made : for they are quite enough to throw light upon the argument concerning Destiny and Providence. As for the rest, probably it was not *fated* for me to hear them.

THE CONVENTION OF THE GODS.[1]

[Zeus, to hush the loud murmurs and growing discontent
of the privileged classes of Olympus at the constant influx
of *novi divi*, which threatens altogether to swamp the
ancient orders of divinity, summons a General Assembly
for the purpose of taking measures to remedy the evil.
After proclamation by Hermes, by permission of the President, Momus, the Censor, or Public Prosecutor, of
Olympus, again undertakes the not uncongenial task of
exposing the patent scandals flourishing in their midst.
He repeats his old complaints,[2] and animadverts sarcastically
upon the scandal, that not only are mortal men deified, but
that they bring with them a whole train of disreputable
followers of low or hybrid origin, whom, surreptitiously,
they introduce into the *haut monde*, and, by corrupt arts,
contrive to get raised to the Olympian peerage; that these
dieux nouveaux insist upon an equal share, with the ancient
aristocracy, of the public feasts and sacrifices.   Here the
President interposes, and calls upon the Public Prosecutor
to proceed from *general* to *particular* charges, and specify
names.   Thus admonished, Momus particularizes the most
conspicuous scandals of this kind, and proceeds (in spite

[1] Θεῶν ’Εκκλησία—the "Popular Assembly of the Gods"—is the
title of this witty piece.   Inasmuch as, however, on this memorable
occasion, the "upper" and "lower" Houses (the *Boulé* and *Ecclesia*)
sat and voted together, the French "National Assembly" or "Convention" more exactly represents the character of the present meeting of
the divinities.   The usual English representative title is "Council,"
which does not accurately express the original.

[2] See Ζεὺς Τραγ.

of a caution from Zeus to except certain privileged personages from his indictment) to insinuate that the case of the "king of Gods and men" himself is not unobnoxious to severe criticism—in particular, in regard to certain events in the island of Krete, the scene of his education and (alleged) decease; and his notorious amours with certain terrestrial mistresses, which were at once hazardous and ridiculous. He does not omit to descant upon a number of other notorious scandals caused by the too free conduct of other deities of either sex, in imitation of their father and sovereign lord. At the urgent interposition of Zeus, passing over the Ganymede scandal, he next attacks the Oriental, and especially Egyptian, interlopers; and, again called to order, passes on to the various *oracular* divinities, and their portentously-increasing number—instancing certain well-known *athletes*, who had received the honours of divinity and immortality. One of the results of this extension of the celestial franchise, according to the Censor, is the increase of perjury. Descending rapidly to human concerns, he severely assails the new-fangled names bandied about in the logomachics, and word-twisting of the "philosophers;" and has a fling at the new fashion of deifying Nature and Destiny, &c., which threatens to divert the old-accustomed rich sacrifices from Heaven to Earth. At this point of his oration, observing signs of weariness from some, of hostility from others, Momus brings his address to a somewhat abrupt close. Leave having been given by the President, he then reads the resolution.

The Decree sets forth, in the approved (Attic) legal forms, the principal cause of the convocation of the Assembly—viz., the intrusion of spurious and barbarous interlopers, the overcrowding of Heaven, and the consequent alarming and extraordinary rise in the market-prices of their ambrosia and nectar, and the arrogance and presumption of the *dieux nouveaux*. It announces the meeting of the celestial Chambers in the approaching winter, when an Inquisitorial Commission is to be appointed for thorough revision and strict scrutiny of the claims of the several more recent and surreptitious additions to the theocracy; when they will be expected to produce credentials, and proofs of the soundness of their claims : the penalty of the flames of Tartarus to be enacted for all who disobey the ruling of the Commission. Also, it is to be within the powers of the same Commission to ascertain and curtail the present pluralities and patronage of the various members of the *ancien régime.*

To this decree Zeus vouchsafes to give his *imprimatur,* and the Assembly is prorogued.]

Zeus, Hermes, and Momus.

Zeus. Have done with your muttering, Gods, and don't crowd yourselves into corners, and take counsel with one another in whispers, in your anger because a number of unworthy *guests* share our table. But, inasmuch as a Convention has been summoned to deliberate about these matters, let each one say openly what he thinks, and produce his charges. And you, Hermes, make your proclamation according to the legal requirements.

Hermes. Oyez! Silence! What God, of full age and qualification, who has the right, desires to harangue? The subject of inquiry is respecting resident-aliens [1] and strangers.

Momus. I do—Momus—if you would give me leave to speak, Zeus.

Zeus. The terms of the proclamation already give you leave. So you will have no need of my *permission.*

Momus. I assert, then, that some of us act in a strange manner—to whom it is not sufficient that they have been themselves transformed from men into Gods, but, unless they render their hangers-on and attendants possessors of equal rights with ourselves, consider they have accom-

---

[1] Μετοίκων. The *Metœci* formed a regular and numerous resident-colony in the Greek States, or cities (10,000, at Athens, in the third century B.C.), subject to severe restrictions and disabilities. They were forced to serve in the armies, but were not admitted to any sort of legislative rights of the State in which they lived. Chiefly engaged in trade, they were always *actually* regarded as ξένοι (foreigners), though *nominally* distinguished from them.

plished no great or gallant achievement. Now I claim,
Zeus, from you the privilege of free speech, for otherwise
I could not venture *upon it*—but all know me, how
free I am of tongue, and that I could not be silent in regard
to any dishonourable action : for I examine everything
critically, and declare my opinions openly, neither fearing
anybody nor disguising my feeling out of *mistaken* modesty.
Thus I have the reputation with the large majority of
being a nuisance, and a calumnious character, and am
entitled by them a sort of public accuser. But, however,
as it is permitted to me, and has been so declared in
the crier's proclamation, and you, Zeus, give me power to
speak out quite freely, I will speak without any sort of
reserve. Well, there are a considerable number, I affirm,
who, not content that they themselves participate in the
same councils with us, and take part in our banquets on
equal terms with ourselves—and that, though they are
half mortals—bring up their servants and Bacchanalian
hangers-on, into the bargain, into heaven, and enregister
them *as Gods.*[1] And now they receive the distributions of
sacrificial meats on equal terms with us, and share in our
sacrifices, without even paying us the foreigners' tax.

Zeus. Give us no riddles, Momus, but speak clearly and
explicitly, and supply us with the names *of the accused.* For
now your statement of the case has been recklessly brought
before the public, so that one guesses at a number of individuals, and fits one individual to one and another individual
to another of your charges. You, who are a bold and independent speaker, ought not to shrink from saying anything
you have to say.

Momus. Bravo, Zeus, for urging me to freedom of speech :
indeed, you act in this right royally, without mistake, and
magnanimously. So I will even out with the names.
Well, that most excellent Dionysus, who is half man (not
even Greek on his mother's side, but grandson of the
daughter of a certain Syrophenician merchant, Kadmus),
ever since he was voted worthy of immortality, what sort of
character he has I say nothing—neither of his hair-fillet,
nor of his drunkenness, nor of his gait. For you all see, I

---

[1] See Ζεὺς Τραγ.

suppose, how womanly and effeminate he is in disposition, only half in his senses, reeking with the fumes of unmixed wine from early morning.[1] He introduced among us a whole tribe *of his relations*, and comes and brings his troop of dancers, and makes Gods of Pan, and Silenus, and the Satyrs, a set of rustics and goatherds, most of them, skittish and goatish, and strange of form—of whom the one has horns, and from the middle downwards, in fact, resembles his own goat, and displays a long beard, and differs but little from that animal; another is a bald old man, with a snub nose, usually mounted upon an ass. He is Lydian.[2] As for the Satyrs, with their pointed ears, and bald heads, with horns, such as grow on recently-born kids—they are by way of being Phrygians. And they are even endowed, the whole lot of them, with tails. You see what sort of divinities this worthy finds for us. And, then, do we wonder that men have contempt for us, when they see such ridiculous and pro-digious Gods? I omit to mention that he brought up, too, a couple of women—the one being his mistress, Ariadne,[3] whose crown, actually, he inserted in the circle of the stars ; the other, a daughter of the Icarian farmer ; and, what is most ridiculous of all, Gods, even Erigone's dog, even him he brought up, for fear the girl might be grieved, if she should not have her accustomed *play-fellow*, and object of her affec-tion, her dear whelp. Don't these things appear to you to be wanton impertinence, and drunken folly, and matter for de-rision ? Now listen, pray, to *the history of* the rest of them.

[1] See Θ. Δ. xviii.

[2] Silenus, as a native of Nysa in Karia, might more properly be termed a Karian. This inseparable boon-companion of the God of the Vine always appears in Art as the personification of coarse and gross sensuality in face and figure, and usually in a state of intoxication. The presiding deity of the Chase and of the Farm does not cut a much more respectable figure. In the famous romance episode of *Pysche and Cupid*, he is repre-sented as acting in the character of protector of the persecuted heroine. Both Silenus and Pan are often pluralized by the poets.

[3] Deserted by her lover, whom she had just rescued from a terrible fate, and left in the island of Naxos, the Cretan princess (so we are in-formed) forgot her grief in a strong attachment to the wine-divinity. The crown, promoted to the stars, was given to her by Dionysus at their union. See *Ariadne Theseo* of Ovid. For the story of Erigone and her faithful dog Mœra, see Apollod. iii. 14. The dog is known to modern astronomy as Procyon.

Zeus. Don't say a word, Momus, either about Asklepius or about Herakles—for I see what is the drift of your speech —for as to them, one of them is a physician and cures men of diseases, and hath "many fighters' value;"[1] while Herakles, who is my son, purchased his immortality by not a few toils.   So don't bring accusations against them.

Momus. I will hold my tongue for your sake, Zeus, though I have much to say. However, if *they have* nothing *to show* else, they still keep the marks of their fire burns.[2] And, if it were allowed me to use freedom of speech in regard to yourself, I should have had much to say.

Zeus. Indeed, you have, by all means, full leave to say your say as far as I am concerned.   But, surely, you are not for bringing an action against me, too, as an alien for usurping rights of citizenship ?[3]

Momus. In Krete, to tell the truth, not only is it possible to hear this *insinuation*, but there is something, besides, they allege about you—they even point out your sepulchre.[4] However, I believe neither them nor the Ægeans of Achaia, who affirm that you were a changeling. But, as to those matters which I consider ought especially to be reproved, those I will venture to speak of. The beginning, surely, of such breaches of the law, and the first cause of our Council being overrun with bastards, you yourself supplied, Zeus, by your familiarity with mortal women, and going down to them now in one shape, now in another; so that we actually fear that someone may get hold of you, and sacrifice you, when you are a bull; or some goldsmith may

---

[1] Parody of part of the Homeric verses :—

    'Ιατρὸς γὰρ ἀνὴρ πολλῶν ἀντάξιος ἄλλων
    'Ιούς τ' ἐκτάμνειν, ἐπὶ τ' ἤπια φάρμακα πάσσειν.

                'Ιλ. xi. 514-515.

" Surely a sage chirurgeon, skilful to cut out arrows,
And overspread assuagements soft, hath many fighters' value."

              (Prof. Newman's *Iliad of Homer*.)

[2] See Θ. Δ. xiii.

[3] Ξενίας διώκεις.   A legal formula taken from the Attic law courts. Cf. Aristoph. Σφ. 718 ; Demosth. *passim*.

[4] This subject for satire is a favourite one with Lucian. See Τίμων, 6 ; Ζεὺς Τραγ. 45; Περὶ Θυσιῶν, 10 ; Φιλοψεύδης, 3. The Ch. Fathers, also, make the most of it. Lactantius gives the inscription on the tomb ; Chrysostom, *Hom.* iii. (as quoted by Du Soul). Cf. Pausanias, vii. 24.

work you up when you are gold, and, in place of Zeus, you
might become either a necklace, or a bracelet, or an earring.
However it may be, you have filled Heaven, at all events,
with these semi-gods, for I cannot otherwise characterize
them. And the thing is most ridiculous, when someone
all on a sudden hears that a Herakles has been proclaimed
divine ; while Eurystheus, who imposed his orders upon
him, has died ; and a temple of Herakles, the servant, and
the tomb of Eurystheus, his master, are adjoining. Again,
Dionysus is divine at Thebes ; while his cousins, Pentheus,
and Aktæon, and Learchus [1] were of all men most
miserable in their fate. From the first moment, Zeus, you
opened your doors to such individuals, and turned your
attention to mortal women, they have all of them set to
imitating your example—and that not the male part of
them only, but (what is most scandalous) the female also.
Who does not know about Anchises, and Tithonus, and
Endymion, and Iasion,[2] and the rest ? So I think I will
pass those particulars by, for it would be a long business to
criticize *them all.*

Zeus. Not a word, Momus, about Ganymedes, for I shall
take it ill, if you cause the boy any pain by reproaching
him with his birth and family.[3]

Momus. Then neither shall I say anything as to the eagle
—how it has taken up its abode in Heaven, and sits upon
the royal sceptre, and all but makes its nest upon your
head, with the reputation of being divine. Are we to pass

[1] Pentheus, the king of Thebes, who made himself remarkably
singular (*rara avis in terris*) by his opposition to the brewers and wine-
merchants of the day, who revenged themselves by holding him up to
future ages as the especial object of the detestation and punishment of the
divinity, by whose frenzied priestesses he was torn to pieces. The
Βάχκαι of Euripides is founded upon this history. Learchus, the son of
Athamas and Ino, was killed by his father in a fit of madness, sent by
the angry divinities Hera and Nephele. See Hyginus, *Fab.* i. 2 ; Ov.
Fasti, vi. 479. For Aktæon, see Θ. Δ. xvi.

[2] For Anchises and Endymion, see Θ. Δ. xx. xi. Iasion, the son
of Zeus and Elektra (daughter of Atlas) was the favoured lover of
Demeter. See 'Οδ. v. 125 ; Hes. Θεογ. 969 ; Ov. *Amores,* iii. 10, 25-44,
Met. ix. 421. According to Apollod. (iii. 12), it was not the Goddess,
but Iasion, who made the first overtures, for which he was struck dead
by a thunderbolt by Zeus.

[3] See Θ. Δ. iv. v. Wieland thinks that Lucian here alludes to the
deified Ganymede of the Emperor Hadrian.

this eagle by, too, for Ganymedes' sake ? Well, Attis,
at all events, and Korybus, and Sabazius [1]—from what part
of the world have *they* been rolled in upon us one after the
other ? Or that Mithras, the Median, with his oriental
mantle and tiara, who does not even speak a word of Greek, so
that, even if one drink his health, he doesn't understand ?
So, of course, the Scythians and Dacians, upon seeing their
characters, bid us a long adieu, and immortalize and elect
for Gods for themselves whomever they may choose; in the
same manner in which Zamolxis,[2] slave though he was,
was enrolled, who crept in I don't know how. However, all
these things, Gods, are comparative trifles. But you, with the
dog-face,[3] the Ægyptian, wrapped up in linen wraps, who
are *you*, excellent Sir, or how do you put in a claim to be
divine with your barking ? And what is the meaning
of this bull from Memphis, that spotted individual, being
worshipped,[4] and delivering oracles, and having prophets ? I blush to speak of the ibises, and apes, and goats,
and other yet more ridiculous *objects of worship*, I know not
how stuffed into Heaven from Egypt ; and how do you,
Gods, submit to see them worshipped upon a perfect equality
with, or even to a greater degree than, yourselves ? Or
you, Zeus, how do you like it, when your ram's horns sprout
out upon you ? [5]

Zeus. These Egyptian facts you mention, of a truth, *are*

---

[1] See Ζεύς Τραγῳδός and ʾΙκαρο-Μεν. Sabazius, a Phrygian divinity,
was identified with Dionysus. Cf. Aristoph. ʾΟρνιθ. 875, Λυσίστ. 388.
Cicero, *De Nat. Deor.* ii. 23, 58. Macrob. *Sat.* i. 1. Korybus may be
either the representation of the Korybantic family, or an individual said
to have been the son of Kybele.

[2] A Thracian divinity, or prophet, who is said to have been a slave
of Pythagoras. See Herodotus (iv. 94, 95), who describes the barbarous
sacrifices to this God ; Apuleius, *De Magiâ*, 290.

[3] Anubis. See N. Δ. xiii.

[4] For the Egyptian worship of and extraordinary reverence for Apis,
or the sacred Bull of Memphis, see Herodotus iii. 27-29 ; Pliny, *Hist. Nat.*
viii. 46 ; Ammianus Marcellinus, *Res Gestæ*, 22.

[5] In the character of Zeus Ammon. He was represented sometimes
as a ram, sometimes as human, excepting the head (or only the horns)
of a ram. The chief seats of his worship were the Egyptian Thebes,
and the famous oasis in the bordering desert. See Herod. ii. 42 ; Lucan,
Pharsalia, ix. 511. Lucian, it seems, had not Plutarch's respect for the
(innocent) non-human species ; or Montaigne's juster estimate of the
relative value of Life (*Essais*, ii. 12).

scandals. But, all the same, Momus, the greater part of them are allegorical; and it is not at all right for an un-initiated person, *like yourself*, to laugh at them.

Momus. We are sadly in want, then, Zeus, of mystic initiation into the Mysteries, so as to know the Gods that are Gods, and the dog-headed that are dog-headed.

Zeus. Have done, I say, with the concerns of the Egyptians : for we will consider about them, another time, at our leisure. Do you go on with the rest.

Momus. About that Trophonius, Zeus, and—what particularly chokes me—that Amphilochus [1] who, son of an accursed matricide, utters his prophecies, excellent man, in Cilicia, lying for the most part, and juggling, for the gain of a couple of oboles. So, forsooth, Apollo, you are no longer in esteem ; but now every rock, and every altar,[2] which may be sprinkled with oil, and have garlands, and can supply an impostor, such as exist in quantities, delivers its oracles. Already, indeed, the statue of Polydamas, the athlete, cures fever-stricken patients at Olympia, and that of Theagenes in Thasos ;[3] and they offer sacrifices to Hektor, at Ilium, and to Protesilaus, over the way, in the Chersonese.[4] Ever since we have become so numerous, perjury has increased all the more, and temple-robbery, and, in a word, they have altogether despised us, and very rightly.

---

[1] See Νεκ. Διαλ. iii.

[2] Cicero characterizes these highly profitable sources, among others, of sacerdotal revenue, as *flexiloqua et obscura, ut interpres egeat interprete. De Div.* ii. 56. By the Christian Fathers they were held to have been directly inspired by the demons (or, rather, devils), who personated the divinities of Paganism : " In oraculis autem," says Tertullian, " quo ingenio ambiguitates temperent in eventus, sciunt Crœsi, sciunt Pyrrhi."—*Apolog.* 22. Lactantius, and St. Augustin (*De Div. Dæmonum* and *De Civit. Dei*), strongly maintained the reality of such diabolic inspiration. Eusebius (Εὐαγ Ἀποδ. Προπ. v.) quotes a number of instances of these tricks of the "juggling fiends." Cf. Bayle, *Sur les Oracles.*

[3] Two famous athletes, the latter of Herculean strength. See Pausanias ('Ηλ. ii.), who states that there were statues set up to the honour of Theagenes in many parts of Hellas, and even in foreign countries, which healed men of their diseases, " καὶ νοσήματα τε αὐτῶν ἰώμενον." The islanders of Thasos enjoyed the privilege of giving birth to this Samson—a somewhat troublesome one, according to the account of the Greek traveller. Cf. Lucian, Πῶς δεῖ Ἱστ. Συγ. 35. For Polydamas, see Valer. Maximus, *De Factis*, etc., ix. 12.

[4] For Protesilaus, see N. Δ. xix.

Thus much as to bastards and fraudulently-registered Gods. For my part, when I hear, as I now do, a number of strange names of certain qualities, which certainly are not found with us, nor can at all agree together; at all that, Zeus, I laugh consumedly. For where is that Virtue, so much in the mouths of all of us, and Nature and Destiny and Chance—without any certain existence, and empty names of things—which have been invented by those stupid dolts, the philosophers ? Yet, though they are plainly fictitious, to such a degree have they influenced the fools, that not one of them cares even to offer sacrifices to us; being well persuaded that, even though he should present ten thousand hecatombs, Chance would all the same effect what was decreed, and what had been spun out from the first for each individual person. I should, therefore, be glad to ask you, Zeus, have you ever *seen* either Virtue, or Nature, or Fate ? For that, in fact, you do *hear* them in the discussions of the philosophers, I know, unless, indeed, you are, in a manner, deaf, so that you don't hear their clamours. Though I have still much to say, I shall now bring my speech to an end. I observe, in fact, that the majority are annoyed by my words, and are hissing : those, especially, to whom the freedom of my address has come home. If, however, you desire an end *to these evils,* Zeus, I will read off a certain resolution in regard to them, composed by me just now.

Zeus. Read : for all your charges are not without some reason. And I must put a check upon the greater part of them, so that they don't come to too great a head.

The Decree.

In the Name of God,[1]
 In a legitimately-convoked Popular Assembly, on the seventh day of the first decade of the month,[2] under the

---

[1] Ἀγαθῇ Τυχῇ. A form used on solemn occasions, and inscribed on public monuments, by Hellenic custom, of which the Latin equivalent was *quod felix faustumque sit.* Cf. Thucyd. iv. 118. Arist. Ὄρν. 435, 675 ; Θεσμ. 283 ; Plato, Νομ. 625.

[2] Ἑβδόμῃ ἱσταμένου. The Attic month was divided into three *decades* —ὁ ἱσταμένος or ἀρχομένος μὴν (the commencing month), ὁ μεσῶν (the middle), and ὁ φθίνων (the concluding decade of the month). Cf. Δίκη Φωνῆ. i.

presidency of Zeus, and vice-presidency of Poseidon, Apollo in the chair, Momus, son of Nux, acting as registrar,[1] and Hypnus brought forward the motion:—Whereas many strangers, not only Hellenes, but even barbarous peoples, not at all deserving to share our rights of *Olympian* citizenship, have been by some means illegally registered, and have got to have the reputation of being deities, and have crowded up all Heaven, so that the banqueting-hall is filled with a tumultuous and turbulent mob, a rabble of people of all sorts of lingos ; there is a failure in the supply of ambrosia and nektar, so that now a half-pint of *the latter* is sold at a *mna*,[2] by reason of the number of the drinkers ; and these, with insolent audacity, have ousted the ancient and genuine deities, and claimed the first places for themselves, contrary to all the traditions *of our constitution*, and wish to have precedence even on the Earth. Be it, therefore, decreed by the Senate and the People, that about the winter solstice a popular Assembly be summoned on Olympus, and seven of the first-class Gods be elected as Inquisitors—three from the old Senate of the time of Kronos, and four from the Twelve, of whom Zeus shall be one. *Be it further enacted*, that these Inquisitors sit *en permanence*, after having taken the customary oath—by the Styx ; that Hermes make proclamation and assemble them all together, as many as put in their claims, as tax-payers, to a seat in the Convention ; and that they bring with them sworn witnesses under oath, and proofs of their birth and family. Thereupon let them appear severally, and the Inquisitors, after close scrutiny, shall declare them to be *bonâ fide* Gods, or shall despatch them down to their proper sepulchres, and their ancestral vaults : And, *be it enacted*, if any one of the rejected Gods once ejected by the Inquisitors, be caught in the act of climbing into Heaven, that he shall be thrown into Tartarus. Further, *be it enacted* that each God employ himself solely about his own proper business : that neither Athena practise Medicine ; nor Asklepius trade in oracles ; nor

---

[1] Ὁ Ζεὺς ἐπρυτάνευε, καὶ προήδρευε Ποσειδῶν, ἐπεστάτει Ἀπόλλων. For the proper meanings of these legal *formulæ*, see Smith's *Dict. of Ant.* (article *Boulé*) and cf. Thucyd. iv. 118 ; Demosth. Λόγοι ; Andokides, Λόγος Περὶ Μυστ. ; Pollux, Ὀνομαστ. viii. 98.

[2] £4.

Apollo have all to himself so many departments, but choose out some one *province*—either be a prophet, a professor of music, or a physician.

Be it further decreed, that the philosophers be warned not to invent empty *names*, nor talk nonsense about what they don't know. And as regards the *disfranchised* Gods, who already have been deemed worthy of temples and sacrifices, their statues are to be thrown down, and *the statue* of Zeus, or Hera, or Apollo, or someone else to be inserted *in the temples, instead* : That, as for those *others*, their State erect a tomb for them, and set up a pillar in place of an altar. And, if anyone disobey this proclamation, and be not willing to come before the Commission, let them give judgment, by default, against him.[1] Such is our Decree.

Zeus. Very just, Momus, and every one who is in favour of it hold up his hand ;[2] or, rather, so let it take effect at once: for I know that the dissentients will be in the majority. The Assembly is now dismissed. But, whenever Hermes shall make proclamation, come each of you with clear testimonials, and plain proofs *of your titles*—the father's and mother's names, and whence, and how, he or she became a divinity, his tribe, and wardsmen.[3] As, in the case of whoever shall not exhibit these, whether a *claimant* has a big temple upon the Earth, and whether he is regarded by men as divine, the Commission will not trouble themselves.

---

[1] 'Ερήμην αὐτοῦ καταδιαιτήσαντων. Sup. δικὴν. Cf. Lucian, Ὑπὲρ Εἰκ. 15—ἐρήμην καταδιαιτήσας τοῦ βιβλίου. The ψήφισμα, "the decree," is the Act passed by the βουλή and ἐκκλησία conjointly : the προβούλευμα, as the word implies, is the *resolution* of the first "house" alone, which had no legal force until ratified by the popular Assembly. It is not uninstructive to remark that, by the Athenian constitution, every Bill to be introduced into the "Commons" was for some time previously exposed to the public view of the *whole* body of citizens.

[2] There were two methods of voting, by "show of hands" (χειροτονία) and by "balloting" (ψηφοφορία). The former was the more usual.

[3] By the constitution of Kleisthenes the whole Attic population was redistributed into ten φύλαι ("tribes"), which were subdivided each into ten δῆμοι ("hundreds"). The term φρατρίαι ("wardsmen"), a significant word, was still retained.

THE FERRY-BOAT: OR, THE TYRANT.[1]

[Charon, ready to set sail, awaits impatiently the appearance of Hermes, who is behind time with his accustomed batch of ghosts; and gives vent to his vexation in complaints to Klotho, his colleague. Presently, the Conductor of the Dead is seen approaching, heated and out of breath, driving the ghosts before him. He accounts for his delay by narrating the attempt to escape of one of his convoy, the tyrant Megapenthes, and the difficulty of the re-capture, which was effected only by the timely assistance of the cynic Kyniskus (a fellow-ghost); and the fugitive tyrant now appears on the scene securely fettered.

Before setting sail for Hades, Klotho receives from Hermes, and enters on his way-bill, the names, nationality, and manner of death of the various passengers. The cynic philosopher complains that she has unfairly neglected him ; and declares that he had long been intending to anticipate her decree. In contrast to the disciple of Antisthenes, the tyrant begs long and vehemently for respite, however brief, on various pretences, all of which are sternly rejected by the Fate. In the end, he is forcibly carried on board by Hermes and Charon, aided by the Cynic, and bound to the mast. At this stage, the cobbler, Mykillus, comes forward to expostulate with Klotho yet more strongly at her long neglect of him, and, to her expressions of astonishment at his eagerness to embark, he replies by narrating,

---

[1] Κατάπλους ἤ Τύραννος. Strictly, " The Putting-in, or Arrival of the Ferry-Boat," etc. For the sake of brevity, the usual title has been adopted here. The opening scene, it is highly probable, was suggested to Lucian by some graphic picture.

at considerable length, his reasons for not shunning Charon's boat; and, at the same time, confesses his previous illusions in regard to the imagined happiness of the despot, Megapenthes.

Klotho now gives orders for weighing anchor; when the cobbler, finding that he was to be left behind until the next day, owing to the crowded state of the boat, struggles hard to get on board, and, failing in the attempt, jumps into the Styx, to get across by swimming. He is, then, perforce, taken into the boat—a place being found for him on the shoulders of the tyrant—which proceeds on its voyage: while Kyniskus, like the cobbler afterwards on landing, declares his inability to pay the small coin required as the fare, and earns his passage by taking an oar.

The tedium of the rest of the voyage he relieves by giving the " time " to his fellow-rowers, to the tune of some popular sea-song, and in jeering at the lamentations of the rich passengers, in which amusement he is joined by the cobbler. Upon landing, the cynic and cobbler join company, and proceed arm in arm towards the tribunal of Rhadamanthys. The Infernal Judge orders that the various dead men be brought before him. The cynic at once demands to be heard against the tyrant; and, after previous satisfactory examination of himself, which results in his receiving a passport for the Elysian Fields, he charges Megapenthes with his foul deeds of cruelty and of debauchery. That royal criminal is found to be covered with the *stigmata* —the brand-mark, of his crimes and vices; and, to establish the accusations of his principal accuser, the tyrant's own lamp and bed are brought forward as witnesses. At the suggestion of his accuser, Megapenthes, in place of being consigned to the flames of Pyriphlegethon, is prohibited from drinking of the waters of Lethe; and his punishment in Tartarus consists in an ever-present recollection of his evil deeds. In accordance with the terms of his sentence, he is now dragged away by the Erinyes, and chained by the side of another royal criminal, Tantalus; who, as a comparatively innocent offender, had some reason to complain of this unexpected addition to his torture.]

Charon, Klotho, Hermes, Megapenthes (a newly-deceased king), Kyniskus (a Cynic philosopher), Mykillus (a Cobbler), Rhadamanthys, Tisiphone, and a number of Dead Men.

Charon (fretfully). Well, Klotho, this little craft of ours long ago has been ready and excellently equipped for putting to sea: for the bilge-water has been all baled out, the mast has been hoisted, the sail spread, every one of the oars supplied with its thong, and as far as I am concerned, nothing prevents our hauling our little anchor aboard, and proceeding on our voyage. But that Hermes is behind his time, whereas he ought to have been here long since. Our ferry-boat, therefore, as you see, has not a single passenger on board, though it might have made the passage three times to-day already. And it's close upon evening;[1] and we have not yet turned over even a penny. And so, I know very well Pluto will suspect me of laziness in the business; and that, though the blame lies with another. Our fine honourable gentleman undertaker, like any mortal,[2] has himself drunk of the waters of Lethe,[3] up yonder, and has quite forgotten to return to us; and, either he is wrestling with his young men in the Palæstra, or playing his lyre, or reciting some oration, and showing off his own silly nonsense. Or, maybe, perhaps, the excellent gentleman is practising his light-fingered art, and outwitting *some one*—for that, too, is one of his accomplishments.[4] And so he takes his liberties with us, and that, while he half belongs to our establishment.

Klotho. But what *would you have ?* How do you know,

---

[1] Σχεδὸν ἀμφὶ βουλυτόν. Lit. "close upon ox-loosing time." See 'Ιλ. xvi. 779 ; 'Οδ. ix. 58. (according to Eustathius, *in loco,* βουλυτόνδε denotes ἡ μεσημβρία ἢ ὀλίγον τὶ μετὰ μεσημβρίαν, "about noon," when they unyoked the oxen to avoid the midday heats) ; Aristoph. 'Ορνίθες, 1500. Cf. Virg. *Ec.* ii. ; Hor. *Car.* iii. 6.

[2] Ὥσπερ τις ἄλλος (Jacobitz), following the principal MSS. Lehmann adopts the reading of the Scholiast, εἴπερ τις ἄλλος, "if any one else."

[3] "The waters of the *upper* Lethe" is Charon's euphemism for the juice of the grape. See Lucian's Περὶ Πένθους, 25 ; Aristoph. Βατρ. 106 (where Xanthias terms the infernal stream τὸ Λήθης πεδίον). The idea of the *river* of Lethe is later than the theology of Homer and Hesiod.

[4] See Θ. Δ. vii.

Charon, whether some pressing business has not been imposed on him, from Zeus wanting to use his services after time, for some commission above? He, too, is his lord and master, you know.

Charon. But not, Klotho, to make despotic use beyond all fairness of a common possession; for, *we* never have detained him when he had to be off. But I know the reason. We have only asphodel,[1] and libations, and cakes, and the offerings to the dead;[2] and all the rest gloom, and mist, and darkness: while in heaven all is bright, and they have large supplies of ambrosia, and abundance of nectar. So I fancy it is pleasanter to linger with them: indeed, he takes wing from us to the upper regions, just as if he were escaping from some prison. But when it is time for him to come down to us, leisurely, and with slow enough steps, and painfully he makes the descent at last.

Klotho. Don't give way to your temper, Charon, any longer: for here is the very person himself hard by, as you see, bringing us a number of individuals; or rather scaring them along *en masse* with his rod, for all the world like a herd of goats. But what's this? I see one of them handcuffed, and another grinning, and one individual with a wallet suspended from his shoulder and with a club in his hand, staring grimly at them, and urging on the rest. And don't you see Hermes himself in a bath of perspiration, his feet covered with dust, and all out of breath? His mouth, anyway, is a regular steam-engine?[3]—what's this, Hermes? what's all this hurry about, for you seem to me to be a good deal put out?

[1] The asphodel, a plant of the lily kind, is one of the few delights of the Elysian fields. See 'Οδ. ix. 538, xxiv. 13; and cf. Hesiod. Ἔργα, 40:—

> Νήπιοι, οὐδὲ ἴσασιν, ὅσῳ πλέον ἥμισυ παντός,
> Οὐδ' ὅσον ἐν μαλάχῃ τε καὶ ἀσφοδέλῳ μὲγ'ὄνειαρ.

For a description of the "Fields of the Blessed," see in the 'Ανθολογία a beautiful epitaph on a girl named Πρώτη:—

> Οὔκ ἔθανες Πρώτη, μετέβης δ' ἐς ἀμείνονα χώραν.

[2] For the use of πόπανα and ἐναγίσματα in the Greek sacrifices to the dead, see the dictionaries of Hesychius and Suidas.

[3] Μεστὸν γοῦν ἄσθματος αὐτῷ τὸ στόμα.—The anachronism may be allowed, perhaps, for the sake of the illustration. Wieland translates: —"wie er keucht und kaum zu Athem kommen kann."

Hermes (*puffing and perspiring*). What else, Klotho, than that, from chasing this runaway sinner here, I was within an ace of being a deserter from my ship to-day ?

Klotho. But who is he ?   Or what was his intention in running away ?

Hermes. That's plain enough—he preferred living.   He is some king or despot—to judge, at least, by his lamentations, and the wailings he gives vent to ; he says he has been deprived of vast pleasure of some sort.

Klotho. Then did the fool run away, as if he could havo a longer lease of life, when his spun out thread had actually failed ?

Hermes. Run away, do you say?   Why, if this most excellent gentleman here, he of the club, had not aided me, and we had not caught and handcuffed him, he would even have got clean off from us altogether.   From the moment, in fact, Atropos had delivered him over to me, all the way he resisted and struggled ; and, firmly planting his feet on the ground, he was by no means an easy charge. Sometimes, too, he would fall to supplications and make vehement entreaty, demanding to be let off for a little, with offers of large bribes.   However, I, as you may well imagine, did not let him off, seeing that he wanted the impossible. Well, when we were now at the very mouth *of Orcus*, while, as was my custom, I was counting over the tale of the dead to Æakus, and he was making up their reckoning by the ticket sent him by your sister,[1] somehow or other, without being observed, the thrice-damned fellow got clean away.   One dead man, accordingly, was wanting to the full tale ; and, says Æakus, raising his eyebrows, " Pray, Hermes, don't practise your thievish art with everyone *you meet :* you have quite enough sport in heaven ; the affairs of the Dead *are managed* with strict attention to business, and by no means can they be slurred over. The ticket, as you observe, has ' one thousand and four ' scratched on it ; whereas you come to me with one short: *this won't do*, unless you tell me that Atropos has cheated

---

[1] *Atropos* ("the Sunderer ") ; *Klotho* being " the Spinner," and *Lachesis* "the Apportioner" of human life. See Hesiod. Θεoγ. 905, Ἀσπ. 258 ; Juv. *Sat.* ix. 135, 136. Hermes appears to have forgotten that to cross the Styx Charon's boat was *de rigueur*.

you." I, blushing at his lecture, quickly recollected what had happened by the way; and when, after a glance around, I saw this fellow nowhere, perceiving his flight, I set out in pursuit with all the speed I could by the road leading to daylight, and this most excellent person followed me quite of his own accord. So, running at a speed as if off from a starting line at a racecourse, we overtake him just at Tænarum [1]—so nearly did he succeed in escaping us.

Klotho. And we, Charon, but now were condemning Hermes's neglect of duty !

Charon. Why, pray, do we longer delay, as though we had not wasted time enough already ?

Klotho. You are right. Let them embark; and I, with my way-bill ready in my hand, and taking my seat, as is my custom, at the gangway, will make my diagnosis of each of them, as he embarks—who he is, and where he comes from, and what the manner of his dèath. And do you take them from me, and pack them together, and arrange them in regular order. And do you, Hermes, first of all, toss in those new-born infants there ; for what could *they* answer to my questions ?

Hermes. There, Ferryman, is the exact number—with the exposed *infants,*[2] three hundred in all.

Charon. A fig for your fine rich haul ! You come and bring me a lot of unripe dead !

Hermes. Will you have us, Klotho, embark the *unwept* next ?

Klotho. Do you mean the old ones ? So do. (*Aside, in disgust*) Why, indeed, should I be troubled with inquiring

---

[1] The south-eastern extremity of Lakonia. The famous cavern, fabled to be the descent to Orcus, was there situated, through which Herakles dragged Kerberus from his infernal post. See Apuleius, *De Aur. Asino*, and Psyche's descent to Hades. Cf. Aristoph. Βατρ. 187 ; Lucian, Νεκυομαντεία.

[2] How prevalent was the practice among the Greeks and Latins of "exposing" infants, whom the parents were unable or unwilling to bring up, and how large the numbers thus inhumanly disposed of in obedience to the oracles, is abundantly evident in their literatures—in particular, in the drama, in the New Comedy, in the imitations of Plautus and Terence, and in the Greek romances. See Aristoph. Νεφ. 522, and the charming pastoral romance of *Daphnis and Chloe,* where both the hero and herione are rescued castaways. The founders of the Roman and Persian monarchies were the same. See Herod. i. 107-117. Livy, *Ann.* i. &c.

into matters which happened before the days of Eukleides.[1]
—You who are above sixty, you come forward now. What's
this? Have they their ears so plugged up by age that
they don't hear me? (*To Hermes*) You will, likely enough,
have to take them up and bring them along.

Hermes. Here, again, are this lot, four hundred all but
two—quite ready to melt in your mouth, all of them, and
full-ripe, gathered in not before it was time.[2]

Charon. By heavens! no, for they are all of them, already,
regular raisins——

Klotho. Bring up next those who received their death-
wounds in battle, Hermes.—(*To the wounded*) And first
tell me, how you met your deaths to come here? Or stay;
rather, I will myself examine you by the written instructions. (*Looking at her way-bill*) Yesterday there must
have perished in battle, in Mysia, four and eighty, and
among them, Gobares, the son of Oxyartes.[3]

Hermes. They are here.

Klotho (*reading again from her tablets*). Seven have
cut their own throats on account of some love-affair, and
the philosopher Theagenes on account of his mistress, the
courtesan from Megara.[4]

Hermes. They are here, at your side.

Klotho (*referring to her tablets*). And where are those
who died at each others' hands, *fighting* for the throne?

[1] After the Peloponnesian War, the Lacedæmonians had imposed
upon conquered Athens the well-known government of the " Thirty
Tyrants." These having been expelled in the archonship of one Eukleides, a general amnesty in regard to all previous offences was
decreed. Klotho means that the Dead, before her, are too old and feeble
for examination.

[2] Hermes derives his forcible metaphor from the vintage. Wieland
has, " alle weich und reif, und zu rechter Zeit abgeschnitten."

[3] Lucian probably alludes to some battle which had been fought about
the time of his writing. As a Syrian, he frequently refers to
Eastern names and events. Perhaps no writer has exposed the *ridicu-
lousness* of War, among the atoms of our " mole-hill," more satirically
than Voltaire (in particular, in his *Micromégas* and other romances), or
Swift, in the *Voyage to Lilliput*.

[4] Theagenes, if not a merely fictitious name, may be the person commemorated by Lucian in his Περὶ τῆς Περιγρίνου Τελευτῆς, as conjectured by Du Soul; or he may be the tyrant of Megara mentioned
by Thucydides (i. 126). There was a distinguished athlete of that name,
recorded by Pausanias.

Hermes. Here they are.

Klotho. And the man who was murdered by his own wife and her lover?

Hermes. There, close to you.

Klotho (referring again). Ah! to be sure, bring up at once those *victims* of the tribunals of justice—I mean, I say, those who have perished by the bastinado, and those who have been impaled alive.[1] And those sixteen killed by pirates—where are they, Hermes?

Hermes. Here they are, those with the death-wounds, as you see.—Is it your wish I bring up the women, at the same time?

Klotho. By all means, and the shipwrecked people at the same time, for, indeed, they perished in the same manner; and the *victims* of the fever, those too—and, with them, the physician Agathokles.   But where is the philosopher, Kyniskus, who was fated to die by eating Hekate's supper, and the purificatory eggs, and the raw polypus, into the bargain?[2]

Kyniskus. I have been at your elbow this long time, most excellent Klotho.   But what wrong have I done, that you left me such a length of time up above?   For you all but spun out your whole spindle for me; although I often endeavoured to cut the thread and come *here;* but, somehow or other, it was not to be sundered.

Klotho. I left you behind as a superviser, and physician, of human wickedness. But come on board, and good health to you.

Kyniskus. In heaven's name, not before we have shipped this fellow here in fetters: for I am afraid he may get over you with his entreaties.

Klotho. Come, let me see who he is.

Hermes. Megapenthes, the son of Lakydas, the despot.[3]

Klotho. Come on board, you.

---

[1] Or "crucified"; 'ανασκολοπίζειν being sometimes used in the sense of ἀνασταυροῦν. See Lucian, Προμ. 7, and Περὶ τῆς Περ. Τελ. 11 (in a celebrated passage referring to Christ's crucifixion). Cf. Herod. i. 128, ix. 78.

[2] Such, according to one account, was said to have been the cause of the death of the Cynic Diogenes. See Πρᾶσις Βίων. 10, and Νεκ. Διαλ. 1.

[3] Probably, a merely typical despot—as no historical personage of that name seems to be known to History. A son of Menelaus so named is mentioned in 'Οδ. iv. 11, xv. 100, 122.

Megapenthes (*imploringly*). No, don't, O my Lady Klotho! pray, suffer me to go up again *to the light* for a little while : then I will come of my own accord, without any one summoning me.

Klotho. But what is it for which you wish to go ?

Megapenthes. Just give me permission to finish my mansion first—for my palace has been left but half completed.

Klotho. You trifle.   Embark, then !

Megapenthes (*on his knees*). It is no long time I ask, O Fate.   Suffer me to stay behind just this one day, until I have given some instructions to my wife about my money, as to where I had that vast treasure interred.

Klotho. Your fate is fixed.   You cannot obtain *your wish.*

Megapenthes (*weeping and groaning*). Is such a vast amount of gold, then, to perish ?

Klotho. It will not perish.   So have no fear on that score, at least : for Megakles,[1] your cousin, will inherit it.

Megapenthes. Alas ! the contumely !   My enemy, whom through indolence I, yes I, did not put to death beforehand ?

Klotho. The very same, and he will survive you forty years, and some little time longer, into the bargain, inheriting your mistresses, and your wardrobe, and all your gold.

Megapenthes. You do me wrong, Klotho, in assigning my wealth to my greatest enemies.

Klotho (*scornfully indignant*). Why, you, did not *you* inherit those very things which were Kydimachus's, most noble Sir, after having slain him, and cut the throats of his little children before his eyes, as he yet breathed ?

Megapenthes. But now they were mine.

Klotho. Nay, your time for possessing them is now over.

Megapenthes (*coaxingly*). Listen for a moment, O Klotho, to what I desire to say to you quite in private, in no one's hearing.—(*To his fellow ghosts*) Do you stand aside for a little.—(*In a whisper to Klotho*) Should you suffer me to run away, I promise to give you this day a quarter of a million pounds sterling.[2]

---

[1] A very aristocratic name at Athens.   *The* Megakles of History was the rival of Peisistratus, in the sixth century B.C.   Alkibiades traced his descent from these Alkmæonids.   Cf. Aristoph. Νεφ. 71.

[2] Χίλια τάλαντα χρυσίου ἐπισήμου.   "A thousand talents of coined gold."

Klotho. What, ridiculous man, do you still keep your gold and your thousands in mind?

Megapenthes. And I will throw into the bargain the two large mixing-bowls,[1] if you like, which I received after putting Kleokritus to death, weighing each a hundred talents of pure fine gold.

Klotho. Drag away and weigh *him*,[2] at once: for he does not look like coming on board of his own accord.

Megapenthes (to his fellow ghosts). I call you to witness —my walls remain unfinished, and my naval docks. I should have certainly completed them, if I had lived only five days longer.

Klotho. Don't fret yourself. Another will build them.

Megapenthes. Well, then, I beg of you this, at all events, surely reasonable request.

Klotho. What?

Megapenthes. For me to live on so long as until I shall have brought the people of Pisidia under my subjection, and imposed tribute on the Lydians, and raised to myself a vast monument, and inscribed on it all the great military exploits of my life.

Klotho. Ah! you fellow, you no longer ask for a single day, but a respite of something like twenty years.

Megapenthes. Indeed, I assure you I am prepared to offer you securities for my speedy return. And, if you wish it, I will hand over to you as my substitute my only beloved son.[3]

Klotho. Abominable villain!—him, whom you often used to pray you might leave behind in the world?

Megapenthes. Those vows I offered up a long time ago: but now I see what is better.

Klotho. He, too, will come to you in a little while, taken off by the new king.

---

[1] Κρατῆρας (κεραννύναι). So called as used for *mixing* the wine and water, which almost invariably was drunk by the Greeks rather than pure wine. They were a common dedicatory offering in the temples, and often were elaborately decorated.

[2] Ἕλκετε. A play upon the word used by Megapenthes—meaning both to "drag along" and "to weigh."

[3] Ἀνταίδρον ὑμῖν ἀντ' ἐμαυτοῦ παραδώσω τὸν ἀγαπητόν. Lehmann detects, in these words, "a not obscure allusion" to the propitiatory sacrifice of Christ.

Megapenthes. Well, then, don't deny me this favour at least, O Fate!

Klotho. Which?

Megapenthes. I wish to know how matters will go on after my decease.

Klotho. Listen, then: for when you have heard you will have the more anguish. Your slave Midas will have your wife; indeed, he had an intrigue with her long ago.

Megapenthes (*furious*). The cursed rascal, to whom, by her persuasion, I gave his freedom!

Klotho. And your daughter will be numbered among the mistresses of the now reigning despot; and the pictures and statues, which the city set up and dedicated to you formerly, will all be overturned, and afford ridicule to the spectators.[1]

Megapenthes. Tell me, and is there not one of my friends indignant at these proceedings?

Klotho. Why, *who* was your friend, or on what account could he be so? Are you ignorant that all, who adored you and eulogized every one of your sayings and doings, did so either from fear or from expectation, from love of your power, and with their looks eagerly fixed on their opportunity?

Megapenthes. Yet when they poured out their libations at my dinner-parties, with loud voice they were accustomed to invoke many blessings upon my head, ready each one of them to die for me, if it were possible. And, in fine, I was the great object of their adjuration.[2]

Klotho. Accordingly, it was when you were dining with one of them, yesterday, you died: for the last goblet

---

[1] Portraits, in the form both of statues, busts, and of pictures, especially the former, as is well known, were exceedingly common methods of self-glorification among the tyrants of Greek and Latin antiquity. Of what vast numbers of them must have been dispersed throughout the Roman empire, some idea may be formed from the records of such writers as Suetonius and Tacitus. As they were usually set up during the life-time of the original, their *testimonial* value is easily appreciated. If the tyrant had made himself especially hated, his splendid images were ignominiously shattered, when he was no longer an object of terror. See Juv. *Sat.* x. 58.

[2] Or, as proper name, "their *Horkus*"—the divinity who punished perjurers. Cf. Hes. Ἔργα. 804., Θεογ. 231. Herod. vi. 86. For a graphic picture of parasitism see Juv. *Sat.* iii. 86-108.

offered you to drink from, that it was which sent you down here.

Megapenthes. That, then, was the taste of something bitter I perceived. But with what intention did he do this ?

Klotho. You ask me a good many questions, when you ought to have embarked at once.

Megapenthes. One thing chokes me most of all, Klotho, on account of which I did long just to have but one peep again into daylight, if but for a moment.

Klotho. And what is it ? It looks like something exceedingly important.

Megapenthes. Karion, my domestic, as soon as ever he perceived me to be dead, late at night went up into my chamber, where I was lying—there being plenty of opportunity, for there was no one even to watch over me—and, fastening the door, enjoyed himself with my mistress Glycerium [1] (and it was not, I suppose, the first time he had made free with her [2]), for all the world as though nobody was there ; then, when he had satisfied his desire, fixing his looks upon me, "You, however, you little paltry scoundrel of a fellow," exclaims he, "many a time you inflicted blows upon me for nothing," and, suiting his actions to his words, he began to pull my beard, and strike me on the chaps; and, finally, making a deep expectoration, he spat on me, with the valediction of "Go to the devil," [3] and took himself off. I was all on fire with rage, and yet could not do anything to him, for I was already as dry as a bone and cold as death ; and the abominable girl, when she heard the noise of some persons approaching, rubbed her eyes with spittle, as though she had been crying over me; and with loud lamentations, and adjuring me by

---

[1] A favourite name of the ἑταίραι or παλλάκιδες, and the heroine of the well-known *Andria* of Menander and Terence : lit. "the sweet creature." The neuter form, and frequently the diminutive, was common to the class—as Erotium, Philocomasium, Philenium, Phronesium, Leontion.

[2] Or reading (with Jacobitz) κεκοινωνήκεσαν, "they had enjoyed each other's society."

[3] Εἰς τὸν τῶν ἀσεβῶν χῶρον ἄπιθι. Lit. "Go to the place of the wicked." The more usual Greek equivalent of our expletive is, ἐς κόρακας—"to the crows," tantamount to "may you be unburied."

name, she slipped away. And if I could but get hold of them——

Klotho. Have done with your threats.—Nay, come on board this instant; it is high time you appeared at the judgment-seat.

Megapenthes. And who will claim the right to cast a vote against a royal person?

Klotho. Against a " royal person " no one, indeed; but against a dead man Rhadamanthys himself, whom you will presently see—a just judge, and who pronounces sentence equitably in every case. But, just now, don't waste time.

Megapenthes. Even make me, if you would, a private person, Fate, one of the crowd of paupers, even a slave,[1] from the king that I was before—only suffer me to live just once again.

Klotho. Where is he of the club ? And you, Hermes, help haul him within by the foot; for he would never come on board of his own accord.

Hermes. Follow me, now, runaway slave. (*Seizing him by the neck*) Take him, you Ferryman, and the other, what's his name, and see that they are safely——

Charon. Don't be afraid—he shall be bound to the mast.

Megapenthes. Surely I ought to sit in the front seat.

Klotho. For why ?

Megapenthes. By heaven, because I was a prince, and had ten thousand body-guards.

Kyniskus. So, then, did not your Karion yonder,[2] properly enough, pull your beard, for a dolt that you are ? A bitter sort of princedom will you have, anyway, when you have had a taste of the club.

Megapenthes. What, will Kyniskus dare to threaten me with his stick ? (*To the philosopher*) Did I not, but the day before yesterday, all but have you nailed up for being over free, and rude, and fault-finding ?

---

[1] See the well-known confession of Achilleus to Odysseus in Hades, 'Οδ. xi. 488-490; and cf. Eurip. Ἰφιγ. ἐν Αὐλ. 1250; Æn. vi. 456; Seneca, *Ep.* 26. Plato (Πολ. iii.) finds fault with the poet of the *Odyssey* for putting such sentiment in his hero's mouth.

[2] A proper name formed from Καρ, a Carian—the slaves from Caria and from Paphlagonia having a pre-eminently bad character. See Eurip. Κυκλ. 647 ; Plato, Εὐθ. 285 ; Cicero, *Pro Val. Flacco*, 27, 65.

Kyniskus (laughing). Accordingly, you will remain, you too, nailed up to the mast.

Mikyllus (pushing to the front). Tell me, Klotho, and am I of no account with you ?   Or, because I am a poor man, must I for that reason be the last to embark ?

Klotho. And you—who are you ?

Mikyllus. The cobbler Mikyllus.[1]

Klotho. And so you are annoyed at waiting about? Don't you see how much this prince promises to give, to be respited for but a brief time ?   I am all amazement, to be sure, that this delay is not liked by you as well.

Mikyllus. Just lend me your ear, most excellent Fate.   The kind gift of the Kyklops does not altogether delight me—the promise, I mean, of "Outis I will last devour."[2]   Whether first or last, the same teeth, I suppose, await me.   Besides, my circumstances are not like those of the rich—for our lives, as the saying is, are "as opposite as the two poles."[3]   The prince, indeed, seeing he had the reputation of being happy in life, an object of dread to all, and looked up to with awe by everyone, and has left behind such a vast amount of gold and silver, and fine clothes, and horses, and dinners, and handsome boys, and beautiful women, was with good reason angry, and vexed at being torn away from them all.   For, somehow or other, the mind clings to such things as to a sort of bird-lime, and is not willing with any good grace to let itself go, inasmuch as it has long been fast glued to them ; or, rather, it is as if it were some unseverable chain, by which it is their fate to be bound.   Of course, should one drag them off by force, they will howl and fall to prayers ; and, while audacious enough in other respects, they are found out to be arrant cowards as respects this road that leads to Hades.   They turn themselves round, forsooth, to regard what they are leaving behind ; and, like unfortunate lovers, would like to gaze even from a distance upon the concerns of the upper world, just as that fool did,

---

[1] Mikyllus, " the dwarf," is the hero of the Dialogue entitled Ὄνειρος ἢ ᾽Αλεκτρύων, who had been instructed by his philosophic feathered friend to entertain that contempt for plutocrats which he now displays.

[2] Οὗτιν ἐγὼ πύματον ἔδομαι μετὰ οἷς ἑτάροισιν.—᾽Οδ. ix. 369.

[3] ᾽Εκ διαμέτρου. Lit. " diametrically opposite." See Erasmus, *Adagia.*

who ran away on the road, and fell to frantic entreaties to you even here.

Whereas I, seeing I had no pledge to hold me to life, no estate, no house-property,[1] no gold, no furniture, no fame, no portraits, naturally I was quite equipped for the journey, and when Atropos simply beckoned to me, gladly I threw away my brad-awl, and shoe-sole—for I had a last in my hands—and jumping up at once I followed barefooted, and without even washing off the black dirt; rather I led the way, with my face to the front : for there was nothing behind to cause me to turn, and to call me back. And heaven be my witness, now I see everything with you to be fair ; for the fact of perfect equality in honour for all, and of nobody being superior to his neighbour, to me, at all events, appears to be uncommonly pleasant. And I guess that debts are not demanded of debtors hereabouts, and that there are no taxes to pay. But what is best of all, is that there is no shivering from winter's cold, nor sickness, nor being beaten by one's superiors.   All is perfect peace here, and things are entirely reversed : for it's we poor devils now who laugh, while the rich plague themselves and make loud lamentations.[2]

Klotho. I have been watching you laughing a long time, Mikyllus. What is it that particularly moved you to laughter ?

Mikyllus. Just hear me, a moment, my most honoured of all divinities. Up above there I used to live near the palace of a prince, and very narrowly observed all his actions, and he seemed to me then to be even, in a manner, a rival of the gods. For when I saw his embroidered purple, and the number of his attendants, and his gold, and his bejewelled beakers, and his silver-footed couches, I thought him happy ; and, moreover, the rich steam from the dishes prepared for his feasts tantalized me to death— so that he appeared quite plainly to me to be some man far above ordinary human clay and thrice-blessed, and almost *I was going to say* the handsomest man alive, and to tower

---

[1] Συνοικίαν. Properly lodging-houses, in which a number of families *lived together*, in separate floors—a common sort of investment of the rich at Athens. See Böckh, *Public Economy of Athens*, 114.

[2] Cf. Ἰακώβου Ἐπιστ. v. 1-6 :—
  Ἄγε νῦν οἱ πλούσιοι, κλαύσατε ὀλολύζοντες, κ.τ.λ.

above the rest of the world by a whole royal cubit; exalted by fortune as he was, with his magnificent strides, with his backward tosses of his head, and inspiring terror in all who accosted him. But as soon as ever he was dead, the great man [1] was seen to be altogether an object for ridicule —when he had stripped himself of his luxuries. And I derided myself the more, such a miserable wretch had I been stupidly gazing open-mouthed at; measuring his good fortune by the steam from his kitchens, and thinking him happy on account of the blood-red liquid obtained from shell-fish in the seas of Lakonia. And, when I saw not only him, but also the money-lender Gniphon, groaning and repenting of his folly, because he had had no enjoyment of his riches, but had died without tasting them, leaving his wealth to the spendthrift Rhodocharis [2] (for he was his nearest relative, and by law had the first claim to the property), I did not know how to stifle my laughter; most especially, when I remembered how pallid he always was, and dirty, with his face full of care, and rich only for his fingers, with which he used to count over his talents and myriads *of drachmas*, scraping together little by little what in a brief time will be squandered by the happy Rhodocharis. [3]—But why don't we set off now? For, faith, while on our voyage we shall be able to have our laugh out, and watch them howling.

Klotho (to Mikyllus). Come on board, that the Ferryman may hoist up his anchor.

Charon (pushing back Mikyllus). Holloa! you there, where are you rushing to? Our craft is full enough already. Stay here till to-morrow: the first thing in the morning, we will take you across.

Mikyllus (struggling to get on board). It is unfair of you, Charon, to leave me behind, an already stale dead man of yesterday. [4] Never mind, I will bring an action against you

---

[1] Αὗτος, Lat. *ipse*. Cf. Juv. *Sat. passim.*.

[2] Evidently, with the poet Anakreon, "a lover of roses" only when conjoined with the wine-cup. Gniphon, or, rather, Gnyphon, the " miser," appears also in the Πρᾶσις Βίων, 23 ; Τίμων, 58 ; and ’Αλεκτρ. 30.

[3] See the *Aulularia* and Euclio of Plautus, and Molière's imitation, *L'Avare*. Fielding has treated the same subject in his *Miser*. Cf. the fine satire of Juv. *Sat.* xiv. 107-254 ; Hor. *Sat.* 1, i.; Cicero, *Ep.* xvi. 26.

[4] Ἔωλον ἤδη νεκρὸν. Cf. Plut. Περὶ τῆς Σαρκοφαγίας, ii. 1.

before Rhadamanthys for unconstitutional procedure.[1]—Out upon my ill-fate ! They are already off ; and I shall have to be left here all alone.[2] However, why don't I swim across after them ? For, as I am already dead, I have no fear of being done up and drowned. Besides, I have not even the penny to pay down for the fare (*jumps into the Styx*).

Klotho. What's this ? Stop a moment, Mikyllus, and wait. It's not lawful and right for you to cross so.

Mikyllus. Indeed, I shall very likely come ashore before you.

Klotho. Not for the world ! (*To Charon*) However, let us sail up to him and take him on board ; and you, Hermes, do you snatch him up at the right moment.

Charon (*helping to drag him overboard*). Where shall he sit now ? Every inch of room is occupied, as you observe.

Hermes. Upon the tyrant's shoulders, if you like.

Klotho. A good idea of Hermes's ! (*To Mikyllus*) Come up, then, and tread on the rascal's neck. And now a fair voyage to us !

Kyniskus (*making up a face*). Charon, it is well at this juncture to tell you the truth. I should not be able to pay you the penny, upon landing ; for I have nothing more than my wallet, which you see, and this club here. But, for the rest, if you would like me to scuttle out the bilge-water, I am quite ready, or to take my place at the oar. And you shall have no cause to find fault at all, only give me a strong and well-fitted oar.

Charon. Row away, then ; for to get even that from you is as much as can be expected.

Kyniskus. Shall I have to give the time to the rowers, too ?[3]

Charon. Do so, in heaven's name, if you really know any nautical tune of the kind.

Kyniskus. Sure enough I know several, Charon (*begins to*

---

[1] Γράψομαι σε παρανόμων, the regular formula in the Attic law-courts.

[2] See Juv. *Sat.* iii. 265, for *horret* reading *optat.* Cf. Aristoph. Βατρ. 190-200. Xanthias solves the difficulty by making the *détour* of the lake.

[3] Ὑποκελεῦσαι, " to hum the song, to keep the rowers to the time," as usual in the Greek ships ; hence ἀπὸ ἑνὸς κελεύσματος, " with one swing," " all at once." Thucyd. ii. 92. See Aristoph. Βατρ. 208, and the κελεύσμα of Charon, on that memorable occasion.

hum the tune). There ! do you see ? these fellows are acting as chorus with their whining. So our song will be rather interrupted.

First Dead Man. Alas ! for all my possessions !

Second Dead Man. Alas ! for my estates !

Third Dead Man. Ah ! ah ! ah ! What a mansion I left behind me !

Fourth Dead Man. How many thousands will my heir receive from me, only to squander !

Fifth Dead Man. Oh ! oh ! my tender infants.[1]

Sixth Dead Man. Who, I wonder, will gather in the harvest of my vines, which I planted for myself last year ?[2]

Hermes. Mikyllus, don't you lament at all ? Upon my word, it is not lawful and right for anyone to make the passage without shedding a tear.

Mikyllus. Get away with you. There's no reason why I should bewail myself for having a pleasant voyage.

Hermes. All the same, make *some* groaning, however little, merely for the sake of conformity.

Mikyllus. I will groan away then, since it's your wish, Hermes.—Alas for my sandal-soles ![3] Alas for my old lasts ! Oh ! oh ! oh ! for my rotten shoes ! Never again, poor wretch that I am, shall I go from morning to evening without a morsel of food, nor in the cold winter shall I wander about unshod and half-naked, chattering with my teeth from cold. Who, I wonder, will have my knife and my awl ?

Hermes. Enough of your dirges; here we are all but across.

Charon (*to the passengers*). Come, I say, first pay me up your fares. (*To a defaulting passenger*) Come, you pay

---

[1] "I could wish," remarks Wieland, "for the honour of Lucian's heart, that these words had not slipped from his pen." But Lucian may have thought them necessary to a complete picture of the lamentations, without intending any unfeelingness.

[2] Holbein, in his famous series of the *Todtentanz*, has graphically presented *oculis fidelibus* this and the similar scenes of the *Dialogues of the Dead.*

[3] Οἴμοι τῶν καττυμάτων, Cf. Aristoph. 'Iπ. 314, 366. Mikyllus seems to play upon the preceding κτημάτων, the object of the lamentations of his fellow-passengers. The "rotten shoes" may be capable of a double interpretation.

too. I have now got the fares from all of them. (*Observing Mikyllus slipping away*) Hand me your obole as well, Mikyllus.

Mikyllus. You joke, Charon, or, as the proverb has it, you are writing on water,[1] if you expect an obole from Mikyllus. To begin with, positively I don't know whether an obole is square or round.

Charon. Ah! a fine voyage and fine profit *I've made* to day. Well, get out all the same, and I will go and look after the horses, and cows, and dogs, and the other animals; for they, too, have now to cross.[2]

Klotho. Take and lead them away, Hermes. I myself will make the return voyage to the opposite shore to bring across Indopatres and Heramithra, the Tartars;[3] for they have died but now by one another's hands, fighting for the boundaries of their territories.

Hermes (*to the Dead*). Ho! you people there, let us go forward; or, rather, do you all of you follow me in order.

Mikyllus. Herakles! what a din! Where now is the beau Megillus? Or by what circumstance does one distinguish here whether Simmiche is fairer than Phryne?[4] For everything is on one and the same footing, and of the same complexion, and nothing is either fair or fairer. Nay, now even the old tattered cloak, which, formerly, for a while seemed to be disreputable, is equally honourable with the purple robe of the king : for both are faded out of recogni-

---

[1] See for similar uses of the Greek adage, Plato, Φαιδρ. 276.

[2] A singular recognition of the right of the non-human species to *posthumous* existence, Cf. 'Αποκ. 'Ιωαν. iv. κ. τ. λ.

[3] Τοὺς Σῆρας, the Seres. Some slight knowledge of the outskirts of the Chinese Empire had been acquired by the western world in the second century; and the great astronomer Ptolemy, a contemporary of Lucian, had embodied all that was known in his geographical work, Γεωγ. Υφηγήσις, vii. MS. authority and the first king's name favour the reading generally adopted, but a conjectural emendation is Σύρας, Syrians.

[4] Phryne, the famous *hetæra*, who made so immense a fortune by her numerous lovers as to offer to rebuild the walls of her country's capital, destroyed by Alexander of Macedon. She is most famous as the original of the *Aphrodite Anadyomene* and the Knidian Aphrodite of Praxiteles, and by the well-known device of her counsel Hypereides (see Quintilian, ii., 15; Athenæus, xiii.). Simmiche figures in the 'Εταιρ. Διαλ. iv. Fontenelle (*Dialogues des Morts*) represents Alexander of Macedon complaining to Plato that the modern imitator of Lucian had preferred, as conqueror, Phryne to himself.

tion, and have sunk beneath the same obscurity.—Kyniskus, where in the world, I wonder, may you be?

Kyniskus. Here, I tell you. Well, if you like, let us trudge on together.

Mikyllus. A good idea! give me your arm. Now, tell me —for certainly you were initiated, Kyniskus, into the Eleusinian Mysteries—does not the state of things here appear to you similar to the condition there, *above?*

Kyniskus. You are right.—But look, there is some female figure approaching with a torch, and with a frightful and threatening sort of look about her. Is it, by any chance, I wonder, an Erinys?[1]

Mikyllus. She looks like it from her dress, at all events.

Hermes (to the Fury). Take over these thousand and four persons, Tisiphone.

Tisiphone. Yes, indeed; Rhadamanthys has been waiting for you this long time.

Rhadamanthys. Bring them up, Erinys, and you, Hermes, make proclamation, and summon them.

Kyniskus. Rhadamanthys, by your father,[2] I beg, have me up and examine me first.

Rhadamanthys. Upon what grounds?

Kyniskus. I am exceedingly desirous to bring charges against a certain person, in regard to evil deeds which I am privy to his having committed in life. I should not, however, be deserving of credit in my report, unless I first myself be tested of what sort I am, and as to what kind of life I have lived.

Rhadamanthys. And *who* are you?

Kyniskus. Kyniskus, most excellent Sir, a philosopher, as he hopes.

Rhadamanthys. Come here, and take your place first for

---

[1] " The persecuting" or "the angry" one. The dire sisters were usually called, in Greek euphemism, *Eumenides*—"the kind" or "well-disposed" divinities. They were distinguished by the names Tisiphone, Alekto, and Megæra, first by Apollodorus; the original plurality of the Homeric conception having been limited by Euripides to a trinity (see Ἰλ. xix. 259-260; Hes. Ἔργα. 39; the Εὐμένιδες of Æschylus, etc.).

[2] This judge of the supreme Court of Hades was son of Zeus by Europa, and brother of Minos. See Apollod; Plato, Φαίδων, ii. 4; Virg. Æn. vi. Juv. *Sat.* xiii. 197. The especial function of Rhadamanthys was inquisitorial, of Minos judicial, of Æacus executional.

judgment. (*To Hermes*) And do you summon the accusers.

Hermes. If any one has any charge against Kyniskus here, let him now come forward.

Kyniskus. No one stirs.

Rhadamanthys. But that is not sufficient. Strip off your clothes, that I may examine you by your brand-marks.[1]

Kyniskus. But why ?   For where did *I* ever become a branded slave ?

Rhadamanthys. Whatever evil deeds any one of you may have done during your life,—in the case of each individual, he carries about invisible brand-marks upon his soul.

Kyniskus (stripping himself). There, I stand before you as naked as *I* was born. So make a thorough search for what you call " the brand-marks."

Rhadamanthys (examining). This man, for the most part, is free *from them ;* with the exception of these three or four very dim and scarcely recognizable ones. (*Scrutinizing more closely*)   What is the meaning, however, of this ? There are traces and many signs of scars; but somehow they have been obliterated, or, rather, excised. How is this, Kyniskus ? how is it you have come out pure, as though you had been born anew ?

Kyniskus. I will tell you. Whereas formerly I was corrupt for want of instruction, and, on that account, contracted many brand-marks; as soon as ever I began to study philosophy, by degrees I cleansed my soul for myself of all its stains, by using a wholesome and most efficacious remedy.[2]

Rhadamanthys. Depart, then, to the Islands of the Blessed,[3] to join the company of the Best, first alleging

---

[1] Στίγματα, the marks branded on a runaway slave. Slaves devoted to the service of the temples, also, were branded. Cf. Herod. ii. 113 ; Ἐπ. Παυλ. πρὸς Κορ.; the *stigmata* of S. Francesco d'Assisi, S. Katerina di Siena, and other Saints.

[2] The last words of Kyniskus here are usually assigned to Rhadamanthys.

[3] For a detailed description of "the place of the Blessed," see the Ἀληθής Ἱστ. and Φαίδων. Cf. Ὀδ. ix. ; Aristoph. Βατρ. ; und Virg. Æn. vi.

your charges against the despot whom you speak of. (*To Hermes*) Call up others.

Mikyllus. Surely my case is a trifling one, Rhadamanthys, and needs but a brief sort of examination. This long time, at all events, I have been quite naked at your service. So inspect me.

Rhadamanthys. And who may *you* be?

Mikyllus. The cobbler, Mikyllus.

Rhadamanthys (after minute inspection). Excellent! Mikyllus: perfectly clear, and without any noticeable mark. Go you, too, by the side of Kyniskus here. Now summon the tyrant.

Hermes. Let Megapenthes, son of Lakydas, approach.— Where are you wriggling to? Step to the front at once. It is *you*, the tyrant, I am summoning. Shove him by the neck, and push him forward into full view, Tisiphone.

Rhadamanthys. Now do you, Kyniskus, produce your accusations, and convict him on the spot: for the man is at your elbow here.[1]

Kyniskus. Indeed, there was no need of words at all: for you will very quickly know him, from his brand-marks, what sort of character he is. All the same, I will reveal the man's life to you by word of mouth, and will show him up still more plainly by my account. Well, all the actions of this thrice-cursed wretch, as a private individual, I intend to pass by. As soon as ever, by attaching to himself the most shameless of men, and collecting a body-guard, he had effected a *coup-d'état*, and established himself as despot, he put to death more than ten thousand citizens untried; and, seizing upon the property of each one of them, and so arriving at the highest pitch of wealth, he has omitted no shape or form of excess. He exercised every sort of cruelty, and insolence, and wrong against the miserable citizens, violating virgins, and foully disgracing youths, in every way grossly insulting his subjects[2] in his drunken debaucheries. Even on the score of his arrogance,

---

[1] The obscurity of the atmosphere of Orcus might well blunt the vision of the unaccustomed guests. According to the poet of the *Odyssey* (xxiv. 6), they are as " blind as bats."

[2] Lucian depicts, with more or less verisimilitude, the origin and character of the old Greek tyrants generally—in particular, of the

full-blown pride, and insolence to all who addressed him,
you could not possibly exact from him any adequate penalty.
One, in fact, could gaze at the Sun without blinking more
easily than at this man. In very truth, his ingenious inventions of cruel punishments, who did not keep his hands
off even his nearest relatives, it would be impossible for
any one adequately to expose. And these charges—that
they are not some groundless calumny against him—you
will soon know, by calling those who have been murdered
by him; or, rather, they are present now, as you see, un-
summoned, and they surround him and are strangling
him (*pointing to the shrieking ghosts*). These all, Rhadamanthys, have died at the hand of the wretched criminal
—some by treachery, for the sake of beautiful women;
and some, because they were indignant at their sons being
carried off to be insulted by his unnatural debaucheries;
others, because they were rich; some, because they were
able, and prudent, and did not at all approve of his acts.

Rhadamanthys. What say you to this, you abominable
wretch, you?

Megapenthes. I have, indeed, perpetrated the murders
which he speaks of: but all the rest—the adulteries, and
unnatural offences, and debauching virgins—in all these
respects, Kyniskus has falsely accused me.

Kyniskus. Then I will bring you witnesses of these
crimes, Rhadamanthys.

Rhadamanthys. Who are they you speak of?

Kyniskus. Summon, Hermes, his lamp and his couch:
for, if they appear, they will testify what sort of deeds they
were privy to his perpetrating.

Hermes (making proclamation). Let the Couch and Lamp
of Megapenthes put in an appearance. (*To the Court*)
They have been so good as to obey the summons.[1]

despots of Sicily, the Dionysii and others, and of the successors to the
various conquests of Alexander. But, doubtless, he had in mind the
still greater enormities of atrocity and licentiousness of the Roman
Cæsars; in particular, of Caligula, as described in the pages of Suetonius,
perhaps the vilest despot who ever ruled the Roman world.

[1] For similar bold *personifications* of Lucian, see his Δικὴ Φωνηέντων.
It is deserving of notice that Lucian has been more judicious in exercising proper reticence, than many of his modern imitators and successors.

Rhadamanthys (to the new witnesses). Tell us, pray, what you are privy to about this Megapenthes. And do you, Couch, speak first.

Couch. All the accusations of Kyniskus are true. I, however, my lord, blush to speak of these things: such were the deeds which he was accustomed to perpetrate upon me.

Rhadamanthys. You certainly give your evidence against him most plainly, seeing you cannot endure even to mention the particulars.—And you, Lamp, now let us have your evidence.

Lamp. I do not know what happened by day, for I was not present: and as to his acts and experiences by night, I shrink from speaking of them. But I saw many indescribable things, and that surpassed all *conceivable* unnatural debauchery; although I would willingly often have not drunk in the oil, and I longed to be extinguished. But he even would bring me up close to the very scene of his acts, and would pollute my light in every possible way.

Rhadamanthys. We have now had enough of witnesses. (*To the officers of the Court*) Well, now, strip off this purple dress, that we may count the number of his brandings. —Ha! The fellow here is livid all over, and everywhere marked;[1] or, rather, he is black and blue from them. In what way should he be punished? Is he to be thrown into the flames of Pyriphlegethon, or to be given up to Kerberus?

Kyniskus. Not so. But, if you will permit me, I will suggest to you a new and befitting kind of punishment for him.

Rhadamanthys. Speak, for I shall acknowledge my extreme indebtedness to you for so doing.

Kyniskus. It is a custom, I believe, for all who die to drink the water of Lethe.

Rhadamanthys. Certainly.

Kyniskus. Then let this man be the exception, and not drink.

Rhadamanthys. Why, pray?

---

[1] Κατάγραφος. Borrowed from Plato by Lucian, from Lucian by Julian (Καίσαρες)—Bourdelotius.

Kyniskus. In that way he will undergo a punishment hard to bear, recollecting, *as he will*, what he was, and how great was his power in the upper world, and pondering over his lost delights.[1]

Rhadamanthys. You are right. Let him be sentenced accordingly, and let him be dragged away and put in chains by the side of Tantalus, and let him retain memory of all his deeds committed in his lifetime.

---

[1] So Dante :—

> " Nessun maggior dolore
> Che ricordarsi del tempo felice
> Nella miseria."
>
> *Inferno, v.*

MENIPPUS: OR, THE ORACLE OF THE DEAD.[1]

[MENIPPUS, the Cynic philosopher, just returned from a visit of inquiry to Hades, meets his friend Philonides, who earnestly begs him to reveal the reasons, and the experiences, of his interesting journey. Thus adjured, with some display of reluctance, Menippus, after having been assured by his friend that human life has not at all improved during his absence, professes that he had been impelled to take so hazardous a journey by an ardent desire to learn the truths of philosophy and life—vainly sought alike in the popular Theology and in the schools of the Philosophers, or Sophists, who were all at variance one with the other, and contradicted themselves; while they failed to practise their own teaching.

Thus forced to trust to his own resources, after much mental inquietude, he determines to go to Babylon, a

---

[1] Μένιππος ἢ Νεκυομαντεία. This Lucianic *Dialogue* (for its genuineness is doubtful, as shewn, among modern critics, by Wieland and Lehmann) borrows its alternative title from the Eleventh Book of the *Odyssey*, of which it is, in great part, a parody. It is a sort of *epitome* of the *Dialogues of the Dead* and other writings of the great master, which satirize the popular theology respecting the Under-World, and is of high interest as a *résumé* of this province of Hellenic superstition.

Rabelais (who is indebted, especially, to the *True History*) borrows one of his most instructive scenes from this *Dialogue*. In the battle with the Dipsodes, on behalf of the Amaurotes (the " shadowy " or "fleeting " people, a name suggested to Rabelais by the *Utopia* of More, himself indebted to Lucian), Pantagruel's companion, Epistemon—who loses his head, but afterwards recovers it through the skilful surgery of Panurge—upon returning from his temporary sojourn in Hades, reports the altogether *reversed* conditions of some of the heroes of antiquity and of later times. (Gargantua and Pantagruel, ii.) The Spanish satirist, Quevedo, also, has obligations to the *Menippus*, in his *Sueños*.

principal seat of the Magi and the Mystics, and by their occult science obtain admission to the Under-World, and, like his prototype, Odysseus, consult the soul of the Theban prophet Teiresias.   Arrived at Babylon, Menippus introduces himself to one of these Magi, named Mithrobarzanes, and, with considerable difficulty, obtains from him promise of assistance.   Under the tuition of the Magus, he enters upon a course of purificatory and mystic rites, and a strict dietetic regimen, until he is properly prepared for the dreadful descent.   Embarking on the Euphrates, they sail to a certain secluded place, where they leave their boat, and begin the prescribed infernal rites and sacrifices—still faithfully following the authority of the poet of the *Odyssey* —invoking Hekate, the Erinyes (or Furies), and all the dæmons.   The Earth opens, and the various infernal sights are revealed. Descending, with much difficulty, the travellers secure places on board Charon's boat, already overladen with dead men, who, for the most part, had received their *quietus* in battle.   The lion's skin, and mane of Herakles, with which the Cynic had provided himself, secure for them places on board, and a courteous reception from the Ferryman of the Styx.   Disembarking, with the Magus for guide, Menippus makes his way, through "squealing" ghosts, to the tribunal of Minos.   There they see the various punishments for crime and injustice administered, and a novel sort of witnesses in the *shadows* of the accused. Among those most severely punished appear the arrogant Rich; and Menippus does not lose his opportunity for the exercise of his satirical faculty.   Leaving the judgment-seat of Minos, they proceed to the scenes of punishment, and view the various instruments and infliction of torture.

In the Acherusian plains, they verify the accounts of the poet of the *Odyssey*, as to the ἀμένηνα καρήνα, and other particulars.   The ἰσοτιμία is found to be complete and indubitable.   Thersites and Nireus, Irus and Alkinous, have nothing whatever to distinguish them one from the other. Under the influence of this spectacle, Menippus compares human life to a gigantic public Procession, and to the Stage, where the several constituents play their diverse parts, for a short time, liable to extremest vicissitudes of fortune.   Mausolus, and other vain-glorious princes, with their " lying trophies " and inscriptions, in particular, fall under the Cynic's satire; and the Earthly kings and potentates who, in the Under-World, cut so abject and inglorious a figure. As for Sokrates and Diogenes, they still pursue their peculiar and favourite occupations. At this point of his narrative, Menippus is reminded that he has omitted to quote the solemn Decree against the Plutocrats, passed by the Popular Assembly of Hades (to which he had referred at the beginning of his report), the purport of which is the apportionment of a severe retribution.

At the point of going back to the Upper-World, Menippus approaches Teiresias, and begs him to reveal the secret, which was the object of his descent. This the prophet's ghost does with laconic brevity. The philosophers then return, by a short cut, to Earth, near to the Cave of Trophonius.]

Menippus and Philonides.

Menippus—
> " Domestic hearth, ancestral palace, hail !
> To light restored, I gladly you salute." [1]

Philonides (*seeing the Cynic at a distance*). Is not this Menippus the Dog ? Surely it is no other, unless my eyes see wrong (*rubbing his eyes*). Menippus every inch of him ! But what means his strangeness of dress—felt hat, and lyre, and lion's skin ? However, I must go up to him. Good-day, Menippus ! And where do you hail from ? Why, you have not shown yourself in the city [2] this long while.

Menippus—
> " I come, th' infernal vault, and Hades' gates
> Deserted, where, apart, dark Pluto broods." [3]

Philonides. Herakles ! Menippus dead without our knowing it.   And so he has come back to life again ?

---

[1]
$$\text{Ω χαῖρε, μέλαθρον, πρόπυλα θ' ἑστίας, ἑμῆς·}$$
$$\text{Ὡς ἄσμενος σ' ἐσεῖδον ἐς φάος μολών.}$$
Eurip. Ἡρακ. Μαιν. 523.

[2] Athens, which, like Rome, was known, *par excellence,* as " the city."

[3]
$$\text{Ἥκω νεκρῶν κευθμῶνα, καὶ σκότου πύλας}$$
$$\text{Λιπών, ἵν' Ἀιδης χωρὶς ᾤκισται Θεῶν.}$$
Eurip. Ἑκαβη. i.
The opening address of the ghost of Polydorus, the son of Hekube and Priam, who had been murdered by his Thracian host.

Menippus—

> "No, but yet alive dark Hades took me." [1]

Philonides. What was the cause of this strange and extraordinary journey of yours?

Menippus—

> "Me youth incited: self-willed more than wise." [2]

Philonides. Stop your tragic style, my fine Sir, and descending from your iambics, speak much as *I am doing*, in simple prose, thus. What was your equipment? What need had you to take the journey below? For anyhow it's not a pleasant sort of thing, nor is the road a usually welcome one.

Menippus—

> "Necessity, O friend of mine, conducted me to Hades,
> The spirit to consult there of Teiresias the Theban." [3]

Philonides. Ah! my good fellow, but you surely are off your head: for otherwise you would not be thus declaiming to your friends in metrical strain.

Menippus. Don't be surprised, my friend, for having lately been in the company of Euripides and Homer, somehow or other I got stuffed full of their verses, and their measures come to my lips, as it were, of their own accord. But, tell me, how go things above on Earth, and what are they about in the city?

Philonides. Nothing new, but just what *they used to do* before—they plunder, perjure themselves, extort interest by hook or by crook, turn "an honest penny" in the most sordid fashion.[4]

Menippus. Poor wretches, and unfortunate devils! They don't know what sort of measures have lately been determined on among the Powers below, and of what sort are

---

[1] Οὐκ, ἀλλ' ἔτ' ἔμπνουν 'Αἴδης μ' ἐδέξατο. A verse, apparently, from one of the lost dramas of Euripides.

[2] Νεότης μ' ἐπῆρε, καὶ θράσος τοῦ νοῦ πλέον. From the lost drama of the 'Ανδρόμεδα of Euripides.

[3]
> χρειώ με κατήγαγεν εἰς' 'Αἴδαο
> Ψυχῇ χρησόμενον Θηβαίου Τειρεσίαου.
> 'Οδ. xi. 165.

The reply of Odysseus to the inquiring ghost of his mother.

[4] Τοκογλυφοῦσι, ὀβολοστατοῦσι. The latter verb (lit. "to weigh obols") is derived, apparently, from Aristophanes, Νεφ. 1139.

the decrees that have been voted against the Rich, which, by
Kerberus, there is no possible means of their escaping from.

Philonides. How? Has any very new decree been passed
by the Powers down below respecting those up here ?

Menippus. Yes, so help me heaven ! and many of them :
but it's not lawful to publish them abroad to everyone,
nor to proclaim the ineffable secrets, for fear that someone
or other might bring an action against us in the Court of
Rhadamanthys for impiety.

Philonides. Don't, Menippus, don't, in heaven's name,
grudge a friend *the narration* of those events ; for you will
speak to one who knows how to hold his tongue, and,
moreover, to one who has been initiated.

Menippus. You impose upon me a hard task, and not at
all a safe one. But, however, for your sake I must run
the risk. It is decreed, I say, that these millionaires and
plutocrats, and those who carefully keep their gold coin
shut up like Danae——

Philonides. Don't tell me the decrees before, my good
Sir, you have recounted that which I would with most
particular pleasure hear from you—what was your intention in making the descent, and who was your guide on
the journey? Next, in regular order, what you saw, and
what you heard among them : for it is reasonable to suppose, surely, that you as a *dilettante* neglected nothing of
what was worth seeing or hearing.

Menippus. I must even do you this service, for what *can*
one do, when a gentleman and a friend urges one ? Well,
then, I will recount to you, first of all, my design, and
whence I got the impulse to make the descent. Well, I, as
long as I was in my teens, when I listened to Homer and
Hesiod recounting the wars and seditions not only of the
demi-gods, but actually even of the Gods themselves before
now ; nay, further, even their adulteries, and violences, and
rapes and feuds, their expulsions of parents, and their
marriages with sisters—all this I used to consider to be
good and right, and I tickled my fancy in no ordinary
degree with it all. But when I began to arrive at
mature age, on the contrary, I then heard the laws en-
joining the opposite to the poets,—not to commit adultery,
nor to engage in civil war, nor to rob with violence, I

stood fixed in great doubt and perplexity, not knowing
where I should turn myself. For, neither could I ever
believe that the Gods committed adultery, and engaged in
fratricidal war, unless they held about these things, that
they were really honourable: nor that the legislators would
encourage the opposite to these practices, unless they supposed *their prohibitions* to be advantageous.   And, when I
continued to be in doubt, I resolved to go to those whom
they call "philosophers," and put myself in their hands,
and pray them to use me as they wished, and to point out
to me some sure and simple way of life.   With this disposition, I say, I approached them ; and I did not know that
I was forcing myself, as the adage is, from the smoke into
the fire itself.¹ For plainly, upon close examination, I found
among them ignorance in a very special degree, and doubt
and uncertainty greater *than elsewhere;* so that very quickly
they proved to me that the way of life of the ignorant and
common sort of people was golden *in comparison.* One of
them would exhort me, you may be sure, to indulge my love
of pleasure in everything, and that only to pursue by all
means: for that that was the being "happy." Another, on
the contrary, *exhorted me* to be laborious about everything,
and to toil, and to restrain, and torture the body, dress in
rags, live in squalor, and to make myself a nuisance to
everybody else, and use vituperative language;² perpetually
declaiming to me those universally known verses of Hesiod
about Virtue, and toil, and sweat, and. the ascent to its
summit.³ Another would exhort me to contemn money and

---

¹ Ἐς αὐτό τὸ πῦρ ἐκ τοῦ καπνοῦ—*Anglice*, "from the frying-pan into
the fire;" *Germanice*, "aus dem Regen unter die Traufe."

² Καταναγκάζειν.   Cf. S. Paul ('Επ. πρὸς Κορ. i. 27.) ὑπωπιάζω μοῦ
τό σῶμα καὶ δουλαγωγῶ, quoted by Origen, Προς Κελσον. v.   The very
opposite schools of Aristippus and Antisthenes are here pointed at.   See
Βίων Πρᾶσις.

³
Τὴν μὲν τοι κακότητα καὶ ἰλαδὸν ἔστιν ἐλέσθαι
'Ρηϊδίως· ὀλίγη μὲν ὁδός, μάλα δ' ἐγγύθι ναίει.
Τῆς δ' Ἀρετῆς ἰδρῶτα θέοι προπάρυιθεν ἔθηκαν
Ἀθάνατοι· μακρὸς δὲ καὶ ὄρθιος οἶμος ἐς αὐτὴν
Καὶ τρηχὺς τοπρῶτον· ἐπὴν δ' εἰς ἄκρον ἵκηται,
'Ρηϊδίη δὴ ἔπειτα πέλει, χαλεπή περ ἐοῦσα.
                              Ἔργα καὶ Ἡμ. 287-292.
Cf. Plato, Πολ. ii. 364 ; Lucian, 'Αλ. 'Ιστ. ii. 18, 'Ερμοτ. 3 (in which

to consider its possession a matter of indifference. Someone else, again, was for proving riches themselves to be "a Good." As for *their theories* of the Universe, what need for me even to speak, who was nauseated in daily listening to their "ideas," "incorporealities," "atoms," "vacuums," and a crowd of such like names? And what was the most absurd of all strange things was—that, while each one of them spoke of matters most opposed one to the other, he would supply exceedingly irresistible and persuasive arguments; so that you could not possibly contradict either him who affirmed the same thing to be "heat," nor him who asserted it to be "cold"—and that, though you knew perfectly well that a thing could never possibly be warm and cold at the same moment. Plainly, then, I was in the same case with those who doze—one moment nodding assent, at another throwing my head back in denial. But still more unreasonable than this—by close observation, I found these same people to follow a manner of life quite contrary to their own precepts. Those, in fact, who urged me to despise money, I observed to cling to it with the firmest grasp, to be quarrelling about their usury, teaching for pay,[1] and ready to endure anything for it. And those who were for rejecting fame, *I found* to be employed in all their words and actions for its sole sake; and, further, while accusing almost all the world of *devotion to* pleasure, to be, in private, firmly attached to that alone.

Deceived, then, in this expectation, I began to be yet more disgusted; while I consoled myself, in some degree, with the fact that I was a fool, and wandering about still ignorant of Truth, in company with many others—learned people, and very much famed for their knowledge : and, as on one occasion, I was kept awake all night, on this account, I determined upon going to Babylon to beg the assistance of some one of their Magi, the disciples and successors of Zoroaster; for I heard that by certain incantations and mystic rites they open the gates of Hades, and

there is allusion to the Stoic metaphor of the Steep Hill of Virtue) ; Κεβῆτος Πίναξ; Χρυσᾶ Ἔπη (" Golden Verses ") of Hierokles. Pythagoras was the first to elaborate these maxims of Hesiod.

[1] It was a chief accusation of Sokrates against the *Sophistæ* that they taught for money.

conduct down whomever they choose in safety, and bring them back again. I considered, therefore, the best thing to do was, to obtain for myself the means of descent from some of these persons, and go to Teiresias the Bœotian, and learn from him, as he is a prophet and a sage, what way of life is the best, and the one which any right-thinking man would choose for himself. And, in fact, jumping up there and then, as quickly as I could, I made straight for Babylon. Upon my arrival I take up my residence with one of the Chaldæans, a learned man, and of preternatural excellence in his art, with white hair, who grew a very venerable beard. His name was Mithrobarzanes. After praying and earnestly supplicating him, I obtained from him with great difficulty *the favour* of conducting me on the route—upon his own terms. This gentleman taking me to his house, in the first place, for nine-and-twenty days, beginning immediately from the *new* moon, made me perform my lustrations, conducting me down, at the first dawn of day, to the Euphrates, and addressing some long speech to the rising sun, which I did not very well understand : for, like incompetent criers at the games, his utterance was rapid and indistinct. However, he seemed to be invoking certain dæmons. After the incantation, when he had spit three times[1] in my face, I returned home, carefully avoiding the gaze of persons I met on the road. Our food was hard-shelled fruits,[2] our drink milk and honey and water, and the water of the Choaspes,[3] and our bed was under the open sky, upon the grass. When there had been sufficient dietetic preparation, about midnight he would lead me to the river Tigris and cleanse me, and wipe me dry, and

[1] Ἀποπτύσας. Used *absolutely*. Ἀποπτύσαντος (sub. αὐτοῦ), is the grammatical construction. But the old reading ἐπανήει (rejected by Hemsterhuis), which obviates a grammatical solecism, is preferable.

[2] Ἀκρόδρυα (ἄκρος—δρῦς), in original meaning *acorns*. By Plato (Κρίτιας. 115) and Xenophon (Οίκον. xix. 12) used for fruit-trees generally. Cf. Clemens Alex. (Παιδ. ii. 1), who informs us that "Matthew, the Apostle, lived upon seeds, and nut-fruits (ἀκρόδρυα), and vegetables, and did not eat flesh-meats."

[3] A tributary of the Tigris : in modern geography, the Kara-Sun. It was famous for the purity of its water, which was so highly esteemed that the Persian despots were accustomed to carry it with them on their campaigns. Cf. Tibullus, *El.* iv. 1 ; Pliny, *Hist. Nat.* xxxi. 3. 23.

he purified me all round with lighted torch, and squill,[1] and
several other *rites*, at the same time muttering the incantation.   Then, having thoroughly charmed my entire person,
and made a pass with his body round me that I might not
be injured by the ghosts, he brought me back to his house
as I was; making me walk backwards.   For the rest of the
time we were engaged in preparations for our voyage.   He
himself put on a certain magical robe, for the most part
like the Persian, and he brought and equipped me in these
things—the felt cap,[2] the lion's skin, and the lyre, to make
them complete.   And he warned me, if anyone asked my
name, not to say Menippus, but Herakles, or Odysseus, or
Orpheus.[3]

Philonides. For what purpose that, pray, Menippus?
For I don't understand the reason either of your dress or
of your names.

Menippus. Yet it is plain enough, and not at all mysterious, for, since they descended alive, before us, to Hades,
he thought, if he made me resemble them, I should easily
escape the observation of Æakus's guard, and slip in without challenge, inasmuch as I should be more familiar to
him in tragic costume, and be well recommended by my
equipment.   Day, then, was now just beginning to appear;
and going down to the river we busied ourselves about
weighing anchor.   There had been got ready for him a

---

[1] Σκιλλy—"sea-leek," used in purificatory rites.   See Arist. Περὶ
Ζώων 'Ιστ. v. 30; Pliny, *Hist. Nat.* xix. 5. 30; Varro, *Rer. Rus.* ii.
7, 8; Mart. *Epig.* x. 4.

[2] Τῷ πίλῳ (Lat. *pileus*), a semi-oval cap of felt, fitting close to the
head—whereas the πέτασος and καυσία were broad-brimmed and served
as a protection from sun or rain, and much resembled the round felt-hat
of the present day.   These broad-brimmed hats were of Thessalian and
Macedonian origin.   It was only in travelling that the Greeks wore a
head-covering of any kind.   Cf. Hesiod. 'Εργα καὶ 'Ημ. 545; Lucian,
'Αναχάρσις, 16; Herod. iii. 12; Tertullian, *De Spect.* 21.   Charon is
usually represented with the πίλος, as boatman.   See Müller, *Handbuch
der Archäol.;* Becker, Charicles.

[3] Because these heroes were privileged, as having already made acquaintance with Pluto and Persephone.   The son of Alkmene had ventured on two descents—one to drag Kerberus off, and the other to
deliver Alkestis.   Orpheus made the terrible journey to rescue his
"half-regained Eurydice."   For a humorous representation of Herakles,
with his club and lion's skin, see Aristoph. Βατρ.

boat, and victims, and honey-cake, and other *offerings*, as many as are serviceable for the initiation. Embarking, then, all our cargo, thus we at length also ourselves—

> " Embark, in soul grief-stricken : down our cheeks coursed many a
>   tear-drop," [1]

and for some time we were borne gently down on the stream ; and after that we sailed into the marshes and lake, in which the Euphrates disappears. Crossing this, we arrive at a certain deserted spot, woody, and impenetrable to the sun, upon which we disembark, Mithrobarzanes leading the way, and dug a pit, and cut the throats of the sheep, and poured out the blood as a libation about the trench : [2] while the Magician, meanwhile, holding a flaming torch, no longer in a subdued voice, but, crying out as loud as he could, invoked all the dæmons together, the Avenging Goddesses,[3] and the Erinyes—

> " Nocturnal goddess, Hekate, and dread Persephoneia," [4]

mixing up at the same time certain foreign, obscure, and many-syllabled names. At once all the neighbourhood was violently shaken, and under the force of the spell the ground was burst open, and the bark of Kerberus was heard in the distance, and the business was exceedingly desperate and gloomy :—

> " Yea, in his underworld-recess Lord Aïdes was frighted." [5]

For now the principal *infernal sights* were plainly revealed —the lake, and the Pyriphlegethon, and the palace of

---

[1] Βαίνομεν ἀχνύμενοι, θαλερόν κατὰ δάκρυ χέοντες.—'Οδ. xi. 5.

[2] Closely following the precedent set by the prototype, Odysseus, which, also, had been too faithfully followed by Virgil's hero :—'Οδ. xi. ; Æn. vi. 243-254.

[3] Ποινὰς. The *Poenæ* were mere personifications of avenging Justice, and were closely allied with and, indeed, were almost synonymous with the Erinyos.—See Æsch. Εὐμεν. 323.

[4] Καὶ νυχίαν Ἐκάτην καὶ ἐπαινὴν Περσεφόνειαν. A parody, apparently, of an Homeric verse.

[5] Ἔδδεισεν δ'ὑπένερθεν ἄναξ ἀνέρων 'Αΐδωνευς ('Ιλ. xx. 61), Prof. Newman's version. The allusion is to the terrific combat among the Celestials, which shook the whole frame of Nature. Cf. *Par. Lost*, vi. " Tantæne animis cœlestibus iræ ? "

Pluto.   Descending, however, through the chasm, we found Rhadamanthys all but dead with fright. Kerberus barked a little, and stirred himself; but, when I quickly struck my lyre, he was at once charmed to silence by the melody.

When we arrived at the lake, we all but failed to get a passage, for the ferry-boat was already full, and resounding with lamentations.   All the passengers were covered with wounds—one in the leg, another in the head, a third mutilated in some other part, having just come, as it appeared to me, fresh from some war.   However, the excellent Charon, when he saw the lion's skin, supposing me to be Herakles, received me on board, and was delighted to ferry me across, and, upon our disembarcation, pointed out to us the path *to be taken*.   As we were in darkness, Mithrobarzanes led the way, and I followed, sticking close behind him, until we come to a very spacious meadow, planted with asphodel.   Here, you must know, there kept hovering about us the shadows of the dead, squeaking.[1]   Gradually advancing, we arrive at the tribunal of Minos : he was seated upon a certain elevated throne, and about him stood the Pœnae, and Avenging Demons, and the Erinyes.   On either side there were brought up, in order, a number of individuals bound with a long chain ; they were said to be adulterers, and procurers, and farmers of the public revenues, and fawning adulators, and public informers, and a similar crowd of such as disturb the whole harmony of human existence.   And, apart, the rich, and hard exactors of usury approached, pale, and with fat paunches,[2] and full of gout, each of them being sentenced to the pillory, and a " crow " of two hundred-

---

[1] Τετριγυῖαι.   So the ghosts of the wicked suitors :—

$$\text{τρίζουσαι ἕποντο·}$$
$$\text{Ὡς δ' ὅτε νυκτερίδες μυχῷ ἄντρου θεσπεσίοιο}$$
$$\text{Τρίζουσαι ποτέονται.—Ὀδ. xxiv. 5-7.}$$

Upon which Barnes, following Eustathius, explains that the poet " rightly compares ghosts to bats, because they appear only at night, because they sleep very little, because they produce a whirring sound, because they are neither animate nor inanimate."

[2] Προγάστορες.   "Montani quoque venter adest abdomine tardus." Juv. *Sat.* iv. 107.   Cf. 'Επ. Παυλ. πρὸς Τιτ. i. 12, γάστερες ἀργαι.

weight.[1] Standing close by, we watched what was happen-ing, and listened to their defence of themselves: while certain strange and unexpected counsel arraigned them.

Philonides. In heaven's name, who were they? Don't, pray, shirk telling me this, also.

Menippus. You know, I presume, those shadows that are projected from bodies against the sun?

Philonides. Of course I do.

Menippus. They, when we die, then, become accusers and witnesses against us, and convicters of *crimes* perpetrated during life; and they have the reputation of being exceedingly trustworthy, inasmuch as they are always associated with, and never separated from our bodies.[2] Minos, however, after careful examination, dismissed each *of the criminals* to the place of the wicked, to undergo punishment proportioned to his deeds. With especial severity did he treat those of them who were swollen with pride on account of their riches and power, and had demanded all but divine worship,[3] from de-testation of their (short-lived) arrogance and haughtiness; and because they did not choose to remember they were mere mortals, and in chance possession of mortal goods. Well, they, stripping themselves of all these splendours— I mean their wealth, and birth, and imperial power—stood by, perfectly naked, and with downcast looks, reflecting on the happiness they had among us as on some dream. So I, observing this, was delighted beyond measure, and, if I knew any one of them, I would approach him in a quiet sort of way, and remind him "what he was in life, and what airs he then gave himself, when numbers of people stood at his

[1] The κόραξ, or *crow*, appears to have been a sort of movable pillory, like the Latin *furca*, with which slaves were commonly tortured, so well known to the readers of Plautus.

[2] This use of the "Shadows," more ingenious than satisfactory, of course fails for the greatest part of human life. "The transformation of the shadows into witnesses is," remarks Wieland, "sufficiently adven-turous. Their only failure is that, just where they would be most useful—viz., in respect of crimes committed in the dark—they are wholly useless." The qualifying τινὲς αὐτῶν, of the common text, is reasonably suspected by Lehmann.

[3] The qualifying "all but" (μονονουχὶ) we must suppose to have been dictated by prudence. The Roman princes, from Augustus, were actually deified, and after death, were entitled *divi*, having assigned to them altars and sacrifices. See Tacitus, *An.* and *Hist.*, *passim*.

gateway, waiting patiently for his appearance, and pushed
about, and shut out by his domestics; while the great man,
in some sort of purple, or gold-hemmed, or variegated robe,
at length, scarcely would rise to them, and imagined he
would render those who addressed him happy and blest, if he
stretched out his hand or foot for them to kiss." Upon
hearing this, they were greatly chagrined.

Meanwhile, one particular case was decided leniently by
Minos. Aristippus,[1] the Cyrenian, came up—they hold him
in honour, and he has the greatest influence with those
below—and obtained the respite of Dionysius the Sikeliot
from his sentence (who had been charged by Dion with many
iniquitous crimes,[2] and had been witnessed against by his
own shadow), as he was within an ace of being bound to the
Chimæra, by alleging that he had been ready and judicious in
his pecuniary gifts to several men of learning. However,
taking our leave of the tribunal, we arrive at the place of
punishment. Here, my friend, many and pitiful indeed, were
the things to be heard and seen ;[3] for, at the same time, was
heard the sound of scourges, and the wailing of those who
were being roasted in the fire, and instruments of torture, and
pillories, and wheels; and the Chimæra tore them to pieces,
and Kerberus gnawed them. All were being punished
together, kings, slaves, viceroys, poor, rich, beggars; and
all repented them of the bad deeds they had committed.
Some of them we recognized at a glance—such of them
as had recently died. These began to envelop their persons, and turned their faces away; but if, by chance,

[1] The disciple of Sokrates, and founder of the Cyrenaic School, as it
was termed from his birthplace. Like others of the *Sokratics*, but to a
greater degree than any of them, he differed widely from his master.
His characteristic teaching was selfish gratification. For some time he
lived in high favour at the Court of Dionysius of Syracuse. See Diog.
Laert. ; Horace, *Ep.* i. 1, 18 ; i. 17, 23. Plato, Φαιδ., Xen. 'Απομν. ii, 1.
Why he was so popular with the authorities of Hades, is not quite obvious.

[2] See Plutarch, Βίοι Παρ.

[3]   " Quivi sospiri, pianti, ed alti guai
                 Risonavan. . . . .
        Diverse lingue, orribili favelle," etc.
                                        Dante, *Inferno*, iii.
Some graphic painting of Tartarus (of a Greek Orcagna or Breughel),
doubtless, was present to the satirist's mind, as well as the *Phædon* and the
Politeia (x. *ad fin.*) of Plato, in writing this highly remarkable passage.

they glanced at us, it was in a very slavish and fawning way : and that, though they had been tyrannical and supercilious, to an extent you cannot conceive. To the poor, on the other hand, remission of half their sufferings was granted ; and, after they had had an interval of respite, their punishments were wont to be renewed. In fact, I saw, too, those *punishments* famous in story—Ixion and Sisyphus, and the Phrygian Tantalus in ill case, and the earth-born Tityus, Herakles ! of what bulk ; he covered, as he lay, you may be sure a whole field's space.[1] Passing these, we enter the Acherusian Plain ;[2] and we find there the demi-gods, and the Heroines,[3] and the rest of the crowd of the Dead living according to their nationalities and tribes— some individuals of ancient aspect and musty, and, as says Homer, a "feeble folk" ;[4] and others fresh and well-preserved, especially the Egyptians among them, on account of the durableness of their preserving, salting, and pickling. The distinguishing each individual, however, was, by no means, at all easy; for all are as like one to another as peas, when the bones have once been stripped bare. However, with difficulty, and after a long time, by narrowly inspecting them, we did recognize *some of* them. They were lying one upon the other, shadowy, dimly seen, and obscure, and no longer possessing anything of what are counted beauties among us. I need not assure you, as there were numerous skeletons lying in the same spot, all alike, and with a sort of horrible and vacant stare, and showing their gumless teeth, I began to be at a loss with myself how I

[1] So Milton's Satan

<blockquote>
"extended long and large,
Lay floating many a rood ; in bulk as huge,
As whom the fables name of monstrous size,
Titanian, or Earth-born, that warred on Jove."
</blockquote>

Cf. 'Οδ. xi. 575, where the giant covers nine acres. For Ixion, see Θ. Δ. vi.

[2] With which Dante's "il primo cerchio" may be compared ; where reside those unfortunate pre-Christian heroes, or saints, who were ex-cluded from Elysium, as not having the baptismal passport :—

<blockquote>
"perch' e' non ebber battesmo,
Ch'è porta della Fede, che tu credi."
</blockquote>

[3] Demi-goddesses, daughters of the Deities who mixed with mortal women.

[4] 'Αμενηνοὺς. See Νεκ. Διαλ., i. xx., etc.

should distinguish Thersites from the handsome Nireus, or the beggar Irus[1] from the king of the Phæakians, or Pyrrhias, the cook, from Agamemnon: for nothing any longer of their old characteristics remained to them, but their bones were all alike, indistinguishable and inscribed with no titles, and impossible any longer to be distinguished by anyone.

So, of a truth, as I looked upon those things, human life appeared to me tó resemble a sort of long public procession, and Fortune *appeared* to have the management of and to arrange every particular, while she assigned to those taking part in the Show various and variegated costumes. One she would take, if so it chanced, and equip in royal fashion, and put a tiara upon his head, and assign to him a number of body-guards, and crown his head with the diadem. Another she would clothe in the dress of a domestic. A third individual she would decorate with beauty; a fourth she turned out ugly, deformed, and an object of ridicule; for it is proper, I imagine, that the Show be composed of all sorts and conditions of men. And frequently, even in the midst of the procession, she would change the costumes of some *of its constituents*, and not permit them to go through with it to the end, as they had been first arranged; but, changing the dress of a Krœsus, she compelled him to receive in exchange the dress of a domestic and a captive: while a Mæandrius,[2] who up to that time had been among the slaves in the Show, she invested with the despotic sovereignty of a Polykrates, and for some time suffered him to use the dress. But, when the time for the Show had passed, at that instant each one restoring his paraphernalia, and putting off his dress with his body,

---

[1] See 'Οδ. xviii. for this counterpart of Thersites of the *Iliad*, an insatiate glutton, who,

$$\mu\epsilon\tau\grave{\alpha}\ \delta'\ \ddot{\epsilon}\pi\rho\epsilon\pi\epsilon\ \gamma\alpha\sigma\tau\acute{\epsilon}\rho\iota\ \mu\acute{\alpha}\rho\gamma\eta,$$
'Αζηχὲς φαγέμεν καὶ πιέμεν οὐδὲ οἱ ἦν ἴς,
Οὐδὲ βίη—

Pyrrhias (Lat. Rufus), " red-headed," is, probably, some *comic* character. It was a common name for slaves from the North. See Τίμων, 23; Περὶ 'Ορχήσ. 19.
[2] The Mæandrius here referred to was the secretary of Polykrates, and is noticed by Herod. iii. 123; Cf. Χάρων, 14.

becomes as he was before, in no respect different from his neighbours.

Some, from folly, as soon as Fortune stands at their side and demands back her decorations, are grieved and are indignant, as though deprived of some of their own property, and as if they were not giving up what they had had the use of for a brief space. I suppose you have often seen of such as are employed on the Stage, those tragic actors, who, according to the requirements of the dramas, become at one time Krœsus and, at another, Priam or Agamemnon; and the same person, if chance so directs, who imitated, a little before, very grandly the dress and bearing of a Kekrops or an Erechtheus, at the summons of the poet, in a little while comes forward as a domestic. And now, when the drama is at an end, each divesting himself of that gold-embroidered garment, and laying aside his mask, and descending from his tragic-boots, moves about in public as a poor and humble individual, no longer Agamemnon, the son of Atreus, nor Kreon, the son of Menœkeus, but now called by his proper name, Polias,[1] the son of Charikles, of the borough of Sunion, or Satyrus, the son of Theogeiton, of the borough of Marathon. Of such sort, in fact, are the affairs of men, as they seemed to me, as I then regarded them.

Philonides. Tell me, Menippus, and they, who possess these costly and lofty tombs above upon the earth, and monumental slabs,[2] and pictures, and inscriptions, are they no more held in honour among them than the plebeian dead?

Menippus. Out upon you! Nonsense! At all events, if you just saw Mausolus himself (the Karian I mean, who is so famous for his tomb) I know well that you would not have stopped laughing—in such humble fashion was he cast away in some remote corner, skulking among the rest of the commonalty of the Dead, getting as much enjoyment, as

---

[1] See Ζεὺς Τραγ. 3, Περὶ τῶν ἐπὶ Μισθῷ Συν. 5. Of Satyrus, little or nothing is found elsewhere. The surnames of Sunian and Marathonian were given to them simply as members of the boroughs of Sunion and Marathon.

[2] Στήλας (Lat. cippos), on which were inscribed the military victories, dedications, votes of thanks, &c., of the dead prince or plutocrat. Cf. Aristoph. ’Αχαρ. 692; Herod. ii. 102 (of Sesostris), iv. 87 (of Dareius), vi. 14; Thucyd. v. 56.

it seemed to me, from his tomb as he was weighed down from having such enormous weight of material pressing on him.[1] For, when Æakus, my friend, measures out for each his place—and he gives at most not more than a foot[2]—he must be content to lie contracted in a very moderate space. But you would laugh, I think, much more, if you saw those who were kings and viceroys with us acting the beggar with them, and either selling salt herrings for want, or teaching the rudiments of grammar, insulted by any common person, and smitten on the cheek as if they were the most despised of slaves. In fact, when I saw Philip the Macedonian, I could not even contain myself. He was pointed out to me in a corner, mending rotten shoes for a pittance. Many others, too, one might see begging at the cross-roads—I speak of the Xerxeses, and Dareiuses, and Polykrateses.[3]

Philonides. The account you give me of kings is a strange one, and all but incredible. But how did Sokrates fare, and Diogenes, and whoever else there was of the philosophic tribe ?

Menippus. Sokrates perambulates there, cross-questioning everyone;[4] and always in his company are Palamedes, and Odysseus, and Nestor, and any other prattler of the dead. His legs, however, were still puffed and swollen out from the draught of poison. The most excellent

---

[1] See Νεκ. Διαλ. xxiv.

[2]
        " Mors sola fatetur
Quantula sint hominum corpuscula."—Juv. *Sat.* x. 172-3.

" Ill weaved Ambition, how much art thou shrunk !
When that this body did contain a spirit,
A kingdom for it was too small a bound,
But now two paces of the vilest earth
Is room enough."
        Shakespeare, *Henry IV.*, pt. i. v. 4.

[3] Rabelais represents (among other distinguished residents in Hades) Dareius as a care-taker in very humble capacity (*cureur de retraicts*); Xerxes as crying mustard ; while Alexander the Great has to take up with tailoring. Sulla acts as assistant (*riveran*) to Charon. Pope Alexander VI. finds a livelihood as a ratcatcher. (Livre ii. 30.)

[4] So he is represented in the Elysian Fields, in the ’Αληθὴς ’Ιστορία— καὶ μοι ἐδόκει ἐρᾶν τοῦ ‘Υακίνθου τὰ πολλὰ γοῦν ἐκεῖνον διήλεγχεν (ii. 221). Rhadamanthys, indeed, was so much bored by this perpetual use of the ἔλεγχος and εἰρωνεία, that he had often threatened to turn him out of Elysium, unless he desisted.

Diogenes resides near Sardanapalus, the Assyrian, and Midas, the Phrygian, and certain other exquisites; and when he hears them wailing and lamenting, and remeasuring their ancient fortune, he laughs and is delighted, and, for the most part, he lies upon his back and sings in a very harsh and savage voice, drowning their wailings; so that the gentlemen are much annoyed, and are seriously considering about moving their quarters, as they cannot put up with Diogenes.

Philonides. Enough of this. But what was the Decree, which you told me, at first, they had carried against the Plutocrats ?

Menippus. Well remembered, for I don't know how I wandered entirely from my story, when I had purposed to speak about that. Well, while I was staying with them, the presiding magistrates proposed a meeting of the Popular Assembly in respect of the common interests. As, then, I observed a number of them running together, I at once mixed myself up with the dead men, and forthwith became myself, too, one of their members of Parliament. Other matters were duly settled, and, last of all, the case of the Rich. When, you must know, many and terrible accusations had been brought against them—violence, arrogance, haughtiness, and injustice—at length a certain popular leader rose, and read the Decree to this effect:—

The Decree.

" Whereas the Plutocrats perpetrate a number of iniquities in life, by plunder, by violence, and in every way utterly despising the Poor, be it enacted by the Senate and the People that, when they die, their *bodies* undergo punishment, just as do those of other worthless people, but that the *souls* be sent up above again into life, and enter into asses,[1] until they have, in such state, passed

---

[1] As is well known, the person of the hero of the Lucianic *Ὄνος* (a curtailed imitation of the *De Aureo Asino* of Apuleius) is bewitched into the form of an ass, and in that quadruped condition meets with a variety of unpleasant experiences, until by eating rose-leaves (the emblem of the secresy of the Mysteries), he is re-transformed into biped and human shape. Bp. Warburton (*Divine Legation of Moses*), with more ingenuity than success, maintains the purpose of *The Golden Ass* to have been a recommendation of *mysticized* Paganism as against the then progressing Christian religion.

through two hundred and fifty thousand years, becoming asses from generation to generation, and carrying heavy burdens, and driven by the poor labourers ; and after that period, that it be permitted them finally to die.

"Dryskull, the son of Skeleton, of the wardship of Deadborough, of the tribe of Corpseland, proposed this bill."

When this bill had been read, the magistrates gave their votes by ballot, and the people by show of hands ; and Brimo[1] roared, and Kerberus howled; for in this way the resolutions, that have been read, became complete and binding. Such, I assure you, were the proceedings in the Popular Assembly. I—in pursuance of the object of my visit —approached Teiresias, and, after explaining everything, begged him to tell me what sort of life he considers to be about the best. Then with a laugh—he is a somewhat blind, little old man, sallow, and shrill-voiced—"My son," says he, "I know the cause of your doubt and perplexity, that it originated with the philosophers, who do not agree among themselves : but it is not permitted me to reveal it to you, for it has been forbidden by Rhadamanthys." "Oh! pray, don't *refuse*, my good little father," said I, "but tell me, and don't despise me who grope about in life blinder than yourself." Thereupon, you must know, he took me aside and withdrew to a considerable distance from the rest, and, quietly stooping to my ear, he says : "The best and soundest life is that of persons in private station. So do you, leaving off the folly of inquiring into transcendental subtleties, and searching into final ends and causes, and rejecting with contempt their learned sophisms and syllogisms, and deeming such things mere trifling and nonsense, search diligently for this one thing alone—how, making wise use of what you have, you may pass by with a smile of contempt most opinions, and pursue nothing with too serious aim."

So spake he, and back he coursed through Asphodelian meadows,[2]

and I—for it was now evening—"Pray, come," say I,

---

[1] "The terrible one," an *alias* of Hekate or Persephone. Cf. Apollonius, Ἀργον. iii. 861.

[2] Ὣς εἰπὼν πάλιν ὧρτο κατ' Ἀσφοδελὸν λειμῶνα. The latter half of this parody is quoted from Ὀδ. xi. 538, 572.

"Mithrobarzanes, why do we longer linger, and not return again to life?" And to this rejoined he: "Courage, Menippus; for I will show you a short and easy path." And, in fact, he led me to a certain spot, darker and murkier than the rest, pointing to a certain dim and faint light in the distance flowing, as it were, through a chink. "That," said he, "is the shrine of Trophonius, and from that place the people of Bœotia make their descent. Ascend, then, by this road, and immediately you will be upon Hellenic soil." Delighted at what he told me was I, and, after taking leave of the Magus, with very much difficulty I crept through the narrow mouth, and here I am, somehow or other, in Lebadeia.[1]

[1] Now Livadhia, a town in Bœotia. The Oracle of Trophonius was situated in a cavern not far distant from the town. See Νεκ. Διαλ. iii.

E.

Echo, a nymph loved by Pan, 52, and *note;* refuses to return the bellowings of Polyphemus, 63.

Eileithuia, the divinity who comes to assist women in childbirth, allusion by Hephæstus to, 17, and *note;* her office transferred to Artemis, 32 *note.*

Eirene, one of the *Horæ,* 21 *note.*

Eironeia ("affected ignorance"), the special characteristic of the Sokratic Dialogue, 144, and *note.*

Eimarmene ("Destiny"), its signification noticed by Wieland, 213 *note.*

Ekbatana, the capital of Media, scene of the death of Hephæstion a favourite of Alexander of Macedon, 126 *note.*

Ekklesia (at Athens), the name given to the Popular Assembly, 179 *note;* the usual translation of the title of Lucian's *Dialogue* Θιᾶν 'Εκκλησία inaccurate, 225 *note.*

Ekklesiastes, its Lucianic tone in regard to Hades referred to, 129 *note.*

"Ελκειν, a play on the word by Klotho, 246, and *note.*

Elektra, daughter of Atlas and mother of Iasion, 231 *note.*

Elenchos, a term used in the Logic of the Stoics, 191, and *note.*

Elenchomenos (Zeus), the title of a Dialogue of Lucian, Wieland's remark on, 209 *note.*

Eleusinian Mysteries (celebrated in honour of Demeter and Persephone at Eleusis), alluded to by Mikyllus, 256.

Eleusis, the famous township of Attica, allusion by Krates to, 156.

Eleutheria, a village at the foot of Mount Kithæron, 156.

Eleven, the, Officers of the Athenian Areiopagus, an allusion by Cyniskus to, 222, and *note.*

Elias (or Elijah), a Jewish prophet, his fire-chariot asserted by St. Chrysostom to be the original of the chariot of Phaethon, 58 *note.*

Elysian Fields, the, Minos dismisses the good to, 165; descriptions in the poets of, 165

note; their delights not valued by the Cynic, 222, and *note.*

Elysium, Lucian's representation in his *True History* of, 119 *note.*

Empedokles, the distinguished Greek philosopher and statesman, insulted by Menippus in Hades, 142; possible origin of the fable of Ætna and the slippers or sandals of, high estimate and eulogy by Lucretius of, 142 *note.*

Empusa, a hobgoblin of the Greek nursery, 37 *note.*

Enagismata, purificatory funeral ceremonies in the Greek ritual, mentioned by Charon, 240, and *note.*

Endymion (a handsome Latmian youth), Selene charged by Aphrodite with her love for, 22-24.

Enipeus, a Thessalian river-god, reproaches Poseidon for his seduction of the nymph Tyro, 78-79.

Entaphia, Greek funeral furniture, allusion by Hermes to, 107, and *note.*

Eos (Aurora), her love and intercession for Tithonus, noticed, 100 *note.*

Epigoni (the name given to the descendants of the Seven against Thebes) referred to, 92 *note.*

Epikurus, his abstinent living noticed, 112 *note;* relieved by Momus of the charge of doing mischief by denial of a divine Providence, 184; allusion by Momus to, 186.

Epikurism, the arguments of, 168-207.

Ephebos, the name given to the Athenian youth at the age of 18, 125 *note.*

Ephialtes, the *incubus* or *night-mare* of the Greek mythology, 37 *note.*

Epistemon (a companion of Pantagruel on his voyage), his temporary sojourn in Hades, 262 *note.*

Erasmus, Desiderius, his interpretation of πηχῦν, 24 *note;* references to his *Adagia,* 89, 98, 100 *notes.*

Erectheus, mythic king of Athens, 277.

Eridanus (the modern Pado), the

105 *note*; one of the "lions" in Hades, 135; disputes with Thersites in Hades, 152-153.

Noce Aldobrandine, a painting of the marriage of Peleus and Thetis so named, 69 *note*.

Nona, the Latin name of one of the Parcæ, 214 *note*.

Notus, the divinity of the S.W. Wind, interrogates Zephyrus as to the fate of Io, 71-72; respecting the rape of Europa, 83-85.

Numphagogos, "the bride-conductor," 48 *note*.

Nux, the divinity of Night, father of Momus, acts as registrar to the Convention of the Gods, 235.

Nysa, Mt., in Thrace (or in India), Hermes carries off the infant Bacchus to, 20 and *note*, 127 *note*.

O.

Obolus, a Greek coin, 88 and *note*, 94, 114, 265 and *note*.

Octopus, or polypus, described by Proteus, 67 and *note*.

Odysseia, the, quoted or referred to, 33, 34, 35, 63, 66, 67, 78, 79, 89, 112, 117, 131, 135, 160, 163, 165, 171, 223, 231, 240, 244, 258, 262, 263, 265, 271, 272, 276 *notes*.

Odysseus (Ulysses), the hero of the *Odyssey*, calls up the ghost of Alkmene in Hades, 22 *note*; his trick upon Polyphemus, 63-64; his visions in Hades, 89 *note*; his prudence, 104; the speech of Aias to, 112 and *note*; the famous speech of Achilleus, in Hades, to, 128, 129; his interview with Herakles, in Hades, 131 and *note*; evokes the spectres of the Dead, 160 *note*; his cool reception by Aias in Hades, 163-164, 249 *note*; his reply to his mother's ghost, 265 *note*; his credit in the Lower World, 270; his company sought by Sokrates in Hades, 278.

Œbalus, king of Sparta, father of Hyakinthus, 27.

Œta, Mt., in Thessaly, the scene of the self-immolation of Herakles, 26.

Olympia, in Elis, 10; a statue of Hermes discovered at, 20, 65, 107 *notes*.

Olympias, the mother of Alexander of Macedon, her decease, 116 and *note*.

Olympus, Mt., in Thessaly, the seat of the third dynasty of the Hellenic deities, 121 *note*.

Omphale (a queen of Lydia, mistress of Herakles), her treatment of that hero, 26.

Oneiros (or *Alektryon*), a *Dialogue* of Lucian, referred to, 250 *note*.

Onion, the, an object of veneration to the Pelusians, 201.

Oppian, a Greek poet, his *Halieutika* referred to, 72 *note*.

Oracles, Greek temples or shrines for delivery of, 92, 105 *notes*; those of Apollo criticized by Momus, 169, 190-192; ridiculed by the Epikurean Damis, 202; by the Cynic Cyniskus, 211, 220, 235.

Orca Marina, the, of Ariosto, 10 *note*.

Orcus (the Lat. poetic name for Hades), 165, 242, 258 *notes*.

Orestes (of Euripides), the, parodied, 172 and *note*.

Oreum, a town, a temple of Poseidon at, 188.

Orcagna, Andrea, an Italian painter of the fourteenth century, alluded to, 274 *note*.

Origen, the Christian Father, his essay *Against Celsus* referred to, 92 *note*; quotes St. Paul, 267 *note*.

Orlando Furioso, of Ariosto, referred to, 80.

Orœtes, a Persian satrap, a fellow-traveller of Krates to Hades, his reluctance to travel on foot, 156-158.

Oropus, a town on the borders of Attica, an oracular shrine at, 92 *note*.

Orpheus, the (legendary) Greek poet, his credit in Hades, 270 and *note*.

sition to the worship of Bacchus,
35-36 *notes.*
Pentekonteros, a Greek "man-of-
war," 199 and *note.*
Pentekosiomedimnoi, a class of Athenian citizens, 178 *note.*
Peplos, the, a dress of Greek ladies,
84 and *note.*
Perdikkas, a Macedonian general,
receives a ring from Alexander,
191 and *note ;* 157 *note.*
Periander, tyrannus of Korinth, a
patron of Arion, 73; one of the
Seven Sages, 142 *note.*
Perikles, the distinguished Athenian
statesman, his funeral oration
quoted, 174, 221 *notes.*
Persephone, queen of Hades, inter-
cedes for Protesilaus, 148, 150.
Perseus, the son of Danae, his exposure related by Thetis, 77-78;
his rescue of Andromeda related
by a Triton, 80-82.
Persius Flaccus, Latin Stoic satirist,
referred to, 88, 123 *notes.*
Pervigilium Veneris ("the Vigil of
Venus "), an anonymous Latin
poem, 184 *note.*
Petronius Arbiter, his *Satyricon* referred to, 87.
Phædrus, a pupil of Sokrates (who
gives his name to a Dialogue
of Plato), attends Sokrates in
Hades, 144 and *note.*
Phaon, of Mytilene, carries Aphrodite in his boat, 103; loved by
Sappho, 103 *note.*
Phædon, the, of Plato, one source
of the Christian *Inferno,* 139 *note ;*
referred to, 258.
Phaethon ("the Brilliant One "),
son of Helios, precipitated from
his father's chariot, 56-58.
Phaethusa, one of three sisters of
Phaethon, 58 *note.*
Phalaris (Prince of Agrigentum),
allusion to the forged Letters of,
167 *note.*
Phalaris, Bentley's, referred to, 203
note.
Phales (unknown object of worship
among the people of Cyllene),
noticed by Damis, 201 and *note.*
Pheidias (the most distinguished

name in Hellenic Art), the Zeus
of, 10; his use of enamel, &c.,
44 *note ;* instanced by Hermes,
176.
Pheidon, a legacy-hunter, 99.
Phersephatte (or Persephone),
Queen of the Under-World, in
love with Adonis, 23 and *note.*
Philenium, the name of a Greek
courtesan, 248 *note.*
Philip (of Macedon), father of Alexander, 115, 120; in Hades ridicules his son for his absurd pretensions, and questions the greatness of his achievements, 124, 127,
181, 221 *note,* 278.
Philocomasium, the name of a Greek
courtesan, 248 *note.*
Philomela (an Athenian princess,
outraged by Tereus), the miracle
of her metamorphosis instanced
by Teiresias, 162 and *note.*
Philonides, an interlocutor of Menippus, 262, 264-281.
Philostrate l'Ancien, a French version of the *Eikones* of Philostratus,
referred to, 19 *note.*
Philotas, son of Parmenion, put to
death by Alexander of Macedon,
116 *note.*
Phineus, a Thracian king and prophet, 160 and *note.*
Philostratus, Flavius, a Greek
writer, his *Eikones* " Pictures " referred to, 19, 21, 27, 61, 69, 72,
76, 81; his *Life of Apollonius,* 85, 92.
Phœbe, the name of one of the
sisters of Phaethon, 58 *note.*
Phœnix, a tutor of Achilleus, 128
and *note.*
Phokion, an Athenian statesman,
his fate instanced by Damis the
Epikurean, 205 and *note ;* by
Cyniskus the Cynic, 221.
Phratria, an Athenian municipal
term, 236 and *note.*
Phrixus, the brother of Helle, 74
and *note.*
Phronesium, a name of Greek cour-
tesans, 248 *note.*
Phryne, a celebrated *hetæra* or courtesan, the original of the "Aphrodite rising from the sea," her
dialogue with Alexander, 127

CATALOGUE OF
BOHN'S LIBRARIES.

735 Volumes, £160 3s.

BOHN'S LIBRARIES.

STANDARD LIBRARY.

334 Vols. at 3s. 6d. each, excepting those marked otherwise. (59*l.* 5*s.*)

ADDISON'S Works. Notes of Bishop Hurd. Short Memoir, Portrait, and 8 Plates of Medals. 6 vols.
This is the most complete edition of Addison's Works issued.

ALFIERI'S Tragedies. In English Verse. With Notes, Arguments, and Introduction, by E. A. Bowring, C.B. 2 vols.

AMERICAN POETRY. — *See Poetry of America.*

BACON'S Moral and Historical Works, including Essays, Apophthegms, Wisdom of the Ancients, New Atlantis, Henry VII., Henry VIII., Elizabeth, Henry Prince of Wales, History of Great Britain, Julius Cæsar, and Augustus Cæsar. With Critical and Biographical Introduction and Notes by J. Devey, M.A. Portrait.

—— *See also Philosophical Library.*

BALLADS AND SONGS of the Peasantry of England, from Oral Recitation, private MSS., Broadsides, &c. Edit. by R. Bell.

BEAUMONT AND FLETCHER. Selections. With Notes and Introduction by Leigh Hunt.

BECKMANN (J.) History of Inventions, Discoveries, and Origins. With Portraits of Beckmann and James Watt. 2 vols.

BELL (Robert).—*See Ballads, Chaucer, Green.*

BOSWELL'S Life of Johnson, with the TOUR in the HEBRIDES and JOHNSONIANA. New Edition, with Notes and Appendices, by the Rev. A. Napier, M.A., Trinity College, Cambridge, Vicar of Holkham, Editor of the Cambridge Edition of the 'Theological Works of Barrow.' With Frontispiece to each vol. 6 vols.

BREMER'S (Frederika) Works. Trans. by M. Howitt. Portrait. 4 vols.

BRINK (B. T.) Early English Literature (to Wiclif). By Bernhard ten Brink. Trans. by Prof. H. M. Kennedy.

BRITISH POETS, from Milton to Kirke White. Cabinet Edition. With Frontispiece. 4 vols.

BROWNE'S (Sir Thomas) Works. Edit. by S. Wilkin, with Dr. Johnson's Life of Browne. Portrait. 3 vols.

BURKE'S Works. 6 vols.

—— **Speeches on the Impeachment** of Warren Hastings ; and Letters. 2 vols.

—— **Life.** By J. Prior. Portrait.

BURNS (Robert). Life of. By J. G. Lockhart, D.C.L. A new and enlarged edition. With Notes and Appendices by W. S. Douglas. Portrait.

BUTLER'S (Bp.) Analogy of Religion; Natural and Revealed, to the Constitution and Course of Nature ; with Two Dissertations on Identity and Virtue, and Fifteen Sermons. With Introductions, Notes, and Memoir. Portrait.

CAMÖEN'S Lusiad, or the Discovery of India. An Epic Poem. Trans. from the Portuguese, with Dissertation, Historical Sketch, and Life, by W. J. Mickle. 5th edition.

CARAFAS (The) of Maddaloni. Naples under Spanish Dominion. Trans. by Alfred de Reumont. Portrait of Massaniello.

CARREL. The Counter-Revolution in England for the Re-establishment of Popery under Charles II. and James II., by Armand Carrel ; with Fox's History of James II. and Lord Lonsdale's Memoir of James II. Portrait of Carrel.

CARRUTHERS. — *See Pope, in Illustrated Library.*

CARY'S Dante. The Vision of Hell, Purgatory, and Paradise. Trans. by Rev. H. F. Cary, M.A. With Life, Chronological View of his Age, Notes, and Index of Proper Names. Portrait.

This is the authentic edition, containing Mr. Cary's last corrections, with additional notes.

CELLINI (Benvenuto). Memoirs of, by himself. With Notes of G. P. Carpani. Trans. by T. Roscoe. Portrait.

CERVANTES' Galatea. A Pastoral Romance. Trans. by G. W. J. Gyll.

—— **Exemplary Novels.** Trans. by W. K. Kelly.

—— **Don Quixote de la Mancha.** Motteux's Translation revised. With Lockhart's Life and Notes. 2 vols.

CHAUCER'S Poetical Works. With Poems formerly attributed to him. With a Memoir, Introduction, Notes, and a Glossary, by R. Bell. Improved edition, with Preliminary Essay by Rev. W. W. Skeat, M.A. Portrait. 4 vols.

CLASSIC TALES, containing Rasselas, Vicar of Wakefield, Gulliver's Travels, and The Sentimental Journey.

COLERIDGE'S (S. T.) Friend. A Series of Essays on Morals, Politics, and Religion. Portrait.

—— **Aids to Reflection. Confessions** of an Inquiring Spirit; and Essays on Faith and the Common Prayer-book. New Edition, revised.

—— **Table-Talk and Omniana.** By T. Ashe, B.A.

—— **Lectures on Shakspere and** other Poets. Edit. by T. Ashe, B.A.

Containing the lectures taken down in 1811-12 by J. P. Collier, and those delivered at Bristol in 1813.

—— **Biographia Literaria; or, Bio**graphical Sketches of my Literary Life and Opinions; with Two Lay Sermons.

—— **Miscellanies, Æsthetic and** Literary; to which is added, THE THEORY OF LIFE. Collected and arranged by T. Ashe, B.A.

COMMINES.—*See Philip.*

CONDÉ'S History of the Dominion of the Arabs in Spain. Trans. by Mrs. Foster. Portrait of Abderahmen ben Moavia. 3 vols.

COWPER'S Complete Works, Poems, Correspondence, and Translations. Edit. with Memoir by R. Southey. 45 Engravings. 8 vols.

COXE'S Memoirs of the Duke of Marlborough. With his original Correspondence, from family records at Blenheim. Revised edition. Portraits. 3 vols.
*** An Atlas of the plans of Marlborough's campaigns, 4to, 10s. 6d.

—— **History of the House of Austria.** From the Foundation of the Monarchy by Rhodolph of Hapsburgh to the Death of Leopold II., 1218-1792. By Archdn. Coxe. With Continuation from the Accession of Francis I. to the Revolution of 1848. 4 Portraits. 4 vols.

CUNNINGHAM'S Lives of the most Eminent British Painters. With Notes and 16 fresh Lives by Mrs. Heaton. 3 vols.

DEFOE'S Novels and Miscellaneous Works. With Prefaces and Notes, including those attributed to Sir W. Scott. Portrait. 7 vols.

DE LOLME'S Constitution of England, in which it is compared both with the Republican form of Government and the other Monarchies of Europe. Edit., with Life and Notes, by J. Macgregor, M.P.

DUNLOP'S History of Fiction. With Introduction and Supplement adapting the work to present requirements. By Henry Wilson. 2 vols., 5s. each.

ELZE'S Shakespeare.—*See Shakespeare*

EMERSON'S Works. 3 vols. Most complete edition published.

Vol. I.—Essays, Lectures, and Poems.

Vol. II.—English Traits, Nature, and Conduct of Life.

Vol. III.—Society and Solitude—Letters and Social Aims—Miscellaneous Papers (hitherto uncollected)—May-Day, &c.

FOSTER'S (John) Life and Correspondence. Edit. by J. E. Ryland. Portrait. 2 vols.

—— **Lectures at Broadmead Chapel.** Edit. by J. E. Ryland. 2 vols.

—— **Critical Essays contributed to** the 'Eclectic Review.' Edit. by J. E. Ryland. 2 vols.

—— **Essays: On Decision of Charac**ter; on a Man's writing Memoirs of Himself; on the epithet Romantic; on the aversion of Men of Taste to Evangelical Religion.

—— **Essays on the Evils of Popular** Ignorance, and a Discourse on the Propagation of Christianity in India.

—— **Essay on the Improvement of** Time, with Notes of Sermons and other Pieces. *N. S.*

—— **Fosteriana:** selected from periodical papers, edit. by H. G. Bohn.

FOX (Rt. Hon. C. J.)—*See Carrel.*

GIBBON'S Decline and Fall of the Roman Empire. Complete and unabridged, with variorum Notes ; including those of Guizot, Wenck, Niebuhr, Hugo, Neander, and others. 7 vols. 2 Maps and Portrait.

GOETHE'S Works. Trans. into English by E. A. Bowring, C.B., Anna Swanwick, Sir Walter Scott, &c. &c. 14 vols.

Vols. I. and II.—Autobiography and Annals. Portrait.

Vol. III.—Faust. Complete.

Vol. IV.—Novels and Tales : containing Elective Affinities, Sorrows of Werther, The German Emigrants, The Good Women, and a Nouvelette.

Vol. V.—Wilhelm Meister's Apprenticeship.

Vol. VI.—Conversations with Eckerman and Soret.

Vol. VII.—Poems and Ballads in the original Metres, including Hermann and Dorothea.

Vol. VIII.—Götz von Berlichingen, Torquato Tasso, Egmont, Iphigenia, Clavigo, Wayward Lover, and Fellow Culprits.

Vol. IX.—Wilhelm Meister's Travels. Complete Edition.

Vol. X.—Tour in Italy. Two Parts. And Second Residence in Rome.

Vol. XI.—Miscellaneous Travels, Letters from Switzerland, Campaign in France, Siege of Mainz, and Rhine Tour.

Vol. XII.—Early and Miscellaneous Letters, including Letters to his Mother, with Biography and Notes.

Vol. XIII.—Correspondence with Zelter.

Vol. XIV.—Reincke Fox, West-Eastern Divan and Achilleid. Translated in original metres by A. Rogers.

—— **Correspondence with Schiller.** 2 vols.—*See Schiller.*

GOLDSMITH'S Works. 5 vols.

Vol. I.—Life, Vicar of Wakefield, Essays, and Letters.

Vol. II.—Poems, Plays, Bee, Cock Lane Ghost.

Vol. III.—The Citizen of the World, Polite Learning in Europe.

Vol. IV.—Biographies, Criticisms, Later Essays.

Vol. V.—Prefaces, Natural History, Letters, Goody Two-Shoes, Index.

GREENE, MARLOW, and BEN JONSON (Poems of). With Notes and Memoirs by R. Bell.

GREGORY'S (Dr.) The Evidences, Doctrines, and Duties of the Christian Religion.

GRIMM'S Household Tales. With the Original Notes. Trans. by Mrs. A. Hunt. Introduction by Andrew Lang, M.A. 2 vols.

GUIZOT'S History of Representative Government in Europe. Trans. by A. R. Scoble.

—— **English Revolution of 1640.** From the Accession of Charles I. to his Death. Trans. by W. Hazlitt. Portrait.

—— **History of Civilisation.** From the Roman Empire to the French Revolution. Trans. by W. Hazlitt. Portraits. 3 vols.

HALL'S (Rev. Robert) Works and Remains. Memoir by Dr. Gregory and Essay by J. Foster. Portrait.

HAUFF'S Tales. The Caravan—The Sheikh of Alexandria—The Inn in the Spessart. Translated by Prof. S. Mendel.

HAWTHORNE'S Tales. 3 vols.

Vol. I.—Twice-told Tales, and the Snow Image.

Vol. II.—Scarlet Letter, and the House with Seven Gables.

Vol. III.—Transformation, and Blithedale Romance.

HAZLITT'S (W.) Works. 7 vols.

—— **Table-Talk.**

—— **The Literature of the Age of** Elizabeth and Characters of Shakespeare's Plays.

—— **English Poets and English Comic** Writers.

—— **The Plain Speaker.** Opinions on Books, Men, and Things.

—— **Round Table.** Conversations of James Northcote, R.A. ; Characteristics.

—— **Sketches and Essays,** and Winterslow.

—— **Spirit of the Age;** or, Contemporary Portraits. New Edition, by W. Carew Hazlitt.

HEINE'S Poems. Translated in the original Metres, with Life by E. A. Bowring, C.B.

—— **Travel-Pictures.** The Tour in the Harz, Norderney, and Book of Ideas, together with the Romantic School. Trans. by F. Storr. With Maps and Appendices.

HOFFMANN'S Works. The Serapion Brethren. Vol. I. Trans. by Lt.-Col. Ewing. [*Vol. II. in the press.*

HOOPER'S (G.) Waterloo : The Downfall of the First Napoleon : a History of the Campaign of 1815. By George Hooper. With Maps and Plans. New Edition, revised.

HUGO'S (Victor) Dramatic Works: Hernani—Ruy Blas—The King's Diversion. Translated by Mrs. Newton Crosland and F. L. Slous.

—— **Poems,** chiefly Lyrical. Collected by H. L. Williams.

HUNGARY: its History and Revolution, with Memoir of Kossuth. Portrait.

HUTCHINSON (Colonel). Memoirs of. By his Widow, with her Autobiography, and the Siege of Lathom House. Portrait.

IRVING'S (Washington) Complete Works. 15 vols.

—— **Life and Letters.** By his Nephew, Pierre E. Irving. With Index and a Portrait. 2 vols.

JAMES'S (G. P. R.) Life of Richard Cœur de Lion. Portraits of Richard and Philip Augustus. 2 vols.

—— **Louis XIV.** Portraits. 2 vols.

JAMESON (Mrs.) Shakespeare's Heroines. Characteristics of Women. By Mrs. Jameson.

JEAN PAUL.—*See Richter.*

JOHNSON'S Lives of the Poets. Edited, with Notes, by Mrs. Alexander Napier. And an Introduction by Professor J. W. Hales, M.A. 2 vols.

JONSON (Ben). Poems of.—*See Greene.*

JOSEPHUS (Flavius), The Works of. Whiston's Translation. Revised by Rev. A. R. Shilleto, M.A. With Topographical and Geographical Notes by Colonel Sir C. W. Wilson, K.C.B. 5 vols.

JUNIUS'S Letters. With Woodfall's Notes. An Essay on the Authorship. Facsimiles of Handwriting. 2 vols.

LA FONTAINE'S Fables. In English Verse, with Essay on the Fabulists. By Elizur Wright.

LAMARTINE'S The Girondists, or Personal Memoirs of the Patriots of the French Revolution. Trans. by H. T. Ryde. Portraits of Robespierre, Madame Roland, and Charlotte Corday. 3 vols.

—— **The Restoration of Monarchy** in France (a Sequel to The Girondists). 5 Portraits. 4 vols.

—— **The French Revolution of 1848.** Portraits.

LAMB'S (Charles) Elia and Eliana. Complete Edition. Portrait.

LAMB'S (Charles) Specimens of English Dramatic Poets of the time of Elizabeth. Notes, with the Extracts from the Garrick Plays.

—— **Talfourd's Letters of Charles** Lamb. New Edition, by W. Carew Hazlitt. 2 vols.

LANZI'S History of Painting in Italy, from the Period of the Revival of the Fine Arts to the End of the 18th Century. With Memoir of the Author. Portraits of Raffaelle, Titian, and Correggio, after the Artists themselves. Trans. by T. Roscoe. 3 vols.

LAPPENBERG'S England under the Anglo-Saxon Kings. Trans. by B. Thorpe, F.S.A. 2 vols.

LESSING'S Dramatic Works. Complete. By E. Bell, M.A. With Memoir by H. Zimmern. Portrait. 2 vols.

—— **Laokoon, Dramatic Notes, and** Representation of Death by the Ancients. Frontispiece.

LOCKE'S Philosophical Works, containing Human Understanding, with Bishop of Worcester, Malebranche's Opinions, Natural Philosophy, Reading and Study. With Preliminary Discourse, Analysis, and Notes, by J. A. St. John. Portrait. 2 vols.

—— **Life and Letters,** with Extracts from his Common-place Books. By Lord King.

LOCKHART (J. G.)—*See Burns.*

LONSDALE (Lord).—*See Carrel.*

LUTHER'S Table-Talk. Trans. by W. Hazlitt. With Life by A. Chalmers, and LUTHER'S CATECHISM. Portrait after Cranach.

—— **Autobiography.**—*See Michelet.*

MACHIAVELLI'S History of Florence, THE PRINCE, Savonarola, Historical Tracts, and Memoir. Portrait.

MARLOWE. Poems of.—*See Greene.*

MARTINEAU'S (Harriet) History of England (including History of the Peace) from 1800-1846. 5 vols.

MENZEL'S History of Germany, from the Earliest Period to the Crimean War. Portraits. 3 vols.

MICHELET'S Autobiography of Luther Trans. by W. Hazlitt. With Notes.

—— **The French Revolution** to the Flight of the King in 1791. *N. S.*

MIGNET'S The French Revolution, from 1789 to 1814. Portrait of Napoleon.

MILTON'S Prose Works. With Preface, Preliminary Remarks by J. A. St. John, and Index. 5 vols.

—— **Poetical Works.** With 120 Wood Engravings. 2 vols.

Vol. I.—Paradise Lost, complete, with Memoir, Notes, and Index.

Vol. II.—Paradise Regained, and other Poems, with Verbal Index to all the Poems.

MITFORD'S (Miss) Our Village. Sketches of Rural Character and Scenery. 2 Engravings. 2 vols.

MOLIÈRE'S Dramatic Works. In English Prose, by C. H. Wall. With a Life and a Portrait. 3 vols.

'It is not too much to say that we have here probably as good a translation of Molière as can be given.'—*Academy.*

MONTAGU. Letters and Works of Lady Mary Wortley Montagu. Lord Wharncliffe's Third Edition. Edited by W. Moy Thomas. With steel plates. 2 vols. 5s. each.

MONTESQUIEU'S Spirit of Laws. Revised Edition, with D'Alembert's Analysis, Notes, and Memoir. 2 vols.

NEANDER (Dr. A.) History of the Christian Religion and Church. Trans. by J. Torrey. With Short Memoir. 10 vols.

—— **Life of Jesus Christ, in its Historical** Connexion and Development.

—— **The Planting and Training of** the Christian Church by the Apostles. With the Antignosticus, or Spirit of Tertullian. Trans. by J. E. Ryland. 2 vols.

—— **Lectures on the History of** Christian Dogmas. Trans. by J. E. Ryland. 2 vols.

—— **Memorials of Christian Life in** the Early and Middle Ages; including Light in Dark Places. Trans. by J. E. Ryland.

OCKLEY (S.) History of the Saracens and their Conquests in Syria, Persia, and Egypt. Comprising the Lives of Mohammed and his Successors to the Death of Abdalmelik, the Eleventh Caliph. By Simon Ockley, B.D., Prof. of Arabic in Univ. of Cambridge. Portrait of Mohammed.

PASCAL'S Thoughts. Translated from the Text of M. Auguste Molinier by C. Kegan Paul. 3rd edition.

PERCY'S Reliques of Ancient English Poetry, consisting of Ballads, Songs, and other Pieces of our earlier Poets, with some few of later date. With Essay on Ancient Minstrels, and Glossary. 2 vols.

PHILIP DE COMMINES. Memoirs of. Containing the Histories of Louis XI. and Charles VIII., and Charles the Bold, Duke of Burgundy. With the History of Louis XI., by J. de Troyes. With a Life and Notes by A. R. Scoble. Portraits. 2 vols.

PLUTARCH'S LIVES. Newly Translated, with Notes and Life, by A Stewart, M.A., late Fellow of Trinity College, Cambridge, and G. Long, M.A. 4 vols.

POETRY OF AMERICA. Selections from One Hundred Poets, from 1776 to 1876. With Introductory Review, and Specimens of Negro Melody, by W. J. Linton. Portrait of W. Whitman.

RACINE'S (Jean) Dramatic Works. A metrical English version, with Biographical notice. By R. Bruce Boswell, M.A., Oxon. Vol. I.

Contents :— The Thebaïd — Alexander the Great—Andromache—The Litigants—Britannicus—Berenice.

RANKE (L.) History of the Popes, their Church and State, and their Conflicts with Protestantism in the 16th and 17th Centuries. Trans. by E. Foster. Portraits of Julius II. (after Raphael), Innocent X. (after Velasquez), and Clement VII. (after Titian). 3 vols.

—— **History of Servia.** Trans. by Mrs. Kerr. To which is added, The Slave Provinces of Turkey, by Cyprien Robert.

—— **History of the Latin and Teutonic** Nations. 1494-1514. Trans. by P. A. Ashworth, translator of Dr. Gneist's 'History of the English Constitution.'

REUMONT (Alfred de).—*See Carafas.*

REYNOLDS' (Sir J.) Literary Works. With Memoir and Remarks by H. W. Beechy. 2 vols.

RICHTER (Jean Paul). Levana, a Treatise on Education ; together with the Autobiography, and a short Memoir.

—— **Flower, Fruit, and Thorn Pieces,** or the Wedded Life, Death, and Marriage of Siebenkaes. Translated by Alex. Ewing. The only complete English translation.

ROSCOE'S (W.) Life of Leo X., with Notes, Historical Documents, and Dissertation on Lucretia Borgia. 3 Portraits. 2 vols.

—— **Lorenzo de' Medici,** called 'The Magnificent,' with Copyright Notes, Poems, Letters, &c. With Memoir of Roscoe and Portrait of Lorenzo.

RUSSIA, History of, from the earliest Period to the Crimean War. By W. K. Kelly. 3 Portraits. 2 vols.

SCHILLER'S Works. 7 vols.

Vol. I.—History of the Thirty Years' War. Rev. A. J. W. Morrison, M.A. Portrait.

Vol. II.—History of the Revolt in the Netherlands, the Trials of Counts Egmont and Horn, the Siege of Antwerp, and the Disturbance of France preceding the Reign of Henry IV. Translated by Rev. A. J. W. Morrison and L. Dora Schmitz.

Vol. III.—Don Carlos. R. D. Boylan —Mary Stuart. Mellish — Maid of Orleans. Anna Swanwick—Bride of Messina. A. Lodge, M.A. Together with the Use of the Chorus in Tragedy (a short Essay). Engravings.

These Dramas are all translated in metre.

Vol. IV.—Robbers—Fiesco—Love and Intrigue—Demetrius—Ghost Seer—Sport of Divinity.

The Dramas in this volume are in prose.

Vol. V.—Poems. E. A. Bowring, C.B.

Vol. VI.—Essays, Æsthetical and Philosophical, including the Dissertation on the Connexion between the Animal and Spiritual in Man.

Vol. VII. — Wallenstein's Camp. J. Churchill. — Piccolomini and Death of Wallenstein. S. T. Coleridge.—William Tell. Sir Theodore Martin, K.C.B., LL.D.

SCHILLER and GOETHE. Correspondence between, from A.D. 1794-1805. With Short Notes by L. Dora Schmitz. 2 vols.

SCHLEGEL'S (F.) Lectures on the Philosophy of Life and the Philosophy of Language. By A. J. W. Morrison.

—— **The History of Literature,** Ancient and Modern.

—— **The Philosophy of History.** With Memoir and Portrait.

—— **Modern History,** with the Lectures entitled Cæsar and Alexander, and The Beginning of our History. By L. Purcel and R. H. Whitelock.

—— **Æsthetic and Miscellaneous** Works, containing Letters on Christian Art, Essay on Gothic Architecture, Remarks on the Romance Poetry of the Middle Ages, on Shakspeare, the Limits of the Beautiful, and on the Language and Wisdom of the Indians. By E. J. Millington.

SCHLEGEL (A. W.) Dramatic Art and Literature. By J. Black. With Memoir by A. J. W. Morrison. Portrait.

SCHUMANN (Robert), His Life and Works. By A. Reissmann. Trans. by A. L. Alger.

—— **Early Letters.** Translated by May Herbert.

SHAKESPEARE'S Dramatic Art. The History and Character of Shakspeare's Plays. By Dr. H. Ulrici. Trans. by L. Dora Schmitz. 2 vols.

SHAKESPEARE (William). A Literary Biography by Karl Elze, Ph.D., LL.D. Translated by L. Dora Schmitz. 5s.

SHERIDAN'S Dramatic Works. With Memoir. Portrait (after Reynolds).

SKEAT (Rev. W. W.)—*See Chaucer.*

SISMONDI'S History of the Litera- ture of the South of Europe. With Notes and Memoir by T. Roscoe. Portraits of Sismondi and Dante. 2 vols.

The specimens of early French, Italian, Spanish, and Portugese Poetry, in English Verse, by Cary and others.

SMITH'S (Adam) The Wealth of Nations. An Inquiry into the Nature and Causes of. Reprinted from the Sixth Edition. With an Introduction by Ernest Belfort Bax. 2 vols.

SMITH'S (Adam) Theory of Moral Sentiments; with Essay on the First Formation of Languages, and Critical Memoir by Dugald Stewart.

SMYTH'S (Professor) Lectures on Modern History; from the Irruption of the Northern Nations to the close of the American Revolution. 2 vols.

—— **Lectures on the French Revolu-** tion. With Index. 2 vols.

SOUTHEY.—*See Cowper, Wesley, and (Illustrated Library) Nelson.*

STURM'S Morning Communings with God, or Devotional Meditations for Every Day. Trans. by W. Johnstone, M.A.

SULLY. Memoirs of the Duke of, Prime Minister to Henry the Great. With Notes and Historical Introduction. 4 Portraits. 4 vols.

TAYLOR'S (Bishop Jeremy) Holy Living and Dying, with Prayers, containing the Whole Duty of a Christian and the parts of Devotion fitted to all Occasions. Portrait.

THIERRY'S Conquest of England by the Normans; its Causes, and its Consequences in England and the Continent. By W. Hazlitt. With short Memoir. 2 Portraits. 2 vols.

TROYE'S (Jean de). — *See Philip de Commines.*

ULRICI (Dr.)—*See Shakespeare.*

VASARI. Lives of the most Eminent Painters, Sculptors, and Architects. By Mrs. J. Foster, with selected Notes. Portrait. 6 vols., Vol. VI. being an additional Volume of Notes by J. P. Richter.

WERNER'S Templars in Cyprus. Trans. by E. A. M. Lewis.

WESLEY, the Life of, and the Rise and Progress of Methodism. By Robert Southey. Portrait. 5s.

WHEATLEY. A Rational Illustra- tion of the Book of Common Prayer, being the Substance of everything Liturgical in all former Ritualist Commentators upon the subject. Frontispiece.

YOUNG (Arthur) Travels in France. Edited by Miss Betham Edwards. With a Portrait.

HISTORICAL LIBRARY.

22 Volumes at 5s. each. (*5l. 10s. per set.*)

EVELYN'S Diary and Correspond- dence, with the Private Correspondence of Charles I. and Sir Edward Nicholas, and between Sir Edward Hyde (Earl of Clarendon) and Sir Richard Browne. Edited from the Original MSS. by W. Bray, F.A.S. 4 vols. *N. S.* 45 Engravings (after Vandyke, Lely, Kneller, and Jamieson, &c.).

N.B.—This edition contains 130 letters from Evelyn and his wife, contained in no other edition.

PEPYS' Diary and Correspondence. With Life and Notes, by Lord Braybrooke. 4 vols. *N. S.* With Appendix containing additional Letters, an Index, and 31 Engravings (after Vandyke, Sir P. Lely, Holbein, Kneller, &c.).

JESSE'S Memoirs of the Court of England under the Stuarts, including the Protectorate. 3 vols. With Index and 42 Portraits (after Vandyke, Lely, &c.).

—— **Memoirs of the Pretenders and** their Adherents. 7 Portraits.

NUGENT'S (Lord) Memorials of Hampden, his Party and Times. With Memoir. 12 Portraits (after Vandyke and others).

STRICKLAND'S (Agnes) Lives of the Queens of England from the Norman Conquest. From authentic Documents, public and private. 6 Portraits. 6 vols. *N. S.*

—— **Life of Mary Queen of Scots.** 2 Portraits. 2 vols.

—— **Lives of the Tudor and Stuart** Princesses. With 2 Portraits.

PHILOSOPHICAL LIBRARY.

17 Vols. at 5s. each, excepting those marked otherwise. (*3l. 19s. per set.*)

BACON'S Novum Organum and Advancement of Learning. With Notes by J. Devey, M.A.

BAX. A Handbook of the History of Philosophy, for the use of Students. By E. Belfort Bax, Editor of Kant's 'Prolegomena.' 5s.

COMTE'S Philosophy of the Sciences. An Exposition of the Principles of the *Cours de Philosophie Positive.* By G. H. Lewes, Author of 'The Life of Goethe.'

DRAPER (Dr. J. W.) A History of the Intellectual Development of Europe. 2 vols.

HEGEL'S Philosophy of History. By J. Sibree, M.A.

KANT'S Critique of Pure Reason. By J. M. D. Meiklejohn.

—— **Prolegomena and Metaphysical** Foundations of Natural Science, with Biography and Memoir by E. Belfort Bax. Portrait.

LOGIC, or the Science of Inference. A Popular Manual. By J. Devey.

MILLER (Professor). History Philo- sophically Illustrated, from the Fall of the Roman Empire to the French Revolution. With Memoir. 4 vols. 3s. 6d. each.

SCHOPENHAUER on the Fourfold Root of the Principle of Sufficient Reason, and on the Will in Nature. Trans. from the German.

SPINOZA'S Chief Works. Trans. with Introduction by R. H. M. Elwes. 2 vols.

Vol. I.—Tractatus Theologico-Politicus —Political Treatise.

Vol. II.—Improvement of the Understanding—Ethics—Letters.

TENNEMANN'S Manual of the History of Philosophy. Trans. by Rev. A. Johnson, M.A.

THEOLOGICAL LIBRARY.

15 Vols. at 5s. each, excepting those marked otherwise.   (*3l. 13s. 6d. per set.*)

BLEEK. Introduction to the Old Testament. By Friedrich Bleek. Trans. under the supervision of Rev. E. Venables, Residentiary Canon of Lincoln. 2 vols.

CHILLINGWORTH'S Religion of Protestants. *3s. 6d.*

EUSEBIUS. Ecclesiastical History of Eusebius Pamphilius, Bishop of Cæsarea. Trans. by Rev. C. F. Cruse, M.A. With Notes, Life, and Chronological Tables.

EVAGRIUS. History of the Church. —*See Theodoret.*

HARDWICK. History of the Articles of Religion ; to which is added a Series of Documents from A.D. 1536 to A.D. 1615. Ed. by Rev. F. Proctor.

HENRY'S (Matthew) Exposition of the Book of Psalms. Numerous Woodcuts.

PEARSON (John, D.D.) Exposition of the Creed. Edit. by E. Walford, M.A. With Notes, Analysis, and Indexes.

PHILO-JUDÆUS, Works of. The Contemporary of Josephus. Trans. by C. D. Yonge. 4 vols.

PHILOSTORGIUS. Ecclesiastical History of.—*See Sozomen.*

SOCRATES' Ecclesiastical History. Comprising a History of the Church from Constantine, A.D. 305, to the 38th year of Theodosius II. With Short Account of the Author, and selected Notes.

SOZOMEN'S Ecclesiastical History. A.D. 324-440. With Notes, Prefatory Remarks by Valesius, and Short Memoir. Together with the ECCLESIASTICAL HISTORY OF PHILOSTORGIUS, as epitomised by Photius. Trans. by Rev. E. Walford, M.A. With Notes and brief Life.

THEODORET and EVAGRIUS. Histories of the Church from A.D. 332 to the Death of Theodore of Mopsuestia, A.D. 427 ; and from A.D. 431 to A.D. 544. With Memoirs.

WIESELER'S (Karl) Chronological Synopsis of the Four Gospels. Trans. by Rev. Canon Venables.

ANTIQUARIAN LIBRARY.

35 Vols. at 5s. each.   (*8l. 15s. per set.*)

ANGLO-SAXON CHRONICLE. — *See Bede.*

ASSER'S Life of Alfred.—*See Six O. E. Chronicles.*

BEDE'S (Venerable) Ecclesiastical History of England. Together with the ANGLO-SAXON CHRONICLE. With Notes, Short Life, Analysis, and Map. Edit. by J. A. Giles, D.C.L.

BOETHIUS'S Consolation of Philo- sophy. King Alfred's Anglo-Saxon Version of. With an English Translation on opposite pages, Notes, Introduction, and Glossary, by Rev. S. Fox, M.A. To which is added the Anglo-Saxon Version of the METRES OF BOETHIUS, with a free Translation by Martin F. Tupper, D.C.L.

BRAND'S Popular Antiquities of England, Scotland, and Ireland. Illustrating the Origin of our Vulgar and Provincial Customs, Ceremonies, and Superstitions. By Sir Henry Ellis, K.H., F.R.S. Frontispiece. 3 vols.

CHRONICLES of the CRUSADES. Contemporary Narratives of Richard Cœur de Lion, by Richard of Devizes and Geoffrey de Vinsauf; and of the Crusade at Saint Louis, by Lord John de Joinville. With Short Notes. Illuminated Frontispiece from an old MS.

DYER'S (T. F. T.) British Popular Customs, Present and Past. An Account of the various Games and Customs associated with different Days of the Year in the British Isles, arranged according to the Calendar. By the Rev. T. F. Thiselton Dyer, M.A.

EARLY TRAVELS IN PALESTINE. Comprising the Narratives of Arculf, Willibald, Bernard, Sæwulf, Sigurd, Benjamin of Tudela, Sir John Maundeville, De la Brocquière, and Maundrell ; all unabridged. With Introduction and Notes by Thomas Wright. Map of Jerusalem.

ELLIS (G.) Specimens of Early English Metrical Romances, relating to Arthur, Merlin, Guy of Warwick, Richard Cœur de Lion, Charlemagne, Roland, &c. &c. With Historical Introduction by J. O. Halliwell, F.R.S. Illuminated Frontispiece from an old MS.

ETHELWERD. Chronicle of.—*See Six O. E. Chronicles.*

FLORENCE OF WORCESTER'S Chronicle, with the Two Continuations: comprising Annals of English History from the Departure of the Romans to the Reign of Edward I. Trans., with Notes, by Thomas Forester, M.A.

GEOFFREY OF MONMOUTH. Chronicle of.—*See Six O. E. Chronicles.*

GESTA ROMANORUM, or Entertaining Moral Stories invented by the Monks. Trans. with Notes by the Rev. Charles Swan. Edit. by W. Hooper, M.A.

GILDAS. Chronicle of.—*See Six O. E. Chronicles.*

GIRALDUS CAMBRENSIS' Historical Works. Containing Topography of Ireland, and History of the Conquest of Ireland, by Th. Forester, M.A. Itinerary through Wales, and Description of Wales, by Sir R. Colt Hoare.

HENRY OF HUNTINGDON'S History of the English, from the Roman Invasion to the Accession of Henry II.; with the Acts of King Stephen, and the Letter to Walter. By T. Forester, M.A. Frontispiece from an old MS.

INGULPH'S Chronicles of the Abbey of Croyland, with the CONTINUATION by Peter of Blois and others. Trans. with Notes by H. T. Riley, B.A.

KEIGHTLEY'S (Thomas) Fairy Mythology, illustrative of the Romance and Superstition of Various Countries. Frontispiece by Cruikshank.

LEPSIUS'S Letters from Egypt, Ethiopia, and the Peninsula of Sinai; to which are added, Extracts from his Chronology of the Egyptians, with reference to the Exodus of the Israelites. By L. and J. B. Horner. Maps and Coloured View of Mount Barkal.

MALLET'S Northern Antiquities, or an Historical Account of the Manners, Customs, Religions, and Literature of the Ancient Scandinavians. Trans. by Bishop Percy. With Translation of the PROSE EDDA, and Notes by J. A. Blackwell. Also an Abstract of the 'Eyrbyggia Saga' by Sir Walter Scott. With Glossary and Coloured Frontispiece.

MARCO POLO'S Travels; with Notes and Introduction. Edit. by T. Wright.

MATTHEW PARIS'S English History, from 1235 to 1273. By Rev. J. A. Giles, D.C.L. With Frontispiece. 3 vols.—*See also Roger of Wendover.*

MATTHEW OF WESTMINSTER'S Flowers of History, especially such as relate to the affairs of Britain, from the beginning of the World to A.D. 1307. By C. D. Yonge. 2 vols.

NENNIUS. Chronicle of.—*See Six O. E. Chronicles.*

ORDERICUS VITALIS' Ecclesiastical History of England and Normandy. With Notes, Introduction of Guizot, and the Critical Notice of M. Delille, by T. Forester, M.A. To which is added the CHRONICLE OF ST. EVROULT. With General and Chronological Indexes. 4 vols.

PAULI'S (Dr. R.) Life of Alfred the Great. To which is appended Alfred's ANGLO-SAXON VERSION OF OROSIUS. With literal Translation interpaged, Notes, and an ANGLO-SAXON GRAMMAR and Glossary, by B. Thorpe, Esq. Frontispiece.

RICHARD OF CIRENCESTER. Chronicle of.—*See Six O. E. Chronicles.*

ROGER DE HOVEDEN'S Annals of English History, comprising the History of England and of other Countries of Europe from A.D. 732 to A.D. 1201. With Notes by H. T. Riley, B.A. 2 vols.

ROGER OF WENDOVER'S Flowers of History, comprising the History of England from the Descent of the Saxons to A.D. 1235, formerly ascribed to Matthew Paris. With Notes and Index by J. A. Giles, D.C.L. 2 vols.

SIX OLD ENGLISH CHRONICLES: viz., Asser's Life of Alfred and the Chronicles of Ethelwerd, Gildas, Nennius, Geoffrey of Monmouth, and Richard of Cirencester. Edit., with Notes, by J. A. Giles, D.C.L. Portrait of Alfred.

WILLIAM OF MALMESBURY'S Chronicle of the Kings of England, from the Earliest Period to King Stephen. By Rev. J. Sharpe. With Notes by J. A. Giles, D.C.L. Frontispiece.

YULE-TIDE STORIES. A Collection of Scandinavian and North-German Popular Tales and Traditions, from the Swedish, Danish, and German. Edit. by B. Thorpe.

ILLUSTRATED LIBRARY.

83 Vols. at 5s. each, excepting those marked otherwise. (20*l.* 13*s.* 6*d. per set.*)

ALLEN'S (Joseph, R.N.) Battles of the British Navy. Revised edition, with Indexes of Names and Events, and 57 Portraits and Plans. 2 vols.

ANDERSEN'S Danish Fairy Tales. By Caroline Peachey. With Short Life and 120 Wood Engravings.

ARIOSTO'S Orlando Furioso. In English Verse by W. S. Rose. With Notes and Short Memoir. Portrait after Titian, and 24 Steel Engravings. 2 vols.

BECHSTEIN'S Cage and Chamber Birds : their Natural History, Habits, &c. Together with SWEET'S BRITISH WAR-BLERS. 43 Coloured Plates and Woodcuts.

BONOMI'S Nineveh and its Palaces. The Discoveries of Botta and Layard applied to the Elucidation of Holy Writ. 7 Plates and 294 Woodcuts.

BUTLER'S Hudibras, with Variorum Notes and Biography. Portrait and 28 Illustrations.

CATTERMOLE'S Evenings at Had- don Hall. Romantic Tales of the Olden Times. With 24 Steel Engravings after Cattermole.

CHINA, Pictorial, Descriptive, and Historical, with some account of Ava and the Burmese, Siam, and Anam. Map, and nearly 100 Illustrations.

CRAIK'S (G. L.) Pursuit of Know- ledge under Difficulties. Illustrated by Anecdotes and Memoirs. Numerous Woodcut Portraits.

CRUIKSHANK'S Three Courses and a Dessert ; comprising three Sets of Tales, West Country, Irish, and Legal ; and a Mélange. With 50 Illustrations by Cruikshank.

—— **Punch and Judy.** The Dialogue of the Puppet Show ; an Account of its Origin, &c. 24 Illustrations and Coloured Plates by Cruikshank.

DIDRON'S Christian Iconography ; a History of Christian Art in the Middle Ages. By the late A. N. Didron. Trans. by E. J. Millington, and completed, with Additions and Appendices, by Margaret Stokes. 2 vols. With numerous Illustrations.
  Vol. I. The History of the Nimbus, the Aureole, and the Glory ; Representations of the Persons of the Trinity.
  Vol. II. The Trinity ; Angels ; Devils ; The Soul ; The Christian Scheme. Appendices.

DANTE, in English Verse, by I. C. Wright, M.A. With Introduction and Memoir. Portrait and 34 Steel Engravings after Flaxman.

DYER (Dr. T. H.) Pompeii : its Buildings and Antiquities. An Account of the City, with full Description of the Remains and Recent Excavations, and an Itinerary for Visitors. By T. H. Dyer, LL.D. Nearly 300 Wood Engravings, Map, and Plan. 7*s.* 6*d.*

—— **Rome :** History of the City, with Introduction on recent Excavations. 8 Engravings, Frontispiece, and 2 Maps.

GIL BLAS. The Adventures of. From the French of Lesage by Smollett. 24 Engravings after Smirke, and 10 Etchings by Cruikshank. 612 pages. 6*s.*

GRIMM'S Gammer Grethel ; or, German Fairy Tales and Popular Stories, containing 42 Fairy Tales. By Edgar Taylor. Numerous Woodcuts after Cruikshank and Ludwig Grimm. 3*s.* 6*d.*

HOLBEIN'S Dance of Death and Bible Cuts. Upwards of 150 Subjects, engraved in facsimile, with Introduction and Descriptions by the late Francis Douce and Dr. Dibdin.

INDIA, Pictorial, Descriptive, and Historical, from the Earliest Times. 100 Engravings on Wood and Map.

JESSE'S Anecdotes of Dogs. With 40 Woodcuts after Harvey, Bewick, and others ; and 34 Steel Engravings after Cooper and Landseer.

KING'S (C. W.) Natural History of Gems or Decorative Stones. Illustrations. 6*s.*

—— **Natural History of Precious** Stones and Metals. Illustrations. 6*s.*

KITTO'S Scripture Lands. Described in a series of Historical, Geographical, and Topographical Sketches. 42 coloured Maps.

KRUMMACHER'S Parables. 40 Illustrations.

LINDSAY'S (Lord) Letters on Egypt, Edom, and the Holy Land. 36 Wood Engravings and 2 Maps.

LODGE'S Portraits of Illustrious Personages of Great Britain, with Biographical and Historical Memoirs. 240 Portraits engraved on Steel, with the respective Biographies unabridged. Complete in 8 vols.

LONGFELLOW'S Poetical Works, including his Translations and Notes. 24 full-page Woodcuts by Birket Foster and others, and a Portrait.

—— Without the Illustrations, 3s. 6d.

—— **Prose Works.** With 16 full-page Woodcuts by Birket Foster and others.

LOUDON'S (Mrs.) Entertaining Naturalist. Popular Descriptions, Tales, and Anecdotes, of more than 500 Animals. Numerous Woodcuts.

MARRYAT'S (Capt., R.N.) Masterman Ready; or, the Wreck of the *Pacific*. (Written for Young People.) With 93 Woodcuts. 3s. 6d.

—— **Mission; or, Scenes in Africa.** (Written for Young People.) Illustrated by Gilbert and Dalziel. 3s. 6d.

—— **Pirate and Three Cutters.** (Written for Young People.) With a Memoir. 8 Steel Engravings after Clarkson Stanfield, R.A. 3s. 6d.

—— **Privateersman.** Adventures by Sea and Land One Hundred Years Ago. (Written for Young People.) 8 Steel Engravings. 3s. 6d.

—— **Settlers in Canada.** (Written for Young People.) 10 Engravings by Gilbert and Dalziel. 3s. 6d.

—— **Poor Jack.** (Written for Young People.) With 16 Illustrations after Clarkson Stanfield, R.A. 3s. 6d.

—— **Midshipman Easy.** With 8 full-page Illustrations. Small post 8vo. 3s. 6d.

—— **Peter Simple.** With 8 full-page Illustrations. Small post 8vo. 3s. 6d.

MAXWELL'S Victories of Wellington and the British Armies. Frontispiece and 4 Portraits.

MICHAEL ANGELO and RAPHAEL, Their Lives and Works. By Duppa and Quatremère de Quincy. Portraits and Engravings, including the Last Judgment, and Cartoons.

MILLER'S History of the Anglo-Saxons, from the Earliest Period to the Norman Conquest. Portrait of Alfred, Map of Saxon Britain, and 12 Steel Engravings.

MUDIE'S History of British Birds. Revised by W. C. L. Martin. 52 Figures of Birds and 7 coloured Plates of Eggs. 2 vols.

NAVAL and MILITARY HEROES of Great Britain; a Record of British Valour on every Day in the year, from William the Conqueror to the Battle of Inkermann. By Major Johns, R.M., and Lieut. P. H. Nicolas, R.M. Indexes. 24 Portraits after Holbein, Reynolds, &c. 6s.

NICOLINI'S History of the Jesuits: their Origin, Progress, Doctrines, and Designs. 8 Portraits.

PETRARCH'S Sonnets, Triumphs, and other Poems, in English Verse. With Life by Thomas Campbell. Portrait and 15 Steel Engravings.

PICKERING'S History of the Races of Man, and their Geographical Distribution; with An Analytical Synopsis of the Natural History of Man. By Dr. Hall. Map of the World and 12 coloured Plates

PICTORIAL HANDBOOK OF Modern Geography on a Popular Plan. Compiled from the best Authorities, English and Foreign, by H. G. Bohn. 150 Woodcuts and 51 coloured Maps.

—— Without the Maps, 3s. 6d.

POPE'S Poetical Works, including Translations. Edit., with Notes, by R. Carruthers. 2 vols.

—— **Homer's Iliad,** with Introduction and Notes by Rev. J. S. Watson, M.A. With Flaxman's Designs.

—— **Homer's Odyssey,** with the Battle of Frogs and Mice, Hymns, &c., by other translators including Chapman. Introduction and Notes by J. S. Watson, M.A. With Flaxman's Designs.

—— **Life,** including many of his Letters. By R. Carruthers. Numerous Illustrations.

POTTERY AND PORCELAIN, and other objects of Vertu. Comprising an Illustrated Catalogue of the Bernal Collection, with the prices and names of the Possessors. Also an Introductory Lecture on Pottery and Porcelain, and an Engraved List of all Marks and Monograms. By H. G. Bohn. Numerous Woodcuts.

—— With coloured Illustrations, 10s. 6d.

PROUT'S (Father) Reliques. Edited by Rev. F. Mahony. Copyright edition, with the Author's last corrections and additions. 21 Etchings by D. Maclise, R.A. Nearly 600 pages.

RECREATIONS IN SHOOTING. With some Account of the Game found in the British Isles, and Directions for the Management of Dog and Gun. By 'Craven.' 62 Woodcuts and 9 Steel Engravings after A. Cooper, R.A.

RENNIE. Insect Architecture. Revised by Rev. J. G. Wood, M.A. 186 Woodcuts.

ROBINSON CRUSOE. With Memoir of Defoe, 12 Steel Engravings and 74 Woodcuts after Stothard and Harvey.

—— Without the Engravings, 3s. 6d.

ROME IN THE NINETEENTH CENTURY. An Account in 1817 of the Ruins of the Ancient City, and Monuments of Modern Times. By C. A. Eaton. 34 Steel Engravings. 2 vols.

SHARPE (S.) The History of Egypt, from the Earliest Times till the Conquest by the Arabs, A.D. 640. 2 Maps and upwards of 400 Woodcuts. 2 vols.

SOUTHEY'S Life of Nelson. With Additional Notes, Facsimiles of Nelson's Writing, Portraits, Plans, and 50 Engravings, after Birket Foster, &c.

STARLING'S (Miss) Noble Deeds of Women ; or, Examples of Female Courage, Fortitude, and Virtue. With 14 Steel Portraits.

STUART and REVETT'S Antiquities of Athens, and other Monuments of Greece ; with Glossary of Terms used in Grecian Architecture. 71 Steel Plates and numerous Woodcuts.

SWEET'S British Warblers. 5s.—*See Bechstein.*

TALES OF THE GENII ; or, the Delightful Lessons of Horam, the Son of Asmar. Trans. by Sir C. Morrell. Numerous Woodcuts.

TASSO'S Jerusalem Delivered. In English Spenserian Verse, with Life, by J. H. Wiffen. With 8 Engravings and 24 Woodcuts.

WALKER'S Manly Exercises ; containing Skating, Riding, Driving, Hunting, Shooting, Sailing, Rowing, Swimming, &c. 44 Engravings and numerous Woodcuts.

WALTON'S Complete Angler, or the Contemplative Man's Recreation, by Izaak Walton and Charles Cotton. With Memoirs and Notes by E. Jesse. Also an Account of Fishing Stations, Tackle, &c., by H. G. Bohn. Portrait and 203 Woodcuts, and 26 Engravings on Steel.

—— **Lives of Donne, Wotton, Hooker,** &c., with Notes. A New Edition, revised by A. H. Bullen, with a Memoir of Izaak Walton by William Dowling. 6 Portraits, 6 Autograph Signatures, &c.

WELLINGTON, Life of. From the Materials of Maxwell. 18 Steel Engravings.

—— **Victories of.**—*See Maxwell.*

WESTROPP (H. M.) A Handbook of Archæology, Egyptian, Greek, Etruscan, Roman. By H. M. Westropp. Numerous Illustrations.

WHITE'S Natural History of Selborne, with Observations on various Parts of Nature, and the Naturalists' Calendar. Sir W. Jardine. Edit., with Notes and Memoir, by E. Jesse. 40 Portraits and coloured Plates.

CLASSICAL LIBRARY.

TRANSLATIONS FROM THE GREEK AND LATIN.

103 *Vols. at 5s. each, excepting those marked otherwise.* (25*l.* 4*s.* 6*d. per set.*)

ÆSCHYLUS, The Dramas of. In English Verse by Anna Swanwick. 4th edition.

—— **The Tragedies of.** In Prose, with Notes and Introduction, by T. A. Buckley, B.A. Portrait. 3s. 6d.

AMMIANUS MARCELLINUS. History of Rome during the Reigns of Constantius, Julian, Jovianus, Valentinian, and Valens, by C. D. Yonge, B.A. Double volume. 7s. 6d.

ANTONINUS (M. Aurelius), The Thoughts of. Translated literally, with Notes, Biographical Sketch, and Essay on the Philosophy, by George Long, M.A. 3s. 6d.

APOLLONIUS RHODIUS. 'The Argonautica.' Translated by E. P. Coleridge.

APULEIUS, The Works of. Comprising the Golden Ass, God of Socrates, Florida, and Discourse of Magic. With a Metrical Version of Cupid and Psyche, and Mrs. Tighe's Psyche. Frontispiece.

ARISTOPHANES' Comedies. Trans., with Notes and Extracts from Frere's and other Metrical Versions, by W. J. Hickie. Portrait. 2 vols.

ARISTOTLE'S Nicomachean Ethics. Trans., with Notes, Analytical Introduction, and Questions for Students, by Ven. Archdn. Browne.

— **Politics and Economics.** Trans., with Notes, Analyses, and Index, by E. Walford, M.A., and an Essay and Life by Dr. Gillies.

— **Metaphysics.** Trans., with Notes, Analysis, and Examination Questions, by Rev. John H. M'Mahon, M.A.

— **History of Animals.** In Ten Books. Trans., with Notes and Index, by R. Cresswell, M.A.

— **Organon**; or, Logical Treatises, and the Introduction of Porphyry. With Notes, Analysis, and Introduction, by Rev. O. F. Owen, M.A. 2 vols. 3s. 6d. each.

— **Rhetoric and Poetics.** Trans., with Hobbes' Analysis, Exam. Questions, and Notes, by T. Buckley, B.A. Portrait.

ATHENÆUS. The Deipnosophists; or, the Banquet of the Learned. By C. D. Yonge, B.A. With an Appendix of Poetical Fragments. 3 vols.

ATLAS of Classical Geography. 22 large Coloured Maps. With a complete Index. Imp. 8vo. 7s. 6d.

BION.—*See Theocritus.*

CÆSAR. Commentaries on the Gallic and Civil Wars, with the Supplementary Books attributed to Hirtius, including the complete Alexandrian, African, and Spanish Wars. Trans. with Notes. Portrait.

CATULLUS, Tibullus, and the Vigil of Venus. Trans. with Notes and Biographical Introduction. To which are added, Metrical Versions by Lamb, Grainger, and others. Frontispiece.

CICERO'S Orations. Trans. by C. D. Yonge, B.A. 4 vols.

— **On Oratory and Orators.** With Letters to Quintus and Brutus. Trans., with Notes, by Rev. J. S. Watson, M.A.

— **On the Nature of the Gods,** Divination, Fate, Laws, a Republic, Consulship. Trans., with Notes, by C. D. Yonge, B.A.

— **Academics,** De Finibus, and Tusculan Questions. By C. D. Yonge, B.A. With Sketch of the Greek Philosophers mentioned by Cicero.

CICERO'S Orations.—*Continued.*

— **Offices;** or, Moral Duties. Cato Major, an Essay on Old Age; Lælius, an Essay on Friendship; Scipio's Dream; Paradoxes; Letter to Quintus on Magistrates. Trans., with Notes, by C. R. Edmonds. Portrait. 3s. 6d.

DEMOSTHENES' Orations. Trans., with Notes, Arguments, a Chronological Abstract, and Appendices, by C. Rann Kennedy. 5 vols.

DICTIONARY of LATIN and GREEK Quotations; including Proverbs, Maxims, Mottoes, Law Terms and Phrases. With the Quantities marked, and English Translations. With Index Verborum (622 pages).

— Index Verborum to the above, with the *Quantities* and Accents marked (56 pages), limp cloth. 1s.

DIOGENES LAERTIUS. Lives and Opinions of the Ancient Philosophers. Trans., with Notes, by C. D. Yonge, B.A.

EPICTETUS. The Discourses of. With the Encheiridion and Fragments. With Notes, Life, and View of his Philosophy, by George Long, M.A.

EURIPIDES. Trans., with Notes and Introduction, by T. A. Buckley, B.A. Portrait. 2 vols.

GREEK ANTHOLOGY. In English Prose by G. Burges, M.A. With Metrical Versions by Bland, Merivale, Lord Denman, &c.

GREEK ROMANCES of Heliodorus, Longus, and Achilles Tatius; viz., The Adventures of Theagenes and Chariclea; Amours of Daphnis and Chloe; and Loves of Clitopho and Leucippe. Trans., with Notes, by Rev. R. Smith, M.A.

HERODOTUS. Literally trans. by Rev. Henry Cary, M.A. Portrait.

HESIOD, CALLIMACHUS, and Theognis. In Prose, with Notes and Biographical Notices by Rev. J. Banks, M.A. Together with the Metrical Versions of Hesiod, by Elton; Callimachus, by Tytler; and Theognis, by Frere.

HOMER'S Iliad. In English Prose, with Notes by T. A. Buckley, B.A. Portrait.

— **Odyssey,** Hymns, Epigrams, and Battle of the Frogs and Mice. In English Prose, with Notes and Memoir by T. A. Buckley, B.A.

HORACE. In Prose by Smart, with Notes selected by T. A. Buckley, B.A. Portrait. 3s. 6d.

JULIAN THE EMPEROR. By the Rev. C. W. King, M.A.

JUSTIN, CORNELIUS NEPOS, and Eutropius. Trans., with Notes, by Rev. J. S. Watson, M.A.

JUVENAL, PERSIUS, SULPICIA, and Lucilius. In Prose, with Notes, Chronological Tables, Arguments, by L. Evans, M.A. To which is added the Metrical Version of Juvenal and Persius by Gifford. Frontispiece.

LIVY. The History of Rome. Trans. by Dr. Spillan and others. 4 vols. Portrait.

LUCAN'S Pharsalia. In Prose, with Notes by H. T. Riley.

LUCIAN'S Dialogues of the Gods, of the Sea Gods, and of the Dead. Trans. by Howard Williams, M.A.

LUCRETIUS. In Prose, with Notes and Biographical Introduction by Rev. J. S. Watson, M.A. To which is added the Metrical Version by J. M. Good.

MARTIAL'S Epigrams, complete. In Prose, with Verse Translations selected from English Poets, and other sources. Dble. vol. (670 pages). 7s. 6d.

MOSCHUS.—*See Theocritus.*

OVID'S Works, complete. In Prose, with Notes and Introduction. 3 vols.

PAUSANIAS' Description of Greece. Translated into English, with Notes and Index. By Arthur Richard Shilleto, M.A., sometime Scholar of Trinity College, Cambridge. 2 vols.

PHALARIS. Bentley's Dissertations upon the Epistles of Phalaris, Themistocles, Socrates, Euripides, and the Fables of Æsop. With Introduction and Notes by Prof. W. Wagner, Ph.D.

PINDAR. In Prose, with Introduction and Notes by Dawson W. Turner. Together with the Metrical Version by Abraham Moore. Portrait.

PLATO'S Works. Trans., with Introduction and Notes. 6 vols.

—— **Dialogues.** A Summary and Analysis of. With Analytical Index to the Greek text of modern editions and to the above translations, by A. Day, LL.D.

PLAUTUS'S Comedies. In Prose, with Notes and Index by H. T. Riley, B.A. 2 vols.

PLINY'S Natural History. Trans., with Notes, by J. Bostock, M.D., F.R.S., and H. T. Riley, B.A. 6 vols.

PLINY. The Letters of Pliny the Younger. Melmoth's Translation, revised, with Notes and short Life, by Rev. F. C. T. Bosanquet, M.A.

PLUTARCH'S Morals. Theosophical Essays. Trans. by C. W. King, M.A.

—— **Ethical Essays.** Trans. by A. R. Shilleto, M.A.

—— **Lives.** *See page 7.*

PROPERTIUS, The Elegies of. With Notes, Literally translated by the Rev. P. J. F. Gantillon, M.A., with metrical versions of Select Elegies by Nott and Elton. 3s. 6d.

QUINTILIAN'S Institutes of Oratory. Trans., with Notes and Biographical Notice, by Rev. J. S. Watson, M.A. 2 vols.

SALLUST, FLORUS, and VELLEIUS Paterculus. Trans., with Notes and Biographical Notices, by J. S. Watson, M.A.

SENECA DE BENEFICIIS. Newly translated by Aubrey Stewart, M.A. 3s. 6d.

SENECA'S Minor Essays. Translated by A. Stewart, M.A.

SOPHOCLES. The Tragedies of. In Prose, with Notes, Arguments, and Introduction. Portrait.

STRABO'S Geography. Trans., with Notes, by W. Falconer, M.A., and H. C. Hamilton. Copious Index, giving Ancient and Modern Names. 3 vols.

SUETONIUS' Lives of the Twelve Cæsars and Lives of the Grammarians. The Translation of Thomson, revised, with Notes, by T. Forester.

TACITUS. The Works of. Trans., with Notes. 2 vols.

TERENCE and PHÆDRUS. In English Prose, with Notes and Arguments, by H. T. Riley, B.A. To which is added Smart's Metrical Version of Phædrus. With Frontispiece.

THEOCRITUS, BION, MOSCHUS, and Tyrtæus. In Prose, with Notes and Arguments, by Rev. J. Banks, M.A. To which are appended the METRICAL VERSIONS of Chapman. Portrait of Theocritus.

THUCYDIDES. The Peloponnesian War. Trans., with Notes, by Rev. H. Dale. Portrait. 2 vols. 3s. 6d. each.

TYRTÆUS.—*See Theocritus.*

VIRGIL. The Works of. In Prose, with Notes by Davidson. Revised, with additional Notes and Biographical Notice, by T. A. Buckley, B.A. Portrait. 3s. 6d.

XENOPHON'S Works. Trans., with Notes, by J. S. Watson, M.A., and others. Portrait. In 3 vols.

COLLEGIATE SERIES.

10 *Vols. at* 5*s. each.*   (2*l.* 10*s. per set.*)

DANTE. The Inferno. Prose Trans., with the Text of the Original on the same page, and Explanatory Notes, by John A. Carlyle, M.D. Portrait.

—— **The Purgatorio.** Prose Trans., with the Original on the same page, and Explanatory Notes, by W. S. Dugdale.

NEW TESTAMENT (The) in Greek. Griesbach's Text, with the Readings of Mill and Scholz at the foot of the page, and Parallel References in the margin. Also a Critical Introduction and Chronological Tables. Two Fac-similes of Greek Manuscripts. 650 pages. 3*s.* 6*d.*

—— or bound up with a Greek and English Lexicon to the New Testament (250 pages additional, making in all 900). 5*s.*

   The Lexicon may be had separately, price 2*s.*

DOBREE'S Adversaria. (Notes on the Greek and Latin Classics.) Edited by the late Prof. Wagner. 2 vols.

DONALDSON (Dr.) The Theatre of the Greeks. With Supplementary Treatise on the Language, Metres, and Prosody of the Greek Dramatists. Numerous Illustrations and 3 Plans. By J. W. Donaldson, D.D.

KEIGHTLEY'S (Thomas) Mythology of Ancient Greece and Italy. Revised by Leonhard Schmitz, Ph.D., LL.D. 12 Plates.

HERODOTUS, Notes on. Original and Selected from the best Commentators. By D. W. Turner, M.A. Coloured Map.

—— **Analysis and Summary of,** with a Synchronistical Table of Events—Tables of Weights, Measures, Money, and Distances—an Outline of the History and Geography—and the Dates completed from Gaisford, Baehr, &c. By J. T. Wheeler.

THUCYDIDES. An Analysis and Summary of. With Chronological Table of Events, &c., by J. T. Wheeler.

SCIENTIFIC LIBRARY.

51 *Vols. at* 5*s. each, excepting those marked otherwise.*   (13*l.* 9*s.* 6*d. per set.*)

AGASSIZ and GOULD. Outline of Comparative Physiology touching the Structure and Development of the Races of Animals living and extinct. For Schools and Colleges. Enlarged by Dr. Wright. With Index and 300 Illustrative Woodcuts.

BOLLEY'S Manual of Technical Analysis; a Guide for the Testing and Valuation of the various Natural and Artificial Substances employed in the Arts and Domestic Economy, founded on the work of Dr. Bolley. Edit. by Dr. Paul. 100 Woodcuts.

BRIDGEWATER TREATISES.

—— **Bell (Sir Charles) on the Hand;** its Mechanism and Vital Endowments, as evincing Design. Preceded by an Account of the Author's Discoveries in the Nervous System by A. Shaw. Numerous Woodcuts.

—— **Kirby on the History, Habits,** and Instincts of Animals. With Notes by T. Rymer Jones. 100 Woodcuts. 2 vols.

—— **Whewell's Astronomy and** General Physics, considered with reference to Natural Theology. Portrait of the Earl of Bridgewater. 3*s.* 6*d.*

BRIDGEWATER TREATISES. *Continued.*

—— **Chalmers on the Adaptation of** External Nature to the Moral and Intellectual Constitution of Man. With Memoir by Rev. Dr. Cumming. Portrait.

—— **Prout's Treatise on Chemistry,** Meteorology, and the Function of Digestion, with reference to Natural Theology. Edit. by Dr. J. W. Griffith. 2 Maps.

—— **Buckland's Geology and Mineralogy.** With Additions by Prof. Owen, Prof. Phillips, and R. Brown. Memoir of Buckland. Portrait. 2 vols. 15*s.* Vol. I. Text. Vol. II. 90 large plates with letterpress.

—— **Roget's Animal and Vegetable** Physiology. 463 Woodcuts. 2 vols. 6*s.* each.

—— **Kidd on the Adaptation of External** Nature to the Physical Condition of Man. 3*s.* 6*d.*

CARPENTER'S (Dr. W. B.) Zoology. A Systematic View of the Structure, Habits, Instincts, and Uses of the principal Families of the Animal Kingdom, and of the chief Forms of Fossil Remains. Revised by W. S. Dallas, F.L.S. Numerous Woodcuts. 2 vols. 6*s.* each.

CARPENTER'S Works.—*Continued.*

—— **Mechanical Philosophy, Astronomy, and Horology.** A Popular Exposition. 181 Woodcuts.

—— **Vegetable Physiology and Systematic Botany.** A complete Introduction to the Knowledge of Plants. Revised by E. Lankester, M.D., &c. Numerous Woodcuts. 6s.

—— **Animal Physiology.** Revised Edition. 300 Woodcuts. 6s.

CHEVREUL on Colour. Containing the Principles of Harmony and Contrast of Colours, and their Application to the Arts ; including Painting, Decoration, Tapestries, Carpets, Mosaics, Glazing, Staining, Calico Printing, Letterpress Printing, Map Colouring, Dress, Landscape and Flower Gardening, &c. Trans. by C. Martel. Several Plates.

—— With an additional series of 16 Plates in Colours, 7s. 6d.

ENNEMOSER'S History of Magic. Trans. by W. Howitt. With an Appendix of the most remarkable and best authenticated Stories of Apparitions, Dreams, Second Sight, Table-Turning, and Spirit-Rapping, &c. 2 vols.

HIND'S Introduction to Astronomy. With Vocabulary of the Terms in present use. Numerous Woodcuts. 3s. 6d.

HOGG'S (Jabez) Elements of Experimental and Natural Philosophy. Being an Easy Introduction to the Study of Mechanics, Pneumatics, Hydrostatics, Hydraulics, Acoustics, Optics, Caloric, Electricity, Voltaism, and Magnetism. 400 Woodcuts.

HUMBOLDT'S Cosmos ; or, Sketch of a Physical Description of the Universe. Trans. by E. C. Otté, B. H. Paul, and W. S. Dallas, F.L.S. Portrait. 5 vols. 3s. 6d. each, excepting vol. v., 5s.

—— **Personal Narrative of his Travels** in America during the years 1799-1804. Trans., with Notes, by T. Ross. 3 vols.

—— **Views of Nature ; or, Contemplations** of the Sublime Phenomena of Creation, with Scientific Illustrations. Trans. by E. C. Otté.

HUNT'S (Robert) Poetry of Science ; or, Studies of the Physical Phenomena of Nature. By Robert Hunt, Professor at the School of Mines.

JOYCE'S Scientific Dialogues. A Familiar Introduction to the Arts and Sciences. For Schools and Young People. Numerous Woodcuts.

JOYCE'S Introduction to the Arts and Sciences, for Schools and Young People. Divided into Lessons with Examination Questions. Woodcuts. 3s. 6d.

JUKES-BROWNE'S Student's Handbook of Physical Geology. By A. J. Jukes-Browne, of the Geological Survey of England. With numerous Diagrams and Illustrations, 6s.

—— **The Student's Handbook of** Historical Geology. By A. J. Jukes-Brown, B.A., F.G.S., of the Geological Survey of England and Wales. With numerous Diagrams and Illustrations. 6s.

—— **The Building of the British** Islands. A Study in Geographical Evolution. By A. J. Jukes-Browne, F.G.S. 7s. 6d.

KNIGHT'S (Charles) Knowledge is Power. A Popular Manual of Political Economy.

LILLY. Introduction to Astrology. With a Grammar of Astrology and Tables for calculating Nativities, by Zadkiel.

MANTELL'S (Dr.) Geological Excursions through the Isle of Wight and along the Dorset Coast. Numerous Woodcuts and Geological Map.

—— **Petrifactions and their Teachings.** Handbook to the Organic Remains in the British Museum. Numerous Woodcuts. 6s.

—— **Wonders of Geology ; or, a** Familiar Exposition of Geological Phenomena. A coloured Geological Map of England, Plates, and 200 Woodcuts. 2 vols. 7s. 6d. each.

SCHOUW'S Earth, Plants, and Man. Popular Pictures of Nature. And Kobell's Sketches from the Mineral Kingdom. Trans. by A. Henfrey, F.R.S. Coloured Map of the Geography of Plants.

SMITH'S (Pye) Geology and Scripture ; or, the Relation between the Scriptures and Geological Science. With Memoir.

STANLEY'S Classified Synopsis of the Principal Painters of the Dutch and Flemish Schools, including an Account of some of the early German Masters. By George Stanley.

STAUNTON'S Chess Works. — *See page* 21.

STOCKHARDT'S Experimental Chemistry. A Handbook for the Study of the Science by simple Experiments. Edit. by C. W. Heaton, F.C.S. Numerous Woodcuts.

URE'S (Dr. A.) Cotton Manufacture of Great Britain, systematically investigated ; with an Introductory View of its Comparative State in Foreign Countries. Revised by P. L. Simmonds. 150 Illustrations. 2 vols.

—— **Philosophy of Manufactures,** or an Exposition of the Scientific, Moral, and Commercial Economy of the Factory System of Great Britain. Revised by P. L. Simmonds. Numerous Figures. 800 pages. 7s. 6d.

ECONOMICS AND FINANCE.

GILBART'S History, Principles, and Practice of Banking. Revised to 1881 by A. S. Michie, of the Royal Bank of Scotland. Portrait of Gilbart. 2 vols. 10s. *N. S.*

REFERENCE LIBRARY.

30 *Volumes at Various Prices.* (9*l.* 5*s. per set.*)

BLAIR'S Chronological Tables. Comprehending the Chronology and History of the World, from the Earliest Times to the Russian Treaty of Peace, April 1856. By J. W. Rosse. 800 pages. 10s.

—— **Index of Dates.** Comprehending the principal Facts in the Chronology and History of the World, from the Earliest to the Present, alphabetically arranged; being a complete Index to the foregoing. By J. W. Rosse. 2 vols. 5s. each.

BOHN'S Dictionary of Quotations from the English Poets. 4th and cheaper Edition. 6s.

BOND'S Handy-book of Rules and Tables for Verifying Dates with the Christian Era. 4th Edition.

BUCHANAN'S Dictionary of Science and Technical Terms used in Philosophy, Literature, Professions, Commerce, Arts, and Trades. By W. H. Buchanan, with Supplement. Edited by Jas. A. Smith. 6s.

CHRONICLES OF THE TOMBS. A Select Collection of Epitaphs, with Essay on Epitaphs and Observations on Sepulchral Antiquities. By T. J. Pettigrew, F.R.S., F.S.A. 5s.

CLARK'S (Hugh) Introduction to Heraldry. Revised by J. R. Planché. 5s. 950 Illustrations.

—— *With the Illustrations coloured,* 15s.

COINS, Manual of.—*See Humphreys.*

COOPER'S Biographical Dictionary. Containing concise notices of upwards of 15,000 eminent persons of all ages and countries. 2 vols. 5s. each.

DATES, Index of.—*See Blair.*

DICTIONARY of Obsolete and Pro- vincial English. Containing Words from English Writers previous to the 19th Century. By Thomas Wright, M.A., F.S.A., &c. 2 vols. 5s. each.

EPIGRAMMATISTS (The). A Selection from the Epigrammatic Literature of Ancient, Mediæval, and Modern Times. With Introduction, Notes, Observations, Illustrations, an Appendix on Works connected with Epigrammatic Literature, by Rev. H. Dodd, M.A. 6s.

GAMES, Handbook of. Comprising Treatises on above 40 Games of Chance, Skill, and Manual Dexterity, including Whist, Billiards, &c. Edit. by Henry G. Bohn. Numerous Diagrams. 5s.

HENFREY'S Guide to English Coins. Revised Edition, by C. F. Keary, M.A., F.S.A. With an Historical Introduction. 6s.

HUMPHREYS' Coin Collectors' Manual. An Historical Account of the Progress of Coinage from the Earliest Time, by H. N. Humphreys. 140 Illustrations. 2 vols. 5s. each.

LOWNDES' Bibliographer's Manual of English Literature. Containing an Account of Rare and Curious Books published in or relating to Great Britain and Ireland, from the Invention of Printing, with Biographical Notices and Prices, by W. T. Lowndes. Parts I.-X. (A to Z), 3s. 6d. each. Part XI. (Appendix Vol.), 5s. Or the 11 parts in 4 vols., half morocco, 2l. 2s.

MEDICINE, Handbook of Domestic, Popularly Arranged. By Dr. H. Davies. 700 pages. 5s.

NOTED NAMES OF FICTION. Dictionary of. Including also Familiar Pseudonyms, Surnames bestowed on Eminent Men, &c. By W. A. Wheeler, M.A. 5s.

POLITICAL CYCLOPÆDIA. A Dictionary of Political, Constitutional, Statistical, and Forensic Knowledge; forming a Work of Reference on subjects of Civil Administration, Political Economy, Finance, Commerce, Laws, and Social Relations. 4 vols. 3s. 6d. each.

PROVERBS, Handbook of. Containing an entire Republication of Ray's Collection, with Additions from Foreign Languages and Sayings, Sentences, Maxims, and Phrases. 5s.

—— **A Polyglot of Foreign.** Comprising French, Italian, German, Dutch, Spanish, Portuguese, and Danish. With English Translations. 5s.

SYNONYMS and ANTONYMS; or, Kindred Words and their Opposites, Collected and Contrasted by Ven. C. J. Smith, M.A. 5s.

WRIGHT (Th.)—*See Dictionary.*

NOVELISTS' LIBRARY.

13 Volumes at 3s. 6d. each, excepting those marked otherwise. (2l. 8s. 6d. per set.)

BJÖRNSON'S Arne and the Fisher Lassie. Translated from the Norse with an Introduction by W. H. Low, M.A.

BURNEY'S Evelina; or, a Young Lady's Entrance into the World. By F. Burney (Mme. D'Arblay). With Introduction and Notes by A. R. Ellis, Author of 'Sylvestra,' &c.

—— **Cecilia.** With Introduction and Notes by A. R. Ellis. 2 vols.

DE STAËL. Corinne or Italy. By Madame de Staël. Translated by Emily Baldwin and Paulina Driver.

EBERS' Egyptian Princess. Trans. by Emma Buchheim.

FIELDING'S Joseph Andrews and his Friend Mr. Abraham Adams. With Roscoe's Biography. *Cruikshank's Illustrations.*

—— **Amelia.** Roscoe's Edition, revised. *Cruikshank's Illustrations.* 5s.

—— **History of Tom Jones, a Foundling.** Roscoe's Edition. *Cruikshank's Illustrations.* 2 vols.

GROSSI'S Marco Visconti. Trans. by A. F. D.

MANZONI. The Betrothed: being a Translation of 'I Promessi Sposi.' Numerous Woodcuts. 1 vol. 5s.

STOWE (Mrs. H. B.) Uncle Tom's Cabin; or, Life among the Lowly. 8 full-page Illustrations.

ARTISTS' LIBRARY.

9 Volumes at Various Prices. (2l. 8s. 6d. per set.)

BELL (Sir Charles). The Anatomy and Philosophy of Expression, as Connected with the Fine Arts. 5s.

DEMMIN. History of Arms and Armour from the Earliest Period. By Auguste Demmin. Trans. by C. C. Black, M.A., Assistant Keeper, S. K. Museum. 1900 Illustrations. 7s. 6d.

FAIRHOLT'S Costume in England. Third Edition. Enlarged and Revised by the Hon. H. A. Dillon, F.S.A. With more than 700 Engravings. 2 vols. 5s. each.
    Vol. I. History. Vol. II. Glossary.

FLAXMAN. Lectures on Sculpture. With Three Addresses to the R.A. by Sir R. Westmacott, R.A., and Memoir of Flaxman. Portrait and 53 Plates. 6s. *N.S.*

HEATON'S Concise History of Painting. New Edition, revised by W. Cosmo Monkhouse. 5s.

LECTURES ON PAINTING by the Royal Academicians, Barry, Opie, Fuseli. With Introductory Essay and Notes by R. Wornum. Portrait of Fuseli.

LEONARDO DA VINCI'S Treatise on Painting. Trans. by J. F. Rigaud, R.A. With a Life and an Account of his Works by J. W. Brown. Numerous Plates. 5s.

PLANCHÉ'S History of British Costume, from the Earliest Time to the 10th Century. By J. R. Planché. 400 Illustrations. 5s.

LIBRARY OF SPORTS AND GAMES.

10 *Volumes at 5s. each.* (*2l. 10s. per set.*)

BOHN'S Handbooks of Athletic Sports. In 5 vols.

Vol. I.—Cricket, by Hon. and Rev. E. Lyttelton; Lawn Tennis, by H. W. Wilberforce; Tennis, Rackets, and Fives, by Julian Marshall, Major Spens, and J. A. Tait; Golf, by W. T. Linskill; Hockey, by F. S. Cresswell. [*Ready.*

Vol. II.—Rowing and Sculling, by W. B. Woodgate; Sailing, by E. F. Knight; Swimming, by M. and J. R. Cobbett. [*Ready.*

Vol. III.—Boxing, by R. G. Allanson-Winn; Single Stick and Sword Exercise, by R. G. Allanson-Winn and C. Phillipps Wolley: Wrestling, by Walter Armstrong; Fencing, by H. A. Colmore Dunn. [*In the press.*

Vol. IV.—Cycling, by H. H. Griffin; Rugby Football, by Harry Vassall; Association Football, by C. W. Alcock; Skating, by Douglas Adams. [*In the press.*

Vol. V.—Gymnastics, by A. F. Jenkin; Clubs and Dumb-bells. [*In the press.*

BOHN'S Handbooks of Games. New Edition. 2 volumes.

Vol. I. TABLE GAMES.

Contents :—Billiards, with Pool, Pyramids, and Snooker, by Major-Gen. A. W. Drayson, F.R.A.S., with a preface by W. J. Peall—Bagatelle, by 'Berkeley'—Chess, by R. F. Green—Draughts, Backgammon, Dominoes, Solitaire, Reversi, Go Bang, Rouge et noir, Roulette, E.O., Hazard, Faro, by 'Berkeley.'

Vol. II. CARD GAMES.

Contents :—Whist, by Dr. William Pole, F.R.S., Author of 'The Philosophy of Whist, &c.'—Solo Whist, by R. F. Green; Piquet, Ecarté, Euchre, by 'Berkeley;' Poker, Loo, Vingt-et-un, Napoleon, Newmarket, Rouge et Noir, Pope Joan, Speculation, &c. &c., by Baxter-Wray.

CHESS CONGRESS of 1862. A collection of the games played. Edited by J. Löwenthal. New edition, 5s.

MORPHY'S Games of Chess, being the Matches and best Games played by the American Champion, with explanatory and analytical Notes by J. Löwenthal. With short Memoir and Portrait of Morphy.

STAUNTON'S Chess-Player's Handbook. A Popular and Scientific Introduction to the Game, with numerous Diagrams and Coloured Frontispiece.

—— **Chess Praxis.** A Supplement to the Chess-player's Handbook. Containing the most important modern Improvements in the Openings; Code of Chess Laws; and a Selection of Morphy's Games. Annotated. 636 pages. Diagrams.

—— **Chess-Player's Companion.** Comprising a Treatise on Odds, Collection of Match Games, including the French Match with M. St. Amant, and a Selection of Original Problems. Diagrams and Coloured Frontispiece.

—— **Chess Tournament of 1851.** A Collection of Games played at this celebrated assemblage. With Introduction and Notes. Numerous Diagrams.

BOHN'S CHEAP SERIES.

Price 1s. each.

A Series of Complete Stories or Essays, mostly reprinted from Vols. in Bohn's Libraries, and neatly bound in stiff paper cover, with cut edges, suitable for Railway Reading.

ASCHAM (Roger). Scholemaster. By Professor Mayor.

CARPENTER (Dr. W. B.). Physiology of Temperance and Total Abstinence.

EMERSON. England and English Characteristics. Lectures on the Race, Ability, Manners, Truth, Character, Wealth, Religion. &c. &c.

—— **Nature:** An Essay. To which are added Orations, Lectures, and Addresses.

—— **Representative Men:** Seven Lectures on PLATO, SWEDENBORG, MONTAIGNE, SHAKESPEARE, NAPOLEON, and GOETHE.

—— **Twenty Essays on Various Subjects.**

—— **The Conduct of Life.**

FRANKLIN (Benjamin). Autobiography. Edited by J. Sparks.

HAWTHORNE (Nathaniel). Twice-told Tales. Two Vols. in One.

—— **Snow Image,** and Other Tales.

—— **Scarlet Letter.**

—— **House with the Seven Gables.**

—— **Transformation;** or the Marble Fawn. Two Parts.

HAZLITT (W.). Table-talk: Essays on Men and Manners. Three Parts.

—— **Plain Speaker:** Opinions on Books, Men, and Things. Three Parts.

—— **Lectures on the English Comic Writers.**

—— **Lectures on the English Poets.**

—— **Lectures on the Characters of** Shakespeare's Plays.

—— **Lectures on the Literature of** the Age of Elizabeth, chiefly Dramatic.

IRVING (Washington). Lives of Successors of Mohammed.

—— **Life of Goldsmith.**

—— **Sketch-book.**

—— **Tales of a Traveller.**

—— **Tour on the Prairies.**

—— **Conquests of Granada and** Spain. Two Parts.

—— **Life and Voyages of Columbus.** Two Parts.

—— **Companions of Columbus:** Their Voyages and Discoveries.

—— **Adventures of Captain Bonneville** in the Rocky Mountains and the Far West.

—— **Knickerbocker's History of New** York, from the beginning of the World to the End of the Dutch Dynasty.

—— **Tales of the Alhambra.**

—— **Conquest of Florida under Her-** nando de Soto.

—— **Abbotsford & Newstead Abbey.**

—— **Salmagundi;** or, The Whim-Whams and Opinions of LAUNCELOT LANGSTAFF, Esq.

—— **Bracebridge Hall;** or, The Humourists.

—— **Astoria;** or, Anecdotes of an Enterprise beyond the Rocky Mountains.

—— **Wolfert's Roost,** and other Tales.

LAMB (Charles). Essays of Elia. With a Portrait.

—— **Last Essays of Elia.**

—— **Eliana.** With Biographical Sketch.

MARRYAT (Captain). Pirate and the Three Cutters. With a Memoir of the Author.